COME MORNING

Also by Pat Warren

Forbidden

Beholden

No Regrets

Published by
WARNER BOOKS

PAT WARREN

COME MORNING

WARNER BOOKS

A Time Warner Company

WARNER BOOKS EDITION

Copyright © 1998 by Pat Warren
All rights reserved.

Cover design by Diane Luger
Cover illustration by Franco Accanero

Warner Books, Inc.
1271 Avenue of the Americas
New York, NY 10020

Visit our Web site at
http://warnerbooks.com

W A Time Warner Company

Printed in the United States of America

First Printing: March, 1998

10 9 8 7 6 5 4 3 2 1

Prologue

On the winding walkway of the Public Gardens on Charles Street across from the Boston Common, Briana Morgan snapped pictures of her seven-year-old son tossing chunks of bread to the sassy ducks in the pond. In the morning sunlight, the child's blond hair shimmered with golden highlights as he watched an elegant swan regard him disdainfully before swimming off. A baby duck upended himself in the blue water, shaking his little tail, and Bobby giggled.

Briana smiled as she lowered her camera, then checked her watch. "It's time to go. We don't want to keep Dad waiting." Every other Saturday since the divorce, her ex-husband picked up their son for the weekend. The arrangement was amicable.

Bobby tossed the rest of the bread at the ducks, then skipped along the walk, his mother following. They hadn't gone far when he spotted a green balloon caught up in the branches of a tree. Without waiting for permission, he started climbing.

It wasn't far up, Briana decided, so she let him go. He was a spontaneous child who loved life and she hated to squelch him in any way. Instead, she took more pictures of her son reaching out to the green balloon, finally freeing it, then carefully scampering back down and looping the string around his wrist. He sent her a triumphant glance, his blue eyes shining, then continued hopping and jumping because merely walking was boring.

They reached the street and Briana looked up and down the block, finally spotting her ex-husband at the corner of Beacon and Charles. He was in an animated conversation with a man whose back was to her. There was quite a lot of foot traffic along the Common, people blocking her view and making recognition of Robert's companion impossible. So she busied herself snapping more pictures of Bobby studying a caterpillar and passersby hurrying to complete weekend errands and tourists enjoying a warm and lovely April morning.

When next she looked up, Robert Morgan was walking toward them with long, angry strides and a dark frown on his face. But when he saw his son running toward him, Robert's smile was genuine and welcoming. Briana snapped father and son sharing a warm hug. She decided not to ask Robert why he'd seemed angry, since he'd apparently put aside whatever had upset him. Instead, she bent down and kissed her son good-bye.

"I love you, Mom," Bobby said, as he always did.

"I love you, too." She watched him reach for his father's hand as they crossed the street together on their way to visit the zoo. "Be careful," she called after them, as she always did.

She'd planned to drive over to Chinatown to take more pictures for a book in the works, but she could find no better subject anywhere than her son. For the moment, she stood next to a lamppost and kept shooting frames, tilting this way and that for better angles. She switched from wide lens to zoom, capturing each small gesture, each nuance and smile, as Bobby chattered away to his father, the green balloon weaving along on a mild breeze.

She shot around a city bus, a yellow cab changing lanes, and a gray sedan barreling up the street in a rush of speed, nearly colliding with a blue van overflowing with children. Then she shifted her attention to a forsythia in full bloom, its golden blossoms a welcome sign that summer was near.

The crackling sounds didn't register at first. Briana didn't even pause in her picture taking, thinking the noise was a car backfiring. It wasn't until she heard people screaming that she lowered her camera. Peering with ever increasing horror through the Charles Street traffic, she could see several people on the ground directly across from her, others scurrying for cover, and a few shouting for help.

No! It couldn't be.

Disbelief clotted the scream in her throat. Terror was an ice-cold hand squeezing her heart. *Dear God, no!*

Dodging cars, Briana raced across the street, not for a moment considering her own safety as a convertible swerved and a Volkswagen screeched to a halt, narrowly missing her. People were gathered around two still figures on the ground, while others got warily to their feet, fear in their eyes. Shoving, she broke through the crowd, looked down, then shrieked as she fell to her knees.

Robert was on his side, not moving, one leg twisted under his body, a horrible gunshot wound in his cheek.

And next to him, lying very still, was her son, his denim jacket soaked through with bright red blood. The green balloon, its string still tied around his wrist, flipped and flopped in a macabre dance.

Oh, Lord, not Bobby! Not her baby!

She gathered Bobby to her and held him close, a keening cry bubbling forth from deep inside. A voice behind her yelled for someone to call for an ambulance, quick.

But Briana Morgan knew it was already too late.

Chapter One

Four months later . . .

It was half a mile from Gramp's house to Brant Point Lighthouse on Nantucket Island, a walk Briana Morgan had taken countless times. There were fewer tourists up that way, the sand not quite so pure, with clumps of grass growing sporadically along the slight incline. The lighthouse itself sported a new coat of white paint and the walkway leading to the front door looked recently renovated. Leisurely strolling along the beach, she noticed a young couple maneuvering a bicycle built for two along the boardwalk, laughing as they struggled for balance. Probably honeymooners, she decided.

She and Robert had never had an actual honeymoon. She didn't count a long weekend at Manhattan's Plaza Hotel as such. They'd vaguely promised each other they'd make the time one day for a really special trip. But he'd been intent on climbing the corporate ladder at his bank and she'd just begun her job at the advertising agency the month before they'd married. The time had never seemed right, and suddenly, they were sitting on opposite sides of the aisle in divorce court.

Briana lifted her face to the warmth of the August sun. She'd flown over from Boston via Hyannis, arriving bag and baggage a mere hour ago, glad to have left behind a chilly three-day rain. It seemed to Briana that she'd been cold a very long time.

It also seemed as if the disturbing memories outnumbered the good ones lately. If only she could turn off her mind, she thought as she trudged along. Dr. Alexander Davis, the physician her mother had insisted she see when her weight loss and sleepless nights had become noticeable, had told her in his best bedside manner to get plenty of rest, eat right, and that time healed all wounds. Perhaps that old adage would apply to most everything except the death of one's child. Seven years old was too young to die.

Maybe some things in life couldn't be healed by time or sleep or good food, by magic potions or even fervent prayer. Maybe there were times when the best a person could hope for was to learn to cope with the ugly hand they were dealt. Maybe just making it through another twenty-four hours without jumping off the Longfellow Bridge was all the victory one could manage. One day at a time, as the saying went.

Briana stopped, squinting up at a cloudless blue sky, feeling warm from her walk. She swiped at her feathery bangs, slightly damp now, and wished she'd brought along a scrunchy so she could twist-tie her shoulder-length hair off her neck. She wished she'd brought along some cold bottled water as well. She kept on going.

Her eyes skimmed the horizon, then drifted to the weathered rocks at the water's edge just this side of the lighthouse, only a short distance away now. She could see a man sitting on one of the higher boulders where she'd daydreamed away many an hour as a teenager. It was one of her favorite spots.

For a brief moment, her hands itched for her camera, her mind setting up the picturesque scene, considering angles. Then she dismissed the thought. She hadn't held a camera in four months.

She noticed that the man was barefoot, wearing jeans and an unbuttoned blue shirt, its open flaps blowing about. His black hair shifted in a playful breeze as he stared out to sea, seemingly lost in his thoughts. Over the years, Briana had come to know almost all the permanent residents, by sight if not personally. She didn't recognize the man, who was likely a summer visitor.

Slowing her steps, she kept watching him, wishing he'd chosen to sit elsewhere. She'd have liked to climb up the steep rocks, carefully avoiding the green moss clinging to the sides, and spent an hour emptying her mind as she gazed at the ever changing sea. But someone had beaten her to it.

As she neared, the man started to rise, then teetered on the slippery rocks for several seconds, and finally toppled backwards. He lay very still exactly where he'd fallen. He might have hit his head, Briana decided as she rushed over, both curious and concerned. Carefully, she climbed up the familiar formation and reached his side.

He was on his back, wedged into a crevice in a semi-seated position, eyes closed. Leaning forward, she pressed two fingers to the pulse point of his neck and felt a strong heartbeat. She slipped her hand to the back of his head, searching for a bump or a cut, but found nothing. Easing back, she stared down into his face.

He had the kind of looks that drew a woman's eye— lean, lanky, athletic. At least two days' worth of dark beard shadowed his square jaw. Ruggedly handsome, most people would call him, with thick eyelashes and a small, interesting scar just above his left brow giving his face a dangerous slant. Unaware of her, he sighed heavily and began to snore lightly. Not injured, but sound asleep. An odd place for a nap, in broad daylight on a pile of uncomfortable rocks decorated with seaweed alongside a fairly remote lighthouse.

Then she spotted a brown paper bag alongside his hip. Checking, she found that it contained half a dozen empty beer cans. Not merely asleep, Briana realized, straightening. Passed-out drunk.

The sun was most decidedly not over the yardarm, yet here he was, an able-bodied man somewhere in his midthirties, drunk as a skunk. What a waste.

She was about to turn away when something made her glance back at him. Even in a deep sleep, his forehead seemed drawn into a frown. There were tiny lines near the corners of his eyes, lines that seemed to her to have been put there more by worry than laughter. There was no relaxation in the way he held his mouth; rather, there was tension evident even in his alcoholic slumber.

Briana sighed. Who was she to judge this stranger? Perhaps he carried burdens as heavy as hers. If she'd thought she could find an answer in alcohol, she might have tried it herself. She had a feeling that, whoever he was, he was going to discover soon that drinking only made things worse. And he was going to have a whopping headache when he finally woke up.

Not her problem, Briana thought, scrambling down. Studying him from the ground up, she decided he was firmly entrenched in his crevice and out of harm's way, with no likelihood of falling off. Even the tide rolling in wouldn't reach him. It wouldn't be dark for another couple of hours and he'd probably awaken before then. Later, after she'd unpacked and returned from getting her supplies, she'd check on him again. Just to be sure.

However, she felt certain that God looked after fools and drunks with equal ease.

She'd almost reached Gramp's house when a high-flying beach ball came out of nowhere and whacked her on the shoulder. Turning, she caught it on the bounce and swung around. A towhead around seven or eight with two front teeth missing stood several yards from her, grinning his apology. For a long moment, Briana just stared at him, at the beautiful young boy gazing up at her, so full of life.

"Hey, lady," he finally called out impatiently. "I'm sorry. Can I have my ball back?"

With trembling hands, Briana tossed him the ball, then turned and hurried into her grandfather's yard and up the stairs. Inside, she leaned against the door, breathing hard. Tears trailed down her cheeks as she swallowed a sob and waited out yet another storm.

Slade had one hell of a headache. Three aspirin washed down with two glasses of water and a hot shower followed by an ice-cold drenching hadn't helped much. The man who stared back at him through the steamy bathroom mirror had bloodshot eyes and foul breath. He'd brushed his teeth twice and still tasted beer.

Moving slowly, like he was eighty-six instead of thirty-six, he pulled on clean jeans and a white tee shirt, then slipped his feet into tan Docksiders. Where his black sneakers were was anyone's guess. He'd been wearing them yesterday when he'd set out for a stroll, carrying along a little liquid refreshment, but he'd awakened sometime in the wee small hours of the morning out by the lighthouse. His beer had disappeared and so had his sneakers.

Slade walked into the kitchen, blinking at the bright sun pouring in through the windows. His sunglasses had to be around here somewhere, but he felt too shaky to look for them just now. He reached up to slant the louvered blinds, but the movement cost him as his whole body protested. Hours spent sleeping it off on a pile of rocks could do that to a man. Suppressing a groan, he opened the refrigerator and gazed inside. Not a lot of choices, but then, he'd only been in Nantucket a week, mostly eating out. He'd have to do something about groceries real soon.

There was milk, but even the thought had his stomach roiling. Juice would have tasted good, but he'd forgotten to buy some. "Oh, well," he muttered, and grabbed a can of beer, of which there was plenty.

Carefully, he made his way out to the front porch, mindful of his head, afraid to jar it unnecessarily. It felt like a percussion band had set up residence inside his brain. Moving closer to the porch railing, he managed to bump his head on a hanging pot filled with nauseatingly cheerful red geraniums. The drumbeat in his brain picked up the tempo. Stepping back, he stumbled into the lone rocker and it went over with a noisy crash. He swore inventively.

Grimacing, Slade righted the chair and eased his aching body into it. Even the popping sound as he pulled the tab on the can had him moaning. He studied the can a moment, some vague memory insisting that beer wasn't the best remedy for a hangover. But he'd already had water and there was nothing else fit to drink. Tipping his head back with care, he drank deeply.

Blinking, he sat waiting for the explosion, sure he'd detonate with the addition of more alcohol to his system. All he could hear was someone banging around something solid and heavy on the enclosed porch next door. Praying his stomach would settle, he set the can onto the floor, leaned his head back, and closed his eyes.

He wasn't a drinker in any real sense of the word, hadn't had more than the occasional beer since his late teens when he'd joined the navy. Most young sailors got drunk on shore leave. It had seemed almost un-American not to. However, most guys outgrew those experimental years. Slade had.

But yesterday, he'd wanted to turn off his brain, wanted a distraction for a few hours, wanted to forget all that coming here had brought to mind. Even so, he wasn't sure that feeling like hell this morning was worth the short respite. And the memory loss worried him. He'd lost whole snatches of yesterday. He had no idea how he'd gotten up on the rocks and had very little recollection of climbing down. Somehow he'd managed to get himself back here and into bed. He'd even had the good sense to lock up.

Good sense. That was a laugh. His was in mighty short supply lately. Unanswered questions had haunted him ever since the letter from the attorney had found him in California. The curt message had advised him to fly to Nantucket without delay. His good sense had cautioned him that answering that directive would probably complicate his already confused life. But as usual, he'd ignored the warning and come anyway. Sure enough, the things he'd learned had brought up more questions than they answered.

Straightening slowly, Slade reached to rub his forehead where most of the pain lingered. How had his mother managed to drink herself into a stupor repeatedly, recuperate the next day, yet decide to do it all over again every evening? The pain of abandonment, of lost love, of gradually losing the ability to cope with a growing son full of questions she couldn't or wouldn't answer had caused her downslide, Slade was certain. Barbara had been a great mother until his father had left them both one sunny California afternoon. After that, the bottle had become her constant companion in a love-hate tug-of-war. In the end, the bottle had won.

Slade glanced down at the half-empty can of beer. Should he or shouldn't he? He'd hated his mother's drinking, had even been ashamed of her as a boy. Was it in the genes, maybe—like mother, like son, each reaching for a drink to soften the harsh realities of problems too difficult to face? Had his father turned to alcohol after leaving them? There were no signs of it around the house, with the exception of an extensive wine collection. Even now, living in his father's home, he sure as hell didn't know much about Jeremy Slade.

Slade contemplated the can again. What the hell. Who was there to care one way or the other? Closing his eyes, he drank the rest, then tossed the can into the tin wastebasket in the corner. The racket echoed through his aching head, but he felt better.

Better, but there was still that burning sensation in his stomach. Slade ground his fist into the spot, but it didn't help. Probably needed some good food. First, though, he needed to ease the pain. He seemed to remember seeing a bottle of Maalox in the bathroom medicine chest. Still somewhat unsteady, he got to his feet slowly and went in search of relief.

Who'd have believed that old wooden porch shutters would be so heavy? Briana thought, as she struggled to remove the third one. Taking several steps backward to keep from toppling over from the shutter's weight, she finally managed to place it alongside the other two. Blowing her bangs out of her eyes, she paused a moment to catch her breath.

Much as she hated to admit it, there were times when a strong man really would come in handy. However, finding a handy man was easier said than done. So she'd learned to manage on her own.

Briana took a long swallow of her bottled water, then glanced over at the house next door. Gramp's neighbor, Jeremy Slade, had lived there as long as she could remember. Somewhere in his sixties now, Jeremy was one of her favorite people, an artist whose work hung in many a Nantucket home as well as being extremely popular with tourists. Watercolors, mostly seascapes, predominantly pastels, peaceful scenes of Nantucket. His home, a sturdy two-story brick house complete with widow's walk and well-tended garden, beautifully decorated inside, was a lovely reflection of the gentle man himself.

Yet, although Jeremy's white Ford pickup was in his driveway, she hadn't seen him around. There'd been no lights on in his house last night, so she'd assumed he'd gone to the mainland on one of his infrequent trips. Then this morning, just as she'd removed the first shutter, she'd seen a man step out onto Jeremy's porch. He'd knocked over Jeremy's rocker, then cursed the chair, the bright sunshine, and the fates in general. Moving closer to the screen for a better look, she'd recognized the man she'd seen on the rocks by the lighthouse yesterday.

Last evening, concerned for his safety, she'd strolled along the boardwalk to check on him after her grocery run, and found him curled up and still sleeping it off. She'd even felt sorry for him, thinking he'd be stiff as a board and really hungover this morning. That is, until she'd seen him come out onto the porch, pop the tab on a can of beer, and drink half down without stopping. A little hair of the dog that bit you, apparently. Some people never learn.

Reaching up to unhook the fourth and last shutter, Briana wondered who the drinking fool making himself at home in Jeremy's house was. He didn't seem at all the sort of guest Jeremy would invite in. Actually, in all the years she'd been on Nantucket staying with her grandparents, she'd never once seen anyone visiting Jeremy. It wasn't that the man was reclusive, for he had a lot of friends on the island. He'd often wandered over and sat alongside Gramp on this very porch, both of them smoking a pipe, conversation at a minimum, as was the habit with many New Englanders. She'd never heard Jeremy speak of family or even mainland friends, and found it difficult to connect the drunken stranger to the gentle man she knew.

None of her business, Briana decided as she freed one hook. Steadying that side, she worked on the other hook, trying to dislodge it so the shutter would release. But the metal was slightly rusty and being stubborn. One-handed, she pushed and poked at it, growing ever more frustrated as she balanced the heavy shutter with her other hand.

Annoyed, she gave the hook a mighty punch and it slipped free. But she lost her balance at the sudden shift of weight and the shutter slipped from her grasp. "Oh!" she yelled as she slammed onto the painted boards of the porch floor, quickly rolling sideways to keep from being hit by the unwieldy shutter as it fell.

Seated once more on the open porch next door, nursing a small glass of Maalox, Slade couldn't help hearing what sounded like a cry for help followed by a loud crash. He felt shaky and decidedly unneighborly; still, his training was too deeply ingrained to allow him to ignore the possibility of someone in distress. Sipping the chalky antacid, he slowly made his way over and entered the enclosed porch.

The woman rubbing her hip looked more embarrassed than hurt, Slade thought as he set his glass on a corner table before picking up the fallen shutter and setting it out of the way. "You all right?" he asked, offering her a hand up.

"I think so." His hand was big, calloused, and strong, Briana noticed as he helped her up. She found herself looking into bloodshot gray eyes. "Thanks. I managed the first three, but this one got away from me."

Face-to-face with her, Slade did a double take. The resemblance was remarkable and quite startling. She was small and slender, but so were millions of women. But this one had the same honey-colored, shoulder-length hair and her face was oval-shaped, just like the one that haunted his dreams. Yet it was the eyes that bore the most resemblance. They were a rich brown, flecked with gold, filled with pain and brimming over with sadness. Intellectually, Slade knew he was looking at a stranger, yet he felt an emotional jolt nonetheless.

Uncomfortable under his intense examination, Briana frowned. "Is something wrong?" She was infinitely more comfortable behind the camera studying people rather than as the subject being scrutinized.

"You remind me of someone." With no small effort, he turned aside. "These are too heavy for a woman as small as you." He began stacking all four of the shutters near the door.

"Yes, well, my grandfather always took them down in early spring and put them back up in late fall. I arrived yesterday and decided to air out the place. The house has been closed up since he moved to Boston."

Just what his pounding head needed, a chatterbox neighbor. "I'm sure he appreciates you taking care of his place." He swung around, unable to resist studying her again. Of all the luck, flying three thousand miles and running into someone who's the spitting image of the woman he couldn't seem to forget.

"Actually, he's in a nursing home now and . . ." Briana's voice trailed off as she remembered her last visit here in the spring. Gramp had already been slipping, having memory lapses, but he'd so enjoyed fishing with Bobby and strolling on the beach after dinner.

A sick grandfather was undoubtedly the reason there was such a sorrowful look about her, Slade decided. "Where do you want these?"

"I can manage from here, really." She hated being thought a helpless, hapless female.

"Where do they go?" he asked again, his patience straining.

Far be it from her to interfere with his need to be macho, Briana decided. "In the garage, if you don't mind." She held the porch door open for him as he picked up two shutters, then led the way around back, yanking up the garage door. "Over there will be fine," she told him, indicating a space in front of Gramp's blue Buick Riviera.

Briana stood aside as he walked past her with his heavy load, then waited while he went back for the others. She was about to close the door after he finished, but he reached past her and pulled it shut himself. Apparently, he thought her not only clumsy but totally inept to boot. "Thanks, I appreciate the help."

"No problem." Slade started back toward her porch, the pain in his stomach a sharp reminder of his antacid. "I left my glass in there."

Following him, she glanced at the solid brick house next door. "Where's Jeremy? I haven't seen him around."

Slade paused at the porch steps. "Jeremy died about a month ago. He left his house and everything in it to me." Hearing himself say the words out loud still shocked him. He stepped onto her porch and picked up his glass, came back out.

"Died? I'm so sorry to hear that." Briana remembered the last time she'd seen Jeremy. It was on Easter week. He'd been teaching Bobby to play chess on his porch, their two heads bent over the board, one gray-haired, the other so very blond. "How'd it happen? Had he been ill?"

"Heart attack, so they tell me. His lawyer phoned with the news." Uncomfortable with the conversation and with being here, he shifted his weight to the other foot. He wanted to go lie down, try to get rid of his headache. But he found it difficult to turn his back on her stricken look. "Did you know him well?"

"Since I was a little girl. He was a real gentleman, unfailingly kind and very talented."

Everything he wasn't, Slade thought without rancor. Maybe if Jeremy Slade had stuck around and helped raise his son, things would have turned out a lot differently. *He* would be different.

"Forgive me for prying, but we never heard Jeremy mention anyone other than his Nantucket friends. You must have known him in another life."

So his father hadn't told his closest neighbor about him, not in all those years. Slade wished the knowledge didn't hurt so damn much. "You could say that. I'm his son, though I haven't seen him since I was ten."

Ten. There had to be a story there, Briana thought, but it was none of her affair. A private person who disliked personal questions from near strangers, she decided to drop the whole thing. If Jeremy's son wanted her to know more, he'd tell her himself. Instead, she glanced at the glass he held, the inside stained with some thick white liquid. "I see you've switched drinks."

About to walk away, Slade turned back. "How's that?"

"From beer. I ran across you yesterday while I was walking on the beach by the lighthouse. You were . . . napping on some rocks."

Terrific. Didn't she have anything better to do than to track his movements? "Yeah, I went there to think, to be alone. Guess it didn't work, since you found me."

Chagrined, she nodded. "Point taken. I'll butt out."

"Good idea." Angrier than the incident called for, Slade marched up onto his father's porch and went inside, closing the door with a resounding thud.

So much for neighborliness, Briana thought as she walked to the front yard. From outward appearances, Jeremy's son had inherited none of the older man's gentle ways. Or good manners. However, she hadn't come here to make new friends, which was a good thing, since she'd just struck out on her first attempt.

She was here instead to let this tranquil island heal her, Briana reminded herself. As she looked around the familiar yard, memories washed over her. There was the picket fence she'd painted the summer she'd turned fourteen. That had been half her lifetime ago, back when her grandmother had still been alive. How Briana had loved spending her school vacations on Nantucket. Even as a college student, she'd come often; then later as a new bride, she'd brought her husband to meet the grandparents she adored. Only, Robert had been too restless to enjoy the peaceful island. After that first visit, she'd left him home and come with Bobby.

But now her grandmother was gone and they'd finally had to put Gramp in a nursing home last month, as Alzheimer's robbed him of his precious memories along with his dignity. And Robert and Bobby were gone, too.

So much sadness, Briana thought as she gazed at the drooping daffodils that her grandmother had taken such pride in. The porch steps were wobbly, the door didn't close quite right, and the lovely gray paint was peeling off the wood shingles, the white off the shutters. Inside, there was a shabby, neglected feel to the house that once had been a proud and happy place. It seemed that with the loss of its occupants, the home had lost its heart.

Briana knew just how that felt.

She let the sea breeze ruffle her hair and breathed in the clean, salty air. Her eyes were shadowed, her heart heavy, and her smiles still infrequent. But yes, she'd made the right decision in coming here to the house her grandfather had built so long ago. The house where she'd always felt safe.

Lord only knew she hadn't been doing well lately in her Boston town house. Most days, she paced the rooms, restless and fidgety, unable to concentrate on even her photography, the second career she'd grown to love. Nights she pounded the pillows, fighting sleep, afraid her dreams would replay her worst nightmares. Dad had suggested a change of scenery, knowing how Briana loved Nantucket, and she'd reluctantly agreed. Perhaps here she'd find peace again. Perhaps here she could come to terms with all that had happened, if that even was possible.

Maybe a walk into town would be good, past Brant Point Lighthouse to South Beach and on to Main Street. She'd clean up and change clothes, take a leisurely stroll, stopping in to reacquaint herself with some of the shopkeepers she'd visited often over the years. Perhaps she'd pop in for lunch at that charming little inn overlooking the ocean, the one that served tiny tea sandwiches and scones with clotted cream.

And, please God, perhaps the people and places along the way would distract her from the pain in her heart that was a living, breathing thing.

Chapter Two

Briana had always enjoyed the shops at the west end of Main Street near North Wharf. She walked slowly, stopping at the Fudge Factory for a bag of candy and at the Nantucket Vineyard to buy a bottle of chardonnay.

Next, she strolled to the Needle Pointe, the little shop her grandmother had opened and operated until her death two years ago. Helen Jaworski, the woman who'd bought the place, said she'd heard rumors but wanted details about the state of Gramp's health. Briana updated her, then hurriedly accepted condolences about the tragedy and moved on.

Farther down, she checked out the window displays at the florist shop and went inside the new Island Book Store, finally choosing the latest Sue Grafton mystery, hoping she could once more concentrate on reading. In recent months, she'd barely gotten through the daily paper.

As she left there, Angelique, the owner of the Cheese Board, stepped outside and spotted Briana. The tiny

French woman motioned her in, slipped an arm around her waist, and led her to the back, murmuring all the way.

"Oh, my dear, it's so good to see you back with us. Gaylord and me, we feel so terrible about your tragedies." Her small face wrinkled in empathy. "First the accident, and now your *grandpère*. It is too much."

Briana felt her eyes fill as she looked down at the floor. "Thank you. You're very kind." Oddly, the kindest sentiments always started her weeping when she should feel grateful that people cared. She glanced around, desperate to change the subject. "I see you've remodeled since I was here last. I like that center display."

Before Angelique could reply, her husband came bustling over, his dark eyes sympathetic. "If there's anything we can do, Briana, you have only to ask."

Briana accepted Gaylord's hug. The two shopkeepers had known her since childhood and were friendly with her whole family. "I know," she acknowledged.

"How are you really doing, *chérie*?" he asked.

"Better. Each day, a little progress." Briana wasn't sure that was so, but it sounded good.

Gaylord's smile was tinged with sadness. "Ah, like it was yesterday, I see Bobby coming in here with you, asking for a sample of the cheese with the holes."

She couldn't do this, Briana thought, nearly panicking. She couldn't be drawn into yet another stroll down memory lane today. She'd been wrong to think she could handle these conversations. She simply wasn't strong enough yet. "Listen, I really must go." She broke away from them, from their good intentions and probing questions, from their puzzled looks and worried faces. "I'm sorry. Please forgive me," she called over her shoulder.

Outside, she hurried past the shop, dabbing at her eyes

with a tissue. How could she forget her pain when everything and everyone reminded her of her loss? What kind of person would even *want* to forget the best part of her life? Yet how could she go on with these tortured memories haunting her every step of the way?

The walk wasn't helping, Briana decided, and turned around, heading back. But she'd scarcely gone a block when she ran into two of her grandfather's old friends, Jake McGrath and Ambrose Whitmore. Both elderly retirees and widowers, they were lifetime residents of Nantucket. Naturally, they'd heard about Gramp moving to the Boston nursing home near Briana's folks, and they had a dozen questions. Shifting from one foot to the other, she answered politely, then begged off, saying she had to get back.

At least they hadn't brought up the tragedy that had changed her life forever, Briana thought as she turned onto Cliffside Road at last. Rounding the bend, she glanced up at the corner house painted Wedgwood blue, the home of one of her favorite people. Irma Tatum's age was a secret she'd likely take to her grave, though Briana knew she was hovering around eighty. She admired the fact that the woman's mind was quick, her humor bordered on the bawdy, and her sense of style was girlishly bizarre.

She'd buried three husbands, Irma was fond of saying, and survived the Great Depression and several smaller ones. Yet she was still here, as solid a fixture as Nantucket's cobblestone streets. She was the kind of person who always made you feel better for having talked with her, and Briana badly needed to feel better.

Before she could knock, the widow was at the door, opening the screen, drawing Briana in for a long look and a comforting hug. Irma was every inch as tall as Briana's five-seven, her back straight and her figure quite slim. Today's outfit was a long, maroon broomstick skirt, a multicolored floral blouse, and silver dangle earrings that nearly reached her shoulders. A bout with cancer and chemo had thinned her hair to near baldness so she'd purchased an assortment of wigs in various colors and styles. This morning's version was an outrageous shade of red, twisted and gathered at the back of her head and anchored with a large mother-of-pearl comb. She owned almost as many pairs of glasses, wearing bright turquoise frames at the moment.

"I'm so glad you're here, honey," Irma said, her throaty voice unable to disguise her sudden emotion. "You look like you could use a good meal. Let's go into the kitchen. My clam chowder should be ready. We'll have a nice lunch."

Dropping her packages on a nearby chair, Briana followed Irma into her big, inviting kitchen. "I'd planned to stop at the inn for lunch, but after walking around the shops, I didn't have the energy." She settled in one of the maple captain's chairs at the round table, feeling at home, remembering how often she'd shared a cup of tea or homemade pastry here with Irma. This room was the heart of her home, with its plank flooring, large oval braided rug, and corner brick fireplace. Even though it was a warm day, there was a fire going. Briana stretched her hands toward the flames and felt herself relaxing.

Irma squinted through her glasses as she reached for two Franciscanware soup bowls. "Did one of those shopkeepers say something they shouldn't? Bunch of nosy busybodies. I hope you didn't let them upset you." She moved to the stove and began spooning chowder.

"Everyone's been very kind. I realize they want to know

about Gramp, a few even want to fly over and visit him. It's so hard, telling people that on a good day, he may recognize them. But most of the time . . ."

"Folks should know that. Don't they read? There're articles in the paper constantly about Alzheimer's." The disease was like a festering fear that hovered over every senior citizen. Two of Irma's lady friends had it, and now Andy Gifford, Briana's grandfather.

She set the steaming bowls on the table along with napkins and silverware, then put the kettle on for tea. "Jake and Ambrose came by last week, wanted to know if I knew anything. Couple of old coots. Once they plop down on your porch, you can't get rid of 'em. 'Specially that Ambrose."

"Maybe he was here for more than information, Irma." Knowing how much the older woman enjoyed men and loved to flirt, Briana felt a smile forming, the first in a long while. It felt good.

"Pshaw! I can do better than either one of those two." Arranging crackers in a dainty Limoges dish, Irma returned to the table.

"Well, you can relax. I ran into them on Main Street and brought them up to date." She inhaled the marvelous aroma of the chowder. "This smells wonderful."

"Dig in, kid. We've got to put some pounds back on you." Irma would have chided her more for not taking better care of herself, but she knew exactly why Briana had lost weight, why she had dark circles under her eyes. Irma didn't have the heart to go on about it. Who could blame the poor thing for her loss of appetite? She bent to taste her own soup, found the chowder to be quite tasty, if she did think so herself. "How's the house looking these days? Your grandfather hadn't done much in months, though we can scarcely blame him. Andy's been ill longer than any of us knew."

Briana let a spoonful of chowder slide down her throat, enjoying the wonderful flavor. "No, we certainly can't blame him, but the house has been neglected for longer than a few months. When I was here last Easter, I did a thorough cleaning but there's so much more that needs doing. The whole place could use a fresh coat of paint, a roof inspection, possibly a furnace check before winter. And the garden! What a mess." She bent to her soup, feeling overwhelmed by such a big project right now. Perhaps if she weren't so preoccupied and restless.

"I could recommend a couple of handymen. Fix the place right up while you supervise from the porch." Irma got up to pour boiling water into her favorite Royal Doulton teapot. Through the years, she'd collected lovely things, not to be admired but to be used daily. After all, who did she have to save them for?

Letting the tea steep, she returned to the table. "I heard Andy say a dozen times that if something happened to him, the house belonged to you because you always loved the place as much as he."

Briana sighed, still touched by her grandfather's generosity. "Yes, Tom Richmond sent me the documents. Gramp drew up the paperwork a while back. He has a life estate until his death, and afterward, it's officially mine. I doubt he'll ever come home again, poor soul." The attorney's notice had jarred her, not because of its message, but seeing it in writing somehow made it seem so final, as if to say that her grandfather wouldn't be around much longer, a fact she didn't want to face.

"Do you know what you want to do? Perhaps fix up the place and move here? Or are you thinking of maybe selling the house?" Irma waited, hoping Briana's answer wouldn't disappoint her.

"Oh, I couldn't sell that house. I'd feel like I was cutting off my right arm."

Irma let out a relieved breath, pleased her assessment had been on the money. "Maybe, under the circumstances, living here away from all the memories in Boston would be a good thing for you right now."

Slowly, Briana set her spoon down. "I have memories of Bobby here, too. No matter where I go, he's with me."

The words were said so softly, so sadly, that Irma took a moment to swallow the sudden lump in her throat before reaching over and grasping Briana's hand. She'd been waiting for an opening, knowing from personal experience that a parent who loses a child wants to talk about it, yet doesn't. She'd walk carefully here, and let Briana lead the way. "He always will be," Irma said. "My Timothy was two when meningitis took him. That's fifty-two years ago, and I still think of him." The grieving and working two jobs to make ends meet had killed her first husband shortly after their son's death. The double sorrow had nearly finished Irma.

Briana squeezed the older woman's hand as her eyes, brimming with tears, met Irma's equally damp gaze. "Tell me, does it ever get better?"

"The sense of loss never, *ever* goes away. It's like an open wound that scabs over, but never quite heals. Yet the pain does ease in time." Irma cleared her throat. "And work, physical work like fixing up that house, can help a great deal."

Briana dabbed at her eyes with a tissue. "I'm sorry. I get like this several times a day, and I can't seem to control it."

"That, too, will let up, honey. I'm living proof that a strong woman can get through a very difficult time."

Briana tried a smile. "I don't think I'm as strong as you."

"Sure you are. Just give it time, and strength will come to you. You're a survivor, Briana. There are two kinds of people in this world, the quitters and the survivors. And it's been my experience you can pretty much tell early on which way a body's going to go." This was turning into a pity party, the last thing her young friend needed. Rising, Irma cleared the soup bowls and busied herself with the tea things. "Just wait until you see what I have for dessert."

"Not for me, thanks. The chowder was just enough."

"You can't turn this down." Irma brought forth a cake dish, setting it on the table. "Chocolate with double fudge frosting. Sinfully delicious. And honey," she added with a wink, "ain't nothing wrong with a little sin now and then."

Knowing when she was defeated, Briana accepted a piece large enough to feed a lumberjack. "Wow, you are generous with that knife."

Irma brought over the teapot, then placed her hands on her hips and stood at an angle in front of Briana. "Well, what do you think? See anything different about me?"

Briana examined her from head to toe and couldn't imagine what Irma had in mind. "Uh, not really."

The older woman patted her rump. "Look, I've got curves back here." She thrust out her rear, then gave an exaggerated bump and grind. "The damnable thing is that after fifty or sixty, you get flat back here. No man wants to pinch a woman who's flat. I remember vacationing in Italy before you were born. Got pinched everywhere I went. Glorious trip. So, last weekend, they had a flea market going on over at the Wharf. I found these padded panties. Don't you think they're wonderful?"

Briana squelched a laugh, somehow managing to turn it into an approving smile. "I see it now. Looks great."

Pleased with herself that she had her friend smiling, Irma sat down and squeezed lemon in her tea. "You better take good care of your parts, honey, 'cause they have a way of disappearing." She patted her chest. "The boobs are the first to go. You dry up and wither away to practically nothing. I've got pads here, too. Why do you think I always wear these busy little blouses? I'd look like a young boy in that lovely little knit thing you have on, even with a little stuffing." She sighed dramatically, picking up her cup. "What nature's forgotten, we take care of with cotton. Or," she went on, pausing to stroke her cheeks, calling attention to her second face-lift, "what nature changes drastically, we correct plastically." She chuckled at her own joke.

Briana shook her head, gazing at the older woman with affection. "I've missed you, Irma. You're one in a million."

The widow sobered. "I've missed you, too. I know I'm being selfish, but I'll say it anyhow. I hope you're here to stay."

"I'll be around awhile." She needed the time to sort out her options. "I think I'll enjoy redoing Gramp's house." Irma was right. A few weeks of hard physical work couldn't hurt. "I've always loved it here." Her grandparents' home had been the one constant in her life, with her parents continually moving while she'd been growing up. After their marriage, she and Robert had lived first in Manhattan, then in an apartment in Boston, followed by a house in Cambridge. And finally, after the divorce, she'd bought the Boston town house that had never truly felt like home, especially now, filled with memories of the son she'd never see again.

Her only real roots had been here in Nantucket. A part of

Briana longed for permanence, a place she felt she belonged, where she felt safe. Perhaps after fixing up Gramp's house, she'd know what she wanted to do with the rest of her life.

"It's even better around here when all the tourists go home, you remember? No need to make reservations at the best restaurants. Hell, they practically give meals away, too. And the traffic slows down to a comfortable crawl."

"I remember. And winters are so beautiful."

Irma picked up her fork, indicating their dessert. "As I recall, chocolate's your favorite, so have at it." She'd baked the cake this morning after hearing via the grapevine that Briana was back. If she hadn't stopped in, Irma had planned to take it over later.

Briana gave in to temptation. "Mmm, this is delicious."

They ate in silence for a bit before Irma began again. "Did you hear about Jeremy dying? That man was a real class act. If I'd have been twenty years younger, I'd have set my cap for him long ago. You know, in the near thirty years I knew Jeremy Slade, I never once saw him with a woman romantically, though there were a few who tried to catch his interest."

"Nor did I. I was very fond of him. When I was a child, he used to let me sit and watch him paint, if I promised to be very, very quiet. Afterward, he'd reward me with a lemon drop from the bowl he always kept on his table. He even let me go with him in his truck when he took his paintings to the gallery." She took another couple of bites, then pushed her plate aside. After eating so little for weeks, she couldn't manage more. "Have you met Jeremy's son?" If anyone knew anything about her new neighbor, it would be Irma, who was privy to everything that went on in the island.

"Oh, yes. I'd heard he was coming because Tom Richmond was Jeremy's attorney, too. At the funeral, he seemed more ill at ease than grief stricken, standing in the back, watching everything, hardly saying a word. Once I ran into him in the market. He bought milk, bologna, catsup, bread, and beer. Lots of beer. Odd, since Jeremy was a gourmet of sorts and an expert on wines. But then, Slade doesn't look anything like his father, either."

"Slade? He goes by his last name?"

"Apparently so. Tom said that Jeremy referred to him as J.D. in the will, but as a grown man, he goes by Slade."

"Do you know anything about him, where he's been all these years, why Jeremy never even mentioned having a son?" Briana couldn't say why Slade aroused her curiosity so. Probably because she hated seeing anyone ruin his life with drink, and naturally wondered what drove him to the bottle.

"Well, you know how closemouthed Jeremy was. Never said much about himself except he'd been a traveling salesman in California, and that he'd walked away from that life and moved here to paint. Tom had quite a time finding the son since he'd moved around a lot. Finally located him in Sacramento, where he's a fireman. After the funeral, he came back about a week ago, but he keeps to himself, hardly ever leaving the house. In that way, at least, he's like his father."

"What about his mother?"

"Tom told me Jeremy never mentioned her. He did say that Slade spent some time in the navy."

"The navy," Briana said. "That's why he moved around a lot, like we did because of Dad's navy position."

"Have you met him?" Finishing every crumb of her cake, Irma sipped tea.

"Sort of. I was taking down the shutters on the porch and having a hard time. He came over and helped. But he was less than cordial, especially when I mentioned I'd gone walking on the beach and run across him yesterday passed out drunk over by the lighthouse. I think he was nursing a monumental hangover."

Irma shook her head. "Damn fool inherits one of the best houses on the island and probably a hefty bank account, to say nothing of a stack of unsold paintings worth a bundle, and he sits around the house eating bologna sandwiches and getting soused all day. Jeremy's probably whirling around in his grave."

"You know, Slade told me he hadn't seen his father since he was ten, and yet Jeremy left everything to him. That seems odd."

"Maybe that's why he drinks so much. Those who lose their parents one way or another when they're young never quite get over it. Still, the man's going to kill himself with all that boozing."

Briana glanced up as the old-fashioned Seth Thomas clock hanging on Irma's fireplace chimed the hour of one. She'd managed to fritter away the whole morning and then some. But she did feel better after her visit. Rising, she carried her teacup and half-empty plate to the sink counter. "This has been lovely and I'm stuffed."

Irma bustled about, finding a covered dish and cutting a large chunk of cake. "You can have some of this with your dinner or tomorrow. And I'm sending some chowder home with you, too."

"That's nice of you, but not necessary. I went to the market and stocked up yesterday."

Irma shoved the first container into Briana's hands.

"Yes, it is necessary. I want to see you regain that weight and . . . and I want to see you smile again."

Briana pulled the older woman into a hug. "I'm working on it."

The phone was ringing as Briana unlocked the front door. Only her folks knew where she was, or even knew the number. She dumped her packages on the kitchen table and answered somewhat breathlessly.

"You sound like you're in training for the Boston marathon," the man said.

"Craig? Is that you?" Briana pulled out a chair and sat down.

"Sure is. I got your number from your mother. I wanted to know how you're doing. Like I've said, I worry about you, Brie."

"Well, you needn't. I'm fine." Which wasn't exactly the truth, but she wasn't about to admit it. "How are things with you?"

"Great. The market's high so things are perking."

Briana pictured Craig Walker, Robert's best friend, leaning back in his swivel chair at Fidelity Mutual Savings, the bank where they'd shared adjacent cubicles. His Armani suit coat would be hanging on his elaborately carved clothes tree and his Ferragamo loafers would be propped on an open desk drawer. A single man, Craig could afford expensive clothes. "I'm glad to hear that," she said.

"You didn't tell me you were going to Nantucket. I could have taken off a couple days and gone with you."

She'd known for some time that Craig was interested in her. He'd asked her out several times even before the ink had dried on her divorce papers. But Briana had told him she didn't want to ruin their friendship by trying to make something more of their relationship. Craig had accepted that good-naturedly and they'd remained casual friends.

It had been Craig who'd somehow learned of the shooting and been there at the hospital during those horrible hours. He'd been wonderful, taking care of notifying people and making the arrangements she'd been too shattered to handle. In the four months since, he'd called frequently, as a friend might, to check on her. However, recently he'd resumed what could only be a more dogged personal pursuit. In coming to Nantucket, she'd hoped to put some distance between them so he'd get the message that she simply wasn't interested. He'd been kind and helpful and she didn't want to hurt him with a blunt rejection, but she also knew they had no romantic future together.

"Coming here was kind of a quick decision. Mom probably told you that my grandfather has Alzheimer's and had to go into a nursing home. He needed someone to look after his house and I felt I needed some time alone. So here I am." That should be clear enough, Briana thought.

"I've never been to Nantucket, but I hear it's a great place to visit."

If he was fishing for an invitation, he would be disappointed. "Yes, it is, but it's really crowded during the summer. I much prefer the off-season, the fall and winter."

"Surely you'll be back before the leaves fall."

Briana found herself frowning. "I really don't have any definite plans, Craig. I have to take things one day at a time."

"Of course you do. Are you sure you're all right? You don't sound like yourself."

Her annoyance rising, Briana got up and walked to the window, trailing the phone cord. "I'm fine, really." She could see Slade stretched out on a lawn chair in the side yard next door, wearing only shorts, his eyes closed. Was he sleeping or passed out again? she wondered.

Craig must have caught the irritation in Briana's voice and decided to back off. "Good. I'm glad to hear it. I'll talk to you when you get back, okay?"

"Right. Thanks for calling." Briana hung up the phone, relieved that Craig hadn't been more persistent. If there was no chemistry, there simply was no reason to pursue a relationship beyond friendship, hoping something magical would happen. Boyishly handsome, a beautiful dresser, and apparently with plenty of money, Craig had his pick of any number of women. She wished he'd find one and soon.

Curiosity drew Briana back to the window. She saw Slade slip on a pair of sunglasses and pick up a book from the grass. She couldn't make out the title, but it was an oversized hardcover. As she watched, he grabbed a tall glass filled with orange liquid and ice cubes. Straight orange juice or laced with vodka? For his sake, she hoped he'd skipped the hard stuff.

Checking her packages, she put the food in the fridge and left the rest on the table. It was too nice a day to stay indoors. Remembering what she'd talked about with Irma, staying in Nantucket awhile and fixing up the house while letting her emotions settle, she decided there was no time like the present to get started.

Changing out of her linen slacks and silk blouse into old cutoff jeans shorts and her comfortably worn college sweatshirt minus sleeves, Briana made a mental list of things to do. She'd put off cleaning the inside until tomorrow so she could get an early start. Today she'd check Gramp's garage and see what he had and what she might need to buy to fix up the exterior.

She knew there was a ladder in the garage. She also

knew she was wary of heights. Maybe she'd call a roofing company to come out. She'd probably need a carpenter to make sure the windows and doors weren't warped, someone who could also fix the gate on the fence. Later, she'd clear out the flower beds, weed the area, maybe get some rich soil to mix in before adding some new plants.

Tying her somewhat beat-up canvas sneakers, Briana felt pleased with her plan. Keeping busy, that was the answer. Seeing progress each day and feeling a sense of accomplishment, something she hadn't experienced in quite some time. She loved her photography, but she couldn't seem to make herself pick up a camera since the day Bobby died.

Photography had become both her passion and her career, one following on the heels of the other. She'd put together her first book of photos as a lark, for her own pleasure. Then a friend she'd showed it to had urged her to send it to a New York agent she knew. To Briana's surprise, Jocelyn Banks had loved her work and sold it to a publisher almost immediately.

That book had been published two years ago under the title *Manhattan Musings,* and been well received, if not spectacularly so. Now she was contracted for another and had deadlines, restrictions, and requirements, diluting some of the pleasure. She'd been working on that, centered around Boston, when her life had changed forever. After Bobby's death, she'd had Jocelyn ask for and get an indefinite extension. She'd go back to her work one day, Briana supposed. But for now, she needed to do something less artistic and more physically tiring.

At the back of the garage, she found several paint buckets, a few with remnants all but dried up in the bottom, one in gray and another in white, plus a couple of smaller cans.

Gramp had probably kept them for touch-ups. The brushes were sitting in some coagulated liquid and too far gone to reuse. Finding a plastic trash bag, she tossed in everything she couldn't use, wound on a twist-tie, and hauled it out to the can at the fence line.

Taking her time, Briana wrote out a shopping list, then circled the house to determine where she should begin. The east side that bordered Jeremy's place was the worst, probably because the wind and rain hit there the hardest, and the sun baked it the longest. She carried the five-foot ladder, the only one she found, out to that side, propped it open, and steadied it on the uneven ground. This was about as high as she felt comfortable climbing. She'd worry about the uppermost part later. With a metal scraper she'd found in hand, she climbed halfway up and went to work grating off the loose paint.

Briana worked slowly, enjoying the warmth of the sun and the sheer effort of working muscles too long neglected. She might be sore later, but it felt good now. After she finished the first section, she went in for the bottled water she kept in the fridge and took a long drink. Outside once more, she set the water on the grass before starting on the second section.

Working on a particularly stubborn bubble of old, dried paint, she hoped that the fall rains would hold off until the job was completed. Then it could storm all it wanted while she remodeled inside.

September was when the rainy season usually began in Nantucket, often lasting for weeks, with occasionally severe storms. Because this had been the pattern for decades, most of the homes were built to be sturdy enough to withstand almost any weather. However, if she planned to linger past the tourist season, she'd best return to her

Boston town house and pack up some of her things to have shipped over by ferry.

Briana was aware that she had a strong nesting instinct. After all the moving around, the many places she'd lived, she needed her own things around her to feel at home. She had no plans to sell the town house and call Nantucket her permanent home, not yet at least. Bereavement advisors always said that it was usually a mistake to make large changes in lifestyle for at least the first year after a death in the family.

Fortunately, money wasn't a worry. She had a good income from a trust fund left by her maternal grandparents, the principal left untouched. And now she had Robert's generous insurance payoff, since he hadn't bothered to change beneficiaries after the divorce. That unexpected inheritance she hadn't wanted to touch, merely depositing the check in the bank and putting off deciding what to do with it. She couldn't help feeling she didn't deserve Robert's money since she was no longer his wife and hadn't been for three years.

When she'd scraped as far as she could reach, Briana climbed down and studied the decorative shutter on the window next to the ladder. It was attached with several screws that had been painted over. After wrestling with the porch shutters, she wasn't anxious to attack this one, but it had to be done. Taking another swallow of water, she stood contemplating the shutter, wondering how best to go about the chore.

"I can help you with that," said a deep voice behind her.

Briana turned and looked up at her neighbor. He was wearing dark sunglasses and baggy, fire-engine red shorts, his bare feet planted in the soft grass. A good head taller than she, his chest was broad, muscular, and covered with dark hair. In one hand, he held a glass filled with orange liquid and ice cubes. Was the man ever without a drink in his hand?

"Thanks, but I think I can manage."

Slade took a sip of the glass he'd recently refilled, enormously glad that his headache was gone. He glanced at the shutter, then back at her. "That's bigger than the ones on the porch, heavier, too." He reached up and scraped a thumbnail over the painted screw. "Whoever painted this last didn't do a very good job."

Briana had to agree. "My grandfather fell and broke his hip a while back and didn't climb ladders after his surgery. I don't know who he hired."

"Not a professional." Slade set his glass on the ground and took hold of the shutter, tugging at it, testing the tightness. "This baby's really up there."

Briana sighed. She'd hoped she could do the job herself, not having to rely on others. "My friend on the corner knows a handyman. I'll get his number." She bent to pick up her scraper and went to work.

"Like I said, I can help."

Stopping, Briana turned to him, wondering why he was offering his services, wishing he'd remove his sunglasses so she could see his eyes.

She wasn't a poker player, he'd wager. Her face gave away her curiosity. Frankly, Slade wasn't certain himself why he'd come out to lend a hand after watching her from the porch. Maybe it was as simple as needing something to do. His whole life, he'd never been one to sit around. He was going stir-crazy inside his father's perfect house.

Slade inclined his head toward the brick house next door. "Not much needs doing over there. Place is like some ad in *House Beautiful.* I'm used to working with my hands, used to hard work and long hours."

Deliberately, Briana glanced at his glass, then back to his eyes, letting the look reveal her doubts about his drinking interfering with his work.

He supposed he deserved her mistrust, Slade thought as he picked up his glass. After all, she had run across him passed out at midday. "This is straight orange juice. I stopped drinking."

She raised a questioning brow. "Really? Just like that?"

Shuffling his bare feet, Slade ran a hand along the back of his neck, unused to having to explain himself. Damned if he knew why he was bothering now. "Yeah. I started just like that and now I quit just like that."

Skeptical, she looked away without commenting.

She didn't believe him, he could tell. Why in hell was he trying to make her see, to understand? Was it the alcohol still lingering in his system? And how could he explain something he didn't fully understand himself? "Look, I wasn't just drinking yesterday to be drinking."

Briana had gone back to her scraping, wielding the hand tool quite well for a novice. She turned back, waiting.

Again, he was reminded of her uncanny resemblance to Rachel, the way she held her head, the unspoken question in her brown eyes. He rubbed the back of his neck, inexplicably wanting her to see—wanting just one person—to know what drove him. "Maybe you don't know what it's like to want more than anything in the world to forget something for just a little while."

Briana's face changed, closing down. "Yes, I do." Did he think he was the only one who needed to forget something hurtful in his past? "But I don't happen to think alcohol's the answer to pain."

Slade's mouth became a thin, angry line. "Well, bully for you. And exactly who appointed you judge and jury for the rest of us imperfect souls?" Tossing the melted cubes and juice on the ground, he marched to his porch and disappeared inside.

Lowering her head, Briana let out a long breath along with her misplaced anger. He was right. She had no business judging him. He wasn't the one she was angry with, either.

It was the fates. Or maybe God himself for taking her child and leaving her so very empty.

Knowing she could get no more done today, Briana left the ladder where it was and went inside.

Chapter Three

It took Slade a full two minutes of steadily staring inside his refrigerator at the cans of beer to realize he didn't want one. Like Pavlov's trained dog, he'd stormed inside and yanked open the door, intending to show that sanctimonious broad next door that she was right as rain. Yes, sir, she'd called it. He'd get roaring drunk and march over there and pass out on her lawn for good measure. If you had the name, you might as well have the game.

Instead, he slowly closed the refrigerator door, disgusted with himself and his juvenile overreaction. What the hell was happening to him lately?

He'd been acting out of character ever since he'd stepped off the plane in Nantucket, defensive and moody, drinking to forget his problems, something he'd never done before. He'd been made uneasy by Jeremy's neighbors, their looks of curiosity and interest as he'd walked through town and shopped in the market annoying him. Who's this newcomer who claimed to be the son of the late, great Jeremy C. Slade? they seemed to ask. A private man, he felt he owed them no explanation. Nor did he have one to give.

In direct contrast, he'd heard the awed respect in their voices at the funeral home when they'd filed past his father's closed casket. What had Jeremy done to earn such esteem? Had the looks they'd given him, the ones that seemed to say loud and clear that the son would have a long way to go to measure up to the father, been only in his imagination?

Thrusting his hands into the pockets of his shorts, Slade walked into the large living room with its wall of windows that looked out on the sea opposite the floor-to-ceiling fieldstone fireplace. He strolled over to the raised brick hearth and stared up at a painting he'd never seen until the day he'd arrived on the island.

A dark-haired boy about five years old sat atop a Shetland pony in a fenced corral. It was a summer scene, very simple, with blue sky, puffy white clouds, and high, green mountains in the background. On the child's face was a look that could only be described as pure joy as he leaned forward slightly, his small hand buried in the pony's shaggy mane.

Slade remembered that pony. His father's boss, the man who owned the electronics firm Jeremy Slade had worked for, had had a big ranch with lots of horses not far from the small California town where they'd been living. He'd also had a son just a little older than Slade and had often invited Jeremy's family over for barbecues. His father had been so proud that Slade hadn't been a bit afraid of the pony, had in fact loved every minute of riding him. He recalled begging his father to buy him a pony, too, unaware at five that their residential neighborhood was no place for a horse.

"One day," Jeremy had promised, "I'll get you a horse all your own." But he never had. Just one of many broken promises, including the one that had hurt the most: "I'll always be here for you, son."

Walking to the window, Slade watched the afternoon sun highlight a boat with billowing yellow sails bobbing along on the waves. The scene could have been a picture postcard, and probably had been. He could readily see why his dad had chosen this place to live. What he couldn't figure out, had never been able to understand, was why Jeremy had suddenly taken off, leaving him and his mother, just like that.

Turning, he gazed around his father's perfect house with carpeting thick enough to sink into, the kind of furniture he'd seen before only in model homes and hotel lobbies, and artwork undoubtedly worth a frigging fortune.

There wasn't one damn thing left to do, not a wall to repaint or a doorknob to repair or a dust mote that dared enter. He who'd never known a stable home, who'd scarcely lived in one place for longer than a year, ought to be grateful, Slade thought. This was a house such as he hadn't figured in his wildest dreams he'd ever live in—and it was all his.

The trouble was, he didn't feel he deserved this house, or the paintings, or even the big-bucks bank account. His father hadn't loved him enough to stay, to help raise him, to guide his formative years. So why should he accept all this from him now?

Slade had systematically schooled himself through the years to hate the man who'd left him and Barbara high and dry like a sailboat twisting in the wind without a rudder. He'd convinced himself the man didn't deserve his absentee love for what he'd done. He'd told himself repeatedly to stop thinking of Jeremy Slade, to stop hoping he'd return one day, to forget him and put him out of mind. It was so much easier to hate than to hurt.

It hadn't worked. Denial, the AA people were so fond of saying, is a nice place to visit, but no place to take up permanent residence.

What to do now? was the question.

Absently, he strolled to the cut glass bowl on the table and reached for a lemon drop, popping it in his mouth. He didn't really want to go back to California to live among the memories that kept him awake nights. He could sell everything here and move to . . . to . . . where? He'd visited a lot of places, but had never particularly longed to live in any one of them.

Drawing in a deep breath, he strolled through the rooms aimlessly. He could stay here, he supposed. Nantucket was about as beautiful a place to live as any he'd seen. The way the lawyer had explained things, with this inheritance, Slade would never have to work again, especially if he was prudent about selling his father's remaining paintings, all carefully stacked in Jeremy's storage room upstairs. They'd be even more valuable once the news spread throughout the art world that Jeremy had died.

But he couldn't just sit and be a beach bum at thirty-six. He'd been here a little over a week and all he'd managed had been two rather spectacular hangovers and to be bored out of his mind. Firefighting was what he'd done best, until that last fire.

The key to firefighting or police work or even career soldiering was to keep your distance. You couldn't be effective, couldn't get the job done if you let the horror, the brutality, the sheer waste of human life get to you. The moment you made it personal, you were no longer useful.

His last fire had been very personal. The idea of returning, of the emotional risks involved, was unthinkable.

What, then? The island had more specialty shops than he'd ever seen in one setting. Maybe something would strike him and he could go into business, something he'd dreamed of a while back and . . . wait!

What in hell was he thinking? Slade scrubbed a hand over his unshaven chin. What made him think this tight-knit community would accept him? Or that he could settle down to a sedentary occupation after years of physical jobs? Maybe he'd had too much booze or sun, to be thinking like this.

He needed to get out of the house, to walk off some energy. Taking the stairs two at a time, he went into the guest room. He'd chosen it rather than the large master bedroom suite, feeling odd about taking over his father's room. He pulled on a shirt and slipped on his Docksiders, and even ran a comb through his hair.

Downstairs, he grabbed his keys and locked up. Maybe he'd stroll into town, talk to a few year-round residents, and see if he could learn more about his father. He hadn't gone through all of Jeremy's papers yet, putting that off until he could accept this new situation. There were many unanswered questions, things he needed to know.

One thing was certain: He wasn't going to be at peace until he figured out why the son Jeremy Slade had denied had inherited his entire estate.

Briana was hot and harried, but pleased with her day so far. It was not yet high noon and all her self-assigned chores were done. She'd awakened early and attacked the house, dusting and vacuuming, scrubbing and cleaning. The faint lingering odor of illness and neglect had been replaced with the lemon waxy fragrance of wood polish and sea air, a noticeable change.

That done, she'd taken a shower, grabbed her list, and set out to do some shopping. She'd found all the supplies she needed to begin painting tomorrow and set them in the trunk of Gramp's eight-year-old Buick. Closing the lid with a thunk, Briana decided she'd done enough work for one day. She'd finish scraping the loose paint tomorrow. It was time to play.

Gramp had always loved fishing off the dock. Often as not, when she'd sat with him, they hadn't caught much. But that wasn't the point. Daydreaming and dozing, chatting and laughing, eating the thick sandwiches her grandmother had packed along with cold lemonade. Those outings had been special.

Occasionally, they'd gotten lucky and caught a small striped bass or a couple of bluefish. Permits weren't required for residents who did recreational fishing. Possibly her old pole was still in the backyard shed. The thought of catching fresh fish for dinner had her jumping in the car and starting back.

Briana turned left onto Beach Road heading north. Gazing toward Steamboat Wharf, she noticed that the sea was calm and the sun high in the sky on what promised to be a scorcher. Already, just running errands, she felt quite warm. It would be slightly cooler on the dock with the sea breezes.

She'd just turned onto Easton and could see Brant Point Lighthouse way off in the distance when she happened to glance to the right. Up ahead just off the road, she saw a man with his feet planted in the sand, bent forward from the waist, his hands braced on his knees. Slowing the car, she saw that he was having difficulty catching his breath. Another jogger who'd likely overdone it in the heat.

With no traffic behind her, Briana coasted along, wanting to make sure he wouldn't keel over with a heatstroke. Almost alongside him, she thought she recognized that tall, broad-shouldered frame, the black hair falling forward.

Her illustrious neighbor. Was he drunk again?

With a glance in the rearview, she pulled off the road and stopped parallel to him. She pushed the button to lower the passenger window. "Hey, are you all right?"

Slade heard the voice, though it sounded as if it came from a long way away. Slowly, he opened his eyes, but the black dots were still dancing, clouding his vision. His legs were trembling so badly he was afraid to take a step. With care, he turned his head, and even in his foggy state, recognized the woman in the car. Wouldn't you just know it would be her?

"Yeah, I'm fine," he said, his voice more shaky than he'd hoped it would be.

Briana shifted into PARK, got out, and walked over to him. His face was dangerously red and she could see his pulse pounding in his neck. He hadn't straightened and had closed his eyes again. She guessed he was trying to ignore her in the hope she'd go away. "Out for a little walk?"

"Yeah," he managed to huff out between heaving breaths.

"I think you may have overdone your run. Let me give you a lift back."

Slade concentrated on his breathing, on tracking the sweat pouring down his face. Stupid. He'd been stupid, running so fast so far. But he hadn't realized he was so badly out of shape. That's what months of goofing off could do to a man. "I'll be fine."

"Sure you will." Briana opened the passenger door. "Get in the car."

Slowly, painfully, his rubbery legs quivering, Slade straightened and opened his eyes. He swiped at his damp face with the back of his hand. This woman was turning out to be his nemesis. "I'll . . . be . . . okay."

She could hear the irritation and chose to ignore it. "I really hate this macho thing, you know. You're at least five miles from your house and in no condition to walk back, much less run." She stepped around so she was facing him, impatience strengthening her voice. "Get in the damn car."

Though he hated to admit it, Slade was too wiped out to argue. His movements slow, he climbed in and grimaced as she shut the door and walked around.

Briana reached into the backseat for her water bottle. "Here. This'll help."

Slade eyed the bottle. That's what he should have brought along. He'd often run five miles, even more, in northern California, cooled down a bit, then turned around and run back. But it had never been this hot or this humid. And he'd been in top shape back then, as firefighters had to be. He took the bottle she offered and sipped, then drank more. The cold liquid tasted wonderful, better than anything he could think of.

Briana watched the muscles of his throat work as he swallowed. His dark hair was damp, falling forward onto his wide forehead. His eyes were closed as he drank and she found herself envying those thick eyelashes she'd admired the day she'd run across him on the rocks. His lips as he lowered the bottle were generous, and looked to be the only soft thing about him. As his eyes opened and met hers, she averted her gaze, uncomfortably aware of him in an unnerving way.

His fingers still curled around the bottle, Slade licked his parched lips. "Thanks," he muttered, then leaned back to the headrest.

"Don't mention it." Briana slipped into gear, checked her mirror, and eased back onto the coastal road.

The ride home was short and quiet. When she pulled into Gramp's garage, she turned to look at him. His face was no longer the color of smashed tomatoes and his breathing had normalized.

"I guess I owe you one," he finally said.

"Consider it payment for your help with the shutters." But she had more to say, remembering their recent encounter at the side of the house. "About yesterday. I owe you an apology. You were right. I have no business judging you."

She'd surprised him. Now that he'd cooled down and was breathing normally, Slade was in a forgiving mood. "Apology accepted." He climbed out of the car, grateful the shakiness had passed. "I probably should apologize, too. I was a little testy. I guess if you pass out on public beaches, people are bound to assume you're a heavy drinker."

Briana opened the trunk and began unloading cans of paint, placing them on a garage shelf. "I shouldn't have assumed. That's generally a mistake."

He grabbed two cans and carried them over, catching her scent in passing. Damn, but she smelled good, while he probably radiated the aroma of week-old gym socks after his long run. "You know, I don't even know your name."

"Briana Morgan." She lifted out the final bag and closed the trunk.

He wiped his damp hands on his shorts, then offered her one. "Slade."

She already knew that, but she shook his big hand anyway. Everything about him was oversized, it seemed, from his shoulders to his running shoes that looked to be at least a size twelve. Jeremy had been only a couple of inches taller than she. Both Robert and her father were of average height. She wasn't used to looking up to well over six feet.

"Now that we're introduced, I have a favor to ask you."

Briana tensed. "What might that be?"

"That you let me help with your painting. I'm pretty good with a roller and brush." He desperately needed something to work on until he could decide what it was he wanted to do, so he'd decided to take another shot at convincing her. "See, I'm a firefighter. Well, used to be. Small town just outside Sacramento. Twenty-four on, twenty-four off. Left me with a lot of free hours. Several of us used to moonlight by painting homes in the neighborhood. We made a few bucks and it was good PR."

She couldn't figure out why he was persisting in this, but she saw no real reason to refuse him. And maybe it would keep him from thinking about what had driven him to drink. "All right. Actually, I could use a hand, especially with the top half. I'm not nuts about heights. As a fireman, you must have done your share of climbing ladders."

"Yeah, I did." He watched her close the garage door, and together, they strolled toward the front. "Do you happen to know Ambrose Whitmore?"

"Sure. He and Jake McGrath are good friends of my grandfather. Did he come by? Ambrose and your father used to play chess together."

"So he said. I ran into him and his friend in town yesterday. They recognized me from the funeral home and stopped to talk." Slade ran a hand along the back of his neck, kneading the taut muscles, an habitual gesture.

"They wanted to know all about me and I wanted them to tell me about my father. I don't think anyone walked away satisfied."

He didn't strike her as the type who'd launch into his life story readily, especially to strangers. "Ambrose and Jake mean well, but they're a bit on the gossipy side." Which was an understatement.

"Did *you* know Jeremy well?" He'd managed to get into three other conversations yesterday in his stroll through town, and each time, the talk inevitably had gotten around to his father. Yet no one had really said much except that they liked and admired him.

Briana adjusted the strap of her shoulder bag thoughtfully. "I'm not sure anyone knew Jeremy Slade well. New Englanders, as you probably know, are reticent by nature, and he fit right in, though he wasn't born here. Your father could talk for hours about paintings or books or gardening. But never a personal word about his past or people he'd known or future plans."

"So I gather." Slade knew he sounded frustrated, which was exactly how he felt.

It must be awful, not knowing someone as important as a father. Briana searched her memory for something more to tell him. "Jeremy was a very generous man. I've been told by several people in town that he'd helped them out, very privately and quietly, when they were in a financial bind. And he was great with kids." She remembered the very adult way Jeremy used to sit with Bobby and explain things, like plant pollination through the bees that hovered around his flowers. "A very patient man. I never heard him raise his voice. And I never heard him say a bad thing about anyone." She shrugged. "I don't know if that helps any."

"Yeah, it does. Thanks." He smiled.

His face changed with that smile, Briana thought. The worry lines disappeared and he looked more approachable, almost gentle. Slade was like the tip of an iceberg; a great deal more probably lay hidden behind those hooded gray eyes.

Jiggling her keys, she took a step toward the back door. "So, do you want to begin tomorrow? There's still a lot of scraping to do before we can paint."

"Sure. Are you an early riser?"

"Yes. I like to run on the beach at first sun, around six. I'll be ready to start around seven-thirty. Is that all right?"

"Fine." He watched her walk away, admiring the way her knit shirt clung to her curves. She was a very attractive woman. He let his eyes slip down to her long, shapely legs and to the white shorts that molded lovingly to her, and wondered if anyone had ever told her she had a great ass.

At his back door, Slade grinned. Hell, yes, they had. A woman who looked like that had had plenty of admirers, he was certain. He hadn't seen a wedding ring and wondered if she was married. Probably not, or the guy would be here with her.

Inside, he let himself remember the way she smelled, like something sinful. He also remembered the way she tilted her head, her brown eyes growing serious as she studied him. Did she also find him attractive? Maybe working on her grandfather's house together, she'd warm up to him. Maybe one thing would lead to another and they'd share a few laughs and a little healthy sex. Something like that could make a man forget his troubles far better than booze.

Maybe he'd even forget the woman in California who haunted his nightmares.

Heading up the stairs, he decided a long shower was in order. Afterward, he'd turn on the fan and lie down, hopefully grab a few winks. The sleepless nights were taking their toll. Perhaps starting tomorrow, if he wore himself out working on Briana's house, he'd be able to manage more than a couple of hours.

And maybe she'd remember more about his mysterious father.

Briana had a quick lunch, then stepped into the backyard carrying the ring of her grandfather's keys, trying to decide which one fit the lock on the white aluminum storage shed where the fishing gear was kept. Even if she didn't get a nibble, just being out on the dock in the sunshine would be enjoyable.

It took several tries before she found the right key. The old lock was rusty, but she finally managed to pop it open. Setting it aside, she pulled on the black metal handle. The door seemed stuck.

Tossing the keys on the grass, Briana took hold of the handle with both hands and pulled. She heard a slight squeak, but it didn't open. Determined, she braced one foot on the shed and yanked again with two hands. Suddenly the door swung open and Briana went down on her rump in the grass, followed by an assortment of beach items that spilled out onto her.

She wasn't hurt, not physically at least. But as she stared at the things scattered about on the grass, she felt a terrible pressure building in her chest. There they were, stark reminders all. The black inner tube Bobby used to love riding the waves in, now deflated. His blue snorkel mask. The striped beach ball, also out of air, as was the inflatable yellow raft they'd used on the freshwater pond near the bicycle path. And the red two-wheeler Gramp had gotten Bobby last summer was leaning drunkenly against the door frame, having broken loose from its constraints.

Her hand to her mouth, Briana staggered to her knees, gazing down at her son's toys, the ones that she'd stored away at the end of their visit last Easter. She'd locked the storage shed then, assuring Bobby everything would wait right there for him to return during his summer vacation. How could she have forgotten? Laden with memories, his things mocked her now like so much shipwrecked flotsam and jetsam.

Her knees too wobbly to hold her, she sank to the grass, one hand landing on something rubbery. Blinking through her tears, Briana closed her fingers around a small swim fin in bright blue. Bobby's, of course.

A pain like the thrust of a very sharp knife stabbed through her chest. She heard a heartwrenching sound, hardly realizing the deep sob had come from her. She bent forward, hugging the rubber fin to herself, rocking through her grief as scalding tears flowed down her cheeks. Overwhelmed, Briana gave in to the wracking spasms. Let it all out, the doctor had advised. It's better than locking it all inside.

Better? She was never going to feel better. Didn't the good doctor know that? Didn't they *all* know that?

How long she sat there letting the tears run their course while she clutched the small, blue fin Briana couldn't have said. Until the pain—that terrible, deep, inside pain—had subsided somewhat. Finally, feeling wrung out, she started to get up.

"Briana?" said a small, hesitant voice behind her. "Are you okay?"

Drawing in an uneven breath, Briana slowly turned

around. Staring at her, her little brow wrinkled with concern, was Annie Reed, the six-year-old daughter of the couple who lived in the house behind her grandfather's place. Gramp had trimmed the shrubbery fence so there'd be a two-foot opening, a pass-through so Annie could come visit him because he enjoyed chatting with her.

Swiping at her streaked face with the back of her hand, Briana nodded. "I'm okay, honey." She glanced down at the scattered toys. "I'm just sad, that's all."

"Oh." Feeling less uncertain now that Briana was talking, Annie hunkered down beside her. "I get sad sometimes, too. Mommy says it's okay to cry when you're sad."

"I guess your mommy's right." Briana found a tissue in the pocket of her shorts and wiped her face.

"Where's Bobby? I want him to come over and meet my new kitten. Her name's Rascal and . . ." Confused anew because Briana had squeezed her eyes tightly shut and bent her head back, Annie frowned. "What's wrong?"

How to tell a child that her playmate's gone forever. Briana pressed her lips together as she searched for the right words. "Bobby won't be coming back here, Annie. He . . . he died." She felt the knife inside slice deeper, deeper. God, how she hated saying those words.

Her brown eyes huge, Annie tilted her head. "How did he die?"

Briana swallowed hard. "An accident. A terrible accident."

"You mean like a car ran over him?" Annie asked, trying to understand.

What did it matter? A random bullet had killed her seven-year-old son, her life, her hopes and dreams. Nothing, nothing would ever be the same again.

"Something like that." She couldn't tell this little girl the truth. No child should have to deal with violence. Children were innocent victims of either careless or evil adults. And their mothers were left to try to put their suddenly meaningless lives back together.

"Is his daddy sad, too? My daddy would be." Annie's lower lip quivered in sympathy.

"His daddy's gone, too." A fresh wave of tears flooded Briana's eyes. For all his faults, Robert Morgan surely hadn't deserved to die with a bullet to the head on a sunny Saturday morning.

Annie stood and slipped one arm along Briana's shoulder. "Please don't cry." Big, fat tears dropped from her own eyes as it all became too much for the little girl to take in. "Bobby's in heaven, you know."

Nothing could have stopped Briana's torrent of tears more effectively than realizing she'd upset Bobby's little friend. She swung about and pulled Annie into a hug, a hug so like the many she'd shared with her son, loving the feel of the small, warm body in her arms. Then she straightened and slowly got to her feet.

Finding another tissue, she dabbed at Annie's cheeks. "I didn't mean to make you cry." She had no business doing this, sobbing out here, she who took pride in controlling herself, most especially in public. Chris and Pam Reed, Annie's parents, wouldn't be pleased to know she'd upset their daughter.

"It's okay," Annie said. "Do you feel better now?"

"Yes, I do." From somewhere, Briana dredged up a smile for the little girl's sake. "Thank you for helping me." She glanced toward the opening in the back shrubs, realizing it was somewhat overgrown and needed trimming. She'd get to it soon. Meanwhile, there was enough room to scoot through and she had some explaining to do. "Is your mommy home?"

"Uh-huh. She's hanging up the wash."

Briana hurriedly stuffed Bobby's things back into the shed, locked the door, then held out her hand. "Let's go talk to her, why don't we?"

"Okay." Holding hands, they walked toward the shrub opening.

In the upstairs bedroom of his father's house, Slade stood at the open window that overlooked Briana's backyard. Through the screen, he watched her walk hand in hand with the little girl. As they disappeared from sight, he let out a long breath.

During his years as a firefighter, he'd seen a lot of people in despair, people who'd lost their loved ones, their homes, their future. There were one or two who stood out in his memory, especially the recent incident. He immediately recognized Briana's pain—it was as soul-deep as any he'd seen.

He'd been lying down trying to sleep when he'd heard her come outside and start fussing around with the shed, pushing and pulling to get it open. He'd almost gotten up to give her a hand when he'd heard her crash-land. The woman seemed prone to falling. Then, almost immediately, he'd heard her wrenching sobs.

He'd risen and looked out the window. She'd been bent over double with toys scattered all around her. For a moment, he'd thought she'd hurt herself on something. But while he was deciding whether or not to go down to her, he realized from the sounds she made that she was hurting, all right, the kind of hurt that came from deep down inside.

Something in the shed had apparently triggered her anguish.

Then the little girl had arrived and he'd unabashedly listened to their conversation.

Slade reached for the glass on his nightstand and drank, tasting bitterness that had nothing to do with the orange juice. Now he knew why she'd been critical of him yesterday about wallowing in self-pity and drinking away his troubles. Briana Morgan had lost both her son and husband, if he'd heard correctly. All the while he'd been wandering around his father's house and all over town feeling sorry for himself, she'd been struggling with far better reasons to weep and complain and seek escape in a bottle than he had.

He stared out the window for long minutes, feeling regret—for her, for himself, for all the sad, lonely people in the world. Despite his earlier annoyance with Briana Morgan, his encounter with her today, and watching her weep, had shifted things for Slade. He was impressed with the way she'd apologized to him—a relative stranger—when she needn't have. And he greatly admired the way she'd pulled herself together for the sake of the little neighbor girl. She was quite a woman and he regretted that he couldn't allow himself to get to know her better.

Briana Morgan needed understanding and support, someone's undivided attention, someone who had his life together and could offer her hope and help. Instinctively, Slade knew that he wasn't that person. Hell, he couldn't help himself, so how could he help her through something as devastating as the loss of her entire family? Besides, after that business in California, he could no longer trust his own instincts.

The last thing she needed was a relationship now, even a purely physical one. She had a lot of healing to do.

As attractive as she was, as vulnerable as he now knew her to be, what made him think he could work alongside her daily and not get sucked in? No, he'd have to back off.

He'd help her with the house for a while. After all, he'd told her he would and he was a man of his word. But after that, he'd find an excuse to stay away. Something, anything.

Because if he didn't, if he let himself care deeply, if he let her snare him in with her needs, like someone had before, this time he might never recover.

Chapter Four

As Briana slowed down from her morning run and went through her front gate, she saw a tall ladder leaning against the side of the house. Standing near the top, Slade was already scraping away. Aretha Franklin was belting it out on the portable wedged into a corner. "Starting off with a little early morning soul, eh?"

"Trying to beat the heat," he answered, glancing down. "I found this ladder in my garage." He had to school himself not to call it his father's garage. When, he wondered, would he be comfortable with the transition? "I think it'll work better than yours."

"Great. I'll be back as soon as I grab a quick shower. Can I bring you out some coffee?" It seemed the least she could do in exchange for his work, though helping her had been his suggestion. Briana still wasn't sure it was the best idea, but when she thought of herself standing on that tall ladder, her stomach became slightly queasy.

"Sure. Black. Take your time." Peering through his sunglasses, he watched her flap the hem of her damp T-shirt in an effort to cool off as she walked around front. How was it that women managed to look good even when hot and disheveled while men just looked sweaty and tired? he wondered. He sincerely hoped she'd cover those long, distracting legs while they worked.

Tipping his head, he returned to chipping paint from the underside of the overhang. With all this sea and sun exposure, he'd be willing to bet that a lot of area homes needed regular painting. Maybe he'd look into starting a handyman service, working outside in season and indoors in winter. Through the years, he'd acquired enough knowledge about carpentry, plumbing, even electrical and heating, to do a variety of repairs, if not major replacement jobs.

Or perhaps he could buy up homes in disrepair, now that he had some capital, refurbish and resell them. The idea of being his own boss held a lot of appeal. Something to think about.

The sound of an inbound plane heading for Nantucket Memorial Airport had him looking up to admire the sleek charter aircraft skimming through the morning sky. That was yet another idea. He had his pilot's license and could apply for a job with one of the four or five private carriers he'd noticed coming and going. There were plenty of possibilities in Nantucket.

The question was, did he want to stay here?

How, he wondered, had his father chosen this island a whole continent away from his former home in California? And how had he accumulated so much? All right, so the paintings sold well. Now. But getting started as an artist, from everything Slade had heard, wasn't easy nor did success usually happen overnight. Had he continued to work as a salesman until his work caught on?

So many unanswered questions whirling around in his brain, he thought. He finished as far as he could reach, then climbed down. Out of the blue, he'd been thrust back into his father's life, only to find the man as enigmatic in death as he had been in life.

As he repositioned the ladder, Slade heard the familiar rumble of a large truck approaching. Moving to the front, hands on his hips, he watched a fire truck whiz by. Only one man in the jump seat and the engineer driving. Not on their way to a fire. Probably heading for a nearby fireplug to practice hose evolutions. No longer his problem, he reminded himself.

"Here's your coffee," Briana said at his elbow, her fingers brushing against his.

"Thanks." Her touch, slight as it was, felt too welcome, her freshly bathed scent snaring him in. Or was it just that he'd been without the softness of a woman in way too long?

She stared after the speeding truck. "I hope they're not rushing to a nearby fire."

"More likely a practice run or an equipment check." He took a swallow and noticed that she liked her coffee as strong as he did.

Turning, she squinted up at him. Lord, but he was tall. "Are you on leave from the fire department or did you quit?"

"On leave. I just haven't gotten around to quitting." But he would, and soon. Walking back, he drank more coffee, then set the mug on the windowsill.

Briana trailed after him. "You won't miss the work?"

"No," he said emphatically. He'd answered his last fire call.

Well, she thought, that was definite enough, and left little room for further discussion. Firefighting had to be a very stressful occupation. Perhaps that stress had gotten to him.

"You know, these shutters are only decorative," Slade said, gazing up at the window, deliberately changing the subject. "The way they're screwed in here, you could never release and swing them over to protect the window in a heavy storm." He nodded his head toward his father's house. "Those kind are better. Decorative *and* protective."

Alongside him, Briana studied the shutters. "You think I should get rid of these and buy new ones?"

"Yeah, I do. You could get aluminum ones, heavy grade. Never need painting. They come in lots of colors."

"All right, then. Let's do it. If you can somehow manage to get these off all the windows, I'll look into ordering the others. There'll be that much less to paint."

He raised a quizzical brow. "Are you always this decisive?"

Briana drained her coffee cup and set it on the ground. "Actually, I haven't been too good in that department lately. But I'm working on it."

Slade thought he knew the reason why, so he decided not to comment. The last thing he wanted was for her to break down again. Picking up his scraper, he angled his head to study the side of the house that was almost ready for paint. "Looking good. Maybe you should take some before and after pictures. You got a camera?"

Scraping away beneath the window, Briana glanced up as he climbed the ladder. "Actually, I have several. I'm a professional photographer."

"No kidding?" He hadn't pegged her as a professional anything. He'd rather imagined she'd graduated from some Ivy League college with a degree in flower arranging or something useful like that before marrying an upwardly mobile type. Just full of surprises, was Briana Morgan. "How'd you get into that?"

Briana's eyes clouded over, remembering how she'd loved staying home after Bobby was born and hadn't thought about working again. He was a year old before she'd gotten restless and started fooling around with photography. Robert had insisted on buying a house in Cambridge and they needed money. He'd refused to accept anything from her trust fund. Commuting to her old job in Manhattan had been out of the question, if they'd even have taken her back. She felt lucky that her hobby had begun to pay off.

"Kind of by accident, I guess."

"Do you have a studio?"

Briana sat down in the grass so she could reach the lowest section. The Boss was hitting the high notes on the radio, telling the world about Philadelphia. "Not that kind of photography. I do coffee-table books, working around a theme, like Manhattan at midnight, which would be night scenes in New York, or Boston by the bay, snapshots taken all around the bay area. Then I pick out the best, write blurbs for each, interspersed with some narrative. I send the package to my agent who then submits to my publisher."

"Have you had any published yet?"

"One. I was working on my second until . . . until recently. I sort of got sidetracked."

Like he'd gotten sidetracked. Funny, viewing the two of them, most people wouldn't think they had much in common. Briana Morgan was upper-crust, educated and sophisticated, someone who looked as if she belonged in a fashion magazine even in her so-called work clothes. He, on the other hand, had spent his life chasing a buck, living in tiny apartments above seedy storefronts, finally earning a diploma after attending nine schools and a college degree attending night school for two years, then finishing in the navy. Yet they'd both been thrown curve balls recently that had changed their lives.

"I'd like to see your book sometime. Is it anything like the art books in my father's house? I tried looking through one of them yesterday. I realized I know very little about art."

"Frankly, I don't know much about art, either. Did Jeremy paint when you lived with him?"

"Not paint, but he used to do pencil sketches occasionally. I don't know what ever happened to those." He remembered his father watching from the sidelines when he'd been in Little League, always with a sketch pad in his hands. He hadn't thought about that in years.

Finishing her spot, she got to her feet, brushing off the back of her jeans. "I spent some time watching Jeremy work. I really liked most of his stuff. His paintings are soothing and peaceful."

"He's got stacks of 'em in his studio and even more in that storage room upstairs. Did you know it's climate-controlled in there so nothing'll happen to the paintings? He even did most of his own framing." Climbing down, Slade shook his head. "The man sure was prolific."

Briana nodded. "And smart. He knew that an artist can't afford to flood the market with too many pieces at once, they'll drop in value that way. He very carefully offered his works to the gallery when he figured the time was right. I don't know how he chose which paintings to sell, but he only took in a few at a time." As Slade stepped off the last rung, she noticed that he was closer than she'd thought. His size was intimidating, the aroma of his sun-drenched skin so very male. She took a step back. "How about a re-fill on the coffee?"

"No, thanks. I'm going to get some tools and start taking down the shutters. Who knows how long they've been up there or what the shingles beneath look like."

Briana brushed paint flecks from her hair. "I think I'll get a bottle of cold water. Want some?"

"Sure." Slade started toward his father's garage on the other side of the house.

Rounding the bend, he came in view of the driveway just as a tan Ford turned in. Pausing, Slade saw a tall, angular man with a pencil-thin mustache, his summer suit quite wrinkled, step out and come around, a smile on his face.

"Are you J.D. Slade?"

Cautiously, Slade nodded.

The man's smile widened. "I'm Nathaniel Evans from the Fern Brokawer Art Gallery downtown. Fern sent me over to introduce myself. You might recall meeting her at your father's funeral. We've represented his work for years." Reaching over, Evans pumped Slade's hand enthusiastically. "So good to meet you finally. We kept hoping you'd drop in."

"I've been a little busy around the house."

"Have you run across our contract with Mr. Slade?" Nathaniel stroked his mustache, his small eyes hopeful.

"No, but then I haven't looked through all my father's papers yet. His attorney mentioned your gallery to me." Slade shuffled his feet impatiently, wondering what this terminally cheerful man wanted and wishing he'd get to the point.

"Good, good." More toothy smile. "We were wondering, Fern and I, when you'd like to bring over the next batch of your father's work. The news of his death has stunned the art world, of course." Then, as if suddenly remembering his manners, his rubbery face sobered. "Please accept my deepest sympathy."

"Thank you, but I haven't gone through the paintings, either. I'll get around to that soon."

Straightening his skinny tie with long fingers, Nathaniel resumed his salesman's smile. "Certainly. We need to make hay while the sun shines, though, you know." He let out a quick chuckle. "We don't want to wait until the market cools. Now, we're down to half a dozen of Jeremy's paintings and . . ."

Slade had had enough. "Look, Mr. Evans, this isn't the best time for this conversation. I'm busy right now, but I'll get back to you." Walking around the man, he headed for the open garage. "Thanks for stopping by."

His expression a mixture of surprise and annoyance, Nathaniel sighed. Jeremy Slade had been polite to a fault, yet his son bordered on rude. "All right. Do call us soon, will you?"

His back to Evans, Slade sent him a careless wave. He found Jeremy's toolbox in short order, but waited until Nathaniel left to walk out to where Briana was leaning against the side of her house, watching Evans drive away. "Do you know him?"

She'd overheard most of the conversation. "Not really, but I've known Fern for years. I used to go to the gallery with your dad when I was a kid. I loved riding in his truck."

"He wants me to take in more paintings. They're down to six." He took the water bottle she held out to him. "I'm not sure if I should." Minutes ago, she'd mentioned that his father had been cagey about releasing his paintings in a timely fashion. Was six an inadequate number at one gallery? If so, how many should he take in? He didn't know one damn thing about the selling of art.

"If you like, I can make a couple of calls. I know someone who owns a gallery in Boston. I trust Doug's advice."

Slade looked thoughtful, then shook his head. "Thanks, but I think I'll look into it myself." He was used to doing things on his own, not relying on others. He'd check at the library and visit a couple of art galleries, learn what he needed to know somehow. At the window, he set down the tool kit and found a screwdriver.

"Okay." Briana watched him for a few minutes, then walked on past him. They'd be finished with this side shortly and ready to start prepping the back. She'd just moved beyond the shrubs when something caught her eye. There on the grass was a beach thong, size one, in seafoam green. Apparently, she'd overlooked it when she'd repacked the shed. As she bent to pick up the small, forlorn shoe that had belonged to her son, she felt a wrenching sob escape from deep within her.

Dear God, not again. How long before she could look at his things or say his name out loud without weeping?

On the side of the house, Slade was climbing down the ladder when he heard an odd sound. Walking around back, he saw Briana standing with her eyes closed, clutching something in both hands. Recalling how she'd lost control yesterday, he debated about whether to get involved or give her privacy. Finally, he stepped closer. "Can I help?"

"No. No one can help." Slowly, her face pale, Briana

straightened, remembering everything she'd been trying desperately to forget.

"I have to go in," she managed, then ran into the house, the screen door banging shut behind her.

As Slade turned, he heard a muffled sound through the kitchen screen. Frowning, he ran a hand through his hair. Damn, but he wasn't good at times like this. He hated seeing a woman cry. He moved closer to the house, trying to decide what to do. Coming to a decision, one he might regret, he discarded his good sense and walked in after her.

She was leaning against the kitchen archway leading into the dining room, small and slender, looking for all the world as if she'd crumble without the support. Acting instinctively, he went to her and patted her back clumsily. A huge sob escaped from her. Feeling out of his element, Slade put his hands on her shoulders, then found himself turning her around, offering a tentative hug. The least he could do was give her a small measure of comfort.

She resisted minimally at first, then released a hiccupy breath and buried her face in his chest, her arms going around him. Slade held her somewhat awkwardly, wishing he had the words that would make her feel better. He had none. Perhaps, with the enormity of her loss, there were none she would believe anyhow.

Briana wept silently, her shoulders shaking, her hands bunched in his shirt. She clung to him, letting wave after wave buffet her. She had to get it out, all out. Oh, God, if only she could get it all out once and for all.

Slade found himself smoothing her hair, brushing back the damp strands, his other hand gently massaging her back. He didn't have words of comfort, but he could show her by touching and holding that he understood. She'd probably never believe how well he understood.

She couldn't keep doing this, a part of Briana's brain told her. She couldn't spend the rest of her days falling into a heap of tears every time she ran across something else that reminded her of Bobby. Burrowing into Slade's chest, she tried to focus on him, on distracting herself from the pain inside herself. She concentrated on the feel of him, the hard muscles of his back where her hands roamed restlessly. The gentleness of his touch on her hair. The steady drumbeat of his heart beneath her ear. The powerful musky smells as she drew in a deep breath.

He represented relief from her pain, escape from her anguished thoughts, an interlude from her ongoing nightmare. Shifting slightly, she moved her face into his throat, wanting to feel that pounding pulse with her lips. She felt his arms tighten around her and closed her eyes, absorbing the comfort he offered. It had been so very long since she'd been held like this, been touched by a man. She'd missed the feel of strong arms and big hands and the scent of musk. Feeling like a desert walker who'd stumbled in and found rain, she slowly raised her head and reached for more.

Then her mouth was on his and she felt the shock of cool lips that wouldn't part, that didn't move. Frantic now, she pressed herself closer to him and suddenly, the response she'd wanted, needed, was there, overflowing. His mouth was softer than she'd imagined and as ravenous as her own seeking lips. She heard a guttural sound and wasn't sure if it had come from him or herself as he took over the kiss, sending his tongue in to mate with hers.

Slade knew what had started this, knew a great deal about seeking comfort and finding passion. He also knew he should push her away and not allow this to continue. And he would. In another minute, after he drank from her a bit longer, after his hands explored a bit more, after his arms grew tired of holding her.

Wild now and desperate, Briana kissed him with all her heart and soul, needing the release, the abandon, the purging. *Make me forget,* she wanted to scream at him. *Hold me tighter and tighter still. Anything, just make me forget, please.* Rubbing against him, she felt his arousal, throbbing and insistent. Mindlessly, her searching hand slipped between their bodies.

His breathing labored, Slade came to his senses with a start and captured her hand with his. No, he couldn't let her do this, not this way. It wasn't a question of wanting, for God knew he wanted her. It was a question of right and wrong, and he wasn't a man who could take advantage. She was too fragile, too upset. So grief stricken was she that she wasn't even aware she'd been ready to use him to forget, if only for a little while.

Shocked and stunned as awareness returned, Briana blew her breath out in sporadic puffs. Raising her eyes to his, she blinked to bring him in focus. But realization had her cheeks flushing as she stepped back, her hands reaching up to cover her face. "Oh, God. I'm so sorry. I . . . I don't know what came over me. I . . ."

"It's all right." He dared to touch her arm gently. "Briana, I understand."

She yanked free of his fingers as shame spread throughout her whole body. "No, no. It's *not* all right. And you couldn't possibly understand. Please forgive me. Please." Eyes downcast, she ran past him and down the hall, hurrying into her room. Slamming the door, she fell on her bed with an agonized groan.

Slade ran an unsteady hand over his face and straightened his shirt. Just as he'd thought yesterday, the woman was terribly needy. Not that he blamed her. He'd been honest when he'd told her he understood, but she didn't believe him. She was too far gone to see past her own need right now. Sex was a powerful escape and her confused mind reached out for that, and not him specifically. He'd been there and done that, and knew how hollow he'd felt afterward.

Leaving by the back door, he only hoped she'd come to that conclusion and forgive herself.

All morning, as she lay on her bed scarcely moving, Briana heard Slade methodically circling the house, scraping loose paint, repositioning the ladder, working the next section. She wanted to close out the sounds of his nearness, but even with her hands over her ears, she couldn't. She wanted him to go away, but she didn't have the strength to go outside and tell him.

It had been a mistake to allow him to help her. She wasn't fit company for anyone. Yet even she hadn't known how low she could sink.

Recalling the outrageous way she'd come on to him, she groaned out loud, drawing her knees up. Had she totally gone around the bend? She'd scolded him for drinking to forget whatever problems he had, feeling superior because she hadn't given in to the escape alcohol offered. Oh, no, not her. Instead, she'd all but raped him, her twisted mind seeking oblivion in sex with a near stranger.

How easy it would be to fall into bed with Slade, she'd thought for those agonizing minutes, to find escape in passion. And passion was what he stirred in her in abundance. But like alcohol, sex like that was a temporary comfort and would solve nothing.

What must he think of her now? How does one apologize for such a loss of control? And Slade didn't even know why she was upset, why seeing Bobby's small shoe had tilted her world yet again, because she'd never told him about her son's recent death. Could she gather up enough energy to explain?

Briana closed her eyes, becoming aware of a headache brewing. What she needed was sleep, hours of dreamless sleep. Then maybe she'd wake up to find today had never happened.

The grandfather clock chiming two woke her. Cautiously, Briana opened her eyes and saw that daylight was still streaming in her window. She hadn't slept the clock around, but she hadn't dreamt, either. Her growling stomach reminded her that she hadn't eaten all day.

In the bathroom mirror, she studied her image. Eyes still puffy, skin blotchy. Not a pretty sight. She splashed cold water on her face several times, brushed her teeth, vigorously dried her face and combed her hair. A small improvement, she noted.

As she hung up the towel, she heard a scraping noise on the other side of the bathroom wall. Everything came rushing back in a torrent of regret. The body repairs were nothing compared to the damage control she had to do with Slade.

In the kitchen, she tipped the slatted blinds upward slightly so no one outside could see in. Feeling cowardly, she put on two eggs to boil and sipped orange juice while she waited. She'd have to face him, of course. First a delayed breakfast, then she'd eat humble pie.

The problem was, she had no excuse to offer, or rather none that she wanted to go into, Briana thought as she dropped an English muffin into the toaster. Then again, how long was she going to use her grief as an excuse for doing crazy things?

Brushing back a lock of hair, she flipped the egg timer, telling herself she simply had to get a grip. She was turning into someone she didn't much like.

A sudden wailing sound from her backyard drifted in through the back screen. Briana went to the window, pulled down one slat, and saw Slade running to where little Annie stood by Gramp's tall apple tree.

"What's the matter there, young lady?" Slade asked her.

Looking uncertain, Annie glanced at him, then peered up into the tree. "Rascal's up there and she can't get down." Her small voice was quivery. "I told her not to climb up, but she's only a kitten and she doesn't know better."

"I see." Hands on his hips, Slade looked up and spotted the calico kitten out on a limb, meowing a mixture of defiance and fear. It was a sturdy limb, but up pretty high. Of all things, a kitten, he thought, staring up, remembering another time, another kitten, one he'd rescued and wished he hadn't. But he couldn't let himself dwell on that.

"I hope she doesn't fall."

"I think I can get her down."

"Oh, could you, please? My daddy's at work and Mommy's going to have a baby so she can't climb. Besides . . ." She glanced nervously toward the opening in the shrubs. ". . . I'm not supposed to let Rascal outside. Mommy's going to be mad."

"Maybe if I get Rascal down, you can get her back into the house before Mommy finds out." Slade positioned Briana's ladder against the thick trunk. "What do you think?"

"Okay." She watched him climb up, then step onto a limb going even higher. "Aren't you scared up there?"

"Nah. I'm a fireman. We're supposed to rescue kittens from trees." Slade reached the leafy branch where Rascal sat eyeing him suspiciously. He'd bet his bottom dollar she wasn't declawed and that this was going to turn into a bloody rescue. "Come on, Rascal," he coaxed. "Annie's waiting down there for you."

"Come on, Rascal," Annie echoed.

The kitten meowed and scooted backward ever closer to the end of the branch as Slade stretched his arm toward her. If she didn't stop soon, she'd either fall or he would, trying to get her. Inching a bit closer, he walked his fingers toward her, trying to make it a teasing game. "Here, kitty, kitty. Come here."

"Don't let her fall, please," Annie begged.

He trailed his hand playfully along the branch, catching the kitten's interest. Finally, she whipped out one paw toward his fingers and Slade's hand closed around her small leg. She meowed frantically, feeling herself falling, but Slade eased her toward him.

Now she was really struggling, whining, scratching. Slade knew the only way he could get back to the ladder was to free his hands and he couldn't do that unless he found a place for the kitten. There was only one way. Gritting his teeth, he stuffed her inside his shirt before starting to scoot backward toward the ladder.

She fought like a tiny tiger, her small claws very sharp and digging into his flesh. Wincing, Slade found the ladder with his foot and eased his weight onto it firmly before letting go of the tree. Another minute and he was down on the ground, opening his shirt.

"Is she hurt?" Annie asked, her big eyes huge. She'd gotten awfully worried when the kitten had disappeared from sight.

"She isn't, but I might be." One hand around the kitten's middle, he pulled, but one tiny sharp claw was still embedded in his flesh. Gingerly, he extracted her paw and handed her over to Annie. "Hang on to her, now."

Meowing, the cat snuggled down into the curve of Annie's arms as Slade studied the scratches on his chest and hands. "Thank you for getting her down." Annie wrinkled up her little face. "Are you really a fireman?"

Solemnly, he raised his hand to his bloody chest. "Cross my heart and hope to die."

Suddenly, Annie remembered a warning she'd heard repeated over and over. "Mommy says I'm not supposed to talk to strangers." She glanced nervously toward both houses. "Briana said you were Mr. Slade's son, so I guess it's okay."

"This one time, I guess it is," Slade told her. "I live over there, so I'm your neighbor and a friend of Briana's. But you listen to your mom and don't talk to strangers, okay?"

"I won't anymore."

At the open window, Briana watched Slade gently pat the top of the child's blond head. "Okay, Annie," she heard him say. "Keep a good eye on her from now on." Annie assured him she would, then ran home through the shrubs as Slade picked up the ladder and walked out of sight.

Briana turned back to the stove and her overcooked eggs, dumping them in the sink. He'd been pretty good with Annie, she decided as she pushed down the toaster lever. She wondered if he had children, if he'd been married. He'd been so gruff the first few days she'd known him, yet he apparently had a gentle side.

And more good sense than she, for he'd grabbed her hand earlier today before she'd made a more complete fool of herself.

Briana broke the eggs into a small dish and peeled the shells. Absently, she buttered the muffin and took her meal to the table, hoping with each bite she took that she'd be able to face J.D. Slade after she finished.

He was working on the front porch when she finally went outside. He'd switched to sandpaper for the older wood around the screens. He glanced toward the door, his face carefully expressionless. "Feeling better?"

"Yes, thanks." Her voice was low, filled with lingering embarrassment. She ran a hand along the wood he'd already sanded smooth as she searched for the right words. She'd begun half a dozen mental scenarios and discarded each. Best just to wing it.

She'd changed into a white top that made her face look even paler than before, and there were dark smudges beneath her eyes, Slade noticed. He wondered if she'd slept at all. "You had a visitor." He nodded his head in the direction of a covered plate on the small table between the two rockers. "Older woman. Said her name was Irma. She brought you some chocolate chip cookies straight out of the oven."

Briana's mind latched onto the diversion. "What color was her hair today?" she asked, a smile playing around the corners of her mouth. The mere thought of Irma had her feeling better.

Slade straightened, wrinkling his forehead thoughtfully. "I guess you'd call it blond. Silver-blond. Maybe platinum. Her glass frames were big and bright red. And her earrings, also red, hung down to here." He indicated his shoulder.

Briana's smile became full-fledged. "She's unique, isn't she?"

"That she is. I told her you were resting. I'm not sure she believed me. Said she'll call you later."

Sobering, she nodded, then thrust her hands into her jeans pockets. "Listen, Slade, about this morning . . ."

He met her eyes, wanting to put her at ease, for he knew what had happened between them earlier had been triggered by grief and a need to forget, not passion or desire. "You owe me no explanation. I understand."

"I don't think you do. I want you to know I don't usually . . ."

He held out a hand, stopping her. "You don't have to go into details. I know." He could see surprise, followed by wariness in her eyes. "I overheard you and Annie yesterday afternoon in the backyard."

"Oh." She ducked her head. Try as she would, she could think of nothing to say.

He'd been right yesterday, Slade thought. He never should have gotten close, not even for one day. The hell of it was that he was here now. "Listen, I'm about ready for a break." He glanced toward the cookie plate. "Do you share?"

She knew what he was doing, offering her an avenue of escape. She would take it gladly, willingly. Perhaps she owed him an explanation and an apology, but they could wait. "I have some fresh lemonade."

"Perfect." He picked up the cookies and followed her inside. While she got out ice and glasses, he glanced around the living room, then trailed through the dining room into the kitchen. "I didn't realize how much smaller this place is than my father's."

A safe topic. She welcomed it. "Jeremy's is one of the largest homes in the area. Have you been out on the widow's walk? He took me up there once when I was about twelve. I was pretty imaginative and after that, I spent hours weaving fanciful tales in my head."

Sitting down at the table, he unwrapped the cookies. "I guess you're a romantic. Do you think women really used those walks to watch for ships?"

"Oh, sure. Nantucket was once the whaling capital of the world. That's why there're so many cobblestone streets, so they could accommodate the heavy oil carts. I'm sure those roof walks were used a lot by worried wives waiting for their men to return." She carried cool glasses of lemonade over and sat down.

"So then my father's house must date back to what, the 1800s?"

"Probably. Renovated several times, of course." She picked up a cookie, bit into it, nearly purring at the taste of still-warm chocolate.

Slade followed suit, watching her. "I see you love chocolate."

"Mmm, nature's most perfect food." She smiled, then brushed crumbs from her lips. Finding them slightly bruised, she felt a blush begin, remembering how they'd gotten that way. Not looking at him, she carefully set down the uneaten half of her cookie. "One more time, then we'll let it go. Thank you for understanding my . . . my actions, for coming to my aid when I sort of lost it there."

"Lady, you don't need this tarnished knight to come to your aid. You're handling things far better than most people could."

She was uncomfortable with that, didn't feel she deserved his praise. So she switched the focus. "I saw you climb the tree for Annie's kitten. It seems you help out damsels in distress and rescue defenseless animals. Do you also leap tall buildings with a single bound?"

But Slade wasn't smiling. "Don't sell yourself short. You're doing an incredible job handling a devastating situation, Briana."

She looked up then, into his eyes. "I wish I thought so. Every time I think I've got things under control, something happens and I lose it."

"You're too hard on yourself." He shifted his gaze out the window, a muscle in his jaw tightening. "I know someone who lost a child a while back and all she's able to do is sit and stare for hours on end. There aren't any guidelines, no right way or wrong way to handle yourself after a personal tragedy. Not for any of the parties involved." Including the person who caused the tragedy.

Briana studied his profile, the stubborn tilt to his chin, the worry lines at the corners of his eyes. "You sound as if you're speaking from personal experience."

Taking in a deep breath, he turned back, picked up his glass. "Bad things happen to good people, haven't you heard? Someone even wrote a book about it. I . . ."

The sharp ringing of the doorbell had both of them turning to gaze through the archway toward the front. "Expecting someone?"

"Not really, but a few of Gramp's friends have been dropping in to ask how he's doing." Briana rose and headed for the door.

Following, Slade looked through the screen door and saw a man of average height wearing a three-piece suit and a big smile. As he watched, the man shoved the door open impatiently and pulled a startled Briana to him.

"Brie, I've missed you." With that, he took her mouth in a hard kiss.

Chapter *Five*

*A*nnoyed and embarrassed, Briana shoved away from Craig and stared at him as she struggled with the urge to wipe away a kiss she'd never wanted. A flush stained her cheeks. "What was that all about?"

"Letting you know how much I missed you." His eyes roamed down to her bare feet and back up. "You look great."

Stepping back, she drew in a calming breath, hanging on to her temper by a thread. In all the years she'd known Craig Walker, going back to when he'd been Robert's best man at their wedding, he'd never kissed her other than on a cheek. What had gotten into him? And why was he here when she'd all but ordered him to stay away? "What are you doing in Nantucket?"

His boyish face turned serious. "Your mother's worried about you. I told her I'd come see how you're doing." As if suddenly noticing they weren't alone, Craig shifted his gaze to the tall man with the cool, measuring eyes and held out his hand. "Craig Walker. And you are?"

"Slade." Reluctantly, he shook Craig's hand, wondering why he'd taken an instant dislike to the man. Obviously he was more than a passing acquaintance of Briana's. That kiss had been much more than friendly, and she'd seemed embarrassed that he'd been here to witness it. None of his business, Slade thought. However, for someone who'd just buried her husband a few months ago, she certainly hadn't wasted much time. Earlier, she'd all but ripped off his clothes, and now this. Maybe he'd been wrong about Briana Morgan. Funny, he wouldn't have figured her for someone loose with her affections.

"Slade lives next door," Briana said absently, still wondering what to make of Craig's unexpected visit. She wasn't fond of uninvited drop-ins. And she didn't buy the story of her mother worrying. She'd just spoken with Martha Gifford yesterday. "He's helping me fix up Gramp's house."

One hand in his trouser pocket jiggling his change, Craig glanced around the room, then back at Briana. "Good idea. Sell it and come home. Everyone misses you."

Not sure exactly who *everyone* was, Briana was nonetheless irritated at anyone trying to make up her mind for her. "As I told you on the phone, I haven't made any definite plans."

Slade decided two was company and three definitely a crowd. "Listen, you two have some catching up to do and I've got to be going. Briana, I'll see you later."

Oddly, she didn't want him to go, but she didn't know what to say to make him stay. "We'll finish later, then?"

"Sure." With a nod toward Craig, Slade stepped out onto the porch.

"Good meeting you," Craig said, smiling now that the guy was going.

"Yeah, same here," Slade called over his shoulder.

Trying to make the best of an awkward, unwanted situation, Briana looked Craig over. His hair was trimmed to perfection, his tanned face radiating good health, his smile confident. His linen suit and paisley tie were gorgeous and as out of place on this resort island as a belly dancer at a bar mitzvah. "Now tell me, what are you *really* doing here?"

Craig managed to look wounded. "I told you the truth. I talked with your mother and she's worried. I offered to fly over and make sure you're all right. Plus, I really do miss you."

They'd hardly ever seen each other when she was in Boston, except that after Robert died, Craig had made it a point to phone more frequently and come by occasionally. What was all this "missing you" business? Brushing back her hair, Briana walked to the kitchen. "Would you like a glass of lemonade?" He had to be hot wearing all those clothes, yet he gave off no sign. Didn't the man sweat?

"Hey, that'd be great." Strolling after her, his gaze slid over old-fashioned wallpaper to the worn linoleum floor and an imitation Tiffany lamp over the kitchen table. "Did you call in a contractor to update this place? Probably won't sell unless you modernize it. As is, you'll undoubtedly take a loss."

Briana's look was sharp as she handed him the lemonade. "My grandfather's not dead, Craig. The home isn't mine to sell."

He had the good grace to look chagrined. "Of course. But your mother did say it would be yours, and I just thought . . . well, surely you don't intend to live here."

She sat down at the kitchen table, trying to come up with words he might understand and believe. "Craig, let's get something straight. I'm a grown woman and I make my own decisions. I may go back, or I may stay. I haven't made up my mind. While I appreciate my mother's concern, I can't run my life based on what she wants for me. Nor on what you think is best."

He took the chair opposite her, gazing down into his glass. "You're right. I was merely voicing her concern. Don't shoot the messenger." He sent her a look tinged with sadness. "And it hasn't been that long since . . . since you lost your family. Forgive me if I worry about my best friend's wife."

Her eyes were steady, unwavering. "That's kind of you, but I'd appreciate it if you'd honor my wishes. I told you back in Boston and again on the phone, stop worrying about me, especially since friendship is all I can offer you. That's all I'll *ever* feel for you. If you can accept that, fine. If you're looking for more, well, you'll have to look elsewhere."

"I have accepted that." Though he was certain, in time, after the grieving, she'd come around. Craig never had trouble attracting women, but *this* woman was truly a challenge. Maybe that's why he wanted her so badly.

"Really? Then what was that kiss all about?"

He ducked his head, again looking down at his glass. "I don't know. I saw you through the screen and I just lost my head." And he'd caught a glimpse of her tall friend and wanted to let the guy know he'd best back off. "You're very beautiful, you know."

Very beautiful, with eyes puffy from her earlier tears, her face too pale, her figure far too thin? There was a time she might have believed herself fairly attractive, but not today, Briana thought.

She waved a dismissive hand. "I'm not in the mood for flattery, especially when it's unfounded. I'm going through a bad time, Craig, and I'm not very good company." As Slade certainly found out.

As if reading her mind, he glanced out the kitchen window where the man who'd just left was setting out a lawn chair, wearing only a pair of cutoff shorts. "I guess your neighbor thinks you're good company."

"I just met Slade a couple of days ago. He offered to help me paint and . . ." Briana got up, her patience gone. "Look, Craig, I don't owe anyone explanations about what I'm doing here or about my neighbors. And I resent—"

"Truce, truce." Craig held out both hands, suddenly contrite. "I'm sorry. I was out of line. Briana, can we begin again? I just flew over for a couple of days in the sun. I landed this morning and checked into this terrific place on Broad Street, the Nesbitt Inn. The owners gave me directions to your place and I walked over even before changing clothes. I was anxious to see you. But if you don't have time for me, I'll just go sightseeing on my own or whatever. I don't want to add to your problems."

How was it that everyone knew just how to push her buttons? Briana wondered. She wanted to work on the house, but what could another day or two matter? Remembering how wonderful Craig had been when she'd badly needed someone after the accident, she relented. "I'm sorry, too. I'm a little on edge. Why don't you go back to the inn, change out of your traveling duds, and I'll come pick you up in about an hour. I'll give you a brief tour and maybe we can have dinner somewhere."

There was relief in Craig's smile. "Great." He spotted a

camera on the kitchen counter. "Been taking any new pictures?" He strolled over and picked up the Nikon, checking it over.

She kept all her cameras loaded and ready in case an unexpected opportunity presented itself. However, picture taking had been the furthest thing from her mind lately. "No."

"Why don't you bring this along, then? I left in a hurry and forgot my camera. I should at least show the folks back home that I've been here."

She hadn't wanted to even hold a camera in weeks, the very act taking her right back to that dreadful morning. Still, she'd have to sooner or later. Perhaps it was time. "All right." She walked him to the door. "I'll see you in an hour, then."

"I'll be ready." Craig paused, his hazel eyes again serious. "Are we all right, Briana? I apologize again for coming on too strong."

"We're fine, really." From the porch, she watched him stroll off down the street, letting out a big sigh. She trailed her hand along the smooth wood where Slade had sanded. Truth be known, she'd prefer finishing up here instead of sightseeing. But the doctor had warned her against becoming reclusive, which usually led to brooding. He'd advised her to get out among people.

All right, she'd go, Briana thought, walking inside to change. And she'd steer Craig away from difficult topics.

Gramp's blue Buick scooted along the coastal road with Briana behind the wheel rattling off bits of trivia for her avid audience of one. "Herman Melville based his novel *Moby Dick* on the *Essex,* a Nantucket whaling ship that was rammed by a whale off the coast of South America in the early 1800s. They say that a mate from the *Essex* who kept the ship's log survived to tell the tale to Melville, who then wrote the book."

"And that's a true story?" Craig said, stretching his arm along the seatback, angling his body so he could look at Briana.

"Absolutely. Two other Nantucket ships, the *Beaver* and the *Dartmouth,* were involved in the Boston Tea Party. Lots of history on this island."

Craig gazed out at the waves rolling endlessly in to shore. "I can see why you like it here."

With the windows down, Briana let the warm sea air blow her hair about. "It's beautiful, sure, but that's not why I love it here. Boston's beautiful, too, in its own way. And so's Manhattan. Nantucket's like a safe haven. Nothing really terrible ever happens here, as it does with alarming frequency on the mainland." Checking the rearview mirror, she changed lanes to pass a slow-moving van.

Craig was fairly certain she was referring to the shooting. "I doubt that there's no crime at all, even here, Briana. What happened on the Common was a freak accident. Bobby and Robert were two people in the wrong place at the wrong time."

Briana felt a muscle in her cheek clench. "I'm aware of that. Drive-by slayings are happening more and more frequently. Ugly, violent people are almost everywhere."

"And you think this place is sacrosanct, that if you stay here, you'll be safe from violence?"

She gave him a quick, disdainful glance. "Hardly. But here, I'm not reminded daily of all the ugliness that's out there. Whether it's true or not, I *feel* safer."

This was a no-win argument, Craig decided, so he

changed the subject. "There's another lighthouse up ahead. Have you ever been inside one?"

"Yes. Gramp got permission to take me into the one near his house at Brant Point when I was ten or so." She smiled at the memory. "Steep, winding staircase, all sorts of equipment at the top to track ships and the weather. And a fantastic view."

"Do you think we could stop and take a picture of this one?"

"Sure. That's Great Point Lighthouse. We're on the northern tip of the island." She glanced down at his Gucci loafers. "I don't know how close you want to get, but it's mostly sand and scrub grass around the base. You might ruin your shoes."

"I'll manage," he answered, reaching for her camera case in the back. "Hey, this is heavy. You have more than one camera in here?"

"I'm not even sure what's in there. I grabbed the case at the last minute when I was leaving Boston and I haven't looked inside except to take out my Nikon. I'd planned to take it on my beach walk the other day, but I got sidetracked." At the last minute, she hadn't been able to make herself pick up the camera. She pulled off the road and brought the Buick to a stop, then took the case from him. Removing the Nikon, she checked the gauges. "This film's been in here awhile, but it should be all right." It actually felt good in her hands, familiar.

"Let me take a couple of you," Craig said, getting out on his side.

"No, this is your vacation. Besides, I'm the photographer, remember?" They strolled toward the deserted lighthouse, Briana's sandals skimming the sand while Craig's loafers were slowly filling up. She tried not to smile.

"You sure can't complain about the weather," Craig commented, brushing back his sandy hair. "Is it this nice always?"

"It gets cold in the winter and there's even snow, but not a great deal. Fall's the rainy season, starting in mid-September. Every couple of years, they get some really rough storms."

Craig spotted a purplish-pink wildflower and stooped to look closer. "What's this?"

"Heather, like on the moors of Scotland. Some long-ago visitor must have brought some over and started a strain." She stopped, placing the strap of the Nikon around her neck, raising the camera up to eye level, testing the light. Her love of cameras, of photography, came creeping back. Yes, it was going to be all right. "Is this close enough?"

"Yeah, sure." He walked over aways, then turned around. "Ready when you are."

Briana took her time lining up the shot, thinking that the camera felt good in her hands. She focused on Craig with his perfect hair windblown, hands crammed in the pockets of his pressed khakis, Gucci's nearly buried in sand, and the lighthouse in the background. She took several shots, then changed the angle, shifted, and took a few more. "There, that should prove to one and all that you were here."

"Is that the end of the roll, or can we take some more in town?"

Climbing back into the Buick, Briana put the camera in her case. "There's more. Do you want to see the other side of the island? There're these great cranberry bogs."

Craig closed his door. "You bet. That is, if you have the time."

She owed him this much, this day, she supposed. He was trying to be a friend, distracting her. "No problem."

"I heard at the inn that the lobster dinners at a place called Vincent's are the best. Have you eaten there?"

"No, but most of the places on the island serve fantastic seafood. We can try Vincent's."

"Great. Let's check out the other side, then I'll take you to dinner. How many lobsters can you eat at one setting?" His smile was teasing.

"Maybe one, certainly not more. How about you?"

"Two, possibly two and a half. I remember once, Robert and I were walking around Faneuil Hall and . . . hey, I'm sorry. I didn't mean to . . ."

"No, it's all right. Tell me." Briana steeled herself for the story, determined to get used to hearing both names without weeping. She simply would have to.

Craig wanted to end their day with a walk on the beach near her house, so Briana led the way, snapping more pictures as they strolled. The sunset was dripping reds and golds through a deep azure sky as seagulls dipped into the water for their fish dinners. Two lovers on a blanket sat with arms around each other, oblivious to the few stragglers left on the beach.

"The shoreline's sure different here than along Hyannis or the coast of Maine," Craig said, gazing toward the west. "Do you ever go over to Martha's Vineyard?"

"I have a friend who lives in Edgartown so I've been there, but not frequently. There's air service and lots of charter boats if you want to check it out."

"Maybe next visit. That is, if I'm invited back."

She hadn't invited him this time, Briana thought, then decided she was being uncharitable. Craig wasn't such bad company, she supposed. He'd entertained her throughout a delicious lobster dinner with funny tales about some of his clients. He'd been gracious and attentive. However, despite that, she wasn't anxious to spend more time with him. "Oh, I'll probably be back in Boston before you think about another trip."

Turning, she gazed toward Brant Point and narrowed her eyes as she noticed a man sitting on the rocks. As they strolled closer, she was certain she recognized him.

"What's that fool doing up there?" Craig asked, following her gaze. "That's quite a fall if he loses his balance."

Briana didn't comment, just kept watching Slade as he sat staring out to sea, his black hair shifting in the breeze. She couldn't help wondering what he was thinking, how long he'd been there. And if he'd taken along a six-pack for company.

"Looks like your neighbor," Craig went on. "Is he a beach bum who does odd jobs for a living?"

Annoyed, she frowned at him. "Why would you think that? Actually, he just inherited one of the best houses on the island and a great deal of money, plus a fortune in art." Ordinarily, she wouldn't reveal the extent of someone's assets to anyone, although Slade's inheritance was common knowledge on the island, but Craig's assumption had raised her hackles.

"Inherited, eh? That's getting there the easy way." Oblivious to her irritation, he pointed to her camera. "Any left on that roll?"

"No, I took the last one of you wading in the surf." He'd actually taken off his shoes and socks, turning up his pant legs. Briana decided that was probably as informal as he ever got.

"I'll get some more film for tomorrow, if you're free."

"I'm afraid not. I've made plans. If I'd known you were

coming . . ." She'd just decided that instant that she'd had enough sightseeing and enough of Craig.

"Hey, that's all right. Maybe I'll go fishing."

She couldn't picture the fastidious Craig Walker on a boat hauling in smelly fish, but she didn't really know the man all that well. The sun was nearly gone, sinking slowly at the horizon. "I think we should head back." One last glance toward the rocks and she saw that Slade had turned in their direction and was now watching them. She had the feeling Slade hadn't thought much of Craig, and vice versa.

Back at the house, Craig sat down to put on his shoes and socks. "If that roll's done, I'll take it in for you tomorrow and get doubles made. There's a camera shop near the inn."

"That's not necessary. I'll get around to it and mail you copies."

He stood, putting on his charming smile. "I insist. It's the least I can do after you gave up most of your day for me."

Briana had a feeling he was looking for another excuse to come by the house, but to refuse again would be rude. She'd already rewound the film and now popped it out and handed it to him. "Leave my copies with Ned Farrell at Island Camera and I'll pick them up later." She noticed a flicker of annoyance in his eyes, and then it was gone.

"I'll do that." He leaned close and placed a very chaste kiss on her cheek. "Thanks for the tour."

"And thank you for dinner. Would you like me to drive you back to the inn?"

Craig licked his lips, a nervous habit he'd been trying to break. Another one was Briana Morgan. He hadn't actively pursued a woman in years. Hadn't had to. But this was different. There was more here than a roll in the hay, not that he'd turn that down, either.

But even a man as stubborn as he could see that he was getting nowhere this trip. "I like to walk. Bye, Briana." He started off undaunted, thinking there was always next time.

"Have a safe trip home, if I don't see you before you leave." And she sincerely hoped she wouldn't. Perhaps she *was* turning reclusive, Briana thought.

Inside, she slipped off her sandals and set down the camera. Maybe it was because Craig reminded her too much of a time in life when she'd been much happier. Maybe it was his aggressive manner, showing up when she'd made it clear he shouldn't, and then that annoying kiss.

Kissing, she'd always maintained, was such a personal act that one ought to be able to choose one's partner. She definitely wouldn't have chosen Craig. Though he'd tried, his kiss had left her cold.

Unlike the stunning kisses she'd shared with Slade.

He had been the unwilling partner that time. At first. Then he'd responded and even taken over. Perhaps he wouldn't have initiated a kiss just then, but he'd nonetheless participated wholeheartedly.

Or was it just because she'd been all over him and he was, after all, a man? She'd probably never know.

Briana poured herself a glass of iced tea and carried it out to the screened-in porch, sitting down in Gramp's rocker. It was something she'd taken to doing most every evening, gazing out at the water, listening to the surf, letting the soothing sounds relax her. Such a peaceful place, she thought, sipping.

A movement to the right caught her attention. She saw Slade climbing the steps to his porch. She waited to see what he'd do, knowing he could see her in the glow of the streetlamp.

Slowly, he looked over and stared for a long minute. "Your company gone?"

"Yes. You want to get back to work tomorrow?"

"Maybe. I'll see how my day goes." With that, he went inside.

Well, fine, Briana thought. Now, why on earth was his nose out of joint? And why should she care? Rising, she went inside and locked her door.

By ten the next morning, Briana had put in two hours scraping paint and sanding around the enclosed porch, yet she still hadn't seen a sign of life next door. Silly to worry, she supposed. Slade was a grown man. A grown man who'd been known to drink his troubles away, whatever they were. Why she should care was a good question, one Briana didn't want to consider for long. Simple human compassion for a neighbor, she finally decided.

Finished, she washed her hands, rinsed off her warm face with cool water, and tied back her hair. After taking a long drink from her bottle of water, she strolled outside. All right, so she'd make a fool of herself yet again, go over and ask him if he felt like painting today since the house was pretty well ready. If he rebuffed her, so be it. At least she'd know.

After all, he'd asked her if he could help. It would be rude to start painting without him, wouldn't it? Of course, something could have come up, an appointment he'd forgotten. It wasn't as if she *needed* his help. Well, only at the top of the house.

Then again, what if he'd tripped and fallen down the stairs, was even now lying there in desperate need? Briana smiled at her rationalizations. The curse of an overactive imagination.

Oh, to hell with it!

The sun was very hot as she stood on the porch and rang his doorbell. She could hear the echo through the rooms, but no footsteps. Fine. He wasn't home. She'd manage just fine without him. She was just about to leave when she heard sounds inside. Then the door swung open and Slade stood there.

For a moment, her breath caught. He was shirtless and shoeless, wearing only gray knit shorts that advertised his sex more enticingly than if he'd been naked. Dark, curly hair was in evidence on his strong legs, his wide, muscular chest, and even his square chin since he hadn't shaved. He was rousingly male this morning, causing her to take a step backward and clear her throat.

"Hi. I was wondering if you were still interested in painting." For a moment there, she'd forgotten why she'd come over.

Slade glanced out and saw that the sun was high in the sky. "I didn't realize it was so late. Time got away from me. Yeah, I want to paint, but first, maybe you can help me with something." He held open the screen. "Have you got a minute?"

Briana hesitated for a heartbeat, then decided she was being foolish. "Sure." She stepped inside, wishing he'd put on a shirt. Why was it that if they'd been out on the beach, she'd think nothing of his outfit, but here, in such close quarters, she found his lack of clothes unnerving? And oddly exciting.

"I've been up in Jeremy's storage room looking over his paintings. Have you ever been in there?"

"No." Glad for the distraction, she gazed around the gracious living room. "Actually, I haven't been inside this house since I was a teenager. Jeremy rarely had guests. It's even more lovely than I remember." Through the archway, she spotted the cut glass bowl on the dining room table and strolled over. "Lemon drops. He always carried some in his pocket, too."

Slade tipped his head thoughtfully. "It's quite possible you have more memories of my father than I do."

His words were said without pity, more as an observance. Yet she wished she hadn't reminded him of the years he'd missed knowing Jeremy. "I'm sorry. I didn't mean to . . ."

He waved a dismissive hand. "Not your fault. It's just that every day in this house—in *his* house—I learn something more about him. Yet I don't feel I'm any closer to knowing him." He ran a hand through his hair. He wasn't a man who verbalized his feelings easily, especially to women. Yet, since witnessing that episode in her backyard and then yesterday when she'd reached out for comfort in the only way she could think of at the moment, he felt he could say things to her he wouldn't have under normal circumstances, and that she just might understand. "Does that make any sense?"

"Yes, it does. There are times when I've wondered if we ever really know anyone." She trailed her fingers along the rim of the lovely bowl, her eyes downcast. "I knew Robert for three years before we married, even lived with him awhile before the wedding. Yet within the year, I knew I'd made a mistake, that I hadn't looked closely enough, that I hardly knew him at all. But by then, I was pregnant with Bobby."

"So you stuck it out."

She turned to him, met his eyes. "For a while. But things got worse and I divorced him three years ago."

That was it, the thing he hadn't guessed, the *something* that explained her behavior. A woman who'd loved her husband and lost him a few short months ago wouldn't have reached out for another man as Briana had yesterday. At least not the kind of woman he felt Briana Morgan was. "That explains it." When he saw her puzzled look, he stumbled about for another explanation. "Your visitor, Craig Walker. You've obviously been together awhile."

Briana shook her head. "No, nothing like that. Craig was Robert's best friend going way back. He was there for me that terrible day, helping with the arrangements. I don't know if I could have gotten through the funeral without him. But we're just friends."

She could tell he didn't believe her and wondered why she wanted him to. Her relationship with Craig was none of Slade's business. Yet knowing he'd witnessed that kiss bothered her. She disliked having given the wrong impression. "I discouraged him from visiting me here, but he came anyhow. I don't know why, since I've told him repeatedly that there can't be anything between us but friendship."

"Why can't there be?" Slade had been watching her closely, wondering if she, too, felt she could somehow say things to him that she might not have before yesterday, when her defenses had been stripped raw. He doubted that she saw Craig Walker the way he did, as a man intent on moving in on a beautiful, vulnerable woman.

Briana shrugged. "Because he was Robert's friend, not mine. And because the last thing I need in this world is to get involved with anyone, much less someone I feel nothing for except gratitude."

Slade's expression relaxed. Maybe she did see through Craig. "I admire a woman who knows her own mind."

She couldn't take credit for that. "I wish that described me. On the subject of Craig I do, but on very little else lately, it seems. Half the time, I feel as if I'm floundering, uncertain which choice is the right one."

Slade nodded. "I understand that perfectly, which brings me to my problem. The owner of that art gallery in town called earlier today. She claims she's got people clamoring for Jeremy's paintings. I've been trying to sort through them, but I don't know which ones to take in. Will you come upstairs and have a look?"

"Sure, although I don't know how much help I'll be." She followed him up the stairs, her eyes straying to muscular legs, her thoughts again giving her pause. Annoyed with herself, Briana walked into Jeremy's storage room, intent on concentrating on paintings.

"Oh, my," she whispered, gazing about the large cool room as Slade turned on the lights. Jeremy had had it customized so that three of the four walls were filled with narrow cubicles, each containing a painting that slid into its own slot and stood upright on the edge of the canvas. Glass doors closed off each section, preventing dust from harming the art. "There have to be over a hundred paintings in here," she commented, awestruck anew by Jeremy's output.

"A hundred eighty to be exact," he told her. "And another fifty or sixty in his studio downstairs where he did his actual painting and framing." Hands on his hips, he gazed around the room. "You see my dilemma?"

"Yes, I certainly do." She walked over to the far end and opened that glass door. "Maybe they're stored according to subject matter or perhaps by date. Did he sign and date all of them, I hope?"

"From what I've checked, yes, he did. Does that make a difference?"

"It sure does." She eased out a large canvas depicting a seascape resplendent with colorful sailboats. "This looks as if it might be a scene he painted right out front here."

"Every one I've looked at randomly appears to be painted around Nantucket." He walked to the opposite wall. "Except for this small group." Opening the glass door, he pulled out a canvas no bigger than nine-by-twelve. "Portraits. Do you know who this fellow might be?"

A soft smile on her lips, Briana walked over and stood gazing at the white-haired man with the craggy, tanned face, a pipe stuck in his mouth, laugh lines crinkling the corners of his blue eyes. "That's Gramp," she said, swallowing around a sudden lump in her throat. "That's how he looked, oh, even last year, before the awareness slipped from his eyes."

Slade put it in her hands. "It's yours."

"Oh, no." She continued looking at the portrait, her admiration for Jeremy's talent evident. "I can't accept this, Slade. It's worth a great deal."

"That isn't the point. It's mine to give, apparently, and I want you to have it."

"Look, I'd like to have this because I believe paintings should reside with people who love them, and I love this. But I'll pay you for it."

"I'll tell you what. We'll arm wrestle for it. Winner gets his way." Slade watched another of her infrequent smiles form, and felt he'd done the right thing. He bent to pull out another canvas of an old man, this one tall and thin, slightly stooped, walking along a tree-lined street using a bentwood cane, a white cap with a dark bill on his head. "Do you recognize him?"

Reluctantly taking her eyes from Gramp's painting, she shifted her gaze. "That's Sailor Bob, a character if ever there was one. He rented boats to tourists as far back as I can remember and told stories about how he used to sail the high seas in his younger days. He died about five years ago. I had no idea Jeremy did portraits, too."

"Do you know if Sailor Bob has family here? They might like to have this."

Setting down the painting she still held, she stared at him. "Are you going to methodically give all these away?"

Slade straightened, gesturing around the room with one hand. "Look at this room, Briana. According to Fern Brokawer, some sell for five thousand, more as high as ten, and a few of the smaller ones go for two or three thousand. And that was *before* Jeremy died. She claims she'll be able to get more for each now. Don't you think I can afford to give away a few?"

"Yes, I guess you can." She had to remind herself that he had no sentimental ties to Jeremy Slade, and the reminder saddened her. "Would it bother you to tell me what happened to estrange you and your father?"

In a way, he supposed it would bother him. But hadn't she opened to him, showed a far more vulnerable side? He rarely talked about Jeremy, but what could it hurt?

He considered her question. "I wish I knew what happened back all those years ago." He returned Sailor Bob to his cubicle. "I'm not trying to be cagey because I honestly don't know." There was only one window in the room, covered with wooden blinds kept closed to keep the light to a minimum. Beneath it were two navy canvas boat chairs. Slade strolled over, lifted a wooden slat, and gazed

out. But instead of seeing blue sky and tumbling waves, he
was remembering another time as if it were yesterday.

"I'd just come home from school and there was my father, back from one of his almost weekly trips. He was a
traveling salesman. Only instead of his usual smiling
greeting, he walked past me all tight-lipped and angry, carrying his bags out and loading them in his car. I knew
something was terribly wrong. I tried to talk to him, but he
wouldn't answer me, so I went inside to get an explanation
from my mother. She was sitting by the window crying,
and she wouldn't talk to me, either. The next day was my
tenth birthday."

Briana wondered if he knew just how heartbreaking he
sounded. She walked over to join him, sitting down in one
of the chairs and looking up at him. "And up to that point,
you hadn't had a clue that something was wrong between
them?"

Slowly, Slade shook his head. "I thought we had an ideal
life, but what does a kid know? We had a nice house in this
small town outside Sacramento, with a big yard and a pool.
Dad was gone a lot, but when he was home, he taught me
to swim, to ride horseback, took me camping. Mom was always laughing. We were happy. Then, without a word of
explanation, without a backward glance, he drove away. I
stood on the porch long after his car was out of sight. I
didn't cry. I think I was in shock."

"And your mother, did she say anything later, give you
some reason? Maybe they had a quarrel?"

"I never heard them argue, not once. I never heard my
father raise his voice, not to me or to my mother. No matter how many times I asked her why he left, she never gave
me a reason."

Briana had known Jeremy to be closemouthed, but to

walk away from his only child like that. It was shocking. "Your mother must have taken it hard, too."

He let out a bitter laugh. "Yeah, you could say that. She'd married young, wasn't trained to do much besides clerical work. She no sooner got a job than she lost it. We moved out of the house, probably because she couldn't afford to keep it. We were always moving after that, one crummy apartment after another." Abruptly, he turned and sat down, feeling weary.

"Surely, if there was a divorce, Jeremy had to pay child support. You were so young."

"He did. The envelopes arrived every month, like clockwork, despite our many address changes. No note, just the check. But still, there was never enough money." He reached for the glass of iced tea he'd set down before answering the door. "You'll be happy to know I'm off the sauce." He swirled ice in the glass, staring at it.

"You see, we kept moving to stay ahead of the bill collectors. We couldn't pay even the rent half the time because my mother decided the bottle was her best escape." He took a long swallow of tea. "Maybe that's why I gave booze a try recently, to see if I could discover what pleasure she found in passing out night after night so I'd have to put her to bed. Or wandering off to bars and forgetting to come home so I'd have to go looking for her." Another grim laugh escaped from him. "Damned if I know what it was because all I found was a major hangover."

"She's not the first person who's tried to find the answer in alcohol, nor the last. What pain she must have been in."

"She suffered, that's for sure." He gazed around, his eyes bitter and angry. "And all the while, he was sitting in this expensive house stockpiling money and paintings."

She studied him as he leaned forward, his elbows on his

knees, his stubborn chin set, his gray eyes stormy. "You hate him very much."

It wasn't a question, he knew. He set down his glass and let out a rush of air. "I've sure as hell spent a lot of years trying. I hate what he did to us, but I keep thinking he had to have had a reason. I need to know that reason."

He'd tried to hate, but wound up hurting instead. It might have been easier on him if he could have kept that edge of anger. "Have you looked through his papers? Maybe he left you a letter or some explanation."

"I haven't gone through everything, but I did separate his legal papers into piles. There's no letter."

She wanted badly to offer him some hope. "Maybe, in reading everything thoroughly, you'll find an answer. I'm surprised your mother, if she drank so much, didn't slip and tell you."

"I used to try to get her to open up when she'd been drinking, thinking the same thing. All she ever said, over and over, was that she loved Jeremy, but he didn't believe her." He looked over and guessed what she was thinking. "You think he came home early and caught her with another guy, right? Could be, I suppose. But I want you to know that never in all the time between him leaving and her dying the week after my nineteenth birthday did I see her with a guy. Not once. Even in the bars, she sat alone, she drank alone, she staggered home alone."

"Heartbreaking. What did you do after she died?"

"I joined the navy to see the world. I pretty much did, too. It wasn't such a bad four years. They let me finish college, taught me to fly." He'd come back stronger, tougher, but just as unhappy.

A misfit, Slade had decided, that was what he'd been. A man without a family, without a home to come back to or a city he could call his own. He'd tried one job after another, one town after another, one woman, then another. Too many. None seemed right, no place ever seemed like home. Then one day, he'd met a guy who'd pointed him in a positive direction.

"After the navy, I became a firefighter, flying planes to put out all those California brushfires. It was exciting work and paid well."

"I had the impression you were a fireman on the ground."

"I was, after I quit flying." That was where he'd found his real calling. For five years, the guys at Number 105 Engine & Ladder Company had been like his extended family. Hell, they'd been his *only* family. Then had come the incident that had sent him into a new kind of hell, one of his own making.

"You said yesterday you wouldn't go back to firefighting again."

Slade sat back, realizing he'd talked more about himself in the last half hour than he had in the last five years. He hadn't even told the company shrink as much as he'd revealed to Briana today. He looked over at her, afraid he might see pity in her eyes with all she'd learned about him. But he saw only understanding and a hint of what looked like admiration. "You listen awfully well, you know. Too well."

She guessed what he was feeling and touched his arm gently. "Do you regret confiding in me? Please don't. It'll go no further. I think my behavior yesterday was far worse than anything you've said today." She saw in his eyes that he was remembering that scene in the kitchen, the one she wished she could erase from both their memory banks. "And don't be ashamed of what you've been through,

Slade. It took courage, a great deal of courage, for a ten-year-old to survive against those odds."

"I didn't feel particularly courageous. I remember being scared shitless most of the time."

"Undoubtedly, but you survived. You're a survivor. Someone recently said that about me, and I wasn't sure I wanted to be. Things happen sometimes and you feel as if it'd be easier to just give up, that it wouldn't hurt so much. But my dear friend, Irma Tatum, said that there are two kinds of people in the world, the quitters and the survivors. And that you can pretty much tell at an early age with a child which way they'll turn out."

"You believe that?"

"Yes, I think I do. Or maybe I just want to. How about you?"

"I'll have to give it some thought." Slade drew in a long breath, then stood. "So, are you going to pick out some paintings for me to take over to the art gallery? Or do you want to get started on the house and we'll do this later?"

"Let's pick out half a dozen paintings now. That should hold Fern for a while." Briana rose and walked to the end row. "Maybe you should choose one from each year, starting with the oldest, for six years. And make them just a little different, a seascape, maybe a street scene, then a lighthouse view. I know Jeremy must have several lighthouse paintings. I used to see him set up his easel down the beach and sit for hours on end."

Slade didn't want to talk anymore about his father. He was all talked out. So they methodically removed several canvases, looked them over, compared them, pushed a few back, picked out more. By the time they'd settled on six, it was noon, the lateness of the hour surprising them both.

"I'll crate these up and take them over to the gallery in the morning," Slade said as he opened the door to the room. "I appreciate your help." He picked up the portrait of her grandfather. "Don't forget this."

"Slade, I don't feel right about . . ." She hadn't realized how close he was as he followed her out.

"Then we arm wrestle for it." He smiled down at her. "But I warn you. I cheat."

"All right, I give up. Then thank you. This portrait means a great deal to me."

His eyes were friendlier than before, she noticed, suddenly a warm gray. Was it because she'd helped him with the paintings, or because she'd listened? At any rate, it was time to go, to leave this close, charged atmosphere and step out into the light of day. "I imagine you'll want to change." At least she hoped he would. Unable to stop herself, her eyes kept returning to those tight knit shorts. "I'll meet you over there."

"Right." He waited at the top of the stairs until she left, then went to his bedroom.

Unlocking her front door, Briana hurried inside, holding Gramp's portrait this way and that, wondering where she'd hang it. She'd just propped the painting on the fireplace ledge when she heard a mewing sound. Frowning, she moved to the kitchen.

A calico ball of fur leaped up onto the chair, then the table, startling her. "Rascal! What are you doing in here? And how did you get in?" It was then that she noticed that her back kitchen window had been smashed in, glass shards everywhere.

Staring transfixed, she saw that her back door was ajar, that once the window had been broken out, someone could easily have reached in and unlocked the door. Who had done it and why? And where was he now?

Oh, God! What if he was still inside?

Heart thundering, Briana ran back out the front door as if she were being hotly pursued and rushed back into Slade's living room, yelling at the top of her lungs. "Slade! Someone's broken into my house!"

Chapter Six

Sheriff Howard Stone had known and admired Andy Gifford as man and boy. Which was why he personally responded to the break-in call to Andy's house. He'd also watched Andy's granddaughter grow into a fine young woman. Smiling down at her from his six-foot height, he patted her shoulder.

"Don't you worry, Briana. We'll find out who broke in here." The sheriff glanced at his deputy carefully dusting the broken glass fragments on the kitchen floor and the table under the window. "You did the right thing, leaving the house as soon as you noticed something wrong. Looks like he broke the window, then reached in and unlocked the door, easy as pie."

"I don't understand who'd want to break in here or why," Briana said, truly puzzled now and less frightened. "I don't recall Gramp ever mentioning burglaries or thefts in this neighborhood."

Stone pushed his rimless glasses farther up on his nose

and sighed. "True enough, but these are rough times we live in. I guess I don't have to tell you that." Like everyone else on the island, the sheriff had heard about the tragic death of Briana's husband and son. "The world isn't an easy place to live in anymore," he added. "When I moved here thirty years ago and signed on as deputy, we had the occasional auto accident, some kids vandalizing now and again, maybe some petty thievery in a hotel once in a while. But now?" He waved a bony hand. "You don't want to know." But he leaned down and told her anyway. "Actually had an elderly tourist assaulted walking along Petticoat Row one evening last month."

Hadn't she just told Craig yesterday that she felt safer in Nantucket than anywhere else? Was her last bastion now gone? "That's terrible."

The sheriff shifted his shrewd gaze to the man in the worn jeans and T-shirt, the one who'd called in the report. "Don't believe we've met, young man, but I knew your father well." He held out his hand. "Sheriff Stone."

Slade shook hands, thinking that if this man knew his father well, he was the only one who did. "Do you know of any other break-ins in this immediate area, Sheriff?"

"No, sir, I don't. Couldn't find any fresh footprints in back. Most of the yard's cement, like the driveway apron, the walkway, and the patio." He glanced over at the deputy, now scooping up shards and fragments. "Hopefully, we'll get some fingerprints off the glass."

"Still, they wouldn't be helpful unless the guy's got a record and his prints are on file, right?"

"Yeah, right." The sheriff sent Slade a look of grudging respect. " 'Course, we could get lucky." He turned back to Briana. "Have you checked yet? Is anything missing?"

"I did a quick inventory, but there really isn't much here

to steal. I brought over only a few things and, as you can see, my grandparents didn't live lavishly." She looked up at Slade. "Kind of makes you wonder, if the thief was after money or something valuable, why he didn't choose your house."

"Jeremy's house is wired for an alarm, but I haven't been engaging it."

"You should," Sheriff Stone said emphatically. "You might want to consider installing one, too, Briana. Though I doubt this fellow will come back. Could be some kid, you know. A prank. Or . . ." He walked to the back and looked out. "Isn't that the Reeds' house past the shrub fence? Maybe their little girl tossed a ball through your window."

"I doubt she'd have the strength at age six, Sheriff," Slade said, wondering just how efficient this man was. "Besides, we didn't find a ball in here."

"Yeah, you're probably right." Annoyed that he'd conjectured aloud, Stone ran a hand over his thinning hair, feeling every day of his sixty years. "You finished, Simmons?" he asked the young deputy.

"Yes, sir." Simmons sealed his evidence bag, nodded to Briana, and left through the back door.

"I'll send someone over to fix your window, Briana," the sheriff offered. "Least I can do for Andy's granddaughter."

"That won't be necessary," Slade answered before Briana could. "I'll fix it and get some better locks as well." He pointed to the flimsy slide-lock on the back door. "That's not good. You need a dead bolt."

"Just like in Boston," Briana complained. "We have to live in fortresses. I hate it."

Stone nodded. "Can't blame you there. I hate it, too. I'll

be in touch." With a nod to both of them, he followed his deputy out.

Briana opened the small kitchen closet and took out the broom and dustpan, wanting to sweep up all that the officer missed. "Thanks. I'm sorry I acted like such a ninny, running over to you. But all I could think of was what if he was still in the house."

"And he could have been. Do you have a tape measure handy? I'd like to take care of this right away."

She let her gaze drift down to his bare feet, knowing he'd been changing clothes when she'd run screaming to him. "Maybe you should get your shoes first."

At least she seemed calmer now. "I will. You want to look around while I do this and make sure nothing was stolen?"

Briana let out a nervous breath as she rummaged through a kitchen drawer, looking for the tape measure. "What's in this house that someone would want badly enough to break in? I'm truly puzzled."

"Did you bring any jewelry with you? Maybe someone saw you in town wearing something valuable."

Her hand went to the gold chain she wore and the small heart that dangled from it. Robert had given the necklace to her when Bobby had been born. She never took it off. And she wore an amethyst ring in a gold setting, a gift from her parents. "I brought only the jewelry I'm wearing. I rarely travel with more. The few other good pieces I have are at home." Which reminded her of something. "You know, my condo in Boston was broken into shortly after . . . after the funeral."

Spotting the tape measure in the corner of the drawer, Slade took it out and walked to the window. "Anything turn up missing?"

"Two cameras from my darkroom."

"That was it?"

Grabbing paper and pencil, she went over to watch him measure. "Far as I could tell."

"You weren't home at the time, I take it."

"No. I'd gone to visit my sister in Florida, mostly because I was such an emotional wreck. But after four days, I flew back. I just wasn't fit company for anyone. And I walked into a real mess. That time, drawers were open and everything spilled out onto the floor. Cupboards and closets had been gone through, everything scattered. But the worst thing was, they'd gotten into the darkroom I'd had built off the kitchen, ruined a bunch of new film and took two of my best cameras. I felt like sitting down and crying."

"Did you report it to the police?"

"Oh, yes. Someone had forced open my patio door and gotten in that way. Easiest point of entry, the officer told me. He took down all the information and to this day, I've never heard from them." She sighed, feeling frustrated. "That's probably what will happen this time, too."

Slade jotted down measurements, stuck the paper in his pocket. "I think Chief Stone's a bit past his prime. Fingerprints rarely get you anywhere unless you're dealing with hardened criminals with a rap sheet. Why would someone like that choose this small, innocuous house to break into?"

"You're right. It doesn't make sense. But then, who else is there?"

"Maybe not a visitor but a resident. Older people often keep cash squirreled away in secret locations. We had a fire once in a home where this elderly woman kept screaming that we had to go back for Mickey. I asked her who Mickey was—her husband, a child, her dog? Turned out to be a Mickey Mouse bank stuffed full of money. Did your grandfather keep cash around and maybe someone got wind of it?"

Briana was already shaking her head. "No. They were both retired business people. He had his own insurance agency and my grandmother had a store off Main Street called the Needle Pointe. They believed in banks. Also, this house stood vacant for several weeks after my parents came over and took Gramp to the nursing home before I decided to visit. If someone suspected there was something worth stealing, that would've been the time to break in, wouldn't you think?"

"You have a point there. I'll get my shoes and keys and run into town for the replacement glass and some sturdy locks."

"I can do that. Give me the measurements and I'll go. I don't want to stay here alone just now." Not an easy admission to make, but it was the truth.

Slade had a better suggestion. "I saw some boards in Jeremy's garage. I'll nail this window shut and we'll both go. How's that?"

"Are you sure? You must have things to do and . . ."

"I'm sure. Sweep up. I'll be right back."

She swept, the work occupying her hands but not her mind. The break-in worried her, yet something else now tangled her thoughts as well. She'd run over to Slade's at the first hint of trouble as if she'd been doing it all her life. That instinctive act had her frowning.

She hadn't leaned on a man in years. Or had she ever, really? Her father hadn't been home enough to count on during her early years. Robert had been too impatient, too occupied, too unsympathetic to even listen to any fears or problems she might have had. No, she'd never leaned on anyone, and she preferred it that way. An independent woman of the nineties, able to care for herself, make her own decisions, take her own lumps.

Except this time, she'd acted on pure instinct. It felt strange, and not at all as unpleasant as she'd feared, to have had Slade come running down, calming her, taking over. Then, while they'd waited for the police, she'd had a delayed reaction and begun to tremble ever so slightly. She'd struggled with an alarming need to be held, just simply to be held.

And somehow, he'd known.

He'd put those strong firefighter's arms around her, eased her close to that solid chest, and put his big hands on her back, stroking her gently. His touch hadn't been in the least sexual in nature, but rather like a big brother might comfort. It had lasted but a few moments, yet she remembered in vivid detail the earthy male scent of him, the feeling of strength he conveyed.

Bending to the trash can, Briana dropped the debris in and put away the broom and dustpan. Her life was in a state of upheaval, she assured herself. That was the reason for her actions and reactions. It was nothing more than that.

Trying to believe that thought, she went to change from shorts to jeans.

In his garage after getting his shoes, Slade was struggling with some concerns of his own. Frowning, he carried boards, nails, and hammer around back to Briana's window. True, the break-in was a mystery and made him uneasy to think she might have walked in on whoever the hell had broken the window and let himself in. But other feelings vied for his attention, feelings that didn't please him.

Having been forced to worry so much about his mother as a boy, he'd shied away from relationships and even friendships that would cause him concern, with one notable and disastrous exception. After Rachel, he'd decided he'd spend time only with lighthearted women, problem-free friends, folks who weren't needy. He'd had no pets, not even plants in his sparse apartment in California. Responsible for no one but himself was the way Slade liked his life. Which was why he was so rattled to find himself suddenly worrying about Briana Morgan.

Was she inside that small house sleeping or crying for her son? Was she eating enough—she was too thin. And now, was she safe in there?

Shit! Slade dropped the hammer and popped the tip of his index finger into his mouth. That hurt. Not paying attention to what he was doing, obviously. He picked up the hammer, found the nail again, and went back to work.

He knew she'd been married, divorced, had a child, buried a child. Yet she had such an air of innocence, of vulnerability about her. Almost from the first day he'd met her, she'd had him wishing he could do things for her. Like chase the sadness from her eyes, make her smile more, hear her laugh out loud. Not once had he ever heard her laugh. He felt the challenge of doing something, anything, just to hear her laugh.

Get over it! he commanded himself. Because not only did she resemble Rachel, but in her own way, Briana was just as needy. And that spelled trouble.

He was just pounding in the last nail when the back door opened and Briana stepped out. Tipping her head, she examined his work. "That looks sturdy enough."

"It'll hold. Besides, I agree with the chief on one thing:

I doubt the thief will return, not after two cop cars came rushing over."

"You know, maybe we shouldn't be calling him a thief. I checked again and nothing's missing." However, she'd noticed that drawers had been searched, closet items shifted, things on shelves rearranged. Even food in the refrigerator had been moved around.

Involuntarily, Briana shuddered. The very thought of someone—a stranger—touching her gowns and underwear gave her an unwelcome sense of violation. What on earth had the creep been looking for?

"Maybe the kitten came bouncing in and knocked something over, the noise spooking the guy before he found anything of value. Let's not overthink it. I'll drive." He headed for the truck. "After we get the stuff, I'll buy you lunch at one of those shrimp stands along the wharf. I'm starving. How about you?"

Her mind hadn't been on food. "I guess I could eat."

"Such enthusiasm."

He was right. She was being a pain. Deliberately, Briana put on a smile. "Okay, upbeat all the way. Better?"

Slade smiled back. "A definite improvement."

Lunch had been eaten, supplies purchased, the window repaired, and new locks installed before Slade opened the bucket of gray paint and stirred the thick contents. Pouring a generous amount into the roller pan, he handed that to Briana. Next, he carefully placed the ladder at the far end of the side facing Jeremy's house and climbed up, the other bucket and brush in hand, to begin the white trim. She'd said she didn't like heights so he'd offered to do the top half. Glancing down, he saw that she was quite contentedly rolling away a short distance over. The old shingles were soaking in the paint.

"You ever paint before?" Slade asked her.

"I did that picket fence out front when I was a teenager. And I painted all the rooms of my town house after the divorce before we moved in. I remember I let Bobby help me and he wound up splattered with paint from his blond head to his sneakers." There, she'd said her son's name out loud without her eyes filling. A definite milestone.

"You're an old pro then, eh?" Looking up, Slade stroked the brush along the boards under the eaves.

"Well, I wouldn't say that. I did the work in the town house as kind of a rebellious thing. I wanted everything in there to be my way. My color choices, my taste, and no one else's."

"I suppose everyone wants to decorate a place their way at least once." Although he never had, mostly because the places he'd lived had never really mattered to him.

"I know I did, mostly because when Robert and I bought the house in Cambridge, he had very definite ideas and he hired the work done a certain way without checking with me." Briana brushed the back of her hand across her cheek where she'd felt spray from the roller splash. Good thing this paint was water soluble, she couldn't help thinking.

"That must have gone over well."

"Yeah, right. We had some serious words over that and he refrained from dictating quite so strongly again."

"Did you disagree a lot?" The only marriage he'd seen up close had been his parents' union. And that had apparently been a lie if it could fall apart so suddenly. He'd never been one to accept invitations to the homes of his married friends, so he was curious in a general way, not just interested in this particular marriage, he told himself.

Thinking, Briana let a minute go by before answering. "Yes, I guess we did. Mostly about his job, his all-fired ambition." In Robert's defense, she felt she should explain that statement. "Robert's father was a state senator from upstate New York, a very successful man everyone looked up to. Robert had badly wanted his father's approval, the same financial rewards his father had, the respect. He felt the way to go about that was to work harder, longer, to climb the ladder, and eventually become a vice president."

"How'd you feel about that?"

"At first, I admired his desire to excel. But each time he got a promotion or achieved another level, he enjoyed it for perhaps a day, then started scrambling for the next mountain to climb. He was rarely home, hardly knew his son, and when he was with us, he was exhausted. In the five years of our marriage, we never once went away together, took a vacation or even a long weekend, not even a honeymoon. I told him his ambition was killing our marriage. He didn't believe me until I filed for divorce."

"So basically you left him because he was a workaholic?"

Briana watched the roller as she swished it in the paint in the pan. "Oh, it's never that simple. There were other things, but that was the crux of it. I didn't go into marriage on a whim, nor did I divorce on impulse. I thought about both long and hard, but looking back, I don't think either of us realized that we didn't really know the other person. We grew apart because we didn't have the same goals. We ignored the signs and never really talked about our problems. A good marriage takes two people working together to succeed. Or so I'm told."

Slade needed to move the ladder, so he climbed down. "Think you'll ever marry again?"

He looked the same, Briana thought, studying him. The same pewter-gray eyes, the wind-tossed dark hair, that rakish scar, the stubborn chin shadowed with two-days' growth. Yet somehow different. Was it because this morning in his father's house, he'd allowed her a glimpse into his past, into what made him the man he'd become? Or was it this odd protectiveness he seemed to feel for her, a kind of shielding she'd never known before?

Tugging her gaze from him, she resumed her painting. "I haven't given it much thought, to tell you the truth."

Slade was considering that when a car turned into the driveway, drawing their attention. Peering around him, Briana recognized their visitor and set down the roller and pan. Wiping her hands on a cloth, she spoke to Slade. "That's Ned Farrell from the Island Camera Shop." She walked toward the short, stout man wearing a white shirt and black slacks held up by bright red suspenders. "Ned, good to see you."

"Hi, Brie. How's Gramp doing?" Carrying a yellow envelope, Ned met her halfway.

"About the same, I guess. What brings you out this way?" Though a lot of friends and neighbors had been stopping by to ask about Gramp, she didn't think the shopkeeper would have driven over just for that.

"A couple of things." He held the envelope out for her. "Young fellow by the name of Craig Walker was waiting at the shop early this morning when I opened up. He had me print two copies of this roll of film and told me to give you one on account of he had to fly back home kind of sudden like. Some minor emergency, he said."

"Really? Well, thank you, but you didn't have to deliver it. There's no rush."

Ned pulled a snow-white handkerchief from his back

pocket and mopped at his damp brow. "I know, but I got something else I want to ask you. Guess you know the Artists' Association Members Exhibition's coming up in September. I've heard rumors you may be staying on through the fall. I'd sure be flattered to display some of your work, if you have any photos available. It's not for another month, so there's time. I'll mat 'em for you and hang 'em. Shucks, it ain't every day we have someone famous in our midst who's published a book."

Briana smiled. "I don't know about famous, but I thank you for the invitation."

"Think you'll have time to get me a few?"

"Let me think about it, okay, Ned? I want to get Gramp's house in shape before the fall rains. I'll look through some I have on hand, though."

"That'd be super." He peeked around Briana at the tall man climbing the ladder he'd finished repositioning. "That wouldn't be Jeremy's son, would it? Heard tell he was here."

"Yes. Would you like to meet him?"

"Sure would. Maybe I can talk him into loaning us a couple of his father's paintings for the exhibit."

Briana introduced the two men and let them discuss the upcoming event. Looking hopeful, Ned left, though Briana noticed that Slade had been about as noncommital as she. She studied the envelope of snapshots. No, not now. She didn't particularly want to see copies of all the pictures she'd taken of Craig, and she had no idea what the photos she'd taken on the beginning of the roll might be of.

Even more than for her work, since Bobby had been born, she'd always kept a loaded camera handy so she could take pictures of his every new accomplishment, each new tooth, all the holidays. She had literally hundreds of pictures, but she hadn't looked at the many albums since that fateful day. She couldn't face seeing any new ones just now, snapshots that undoubtedly would have been taken weeks, perhaps mere days, before he died. Perhaps when she was stronger.

Briana placed the envelope on the grass at the corner and resumed her painting.

Slade had been watching her carefully without seeming to, and had noticed the way she'd studied the envelope of pictures before she'd set it aside. He remembered seeing her and Craig walking on the beach last evening, with Briana taking pictures of him. Why, he wondered, didn't she want to see them?

"So your friend took off in a hurry this morning?" he asked.

"I guess so. Can't imagine what kind of emergency he'd have on a Saturday. Not work connected. Maybe it's his mother. She's got a weak heart."

Or was it just that Craig hadn't gotten to first base with Briana so he'd decided to back off for now and try again later? Slade wondered. Craig seemed like a man who wouldn't give up even against tough odds. Still, Briana had seemed adamant that they were just friends.

Why the hell was he pondering that relationship? Slade asked himself, swiping the brush overhead almost viciously. It didn't matter one bit to him whether she sent that geek in the linen suit packing or married him. Did it?

Time to switch the focus. "Hey, boss, how long do we have to work in this broiling heat? Do we get combat pay for sunburns?"

"What a baby! Want me to get you some sunblock?" She'd smeared some on her face and arms before coming out. Fair as she was, the sun was rarely kind to her, even after she'd built up a season's tan, which she hadn't managed to do this year.

"Nah, I'd rather complain." He never burned, just got tanner. Must have been some Mediterranean ancestors in the old family tree, Slade had always thought. Neither of his parents had been as dark as he, not their skin or hair. A small piece of biological luck, but he'd take it.

"Complain away. This was your idea, helping me, you know. You want to quit, you certainly can. The pay doesn't get any better." Only after she'd said the words did she realize she hoped he wouldn't take her up on her impulsive offer. It was hot out and slow going. She just might quit herself if he did.

"You can't get rid of me that easily." Dipping his brush into the bucket, his arm twitched just as he reached to tap off the excess. A healthy dollop fell straight downward right onto Briana's head. "Whoops!"

"Hey!" She'd wrapped a scarf she'd found in a drawer around most of her hair, but as luck would have it, the blob of paint fell on a section uncovered. She scowled at the sticky mess. "This may mean war, Mr. Slade."

His lips twitching, he climbed down. "Here, let me get that off for you."

"How do you plan to do that, exactly?" Head angled to the side, she held the lock of hair soaked in white paint out from her shoulder. "So this is how I'll look in another twenty years, eh? Maybe sooner." She gave him a mock frown as he stood looking down at her, trying not to smile. "Maybe in the next hour, if you have your way. Perhaps we should switch places and I can drip down on you."

Slade had a clean corner of his rag in his hand. "Here, just hold still."

She pulled away out of reach. "Never mind. You'll just rub more in. I'll wash it out when we're finished."

"Then at least let me wipe off this smudge that's near your eye before you manage to smear it in." Holding her steady with one hand on her shoulder, he bent to the task, concentrating on the spot, moving carefully so as not to rub too hard on her soft skin.

For a heartbeat, two at the most, time stood still for Briana and suddenly she was engulfed in feelings. Everything was magnified, exaggerated, making her aware. His touch, surprisingly gentle. The smell of paint rising between them in the hot sun. Streaks of perspiration sliding down her back beneath her shirt. His tan skin shiny and damp and utterly masculine. The tiny gold flecks in the depths of his gray eyes that she'd not noticed before. And the heat that shimmered between them that had nothing to do with the temperature of the summer day and everything to do with the way he looked at her as he slowly lowered his hand.

Then it was over, and she stepped back, swallowing hard. She'd probably imagined the moment, Briana decided, bending down to add more paint from the bucket to her roller pan. She'd always been highly imaginative, her mother had said.

But when she rose and glanced over her shoulder, she saw that he was studying her with an intensity she couldn't mistake, and she knew she hadn't imagined what she'd felt. She knew Slade had felt it, too.

Slade whacked the lid onto the can three times with the heel of his hand and carried the paint bucket into Briana's garage. The brushes, pan, and rollers had been washed and were drying in the yard. Briana gathered up the rags and gave him a weary smile.

"Thanks. I couldn't have done it without you." From the corner of the yard, she gazed up at both sides of the house. "I can't believe we did so much in just, what? Six hours?"

"Teamwork," he said, rolling his shoulders. "I used to work twenty-four- hour shifts and not get this tired. I'm really out of shape."

Watching his powerful muscles moving in perfect rhythm, she didn't think so, but wisely kept quiet. "I think I need a very long, very hot shower." She glanced at the clump of painted hair. "And a thorough shampoo."

He grinned. "Occupational hazard. Happens to all good painters."

"Uh huh." Almost moaning out loud as her muscles protested, she walked to her back door. "Tomorrow?" she asked.

He nodded, then glanced up at the sky. "What are you planning to do after you clean up?" Now, why had he asked her that?

She studied her paint-spattered hands and arms. "That may be hours from now. Why? What'd you have in mind?" Without Briana's permission, her heart picked up its rhythm.

"Nothing too strenuous. Maybe a walk on the beach. If you're up to it." He saw her skeptical look. "Never mind," he said, backtracking. What was wrong with him? Talk about crowding someone. He'd been with her since ten and now the sun was setting, slowly slipping into the sea. Hadn't he been the one who wanted to steer clear of involvements? He started to walk away. "See you tomorrow."

"How long before you'll be ready?"

Slade turned back slowly. "An hour?"

"An hour and a half and you buy dinner." She'd insisted on paying for lunch since he was the one helping her. But this was different. This was evening and besides, she reminded herself, he could afford one small dinner. "I mean, if we're going to work this hard, we need to keep up our strength, right?"

He didn't smile, his look thoughtful. He should speak up now, say he was too tired or that he'd simply changed his mind. "I'll knock on your front door."

Briana smiled all the way inside, all the while she stripped and threw her paint-covered clothes and the rags into the washer, and well after her sprint into the bathroom. It was only when she met her own eyes in the medicine chest mirror that the smile slipped.

What in holy hell was she doing?

Chapter Seven

Sitting cross-legged on the plaid blanket spread on the sand, Slade looked over at Briana. "I know you're not much of a drinker, but a cold beer just seems to go with fish and chips, don't you think?" He was still trying to explain away or justify or whatever his short but memorable drinking binge. The fact that he felt it necessary annoyed him.

Briana lowered the brown bottle she'd been sipping from and nodded. "I agree." She glanced into the carry-out basket they'd gotten from the Fog Island Cafe and saw that only one roll and a few straggly fries remained. "I can't believe we polished off all that food."

They'd strolled into town, but vetoed a restaurant in favor of fast food, then walked to a fairly deserted strip of beach to have their picnic. It had been Slade's suggestion and he'd been glad she'd gone along with it. He simply hadn't felt like sitting at a table where every other diner knew Briana or recognized him, and felt it their duty to stop to chat. "How is it that you know nearly everyone on this island?"

Briana nibbled on a final fry. "I don't, but most of them knew my grandparents because they'd lived here most of their lives. And they've seen me visiting on and off. I recognize their faces, though I can't always remember names." She sighed, then leaned back on her elbows, staring out to sea where the sun had all but disappeared from sight. "It's hard for me to imagine living in the same place, even the same house, for that many years. Yet I envy the stability, that one constant in life—the home. There's a lot to be said for the familiar, for lifelong friends."

Slade wrapped up their trash and stuffed it into the large brown sack before finishing off his beer. "I wouldn't know what that feels like, either. Even before my father left, we'd moved three times, always to a better house, probably because his income went up. I find it hard to believe he came to Nantucket and stayed put for nearly thirty years."

She shifted her gaze to him. "Do you think you'll stay here in his house?"

"I haven't decided," he said, giving her the same answer she'd given him. His eyes narrowed, skimming the horizon, the restless sea, the pristine sand, then back to the woman watching him. "Nantucket's got a lot going for it. It's just that I don't feel as if I fit in here. Work has always defined me, and I'm not working at anything."

"You could find something. Start a business, open a shop. What is it you want? What do you like to do?"

A good question. "Mostly I like to work with my hands. And I like to fly."

"There are several charter airlines operating out of here. Or you could start your own construction company. And there's always just kicking back and being a man of leisure." She'd seen the restlessness in his eyes and doubted that last suggestion held much appeal, but she wanted to know what he'd say.

"I couldn't handle a steady diet of leisure. I've already had too much. Sitting around makes me nervous. Especially in Jeremy's perfect house."

She sat up, angling toward him. "You know, that's the second time you've said that. If you don't like the way the house is, why don't you change it?"

He shrugged, watching his hand trace the design on the blanket. "It seems such a waste to mess with his *House Beautiful* decor."

"But a house should reflect the owner's personality and taste. Whether I go or stay, I intend to redo the inside of Gramp's house from top to bottom. I might live in Boston and use this place as a summer home. But even for a few months of the year, what suited my grandparents doesn't appeal to me at all."

"Yeah, but that house needs redecorating and modernizing. Jeremy's is the kind most people would kill to live in."

"That doesn't matter if it doesn't please you." She adjusted her position, really getting into the idea now. "Think about what you would want in your ideal house. What would it be like?"

His eyes thoughtful, Slade let his mind wander and imagine. "I like California casual. Tiled floors in the kitchen, light wood cabinets instead of all that dark walnut. I'd have terrazzo in the front of the house, or maybe plank flooring, with lots of colorful area rugs. His white carpeting and white painted brick fireplace are too antiseptic for me. I'd use some rich wood paneling, get rid of all that period furniture, and get some big, comfortable couches and chairs. I like sturdy, serviceable tables, maybe in pine, something you can put your feet up on if you like. Everything in the house looks like it's too delicate to touch for fear it'll break. I've never sat in the living room, not once. I feel like a bull in a china shop in there."

"You're a much bigger man than your father was. He liked French provincial furniture, cut glass, and bone china. That doesn't mean you have to. You've got the money. Why not change things so you're comfortable?" The things he had in mind would be quite a change, she thought, but whose business was it, anyway?

He frowned, considering. "I don't know. It seems like such a waste to get rid of perfectly fine, hardly used furniture."

"You can donate it. Lots of places, like homes for abused women and children, need things always. It wouldn't go to waste."

He turned to her, his expression serious. "I guess I've been putting off any changes because once I start, it'll be like a commitment to remain. And I'm not sure I should."

"I know how you feel. I seem to be having a hard time making up my own mind. In my case, I don't have much I want to go back to. Of course, my family's in the Boston area, and some lifelong friends. Still, I just don't know."

Slade braced his arms on his bent knees. "Me, either."

"It feels strange, starting over yet again. I did that when we moved from Manhattan, then after the divorce, and now this time. And countless times with my parents. I wonder how many times I'm going to have to regroup before I can finally feel I have a permanent home."

"My feelings exactly. I'm so sick of bouncing from place to place. Yet that house, *his* house, doesn't feel like home to me."

Briana was aware that he never referred to Jeremy as his

father or dad, always by name or by the pronouns *his* or *him*. On one level, she understood the sense of abandonment that still lingered after all these years. On the other hand, she wondered if he could truly get on with his life until he let go of all that pent-up resentment and anger. "Maybe if you thoroughly search through your father's things, if you find some answers, you'll be able to come to grips with your feelings about Jeremy. Putting that to rest might make you more comfortable in that house. And redecorating it might make it feel like it's yours, not Jeremy's."

"Maybe." Squinting off into the distance, he spotted what looked like a bonfire. "I didn't know they'd allow fires on the beach. Pretty dangerous with the wind changing so frequently here on this side of the island."

She followed his gaze. "Actually, they don't. That's probably some kids hoping they don't get caught."

Slade yawned, realizing he was more tired than he'd thought. "Are you ready to head back?"

"Sure." She added their empty bottles to their trash bag and tossed the whole thing into a nearby container while Slade shook out the light blanket and draped it over his shoulder.

They walked along in companionable silence, both lost in their thoughts. The sand kept oozing into her sandals so Briana bent to remove her shoes, carrying them as they strolled.

On the edge of the sea on a spit of land just ahead, Slade spotted a large gray two-story house with a widow's walk like Jeremy's place had. Not a single light glowed from its many windows. There was a deserted air about the home, yet it appeared to be in good repair. "I wonder who lives there," he commented.

"No one. Not anymore. That's Mayberry House." They drew closer and Briana stopped to stare up at the building, eerie in the moonlight. Half a dozen scrub pines stood to each side, swaying in a slight sea breeze. Rocks barely visible in the surf shimmered, beckoning dangerously. "There's a legend about that place. Everyone on the island knows it."

"A legend. You mean like a folk yarn?" His dubious expression told her what he thought of legends.

"Sort of, although the longtime residents swear there's truth to the story. They say that if you listen to the legend with your heart and soul, you'll become a believer." Her look challenged him.

"Listen with my heart and soul, eh?" He tossed down the blanket. "All right. Let's hear it."

"If you insist. It seems that Josh Mayberry and his father, Ira, owned a whaling ship named the *Winston*. They were on their return trip when a huge storm came up. Josh's wife, Annabel, always waited for her husband on the roofwalk on days he was due home. She never missed one, even this time when she was pregnant. There's a bell in that tower up there, though you can barely see it from this direction." She pointed as they strolled closer. "See?"

"I think so."

"Annabel would ring that bell the moment she spotted the *Winston* heading for the dock. Only this time, she waited all day and into the night, wearing a hooded raincoat, unmindful of the rain."

Slade watched Briana as she gazed up at the big old house, his expression one of amusement. She actually believed all this.

"By the next morning," Briana went on, "another ship, the *Algonquin*, hobbled in. The owner, Ethan Quish, rushed over to tell Annabel that he and his crew saw the *Winston* go down. There were no survivors."

"I had a feeling that would be the case."

She ignored the mockery in his voice. "Josh's mother, grieving for her son and husband, tried to persuade Annabel to come down, fearful for the baby as well as her daughter-in-law. But Annabel stayed, pacing and praying. The next night, the rain slowed and finally stopped, but still she kept her vigil. However, just before dawn, finally admitting that Josh was lost, Annabel flung herself onto the rocks below, where they found her the next morning. It was two days later when another ship limped back to port, carrying Josh, who'd managed to stay afloat until rescued. When he heard of Annabel's death, he quietly walked into the sea the following night."

"Cheery little tale."

"Now, on rainy nights, you can hear Annabel's cries and Josh moaning. No one's lived in Mayberry House since."

"Who maintains it?"

"The Nantucket Historical Society. It used to be on the list of tourist attractions, but because of its age and the proximity to the sea, they decided it was dangerous to let people wander around inside and climb up to the roofwalk. They only let visitors walk about outside while a guide tells the legend."

"Do you believe that story?" Surely she was too intelligent to put much stock into such an obviously fictionalized romantic yarn.

Briana turned to look up at him. "I've walked out here on rainy nights and I've heard the cries and moans. Yes, I believe the story. Like all good legends, it's more truth than fiction."

"Uh-huh. Spoken like a true romantic."

"Sometimes you have to suspend reality and go with the flow, as the saying goes."

"I've spent my life facing reality and its grimmer aspects. I'm not sure I can make the switch."

"Sure you can. Think about how you wish things were instead of how they really are, for a moment. Then put a pretty spin on them. Imagine how Annabel felt, loving Josh so much that she didn't want to live without him, even sacrificing her baby to be with him."

"Pretty selfish, I call it."

Briana dropped her shoes. "You're not concentrating. In her anxiety, she felt as if she and the baby were joining Josh for eternity, that the three of them would be together for all time. And when Josh came back and found her gone, he felt the same way and hurried to join them. *That's* what the legend teaches us, that love can be strong enough to overcome anything, even death."

Slade had the feeling they were no longer talking about the legend. "Do you believe there is a love that strong?"

Briana met his eyes, silvery in the moonlight. The night was heavy with humidity, with sudden sensual tension. "I'd like to think there is."

Slade saw the wind blow her hair around her face, watched her reach up to try to tame it. "It's an interesting story," he said, suddenly wanting desperately to touch that lovely hair, to shove his hands into its thickness, to bury his face in its feminine fragrance. "But I still prefer reality."

Looking up at him, Briana saw his eyes change, darken, grow heated. Or was it just a trick of moonlight? Emotions, so close to the surface lately, swirled around inside her, all tangled together, needs and longings and desire, thickening her voice. "What is reality?"

Slowly, he placed his hands on her shoulders, his eyes on hers. "This." Lowering his head, he pressed his lips to hers.

Though he'd kissed her before, this was really the first time. In her kitchen that day, she'd been an overwrought, grieving woman latching on to someone handy, not caring who, reaching out to the only one there. But not this time.

This time, Slade knew she was fully aware of who was kissing her. His touch was light, his lips gentle, letting her decide, giving her ample time to pull back.

Only, she didn't. She let his lips caress hers slowly, seemingly suspended in time, perhaps waiting for her own reaction. She had to have seen the kiss coming yet hadn't stepped away. He dared to increase the pressure ever so slightly. Then he heard a low sound from deep in her throat and it was like a signal, a go-ahead sign. His arms slipped around her and his hands urged her closer.

Briana did what she'd advised him to do, suspended reality for this one special moment. Her arms encircled him, her hands fisting in the material of his shirt as her mouth opened to him, inviting easier access. She could no longer deny, could even finally admit to herself, that ever since those feverish kisses in her kitchen, she'd been wanting to kiss him again. Wanting to find out if the feelings he'd stirred inside her had been because of her emotions that day or simply because it was Slade's mouth on hers.

Pressed close to him, his breath mingling with hers, his tongue sparring with hers, she finally had her answer.

Passion. It was what had been missing from her life, even with Robert. She'd acknowledged the absence of it then, as she now recognized its very real presence. And she reached out with both hands for more.

She hadn't wanted to need again, the very thing she'd

schooled herself to live without for three long years, Briana thought. But the chemistry between Slade and her was too obvious to ignore, too real to question, too volatile to disregard. A mere look from him sent awareness shimmering through her. The more she denied that fact, the stronger her reaction.

Slade shifted, slanting his mouth across hers, taking her deeper, and Briana felt her stomach muscles clench. How long had it been since a man had held her like this, had wanted her so obviously, had made her feel so much? Almost more important, how long since she'd looked at a man and felt desire awaken inside? How long since she'd wanted to touch and be touched like this? Months, years. Maybe since forever.

She forgot that she was on a public beach where anyone could come strolling by, in a town where hundreds knew her by sight, although it was quite dark. She forgot she'd considered living a solitary life because wanting someone inevitably led to disappointments. She forgot she'd known this man less than a week and she was kissing him as hungrily as if they'd been lovers for years. She filled her arms with the reality of him and emptied her mind of everything but this wondrous feeling.

Slade knew he should stop. Even as his hands slid along her rib cage, then slipped between their bodies until his fingers found her breasts, sweetly heavy, unbearably exciting, he told himself he should back off. He felt her draw in a sharp breath and swallowed her soft moan as he caressed the soft flesh straining into his touch.

Maybe she was as physically needy as he. He couldn't even remember the last time he'd been with a woman. Perhaps she was as ready for sex as he, divorced for years and only occasionally seeing the creep in the suit who was "just a friend." Maybe she'd be willing to take this little experiment down the beach to her house, her soft bed, and invite him in.

The hell she would.

The cold voice of reason intruded on Slade's thoughts and had him pulling back, breathing hard, buying time. Opening his eyes, he saw that hers were hazy with passion, her cheeks in the moonlight flushed, her breathing uneven.

Briana took a step back, struggling for control. She hadn't expected her body to overrule her mind and react so quickly, so fiercely. She'd never trusted the fast and furious. Yet here it was, and it was overwhelming. "So, that's reality. Whew! Packs a wallop, doesn't it?"

He wasn't in the mood for levity. His erection was huge and hurting, yet he had no one to blame but himself. He was pretty damn sure, despite her effort to lighten things, that she'd gotten more than she'd bargained for. "It probably wouldn't be wise for you to get involved with me, Briana."

"You're probably right." She was having trouble sorting out her feelings with residual desire clouding her mind. Why would he kiss her like that, then issue a warning? And why wouldn't a smart woman, as she thought herself to be, heed that warning?

He did a half turn, feeling the need to expand on what he'd said. "You don't know me very well. I've done things, things I'm not proud of. And you're vulnerable right now."

"Oh, bull! When aren't we vulnerable when we run across an overwhelming attraction?" She raised her eyes to his, suddenly wondering if she was the only one feeling so bewildered. "Or is it just me feeling so much?"

God help him, he could think of no better way to show her. He gripped her shoulders again and brought his mouth down hard on hers. He kissed her deeply, thoroughly, forgetting all the reasons he shouldn't. This kiss was shorter but the message was clear. He let her go abruptly. "Any questions? If so, give me your hand and I'll show you more."

Locked close against him, she'd been very aware she was wrapped around a fully aroused man. Briana took several steps back and drew in a deep breath, buying a little time.

There was no question that physically he wanted her, Slade thought. And he knew she felt the same. If he could just keep his feelings under wraps and concentrate on the physical, they could be good for each other. But more than that he couldn't handle, couldn't allow. Because if Briana Morgan knew the whole truth about him, she'd turn from him. "Maybe it's best if we back off for now."

Was it? Briana wasn't sure. He was sending her mixed messages. "I don't know." She was being brutally honest. "I do know I'm not prepared to deal with this right now." A simple kiss. She'd been so certain she could handle a simple kiss. Only, there'd been nothing simple about that kiss.

Slade ran a hand along the back of his neck, massaging the knot of tension there. "Me, either." Again, he draped the blanket over his shoulder, struggling with emotions he didn't want to face just now.

Taking her cue from him, Briana stepped into the shoes she'd dropped and fell in step.

They walked in silence, which seemed unnatural after the closeness they'd shared mere minutes ago. Slade gazed up at the stars, winking and blinking overhead. "Nice night," he finally got out. The weather, always a safe topic.

"Yes." She couldn't think of anything bright or clever to

add. They were near enough to the bonfire to smell the acrid odor and hear the small cracklings as the blaze slowly died out. "Looks like the party's over."

But Slade spotted a big man with beefy hands planted at his waist, standing downwind and watching the fire closely. "Not quite. Do you know that guy?"

Briana squinted through the lingering smoke. "Oh, yes. That's Jimmy Kendall. He's with the fire department. Probably came along, spotted the fire, and ran the kids off."

Just what he needed, Slade thought, hoping the man wouldn't notice them. But his luck wasn't holding.

Jimmy spotted them, recognized Briana, and with a glance at the dying embers, walked over to intersect their sandy path. "Hey, Briana. How're you doing?"

"Getting by, Jimmy. How about you?"

He indicated the bonfire still smoldering. "Damn kids. Never use their heads, even though we've got signs all over warning people about the danger of fire."

"That's teenagers, I guess."

"Yeah." Jimmy brightened. "My daughter finally had her baby. Nine-pound boy. Thought he'd never get here." Jimmy hitched up his low-riding pants.

"Congratulations. Give Colleen my best." Briana wasn't feeling chatty. All she wanted to do right this minute was get home, lie down, and mentally go over the unsettling events of the evening.

Jimmy's dark eyes examined Slade. "Say, aren't you Jeremy Slade's son? Heard you were here. Damn shame about your father."

"Thanks." Slade took a step, hoping to discourage more talk.

But Jimmy was nothing if not persistent. "Heard you were a firefighter in California."

"Yes, I was." Slade emphasized the past tense, hoping that would put an end to the man's curiosity.

"Now that you're settled in," Jimmy went on, "maybe you'd like to stop in and meet the guys. We've got three stations on the island. I heard your father left you well set, but I also know that firefighting gets in your blood. We're kind of shorthanded."

Slade was unaware his expression had hardened. "Thanks, but I'm not interested."

"Bet you'd change your mind if you came by. We've got a great bunch of fellows. Why don't you come join us, son?"

Slade's eyes turned as cold as a wintry sea. *Son!* He'd been no man's son for years now, had had no father who wanted him. The very word had him seeing red. "I said no. And don't call me that. I'm not your son."

Taken aback, Jimmy looked from one to the other. "Yeah, sure, okay. Sorry." He backed up, then turned away.

Slade set out, his strides long, his need to move on obvious. Briana kept up, but her own temper was frayed.

"That was pretty rude."

Drawing in a deep gulp of sea air, Slade was sure she was right. "Yeah, I guess it was." He wasn't in an apologizing mood.

"Jimmy's a nice guy. He didn't mean any harm. Would it hurt you to stop at the station and meet the men?"

He stopped abruptly and faced her. "Yeah, it would. You don't seem to understand, I left the fire department for good. Period. End of story. I'm sick of everyone on this island either telling me what a great guy my father was when I know he deserted his family or asking me why I don't rush over and join the fire department. I wish everyone would just back the hell off."

"That's an excellent idea." Briana turned and started walking toward the coastal road, leaving the beach.

Furious—at her, at Jimmy Whatever-his-name-was—but mostly seething at himself for a long list of sins, Slade went after her. His longer legs had him alongside her in no time. "Look, I didn't mean you."

"I'm flattered."

He gritted his teeth. "Listen, I'm sorry. Is that what you wanted?"

Whirling about, she glared up at him. "What I want is for you to go on your way and I'll go on mine. All right?"

"No, damn it, it's not all right. I'm seeing you home. Did you forget your house was broken into this morning?"

"No, I didn't. Thank you for your concern, but I'll manage. I've taken care of myself for a lot of years now and I think I can handle one more evening. Good night." And she took off at an angry pace.

He let her go, walking a short distance behind her, overseeing her to safety even if she didn't want him to. He'd be damned if she was going to dictate what he'd do. What got into her, anyway? One minute she's kissing him like there's no tomorrow, confessing that she's got this overwhelming attraction to him, and the next she's marching away from him like he'd done something really terrible.

So what if he was rude to that clown, Jimmy? The man had no business hanging around the beach trying to recruit reluctant applicants. Is that the only way this island could get help, bully or coerce or shame someone into applying?

Patchy clouds had drifted through the evening sky, almost blocking the moon. All right, so he'd been out of line. Jimmy Whatsit couldn't have known that *son* was a four-letter word to him, one that triggered his temper. He'd apologized to Briana. What more did she want?

Slade noticed that they were almost in front of their houses. He slowed his steps when he saw that Briana had stopped by the mailbox and was standing utterly still, her back to him.

At first, he couldn't figure out what she was focused on. Then he saw the balloon tied with a string to Gramp's mailbox. A silvery color, it danced and swayed in the ocean breezes. He glanced up and down the street and saw that each mailbox had a balloon on a string tied to it. Squinting in the faint light, he saw that the logo of a local real estate office was imprinted on the balloons. Just a silly advertising gimmick.

Wondering why the sight of a balloon seemed to stop her cold, he moved around her. She was fixated on the balloon, watching its jerky little dance, her face pale, her expression like glass that was about to shatter. He decided he'd better get her inside before her emotions burst free and she had another crying jag.

Slipping an arm around her shoulders, he started her forward. "Let's go inside, Briana."

She took one, two lurching steps, then dug her heels in, her eyes still on the balloon. "I'm all right," she whispered, her voice so low he had to duck his head to make out the words.

"Sure you are, but you'll be better inside." He tugged on her, urging her through Gramp's gate. Finally, she allowed him to move her along, but her steps were reluctant and her head was turned so she could still see the balloon over her shoulder.

Up the walk, up the steps, inside the porch. "Where's your key?" he asked, but when she turned to him, her eyes were dazed, as if she wasn't picturing him but another scene in her mind's eye. "Okay, let's see." He slipped a hand into the pocket of her slacks and came up empty. In the second pocket, he hit pay dirt. The key was large and old-fashioned, but he finally managed to get the door open and Briana inside.

He sat her down on the couch and switched on a table lamp, which gave off a soft light. He watched her blink, as if orienting herself, while she rubbed at her forehead. She'd had a shock of some sort that had conjured up a disturbing memory, he guessed. He'd seen fire victims like that, days later blanking out, reliving the blaze.

Leaving her momentarily, he found the bathroom, wet a washcloth, and went back to place it on her forehead. She was warm to the touch, but not overly so. His arm around her shoulders drew her close. He held her there for long minutes, and finally, he felt the tension ease out of her, felt her muscles relax.

Several minutes later, Briana straightened, removed the cloth, and leaned forward. Her voice was just the slightest bit shaky. "I wonder if it's *ever* going to get better."

Slade thought of another woman in another town, the shrill voice of her mother asking him the same question, accusation inherent in every word. In his nightmares, he heard Rachel's cry: *"It's your fault, all your fault. I told you and you didn't listen. Why didn't you listen?"*

To Briana he said, "It's supposed to."

"That's what the doctors tell you." She scooted away from him, settling in the corner of the couch, pulling her legs up under her, facing him. "You must be convinced by now that I'm a certifiable nut case."

"Far from it. In my line of work, I ran across a lot of vic-

tims and their relatives. Believe me, I know strong when I
see it."

With both hands, Briana brushed back her damp hair. "I
wish I felt strong."

"There's a significance to the balloon, I gather." Maybe
if he could get her to talk about the hard parts, she could
accept things more readily.

Briana supposed she owed him some explanation since
he'd witnessed her emotional reaction several times now.
She kept her eyes downcast as she forced herself to remember. "The day it happened, Bobby and I were in the
Public Gardens across from the Boston Common when he
found a balloon caught in a tree. He climbed up and got it,
then tied the string around his wrist. He skipped along the
walk, so happy that day." Briana choked on a sob, but
forced herself to go on.

"Robert was picking him up and he was late. They were
going to the zoo. Finally, he arrived and I said good-bye to
Bobby." The very last time she'd kissed that freckled face
and hugged that warm, energetic little body. Briana swallowed hard. "They crossed the street and I was taking pictures. Snapping away at this and that. Suddenly I heard
sounds, like a car backfiring. Only it wasn't that. It was
gunshots."

"Gunshots? I thought they'd died in an auto accident."

Briana shook her head. "That might have been easier to
handle. Maybe not. Anyway, I heard people screaming,
brakes screeching, and a car speeding by, but I wasn't
looking at the street. I was trying to spot Robert and Bobby
but I couldn't, so I raced across the street. And . . . and my
son was lying there on that dirty sidewalk, so very still.
The balloon was still tied to his wrist, still dancing and
whirling. The string stayed tied to his wrist even in the am-

bulance as I rode along, praying harder than ever before. But I knew it was too late."

Slade edged closer. "Did they find whoever did the shooting?"

Again, she shook her head, more slowly this time. "The police talked with me repeatedly. Did Robert have any enemies? Did I? Or our families? I couldn't come up with a single name. Finally they called it a random drive-by shooting. Two lives snuffed out and several more ruined. Just one of many random acts of violence happening all over the world in these terrible times, the officer told me. Two people in the wrong place at the wrong time."

Slade didn't know just when he'd taken her hand, only knew that he held her chilled fingers wrapped in his own warm palm. "And no one saw the car or got the license plate number? I mean, isn't it usually crowded along the Common?"

"It was very crowded, Saturday morning. But at a time like that, everyone's intent on saving themselves, not in jotting down numbers, I guess. Besides, I've come to realize it doesn't matter. Knowing the shooter's identity wouldn't bring Bobby back, nor Robert either." She thought of the reason she'd begun this explanation and raised her eyes. "Then at the service in the cemetery, the minister's wife had dozens of balloons released into the sky as her husband spoke. Apparently, it's a tradition with them whenever a child dies, as sort of a sign of hope rising to the heavens, or whatever. I'd been holding up fairly well until then. I saw those balloons and I collapsed. Dad caught me and took me out of there."

She let out a ragged breath. "I've simply got to get a grip. The trouble is that when you lose someone you bring into the world, there's a disruption of the order of things. Our children aren't supposed to die first."

"And then I add to your problems. I'm sorry about losing my temper back there, Brie." He rather liked the nickname he'd heard several people call her. Briana seemed too formal, somehow. "You're right. I had no business being rude to Jimmy. I'll go apologize to him if you think I should."

She studied him, noting his sincerity, yet seeing more. "You know, I think there's more to that encounter than you taking offense at Jimmy pressuring you. I think there's something in your past, something involving being a firefighter, that triggers a response in you as upsetting as balloons are to me."

He should have known she'd figure it out. He patted her hand. "You know what they say: there're a million stories in the big city. But we'll save that one for another day. I'd better go so you can get some rest." He rose and walked to the door.

Briana followed. "Thanks for yet another rescue. And for a great beach picnic."

"Will you be all right now?"

"I'll be fine."

"Good night, then."

Long after he'd walked out of sight, Briana stood in the doorway, sliding her tongue over her lips, tasting him.

In the morning when she went out, she saw that not a single balloon was visible from any of the mailboxes up and down her street.

Chapter Eight

"I can't believe how much you've managed to accomplish since I saw you last," Irma said. She was standing in the archway of Briana's kitchen, where two workmen were installing new cupboards. "First the entire house painted inside and out, and now this." She swung back to smile at her young friend. "Maybe you should come down to my place and help me make some changes."

"Your home is lovely and perfect as it is, Irma," Briana answered, leading the way to the front porch. "I hope you don't mind sitting out here, but I've given away most of Gramp's furniture except in the bedroom I'm using."

"This is fine." Irma settled herself in the cushioned wooden rocker, adjusting her gauzy burnt orange harem pants and billowing black top as she sat back. Poking at her ebony black upsweep with a long crimson fingernail, she eyed Briana. "Well, this extensive renovation must mean you're planning on staying."

Briana toed off her white canvas shoes and drew her legs

up under her as she made herself comfortable in the companion chair. "Don't you start, too. I hear that from everyone I talk with, it seems." Everyone except Slade, who seemed convinced that she'd be returning to Boston. "The truth is, I'm still not sure what I'm going to do."

"Waiting for divine inspiration, my dear?" Irma asked, not unkindly. She'd been by once when Jeremy's son, definitely sober, had been preparing the house for painting and had told her that Briana was resting, an odd occurrence in midmorning, to be sure. She'd driven by the following week and seen both of them painting away, so busy they hadn't spotted her. And finally, she'd run into them shopping together in town several days ago, so thoroughly wrapped up in a discussion they were having that neither noticed her. Irma was beyond curious and had moved into downright nosy. This afternoon, she'd simply had to stop by and find out for herself. "Or has Slade something to do with your ambivalance?"

Briana wrinkled her forehead. "What makes you ask that?"

"Oh, I don't know. I rather had the feeling the two of you had become friends. Good friends." Irma was careful not to put too much inflection in her voice.

Briana shrugged. "I suppose we have. But certainly not close enough that he would affect my decision to go or stay. The fact is that right now, I'm having a great time redoing this house." She glanced over her shoulder through the open door into the living room at a pile of large books and design sketches. "Those are carpet samples and drapery swatches. I think I've finally settled on the right selection. I never realized how exciting it can be to all but gut a house and redo it from the ground up. And do it my way."

Irma raised a penciled brow. "In all the times you moved, you never redecorated a place?"

"Oh, sure, some. New curtains, a paint job, my own furniture. But here, I kept only a few special mementos of my grandparents and the rest I gave away. When I finish, whether I use this house as a vacation home or a permanent residence, it'll be just as I want it. I even had them take down a wall in back so I could enlarge the bathroom. I'm having a sunken tub installed with Jacuzzi jets. How's that for decadence?"

"I love it!" Irma declared. "It's so good to see you smiling, Briana. And I do believe you've picked up a bit of the weight you lost."

"Probably." Working alongside Slade over the past couple of weeks, he'd insisted they stop regularly and often for meals. "It's Slade's fault. The man's appetite is huge."

"Is that a fact?" Irma's expression turned speculative. "Personally, I've always preferred men with huge appetites."

Her friend had chosen to deliberately shift the meaning of her words, Briana thought, and they both knew it. But she smiled nonetheless. "You're terrible, and for your information, I wouldn't know about his *other* appetites, but he sure likes to eat."

"How about the drinking?" Irma asked. Her second husband had been altogether too fond of alcohol, which had hastened his demise. She'd hate to see Briana, who'd had more than her share of problems, get involved with a drinker.

"I haven't seen signs of it since those first few days. I think he was out of sorts, suddenly finding himself here in an unfamiliar place where he knew no one, not even the father who'd left him everything. He tried drinking his troubles away and quickly discovered that was no answer."

Although Slade's estrangement from his father and his unsettling upbringing were problems enough, Briana felt there was something more, some incident or event that happened to him, likely connected to his work as a firefighter, that was the true basis of his melancholy mood swings. She couldn't forget his words the night they'd kissed by Mayberry House. *I'm not a very nice man. I've done things, things I'm not proud of.* What could he have meant? She'd tried to segue into a discussion on those disturbing statements several times over the past couple of weeks, but Slade had danced around the topic. She had no choice but to bide her time.

"We had beer together once and shared some wine at dinner, but that's the extent of his drinking these days."

Irma tipped her head, her large gold hoop earrings grazing her shoulders. "It takes a good woman to show a man the error of his ways."

Briana shook her head. "I doubt I'm in any shape to influence anyone these days. Besides, Slade's very much his own person."

Reading between the lines of what her friend was saying, Irma wasn't so sure Briana was seeing everything clearly. She'd heard so many conflicting stories around town about Jeremy's son. There were those who said he was rude, tactless, and arrogant. Jimmy Kendall, who was sort of a liaison for the firemen, said he wouldn't have the man on his team on a bet.

Others felt Slade had lightened up, actually chatting with shopkeepers in a friendly way, even smiling and being polite now and then. And Irma's friend, Dottie, who worked with abused women and children, had told Irma at bridge last Friday that Slade had not only donated several truckloads of furniture to the shelter, but had spent two days doing badly needed repairs. The word in some quarters was, the man had gone from surly and reclusive to helpful and accommodating in less than a month. If that was so, something had to have motivated him, and Irma felt sure she was looking at the reason. "Do you like him, Briana?" she asked finally, blunt as always.

Taken aback, Briana frowned. She should be used to her elderly friend's ways, yet she hadn't been prepared for the question. "Yes, I like him. He's had his problems, like most of us." Some, told to her in confidence, she wouldn't repeat, while others were common knowledge around town. "He's trying to get past that, as we all are. He's a hard worker—I don't know how I'd have managed all this renovating without him." *And he's softhearted when it comes to little girls and stranded kittens,* she thought, *and much bigger girls who have a tendency to indulge in crying jags.*

Plus, when he kissed her, she forgot her own name.

Briana felt the heat rise in her face. She stood, walking to the doorway, presumably to check on the kitchen's progress, and attempted to change the subject with her back turned while her skin cooled. "I sure hope they finish today. The tile people are scheduled to do the floor in there tomorrow."

Irma's shrewd gaze stayed on the back of her head for long minutes, then she decided to plunge in. After all, what were friends for if not to meddle in their lives? "Briana, you're not getting seriously involved with Slade, are you?"

Swiveling about, Briana frowned. "That sounds very much like a warning. Is there something I don't know about him that worries you?"

Irma waved a bony hand. "Not specifically. I've only

had two conversations with him. It's his eyes more than anything. Even when he smiles, there's a dangerous cast to his eyes. Perhaps you should have a chat with Medea."

Briana shook her head, dismissing the suggestion of talking with Irma's fortune-teller friend. "I think I'll pass. But you can stop worrying about me. I'm hardly the impetuous type."

"Mmm, I wonder if all women aren't impetuous around certain men." She studied her young friend. Though Briana had said she didn't know about Slade's "other appetites," Irma wasn't convinced. "Tell me, are you sleeping with him?"

Briana's eyebrows shot up. "Well, that's blunt enough. Honestly, Irma!"

Irma waved a manicured hand. "At my age, I don't have time to beat around the bush. I know you've lived alone for several years, and that's not healthy. I ought to know, I've been alone for twenty years. It's not natural. So, are you?"

Briana knew if she didn't answer, Irma would just keep it up. "No, I'm not."

"Maybe you should. You can learn a great deal from pillow talk. A little healthy sex wouldn't do you any harm, either." Rising, she adjusted her tiny granny glasses. "Well, I've got to run along. They're having a sale at Bonaventures that I don't want to miss."

Brushing back her hair, Briana wondered if there wasn't some truth to Irma's observation. "Are you looking for something in particular or just a new fall wardrobe?" Bonaventures was a shop specializing in women's clothes.

Irma went down the steps carefully. "They've got these great new padded bras. Imported. They have this plastic insert in each cup and it comes with a strawlike gizmo. You blow in as much air as you wish, then seal it like an inner tube. With some outfits, you know, you need a little more chest, and with others, less. They're wonderful and you can't always find them."

"I'll bet not," Briana commented, standing at the picket fence with her. She leaned to hug the older woman, her smile in place. "I'm so glad you stopped in."

"Me, too, darlin'. You know I only meddle because I love you, don't you?"

"I love you, too." She watched Irma start back the one-block walk to her house, her pace belying her age. She was definitely one of the world's wonders, Briana thought as she turned back. But before she reached her steps, she caught sight of a familiar figure riding a bicycle heading her way, a bulky package anchored behind the seat.

Pulling up alongside her fence, Slade braked. "Like my new bike?"

"Pretty sharp." She examined the bike, noting it was built for speed. "When did you get it?"

"Bought it this morning. I used to have a Harley in California, but I've never had a speed bike, so I thought I'd indulge myself." He glanced toward her garage. "I noticed there's a girl's bike in there. Maybe we can go riding one day. Good exercise."

"Mmm hmm." She sniffed the air, wondering at the source of the familiar smell as she leaned closer to the package wrapped in white paper. "You've been shopping."

"Yeah. I rode my bike into town and decided to get us a couple of lobsters for dinner." Scooting to the back edge of his seat, he raised the front wheel off the ground, then let it drop down with a bounce before grinning at her. "Neat, eh?"

She had to smile at him. Like a little boy with a new toy, one he'd obviously missed out on in his teens. "Lobsters, did you say? Well, guess what? My cupboards should be in by day's end, but my new stove won't be delivered for another day or two. That means you're the chef tonight." They hadn't eaten every meal together over the last couple of weeks since their beach picnic. But most of them.

"I'm planning on it." He got off the bike and turned it around. "See you around six?"

"That's good. Do you have a pot big enough?"

"I imagine so. I'll poke around and find one."

"How would it be if I bring the wine?"

"Nope. I've got it covered. Just bring yourself." He walked the bike toward his garage.

Briana watched him go and wandered back up onto the porch. The weather was cooler since Labor Day had passed. There were fewer people on the beaches. Only a couple of diehards actually braved the chilly waters and already the days were getting shorter. But the rains had held off and for that she was grateful. Sunny days were cheerier and she needed all the mood elevators she could find.

But the best one of all was Slade.

By unspoken agreement, they'd behaved as friends— good and true friends, not as sweethearts, and certainly not as lovers—since that last soul-searching evening of the balloon incident. There'd been no unnecessary touching, not since that stunning kiss in the sand. Their conversations had centered around the projects they were working on together, her house and his, and rarely got personal, as it had that evening. They'd even managed to leave the past at rest for a while, both his situation with his father and hers with the loss of her son. It had been a healing respite for both of them, Briana felt. No touchy-feely stuff to cloud their minds and no mention of uncomfortable subjects, like his firefighting career.

They'd gotten to know each other better, through actions and deeds rather than words and confidences shared. It had been an experience like no other she'd ever had. If occasionally she recalled with longing the feelings he'd aroused in her by taking her in his arms, she'd managed to relegate those thoughts to the back of her mind. She was aware that Slade, too, remembered those moments, for she'd catch him looking at her when he didn't think she noticed, and there'd be such heat in his eyes. But then he'd turn aside, putting his feelings on hold.

Civilized was what they were, Briana decided. While the approach gave her breathing room at a time when she needed it, she also wondered how long this unusual alliance could reasonably continue. An attraction so strong was bound to rear its head again, yet neither of them was willing to push the issue right now. Relationships, in order to survive and thrive, needed a great deal of time, attention, and nurturing. And they required two people who had their heads on straight and their emotions under control.

Briana doubted if either of them had those two prerequisites.

She heard her name called and turned to see one of the workmen in her kitchen signaling her. Time to stop daydreaming, she told herself as she went to see what he wanted.

It wasn't a date, Briana reminded herself as she brushed out her hair. They'd shared many a meal together by now, so one more could hardly be called a date. It was just a lobster dinner for two friends.

Then why was her stomach all jittery?

Because she'd skipped lunch, since workmen had been all over her kitchen most of the day. Zippering up her yellow linen slacks, she turned in front of the full-length mirror, examining her image. Irma was right, she had picked up a few pounds. Not enough to make her slacks tight, but rather enough so her clothes were no longer so loose. She actually had a few curves again.

At the closet, Briana removed two sweaters, angling her head, trying to decide. Yes, the matching cotton sweater would be best. Slipping it on, she shook out her hair and finger-combed her bangs. She'd have to think about a haircut soon. Time was getting away from her.

Sliding her feet into leather flats, she stopped to review the finished product. A touch of makeup, which she so seldom wore, made her eyes seem larger and her mouth fuller. Not exactly a knockout, Briana decided, but she'd do. The last thing she did before leaving her bedroom was to dab on some cologne. Might as well go whole hog tonight.

Pocketing her key, she left the house and crossed over to Slade's lawn, climbing onto his porch. Surprised that he hadn't left the door ajar for her as he usually did, she gave two sharp raps and waited. No answering sounds from inside. She knocked again, then wandered across the porch to the window and peered inside. No sign of life.

Her heart stuttered for just a beat. Where could Slade be—was something wrong? When he didn't appear after another minute, she tried the knob and found the door unlocked. Inside, she called out his name.

Briana heard a chair scrape back, the sound coming from the kitchen. Heading that way, she walked through the empty living room and on into the dining room with its table set for two. Slade was sitting at the small table by the window. Its entire glass top was covered with envelopes and letters in a state of disarray. A large blue ribbon had been carelessly tossed aside.

Slade looked up, his expression a little dazed, as if surprised at seeing her, and set down the letter he'd been holding.

Pausing in the archway, Briana glanced at a big pot on the floor by his feet, then at him. "Is something the matter, Slade?"

"I'm not sure." His voice sounded rusty, as if it hadn't been used in a while. He glanced down at the pot, the scattered letters, then at Briana. "I was looking for a lobster pot and found this one up on the top shelf in the pantry. I was about to wash it when I found these letters inside."

Briana sat down in the only other chair. "Jeremy's letters?"

Gazing down at them, he fingered one or two, then nodded absently. "They're all from my mother." His expression changed, turning bleak. "My poor, sad, faithless mother."

Briana had wondered if going through Jeremy's papers would shatter even more of Slade's illusions. It might have been less nerve-wracking to let things be, though there were those who preferred knowing the truth no matter the price.

"I take it she confessed to an affair and that's why Jeremy left."

He let out a short, bitter laugh. "Not just an affair, bad as that would have been. An affair that produced a child. Me." Slade saw her eyes widen. "Yeah, that's right. Jeremy wasn't my real father. Small wonder he could no longer stomach the sight of me after he found out."

This wasn't the way he should be viewing this, not after all this time. "Slade, he could hardly blame you. You were an innocent child. Your mother may have hurt Jeremy with such a betrayal, but none of that was your fault."

"Apparently that's not how Jeremy saw it. Punish the mother, punish the son." He grabbed one of the letters, the first he'd read. "She sent him this one just six months after he left us, which was when the checks had begun arriving, when he'd settled here in Nantucket. Probably that was when she first learned his address. She begs him in this letter to forgive her, but that if he can't do that much, at least to not shut me out of his life. She goes on to say how much I missed him."

Briana watched him swallow a lump in his throat and knew how very much he was hurting.

"What did high-and-mighty Mr. Jeremy D. Slade do about her pleas? I ask you. Exactly nothing. Her next letter, and the next, and the ones after that, all beg him to write to the son who's too young to understand an adult situation. But he never did." Viciously, Slade kicked the pot by his feet. "He never did."

Briana understood his anger and wished she could do something to ease it. "How did he find out? I mean, you were already ten."

"Before I got home from school that day, they must've had some sort of argument and she blurted out the truth. We'll never know why. And the great man couldn't handle it, could no longer accept the boy he'd once professed to love. Which translated means he never loved me at all."

"I'm not so sure."

Slade raised his head to look at her. "Not sure? Read these letters and you'll be sure."

But Briana remained unconvinced. "Slade, there had to be a reason Jeremy didn't destroy these letters. He didn't put them with his other papers, or in a lockbox or even a bank safe-deposit box. No, he tucked them away where you probably wouldn't find them for a while. But eventually you would. I have a feeling he hoped by then you'd understand him a little."

He kept staring at her, his brow wrinkled. "Just what is it I'm supposed to understand? That he was small and mean and petty? That he left a woman he knew to be weak to fend for herself, never once contacting her to see if she was alive or dead? That he turned his back on a boy who adored him because of *wounded pride*? Jesus, Briana! I'm glad none of his blood flows in my veins."

No, he wasn't, but right now, he surely thought so.

"Slade, your father could have destroyed these letters. You'd have come here at his death when his attorney contacted you, and never learned the truth. You'd go along believing a lie. But Jeremy hadn't been able to live a lie, to pretend he still cared for your mother after such a serious betrayal, and he probably assumed you wouldn't want to, either. So he made sure you found them."

She couldn't tell if he was listening or ignoring her, but she went on anyway. "Maybe he wanted you to know because it was his way of apologizing for the hurt he'd caused you. Maybe he hoped you'd understand, man to man. We can't know what he was thinking. Yet there's still one important unanswered question: Why did he leave not only these letters for you to find, but everything—his house, his paintings, his money—all to you, that boy he walked away from without another thought, as you say?"

"Damned if I know." He ran long, agitated fingers through his hair.

"Because even though, right or wrong, his pride wouldn't let him return to the family he'd left, he never forgot you. He couldn't erase the love he felt for that boy."

Slade thought of the boy on the pony in the painting over the fireplace. It seemed to have been painted with a lot of love. Or had Jeremy been incapable of feeling the real thing, but damn good at faking it on canvas?

Briana saw a flicker of doubt in his eyes and went on. "I believe that leaving you everything, after all the bitter, lonely years, was Jeremy's way of telling you he'd loved you after all."

But Slade wasn't ready to buy into her theory. "Well, it comes a bit late now, doesn't it?" Slade shoved to his feet and began gathering up the letters, shoving them into old, yellowed envelopes, straightening the pile. When he finished, he wound the blue ribbon around the packet and walked over to the counter, thrusting the bundle inside a drawer. His back to Briana, he stood looking out the window over the sink, letting his emotions settle. Hoping they would.

The sun was lowering, light and shadow dancing around the kitchen. Still seated, Briana watched the powerful muscles of Slade's back bunch and clench as he struggled for control, his big hands clutching the counter's edge. Then she saw a single tear slide down his cheek, but it disappeared so quickly she wasn't certain if she'd imagined it. She wondered if he'd weep all the more if she weren't there.

Tears or not, he was grieving, Briana realized, recognizing all the familiar signs. He hadn't known the man he'd been named after, but Briana knew that Slade grieved for him now all the same, despite his words to the contrary. As he'd once told her, he'd tried all these years to hate Jeremy and could never quite pull it off. He grieved for his mother as well, as he'd probably been unable to do at her funeral, weighed down with sadness at how early her life had ended, and how alone her death had left him. Infidelity was a terrible thing, and discovering it about a parent was even worse. Yet Slade had to feel that his mother had paid a very high price for one mistake. And he was probably grieving for what might have been, for lost opportunities, for the high price of pride.

Rising slowly, she went over to him and slipped an arm around his waist, wondering if he would reject her.

With a deep sound from his throat, Slade turned and gathered her to him, holding her tightly. Very tightly.

God, how he'd love to take Briana upstairs into his bed and bury himself deep inside her. Or into that empty living room on the plush carpeting and ravish her right on the floor. She could make him forget all he'd read just now, everything he'd learned over the last hour. Making love to her, he would think of nothing but pleasing her and being pleased. There'd be no yesterdays, not even today, and no tomorrow.

Only, there was always tomorrow.

Easing back from her, Slade knew he couldn't use her like that, couldn't escape from his problems in her arms, though he was sorely tempted, as she'd been tempted that morning in her kitchen. But Briana wasn't just some woman he'd picked up. She was his friend and his . . . his what? He didn't know what else, didn't want to put a name to any of his feelings right now. He only knew he felt better holding her.

"Thanks," he said, his eyes on her hair, her lovely hair, her face. Anywhere but meeting her serious gaze.

"For what? Turnabout is fair play, wouldn't you say?" She reached up, brushed a lock of hair from his forehead. "Are you okay?"

He tried for a smile he couldn't quite pull off. "Yeah, for a bastard kid, I'm doing okay."

Briana's frown was swift and fierce. "Don't! Don't ever

say that and don't think it. You're no different a man than you were before you read those letters. If Jeremy had been a bigger man and stuck around, he'd be proud of the man you've become. You served in the navy. You've put out fires and saved lives. You . . ." She saw his expression turn stricken and wondered what she'd said. "What is it?"

Slade pulled back, turning away, rubbing the back of his neck. "I need some air." He waved a hand at the dining room table, at the oven where potatoes were baking, and the refrigerator where a salad was cooling and a bottle of wine chilling. "Can I have a rain check? I don't feel up to this dinner tonight."

"Of course. Can I do anything?" She'd inadvertently said something, but what? What *else* was bothering him?

"No, I'll be all right." He headed for the door. "I need to take a walk. Lock up when you leave, will you?" Almost at a run, he left the house, jogged across the narrow street, and headed down the beach toward the lighthouse.

Stunned and confused, Briana stood looking after him for long minutes, wondering what on earth had happened here tonight. She understood his shock over learning his mother had cheated on Jeremy, which had caused the man he'd known as his father to leave them both. But he'd been all right in her arms until she'd tried to bolster his trampled ego.

What words had triggered such a sudden exit? Or had it all just become too much for him? Information overload, perhaps.

Fixing the lock on the door, Briana closed it behind her and slowly walked back home. This hadn't exactly been the evening she'd envisioned when she'd dressed so carefully. She could have had on a sackcloth for all Slade had noticed tonight. Not that she blamed him.

There was a brooding nature to Slade that she'd spotted the very first day they'd talked. He tended to be introspective, to overthink things too much, yet he accused her of that very thing. In that way, he was more like Jeremy than he knew, though they apparently hadn't been related.

Stepping onto her porch, she decided to sit in the rocker and gaze out to sea for a while. Her appetite had fled and she still had trouble concentrating on reading for very long. Inhaling the salty air, she drew up her legs and hugged them, aware of the chill moving in. Still, she didn't go inside, content to let her thoughts wander.

It was a good night for thinking.

Two miles down the beach, Slade slowed his steps gradually and flung himself onto a small sand dune, breathing hard. The waves were rolling in and out in their tireless rhythm. The night sky was inky with only a sliver of a moon but dotted with a myriad of stars. There was a faint lingering smell of fish out this way where a dock trailed into the frothy water. He lay back on the cool sand, propping his hands behind his head.

What must Briana think of him now? Too damn bad he hadn't stumbled on that pot when she wasn't due over. Too late. Damage done. Now she thought of him as the son of a drunken, faithless mother and a judgmental, unforgiving father. Stepfather, he corrected. Or was that even right? Whoever the hell his real father was would always be Barbara's little dirty secret that she took to her grave.

But at least none of that shoddy past was of his doing. If Brie knew the rest, the sorrow he'd caused, the pain he'd brought to others, she'd never darken his door again.

Poor Barbara. Yes, she'd broken her marriage vows. One time, according to the letters. And ten years later, she'd spit the truth in Jeremy's face. Why, mother, couldn't you have kept still?

He was undoubtedly a hypocrite, Slade decided. He was ready to forgive infidelity but not a breach of etiquette, such as the revelation of the deed. Which was worse, screwing around or blabbing about it? Hell, he didn't know.

For one long minute, he tried to put himself in his father's shoes, to picture the scenario. He's a hardworking man, devoted (for all anyone knew) husband and father, and one day during a quarrel, he learns his wife cheated on him, that his son was the result of a one-night stand with a man whose name Barbara probably couldn't even remember. Would he react as Jeremy had? Would he hate the wife? Would he turn away from a boy he'd loved for ten years?

Slade didn't think he'd do either. To be fair, a person should consider all sides of a question. So why had Barbara cheated on Jeremy? There surely had to have been a good reason. Had Jeremy been a cold fish, indifferent to her sexually? As a child, he'd witnessed affection between them, but what did a kid know about what really went on in the bedroom? To her credit, not in a single letter—and Slade had painstakingly read them all—had Barbara defended herself. She'd given no excuses, no reasons, no alibis. She'd merely asked Jeremy's forgiveness, saying she loved him and that she was desperately sorry.

She might as well have been whistling in the wind.

A sudden possibility occurred to Slade. Had perhaps Jeremy been the typical traveling salesman with a woman in every port, so to speak, and had Barbara learned of his affairs, and thrown out a zinger of her own to hurt him back? Had her story even been true? Both dead, no blood tests here, no DNA testing available. He'd never know all the truth.

Slowly, Slade sat up. What did it all matter anyway? The bitter truth was, his parents had both been human, and being such, they'd both made mistakes. But whose had been the greater, the wandering wife or the deserter husband?

His head was beginning to hurt with all the unanswered questions whirling around inside. He stumbled to his feet and started back, walking this time. Another disturbing thought. Would history repeat itself? Would he wind up alone, as Jeremy had? As Barbara had?

Two days ago, while finishing up painting the walls in Briana's living room, the phone had rung and he'd had no choice but to listen to her end of the conversation. The caller had been her agent in Manhattan asking how she was doing, when she thought she'd be able to finish the book in progress. The book that involved photos around Boston bay. Which meant she'd of course have to return to shoot the rest, mount them, do the story line, and whatever else was involved.

Briana's answers had been vague, but he'd seen a spark in her eyes for a moment. Renewed interest in returning to work. And why not? She was probably very talented. Anxious to get back to family and friends. Where she belonged.

He'd known she'd be leaving one day. Just not which day. As well she should. He was hardly someone to pin her future hopes on. She was young, not yet thirty. She undoubtedly wanted to remarry and possibly have more children. Why would she want to stay around a sorry wreck like him?

You're a good man. You've saved lives, she'd told him

tonight. If she only knew. Slade felt the guilt of the masquerader rise like bile in his throat. He'd always hated deception. Perhaps in that way at least, he was like Jeremy. Yet here he was, a living, breathing deception.

His guilt followed him around like a stray dog scenting a meaty bone. Always close, always waiting.

He lived in fear that Briana would find out, that others in Nantucket would know his secret sin. Of course, the story could be glossed over, but inside, he knew. He knew he was guilty as sin.

Gazing out at churning waves, Slade recalled the legend of Mayberry House and the shattered young man who'd walked into the sea because he couldn't stand living without his wife and unborn child. There was a time he'd have thought only cowards took their own lives.

Lately, he wasn't all that certain.

Chapter Nine

The weekend of the Artists' Association Members Exhibition arrived with plenty of sunshine cooled down by balmy ocean breezes, not unusual for mid-September. Briana had taken eight photos to Ned Farrell at his Island Camera Shop for matting and display preparation. He'd told her at the time that so far Slade hadn't shown up with the paintings he'd promised, but Ned hoped he would before the big day. To all intents and purposes, she should have been happy and looking forward to the annual show she'd never before attended or exhibited in.

Instead, she was worried.

She hadn't seen Slade for two days, not since the evening he'd hurried out and left her in his house after reading the letters he'd found. His doors had remained closed and she hadn't seen him coming or going. It troubled her, especially since he hadn't been by Ned's place yet. She considered Slade to be a man of his word and wondered if he'd found something more that had upset him further.

Was he hiding out inside that fortress of a house, brooding over the discovery of his tangled parentage, rereading the letters and cursing both Barbara and Jeremy? Or was he hurt and trying to cope, perhaps turning to booze again for consolation? Briana was well aware he'd told her he wasn't really a drinker, but she couldn't dislodge the image from her mind of Slade passed out on the beach rocks at midday.

If none of those things, then what *was* he doing? she wondered, as she fastened her hair with a gold clip at the nape of her neck. Grabbing her navy blazer, she walked to the front, checking her watch. It was quarter to four. She'd promised Irma she'd pick her up around four so they could stroll the North Wharf area where the exhibit was being held this year.

Stepping out onto the porch, she wondered how much longer these fall days would last before she'd have to think about putting up the heavy storm windows again. With the thought came a picture of Slade that first day when he'd reluctantly come to her aid while nursing a hangover. Five weeks had passed since then. Five weeks on the island, healing, working on Gramp's house, trying to make decisions about her uncertain future.

Irma had been right. Her memories of Bobby came just as frequently, saddened her constantly, and the tears still flowed occasionally, but the pain wasn't quite so sharp these days. Keeping busy helped. The house was coming along nicely, with the kitchen almost completed, the tile floor laid, and all the new carpeting in place. There was still much she wanted to do, but she welcomed each chore. It gave her a reason to get out of bed each morning.

What she was going to do when the house was finished Briana still wasn't certain. She'd cross that bridge when she came to it.

She'd even toyed with the idea of returning to work. Her agent had called with a gentle reminder, prompting her to give serious consideration to fulfilling her commitment. Her publishers had been both kind and patient, but they wouldn't be forever. Soon, Briana decided.

Shrugging into her jacket, she stepped out into the front yard and studied Slade's place. All unusually quiet, blinds closed, the truck in the driveway. Should she just let him be, or dare she intrude where she probably wasn't wanted? A while back, he'd said he would go with her to the exhibit. But that had been before his little family shocker.

Coming to a decision, Briana walked over. What could he do except tell her to get lost? She knocked several times quite loudly. It was a full minute before she heard footsteps, then the door swung open.

He stood there clean-shaven, dressed in a white cable-knit sweater, khaki slacks, and Docksiders, with a welcoming smile on his face. "Hey, I was wondering if you still wanted to go to the exhibit?"

More surprised than anything after her worrisome thoughts, Briana knew her concern must be evident. "I was wondering the same about you."

He stepped out. "I said I would go, didn't I?" He finished locking the door and turned to face her, noticing her frown, the shadows in her eyes. "What is it?"

"I haven't seen you since . . . in several days. I was worried about you."

Different emotions vied for attention inside Slade. Worried? About him? He couldn't honestly remember the last time *anyone* had worried about him.

"I'm sorry if I worried you. It never occurred to me that you would. I mean, I've been on my own so long that . . . well, never mind. Is Irma going with us?"

"I told her we'd pick her up." Actually, she'd told Irma that *she'd* pick her up, but she knew that her friend would roll with the punches. "I can drive." There was more room in her car.

"I've got Jeremy's paintings wrapped and in the truck. Do you think Irma'll mind?"

She'd probably love climbing up into the high cab, Briana thought, and told him so as she followed him to the driveway.

Slade started the engine, then paused. "I want to thank you for being so understanding the other night. As you discovered, I don't respond well to shock. I hope I didn't freak you out."

So he wasn't just going to ignore that evening. Good. "No, but I have been concerned."

"Yeah, well, my way of coping with startling pieces of news is just to sleep a lot, spend some time thinking things through, and not foist myself on others until I've come to grips with things."

"And have you?"

Slade shrugged. "More or less. I think both my mother and Jeremy made some heavy-duty mistakes, but they each in their own way paid for those errors in judgment. God knows, I've made more than my share. I don't want to be as judgmental as Jeremy was. Whatever happened happened. I just have to learn to let it go."

The complete about-face from his anger two evenings ago was surprising, but she welcomed the change. "I think that's wise."

He shifted into reverse. "Don't go handing me any

prizes. It's self-preservation and nothing more. Blaming two people who're no longer with us for things they did years ago would be pretty stupid." He shot out into the street.

"A lot of people do it. I'm glad you decided not to. They can no longer be hurt by anything you might do, but you can be."

Enough talk. It was a beautiful day and Slade wanted to put all troubling thoughts aside. "You know another reason I wanted to take the truck?"

"No, why?"

He pulled up in front of Irma's house and saw the older woman waiting on her porch. "Because you'll have to scoot over real close to me in order to give Irma room to sit." His grin was wicked.

Surprised and somewhat amused, Briana looked away from his laughing eyes. Now, where had that come from?

It was dusk by the time the three of them settled at an outdoor table in front of Ricardo's Mexican Restaurant two blocks from the exhibit. Mariachi singers with guitars wandered about, serenading the late diners. The red lanterns strung along the fenced-off area added sparkle to Irma's auburn hair as she gazed up at the mustached waiter and insisted on ordering for all of them.

"We'll have black bean nachos for starters, young man," she began. "With extra hot sauce. Then jalapeno chicken, cheese enchiladas, and a double order of chile rellenos. Of course, you'll bring rice and refried beans as well, yes?"

"Yes, madam." The young man smiled broadly.

"Aren't you going to write down the order?" Irma asked him.

The waiter pointed to his head. "All in here, madam. And to drink?"

"A big pitcher of margaritas, of course. No salt. Bad for you." She winked at him, then watched him walk away. "Nice buns, don't you think, Briana?"

"Irma, behave." But she was smiling as she dipped a tortilla chip in a bowl of salsa.

Irma frowned. "Why would I begin now?" She smiled over at Slade, impressed with the fact that he'd spent the last several hours strolling around with them, not saying much but seemingly interested in everything on display, stopping occasionally to answer a question about Jeremy's paintings. She was determined to make the most of this opportunity and find out more about J.D. Slade. For Briana's sake, of course. "Now, remember, this dinner's on me. To thank you both for dragging me along."

"No one has to be forced to take you anywhere, Irma," Briana commented, meaning it. "You've got friends on every street in Nantucket."

"Longevity, my dear, is its own reward. The secret is outliving people. Then there's no one left to correct your ramblings or your memory."

Slade had to smile. The woman was irrepressible. "You mean there are those who would dare correct you?"

"Used to be," Irma answered as their waiter set frosty glasses in front of them, then filled each to the brim with frothy liquid. "Very few of my contemporaries left, don't you know." She held up her glass. "Here's to friendship."

"Friendship," they both echoed, then everyone drank.

"Mmm, that's tart. Wonderful." Irma set down her glass carefully. Time to test the waters. "You know that painting of Jeremy's that Ned had on display, the one that looked like a sea of daffodils?" she asked, looking at Slade.

"I know the one."

"How much is that, or do you want me to go through the gallery?"

"No, I want you to have it, as my gift."

Irma wrinkled her forehead, then thought better of it. The doctor had told her after the last face-lift that a wrinkled brow would negate all of his fine work. "I wasn't fishing, young man. And I won't accept such an expensive gift. Just tell me the price. I'm not without resources."

"I'm sure you're not. Nor am I. It would be my pleasure to give it to you." He glanced at Briana, then back to the older woman. "Someone told me that paintings should reside with people who love them. I thought at the time it was an odd concept, people loving paintings. Most places I've lived, people hung paintings to cover the cracks in the wall. But I think I understand more now. Please, allow me to give it to you."

"Well, if you insist, but I have a feeling I'm getting a real bargain in exchange for this measly meal." The measly meal arrived then and was anything but, the huge platter-like plates taking up nearly every square inch of table space. "Oh, doesn't this smell heavenly?"

"I love Mexican food," Briana commented, picking up her fork. She was pleased that Irma seemed able to get Slade to open up.

"The best I've ever tasted was in California," he said, "in this little dive of a place south of San Diego. Their salsa would bring tears to your eyes."

"Were you stationed there in the navy?" Irma asked, glad he'd unknowingly given her an opening.

"Part of the time." He took a bite of steaming, fragrant enchilada and felt fire ripple along his tongue.

"Where else did you go in your travels?"

Briana glanced up, hoping Irma wasn't going to give the poor guy the third degree, as she seemed destined to do. But the older woman avoided her eyes.

"Oh, here and there, wherever they sent me," Slade answered.

"My, you're as reticent as your father was." Undaunted that Briana was sending her disapproving looks, Irma swallowed a bit of rice and moved on. "I thought all men liked to talk about themselves."

Slade looked into sly eyes behind glasses framed in exotic turquoise. "All right, let's see. I spent four years in the navy, visiting Germany, Hawaii, the Philippines, and Korea, courtesy of the government. After that, I became a fireman in the Sacramento area. I've never been married, have no children, but I do have all my own teeth. My health is excellent, my shoe size twelve, I prefer Colgate toothpaste, and my intentions are strictly dishonorable. Did I leave anything out?"

Cute, Irma thought, with admiration. "I like this man," she told Briana, who wasn't smiling. Irma ignored her friend. "Why'd you quit the fire department?"

Briana's gaze flew to Slade's face, noticing only a flicker of reaction in his eyes, but he recovered quickly.

"Wouldn't you if you inherited all of Jeremy's worldly goods?"

A great evasive answer, Irma decided. "Maybe. I rather thought that firefighting got into your blood. Not so?"

"Not everyone's blood."

"Since you've never married, then have you ever lived with anyone? A female, I mean. You're not kinky, are you?"

"Irma, honestly. That's enough." Briana was truly embarrassed at this point. Some gentle old ladies thought their age gave them permission to ask personal questions they'd have thought rude forty years ago.

"That's all right," Slade said, because to be ungracious would just whet her appetite. Irma was like a dog with a juicy new bone, not about to let go despite Briana's discomfort. "Yes, I lived with a woman once, for about half a year."

Finally, pay dirt. "Six months isn't very long. What happened?"

Before Briana could lodge a new protest, Slade answered. "She kicked me out." He had no intention of telling her more, so while Irma thought that over, he grabbed the conversational ball. "Tell me about your husbands, Irma. I understand you've had three and outlived them all."

A neat turnaround, Irma thought. The man was probably great at board games. "Do you play chess, Slade?"

"Yes. Jeremy taught me when I was quite young. Want to take me on?"

It was on the tip of Irma's tongue to give a cheeky reply reeking with sexual innuendo, but she didn't want to irritate Briana any more than she already had. She'd back off. For now. But there was something lurking behind those hooded eyes, she decided. One day, she'd find out what it was. "Name the date and hour and I'll be there. As to your question, Oscar was my first husband, a workaholic. Carter was my second, an alcoholic. And Mac Tatum was my third, a sweet man except for his love of gambling." She sighed lustily. "I married three men with different addictions. I haven't been lucky in love, Slade." Her past was no one's business but her own, which, Irma had just learned, was exactly how J.D. Slade felt. "Does that give us something in common?"

"It certainly does."

A lucky thing for Irma that respect for her elders had been drilled into her by a military father, Briana thought, or she'd have kicked the older woman under the table for grilling Slade under the hot lights. She knew Irma meant well, that she didn't trust Slade and wanted to reveal his bad side, if he had one, before Briana got too involved. But she hated inquisitions and meant to let Irma know just how displeased she was at the first opportunity. There was a time to protect someone and a time not to. She was, after all, a grown woman and not some teenager.

Only half listening to one of Irma's dead husband stories, Briana poked at her remaining food, filling up fast. She leaned back for a breather and took a sip of her margarita. Gazing out past the half wall surrounding the outdoor section, she noticed Pam and Chris Reed walking toward them, their faces anxious. She raised her hand to wave.

"Hey, you two, what's up?"

"Oh, God, Brie," the very pregnant Pam said, coming up to the partitioned-off table. "It's Annie. We can't find her. Have you by any chance seen her?"

"She's wearing a red sweatshirt, jeans, and plaid sneakers," Chris interjected, brushing back a lock of curly red hair.

Catching their anxiety, Briana stood. "No, not since we ran into the three of you buying caramel corn, remember?"

"That has to be at least two hours ago," Irma added. "When did she come up missing?"

There was an edge of panic to Pam's voice. "About twenty minutes now, right, Chris? We'd gone into this pet store and I reminded Annie to stay close to me because it was really crowded in there. Then Chris called me over to look at this adorable puppy and when I turned around to point him out to Annie, she wasn't there." Pam's hands were trembling as she stuffed them in the pockets of her jacket that she could no longer zip over her belly. "Oh, God, where did she go?"

"Now, honey, don't cry." But Chris's voice was quivery, too. "She's *got* to be here somewhere." He was a tall man, with blue eyes that scanned the people milling about, some friends and neighbors, others visiting strangers, looking for that little blond head.

"Have you notified the police?" Slade asked, remembering having seen several officers strolling past.

Pam's eyes grew huge. "The police? You don't think . . . I mean, surely no one would . . . oh, God!" She crammed one hand to her mouth, too upset for words.

Briana quickly introduced Slade to the Reeds. "We'll help you look, and we'll round up others." She walked around the restaurant's barrier wall while Slade threw some money on the table. Irma moved to put a comforting arm around Pam.

"Let's go back to the spot where you last saw her, and then fan out from there, each of us taking a different path," Slade suggested. In step with Chris, who seemed relieved to have someone, anyone, take over, he asked a few hard-ball questions out of earshot of Pam. "Did you see anyone suspicious hanging around that pet store?" A store with puppies would be an ideal place for a child to be snatched, since animals fascinated kids.

"No, no one. There's my friend, Pete Wilder. I know he'll help." Chris hurried over.

At the pet store, Pam tearfully informed the owner what had happened. To Briana's amazement, in a matter of minutes, Slade had eight people organized, each going off to search a different area.

"I'd better go with you, Irma," Briana told her. People were still out and about and the streetlights were on, but the side streets especially around the wharf area were quite dark. She didn't want the older woman falling and adding to the problem.

"Briana," Irma said, pulling herself up to her full five-seven height, "I'm perfectly capable of walking these streets alone." With that, she turned, skirts swirling, and headed in the direction she'd been assigned.

"Okay, you win," Briana muttered, walking over to Slade. "I'm going down toward town, then. Where'll you be?"

"I'm staying right here in case Annie comes back. I'm better at coordinating than searching."

She took a moment to study his face, wondering why he wouldn't meet her eyes. His mouth was a thin line and he seemed paler in the artificial light. "Are you all right?"

"*Yes*. Will you get going? We've got to find her. We've got to find Annie."

Moving off hurriedly, Briana wondered when Slade had become so attached to little Annie. Of course, they were all anxious to find her. When a child became lost or was in danger, she was everyone's child. But to the best of her knowledge, he'd only had that one conversation with the little girl when he'd rescued her kitten from the tree.

Perhaps Annie reminded him of someone, she decided as she rushed into a toy store, peering down all the aisles. Finally, she asked the owner to make an announcement, but although she waited several minutes, Annie didn't show. Briana walked on to the next establishment.

Slade didn't give a damn if it upset the Reeds, he decided it was time to involve the police when he saw an officer stroll around the corner of the pet store. He signaled the man over.

Within ten minutes, the officer had a much larger search party organized, having radioed for backup. Slade gave them a detailed description, then tried to calm Pam, who'd wandered back. Noticing her strained pallor, he insisted she sit down on a bench just outside the shop. Her pregnancy looked to be quite advanced.

"When are you due?" he asked, trying to distract her.

"Six weeks." She sniffled into a tissue. "Annie never does this. I can't imagine what possessed her to wander away." Horrified eyes looked up at him. "You don't suppose someone . . . that she might have been . . ." Pam couldn't finish the thought out loud.

"Let's not jump to conclusions. We need to stay calm." But inside, Slade was anything but calm, remembering another night, another frantic mother, another child in danger. He felt sweat break out on his neck and trail down between his shoulder blades.

Pam clutched at his sweater's sleeve, recalling that she'd been told Slade was a fireman, a man sworn to help people. "Please, help me find my little girl. I knew your father. He was a good man. He'd help us if he were still alive. Please, bring me my baby."

The words echoed in Slade's head, their meaning cutting through to his core. *Please, bring me my baby.* Oh, God, not again.

Unable to look at her another minute, Slade walked away, then broke off in a run. He didn't know where he was going, only that he couldn't stay there, couldn't hide out *organizing* when what he really needed to do was search like everyone else. Maybe he'd get lucky. Maybe this time, the gods would be with him.

Briana slowly walked back to the pet store, her steps dragging. She'd been up and down the streets, in dozens of shops, talking with countless people, asking if they'd seen a small, towheaded little girl about six. No one had. As she approached, she saw Pam sitting on a bench, Chris crouching in front of her as she wept. Several police hovered around together with onlookers and members of the search party who'd returned.

But no sweet, freckle-faced child.

Almost in tears, she joined them, seeing by their faces that no one had gotten lucky. Irma had lost her bounce as she moved to sit alongside Pam, to pull her close and lend a measure of comfort. Behind her glasses, her blue eyes were swimming with tears.

The senior officer's name tag read "Sgt. Bremer." He turned to Chris Reed and Briana, who was standing with him. "I think we're going to have to face some harsh facts. We could be looking at an abduction." He kept his voice low.

Chris turned even paler as he glanced at his wife, making sure she hadn't heard. "Why would someone abduct our child? We don't have that kind of money."

"Well, sir, not all abductors are interested in ransom money."

His mouth a grim line, Chris closed his eyes as the unspoken fear washed over him. "What do you want us to do?"

"I'm going to ask you and your wife to . . ."

"Look!" Irma cried out loud enough to be heard above the hum of voices as she squeezed Pam's hand. "Do you see what I see?" Everyone turned toward the direction she was pointing.

Briana gasped as she recognized the tall man carrying a blond little girl wearing a red sweatshirt and jeans. He was hurrying down the hill. For just a moment, with his head backlit from a glowing streetlamp, Briana could imagine Slade carrying someone else's child out of a burning building, rescuing, helping. She felt he must have done just that countless times, yet he'd walked away from his profession. The thought didn't sit well with her.

"Annie!" Pam screamed, getting clumsily to her feet as her husband rushed to her side. Together, they hurried to meet Slade.

He handed the child over to Chris, then stepped aside so Pam could embrace her daughter, too. For a moment, he stood watching the small family sob with relief. Then he turned and walked toward Briana, who quickly put her arms around him, her damp face burrowing into his shoulder.

"Thank God you found her," Briana whispered.

He'd found her crouched behind a big old evergreen on a side street four short blocks from the pet store. In her arms, she'd been cradling a calico cat, a stray she'd spotted while her parents had been occupied, one she'd mistaken for Rascal. So of course, she'd had to go after her. By the time she'd caught the kitten, Annie had gotten confused and lost. She'd heard people walking by and calling her name, but they were all strangers and she'd been afraid. It wasn't until Slade showed up that she recognized someone and crept out.

"Dumb luck, Briana, that's all," he told her after finishing the story. "A stroke of dumb luck that she recognized me in the dark."

"We'll take it," Briana answered, watching the Reed family.

"Mommy, I'm sorry. I thought the kitten was Rascal and . . ."

Pam hugged her daughter tighter. "It's all right, honey. Everything's all right now."

Several people hovered around, offering their good wishes. Quite a few stopped to slap Slade on the back and congratulate him on a job well done. Still, it wasn't enough to make up for the other time, he knew. Nothing he did would ever be enough.

Finally, he took Briana's hand and pulled her aside. "Let's get out of here." He'd had enough. This was not a scene he enjoyed, despite the relief and happy ending. He didn't want credit. He wanted to erase the memory of another time, another child.

"I have to find Irma."

"All right, but then let's go."

Briana located Irma, but the older woman decided she wanted to stay and chat with a friend who'd drive her home later. She hurried back to Slade, then followed him to where he'd parked the truck, barely able to keep up with his long strides. Finally seated, she huffed out a jagged breath. "What's your rush, fella? You're a hero now, you know."

His head swiveled toward her, his eyes bleak. "Don't call me that. I don't deserve it." He started the motor and lurched out into traffic.

Thoughtfully, Briana watched a muscle in his hard jaw twitch, and wondered not for the first time what he was thinking, and what had triggered this particular reaction. A man of many moods, most of them enigmatic, she decided. Would he even confide in her if she asked? Doubtful.

In his driveway, outside the parked truck, Briana decided to try. But she'd have to go slowly, using caution. He was as skittish as a newborn colt. "Will you come in and have coffee with me?"

Slade rubbed a weary hand along the back of his neck. "Brie, I'm a little tired tonight and . . ."

"Please?"

He knew what she wanted from him, and it wasn't coffee. He knew he hadn't revealed much about his recent past in words, but his actions, his reactions, had disclosed a great deal. Briana Morgan was very good at reading between the lines.

He also knew he was scared to death.

He'd come to this island a skeptic, a loner, a man unwilling to let anyone get close to him, with good reason. He'd grown up ashamed—that his father had left them, that his mother drank, that they'd had to live hand-to-mouth, none of which had been the fault of a young boy. As a defense mechanism, he'd done everything he could to protect himself from people who would judge, who would criticize, who could hurt him.

Then, as an adult, he'd done something that had brought disappointment, pain, and disgrace on himself. After that, he'd bottled up his feelings, sharing them with no one except in the most casual way, living with a loneliness so entrenched that at times he'd felt desperate.

Then Brie had come into his life, a beautiful, vulnerable woman whose pain was as deep as his own. Only, she hadn't set into motion the cause of that pain. She was an innocent and he was a guilty man. How could she understand what he'd done and forgive him when he couldn't forgive himself?

"I'm not very good company tonight, Brie."

But he had been until the incident with Annie. Briana was certain that whatever triggered Slade's reaction to that missing child held the key to his past problems. Without asking herself why, she knew she had to find out what that was. "You're afraid to trust me, is that it?"

"No!" Slade scrubbed a hand over his face, wishing he'd said goodnight and gone inside. Better to be thought unfriendly than to strip yourself down to a raw and aching soul. "I can't tell you."

"Why?"

"Because I don't want anything in my past to hurt you."

That surprised her, but she remained unconvinced. "It's not your call. I'm a big girl. I can handle more than you think I can."

Slade shifted his feet on the grass. In a distant yard, a dog began barking, vying with the sound of the relentless waves rushing in to the sandy shore. He felt his stomach muscles clench. God, when had he become such a coward?

He wanted to tell her, but he also wanted her to understand, and there were no guarantees that she would. He hadn't been aware that the need to share his feelings had been steadily growing inside him, and that Brie was the one person he wanted to confide in. But what if she turned from him? He'd already lost so many. He wasn't certain he could handle losing her, too.

Maybe he could talk her out of this. "What happened to me in the past shouldn't have anything to do with you and me now."

"But it does. Everything that happened to form us before we met and since is what makes us what we are. I saw my son die. That experience changed me forever. I'm not the person I was before then. Just this week, you learned that the man you thought all your life was your father wasn't.

You're a different person knowing that." Suddenly, Briana felt tired. Why was she pushing him? It was obvious he didn't want to confide in her. She had no business badgering him.

"Listen, let's just forget it. You have a right to your privacy. I told you weeks ago that I'd butt out, but here I am, doing it again. I'm sorry. I'll talk with you tomorrow." She started to walk toward her house.

"You'll hate me if I tell you everything."

Briana stopped, then slowly turned back, meeting his eyes in the patchy moonlight. "I could never hate you," she said, her voice whisper-quiet as she realized she spoke the truth.

"Why not? There are those who do."

"Because . . . because I care about you." She took a step closer, well aware that what she'd said could send him scurrying for cover. "I know what you're thinking, that if I learn what's bothering you, I'll walk away. All your life, people have abandoned you. I'm not like that, Slade. When I care about someone, I'm in for the long haul. There's precious little they could do that would cause me to leave."

"You walked out on your marriage, on Robert."

"Yes, I did, because it was no longer a marriage in any sense of the word. I didn't know it when I met him, but Robert was already married—to his work. I couldn't compete. Indifference kills even the strongest love."

Opposing emotions warred in him, yet the overriding one was fear—fear of losing her before he really had her. Not until he'd faced the possibility of that loss tonight did he even realize that he wanted her. Maybe a clean break would be best before things got out of hand. "I told you once before, it would be unwise of you to get involved with me. I warned you. You should have listened."

"I remember and I gave you some breezy answer. But the truth is, admit it or not, we're already involved. Aren't we, Slade?" She kept her eyes steady on his. Showdown time, Briana thought. She'd never been much of a gambler, but she'd put a lot on the line this time.

Slade stared back. There was nothing to do but tell her the truth. Then watch her walk away.

"Maybe. The question is, do you want to be involved with a man who's responsible for the death of an innocent child and the utter ruin of her mother?"

Chapter Ten

It was several seconds before Briana could speak. Her first thought, irrational as she knew it to be, was that she'd heard wrong. Slade couldn't have caused someone's death. He was a firefighter sworn to save people's lives.

She was aware he was watching her closely and knew that her first reaction was one he'd remember. "Come with me," she finally said. "I'll make coffee. I want to hear the whole story."

Slade didn't move. "It's not going to make any difference. The bottom line is that a four-year-old died because of me and her mother's a basket case. Period."

"Nothing is that simple, Slade. Certainly everything isn't all black or all white. You told me you didn't want to be judgmental like Jeremy. I'm not quick to judge, either." She touched his arm. "Come with me, please."

He let out a shuddering breath. It was bad enough that he'd blurted out the end result. He didn't know if he had the strength to tell the rest. Or rather, he didn't know if he could stand watching her face while she heard the terrible details. "Maybe it's best if we just leave it alone. I told you I'm not a good person, that I've done things."

"I wish you'd stop trying to make up my mind for me. Are you so certain I'm incapable of listening and deciding for myself what to believe?"

"It's cut and dried, Brie. A done deed."

She was tired of fencing with him on the front lawn. Taking his arm, she pulled him along the walk to her front porch, leading him inside. "The best I can offer you is the floor. Sit down. I'll be right back."

In the kitchen, Briana busied herself with the coffeemaking, her thoughts on his words. She could tell he firmly believed that he was responsible for the child's death, the mother's devastation. But was he? There had to be extenuating circumstances. If he were guilty, wouldn't he be in prison? Chances are he only *thought* he was responsible.

The whole thing had to be tied in to his work. She knew he'd been with the fire department over five years. Surely in that period of time, there had to have been some casualties. Surely Slade couldn't take full personal responsibility for those deaths.

Plugging in the pot, she went into the living room and joined him as he sat cross-legged on the floor, staring at her new blue carpeting. "Are you all right?"

Slowly, he raised bruised eyes to hers. "I'll never be all right again, Brie."

She nodded, understanding. "I remember saying those very words after Bobby died. Was this child a stranger or someone you knew?"

"Oh, I knew her, all right. That makes it much worse."

Briana waited, hoping he'd go on without her prompting.

Finally, like a man reciting a bad dream, Slade began to talk. "The woman I mentioned living with earlier tonight, the one who threw me out? Her name is Rachel. You remember when we first met, I said that you reminded me of someone?" When she nodded, he went on. "I thought you resembled Rachel more then than I do now. Same hair coloring and eyes. But there it ends."

He cleared his throat. "Anyhow, I worked with Rachel's brother, Alex, and he introduced us. She was a single mother, married and divorced real young, and she had this really cute little girl. Megan. She wasn't quite four then, blond hair, big blue eyes. She was on the shy side, loved to be read to."

Briana listened, not wanting to interrupt, allowing him to tell it at his own pace.

"Rachel and I started dating and we hit it off right away. After about a month, she asked me to move in with her. She was always short of money because her ex-husband had skipped the state and never paid child support. So I sublet my apartment and we split the expenses on this older house she was renting. Things were okay for several months, then I began to see signs of restlessness in Rachel."

"What kind of restlessness?" Briana asked as she rose to get their coffee. She brought back two steaming mugs.

"She didn't like being alone so much when I worked my twenty-four-hour shifts, but I explained that there wasn't anything I could do about that. She wanted me to put in for a desk job and regular hours, but I didn't want that. She told me she wanted a better life, a nicer place, money in her pocket. Unfortunately, I'd never gotten into the habit of saving much."

"So she was unhappy, discontented?"

"Oh, was she ever. Next thing I know, she quit her job and told me she wanted to stay home, wanted us to get married so she could have another baby. We were already fighting most of the time. I told her no way was I getting married just then, and I made damn sure she didn't get pregnant. Things went from bad to worse and I was about to pack up and leave her, but I was nuts about Megan. I didn't know what would happen to her if her mother didn't grow up." Slade shoved both hands through his already mussed hair. "I should have tried harder."

"Don't," Briana said. "Don't start the should-haves, could-haves. We *all* might do things differently if we could foresee the future. Countless times, I've said to myself, why did I let Bobby go with Robert that day? I could have begged off and he'd have probably agreed. Or why didn't I go along and take the bullet that killed my son? You can drive yourself crazy with those thoughts."

Slade sighed heavily. "Yeah, I guess you're right. Anyhow, I did finally make up my mind to pull out. I went home after my shift one early morning and found that my key wouldn't fit. Rachel had had the locks changed. I was furious and started banging on the door. She finally answered, wearing her robe, her hair all wild like she'd just climbed out of bed."

He gave a mirthless laugh. "Because she had. She had my bags packed and waiting at the door and the other guy already moved in. He was someone Rachel said made more money than I did, enough so she'd never have to work again. Good for you, I told her and grabbed my bags. But before I could leave, Megan came running out and threw herself at me. That was the hard part, walking away from that little girl."

Briana had a feeling there were even harder parts yet to come, but she kept still. She badly wanted to reach out and touch his hand, just to let him know she was listening with an open mind. But his head was bent and he was staring into his mug, the coffee untasted. "So she threw you out, so to speak."

"Yeah." Slade forced himself to go on, to finish. Briana had wanted to know, and by God, he was going to tell her every rotten, ugly detail. "Alex, her brother, got transferred across town to a different station, so I didn't see much of him after the split. That was good because he used to bring Megan down to the station occasionally. It would've been hard, seeing her like that.

"One night about six months later, I was on duty when we got a call—a one-alarm fire. That usually means two engine companies, two four-men teams plus a battalion chief. A pretty serious blaze. A neighbor had phoned it in and I recognized the address right away, Rachel's house. As soon as we pulled up, I saw flames shooting out of the back bedroom. Rachel's room."

Lifting his mug, Slade drank, needing the momentary diversion. He didn't even glance at Briana, so anxious was he now to finish. "Two of us went barreling in, the other two on hoses. I knew the layout best so I went first. The whole place was filled with smoke and it was hotter than hell. I found Rachel on the floor in her bedroom. Later we learned she'd fallen asleep smoking."

"The new man who lived with her, was he there?"

"No. Apparently he'd moved out about as fast as he'd moved in. Maybe he hadn't lived up to Rachel's expectations, either. Anyway, I picked her up, saw she was breathing, and handed her over to my partner because I knew Megan had to be in there somewhere. Rachel started coughing so I got in her face and asked where Megan was. In the closet, she finally said."

Shaking his head, he struggled for composure. "I didn't believe her. God, I wish I'd believed her."

"What do you mean? What happened?"

"I went back down the hallway toward the bedrooms, but I thought that Rachel had been too foggy and disoriented to know where her daughter was. You see, Megan was scared to death of closets. She'd managed to lock herself in one once, and her mother hadn't heard her yelling right away over the sound of the television. By the time I got to her, she'd been hysterical. But I went into her room anyway because I'd heard a sound, something that sounded like a child's cry. I opened her closet and her kitten jumped into my arms. I'd heard the cat's cry, not Megan's."

Briana was puzzled. "I've read that young children often hide in closets when there's a fire, thinking they can escape that way. But since Megan was afraid of closets, why would she hide in one for any reason? And why would Rachel tell you to look for her in a closet unless she *knew* Megan was in there?"

"I don't know. It doesn't matter. I should have searched *all* the closets. But I didn't. I put the cat inside my coat and started searching, but she was nowhere. The smoke was so thick I could barely see. And hot! My God, it was like an inferno. My air bottle was running out and I knew I'd soon be in trouble. I was moving along the hallway, keeping low to avoid the worst of the smoke, when Rachel's bedroom ceiling collapsed, the walls caved in, fire shooting up all around. That was the room hit the worst because that's where the fire had started. The rest of the crew were pouring on the water, a couple on the roof ventilating, cutting holes to let out the smoke and heat. Still, I kept on looking for Megan, crawling along the floor, calling her name, until the kitchen burst into new flames."

Slade shifted, rubbing a hand over his tired eyes. "It's called a flashover. Heat builds in a room where there's lots of smoke, it gets hotter and hotter, then suddenly erupts into new fire. The impact threw me into a corner. A couple of the guys came in and dragged me out. My air was used up. Another minute and the whole side of the building fell in."

Briana did reach out then, moving closer, putting her hand on his arm, squeezing it to let him know she was there.

Slade drew in a deep breath. "They tried to put me into an ambulance because of smoke inhalation, but I wouldn't go. I had to find Megan." He shook his head. "But I knew. I knew it was too late." He'd made himself stay until they'd carried out the small, charred body of what had once been a vibrant little girl. She'd looked no bigger than a blackened rag doll. Helplessly, he'd watched them bag her, knowing his life would never be the same.

He turned to Briana, his eyes bleak and empty. "Do you know where they finally found her poor little body? On the floor of Rachel's closet. Her mother had trusted me to get her child out, told me she was in the closet, but like a stubborn, arrogant fool, I didn't believe her because I was so sure Megan wouldn't go into a closet."

"But you *did* go look in the closet. *Megan's* closet, which was the logical one to search. Rachel never indicated she meant *her* closet, did she?"

"No. She just said, 'She's in the closet.' But I was the

firefighter, the professional. I should have looked in *every* closet. You can't assume anything, especially when a victim is near hysteria." He rubbed a hand over his eyes, suddenly aware he had a pounding headache. "When I finally saw Rachel outside in an ambulance after the medics had worked on her, she asked where Megan was. I had to tell her I hadn't been able to find her. She screamed and screamed and screamed, then she collapsed. I'll never forget that sound. I hear it in my sleep."

Of course he would. He'd probably witnessed many burned and hysterical survivors, but none as personal as this one. "How badly was Rachel hurt?"

"Not much. They investigated and found she'd dozed off, the cigarette had fallen onto the bed and started the fire, but somehow, she'd rolled off the bed. The floor's the safest place to be in a room that's on fire. The best guess was that Megan had awakened in her room and wandered into Rachel's, got scared when she saw the fire and crawled into her mother's closet. Rachel had only minor burns, some smoke inhalation."

"Didn't you tell her how you'd searched everywhere for her daughter?" Briana saw a muscle in his jaw twitch as he fought for control.

"Yeah, but she kept screaming over and over that she'd told me Megan was in the closet, why didn't I find her? She got so agitated that the EMS guys asked me to leave." Even in the hallway, I could hear her. *You let my baby die*."

"Oh, but you didn't, Slade." Briana scooted so she was directly in front of him, forcing him to look at her. "You did everything you could. The walls collapsed. You couldn't go in there. You did your best. It wasn't your fault."

But he was shaking his head. "I followed the sound, the cry, and it was the cat, not Megan. I should have immediately gone to Rachel's closet and checked. But I was so sure Megan wouldn't be there."

"Have you considered getting some counseling about this?"

"The battalion captain debriefed me, took me off active duty, and ordered me into counseling. I went on and off for two months, but I don't feel any differently about what happened." He met her eyes, his face weary. "It was my fault, Briana, plain and simple. I have to live with that the rest of my life. Now do you see why I don't want to be a firefighter ever again?"

She nodded. "Yes, but I don't believe Megan's death was your fault. It was an accident, Slade. Weren't you the one who told me that bad things happen to good people?"

It was as if he hadn't heard her. "Do you know what Rachel's like these days? I went to see her again about a week before I came here. She's moved in with her mother, who also blames me. Rachel sits staring off into space, rocking in an old chair, rarely speaking. Scarcely living. *She's* on my conscience, too."

Briana had listened carefully, but still didn't think he should shoulder all this blame. Rachel, after all, had been the one who'd been smoking in bed, fallen asleep, and caused the fire that killed her daughter. How can she blame the firefighters, most especially one she'd cared for once and who obviously loved Megan?

She searched her mind for words of comfort. "Slade, when we're hurting, we want to blame someone, anyone, to lift the burden of guilt from ourselves. It's only human."

"You didn't do that in Bobby's death."

"Because there was no one tangible to blame. If the police had caught the person in the car that had driven by and shot my son, I'd be at that courthouse, at his trial, wanting to see him punished. Rachel doesn't sound very strong to me. She doesn't accept responsibility for causing the fire in the first place, but rather blames you for not finding her child. That's not right."

Slade shrugged. "Right or wrong, the fact is that even if she forgave me, I'd still blame myself. I *loved* that child, Briana, and I couldn't save her. I made a bad decision, looked in the wrong closet. Rachel trusted me to get Megan out and I failed her."

"No! You didn't fail anyone. You did your best. No one can ask more of another human being. If a policeman's called to a house to settle a domestic squabble and the husband pulls out a gun and shoots his wife, is it that officer's fault that he didn't prevent that from happening? Absolutely not. You're human, not superhuman. You can't protect everyone or prevent everything bad from happening. You're *not* to blame."

He studied her face a long moment, so serious, so intent. How had he come to deserve someone like this championing him? And here he'd tagged her as the needy one. "I appreciate your faith in me. I wish I had a small measure of it."

Briana set both their mugs aside, then moved closer to him, straddling his lap so they were torso to torso. "You have to find a way to forgive yourself. You can't carry around this burden." She framed his face with her hands, looking deeply into his eyes. Maybe if she could ease his pain, she could ease her own. "I believe you're a good, honorable man. *You* need to believe it, too."

Gently, Briana touched her mouth to his, her lips soft on his, slowly brushing, coaxing. Her hands slipped to his shoulders as she rained small, healing kisses on his chin, his cheeks, up to his closed eyes, then back to his mouth.

He wasn't indifferent, but he wasn't responding. Yet. She'd run out of words to convince him; perhaps she could let him know in another way that she cared, that she saw only good in him.

She kept up the onslaught, circling his face again, pausing to plant warm, wet kisses at his ears, then pressing her mouth to the pulse point now throbbing at the base of his throat. She felt his arms slide around her, slowly drawing her nearer, and became bolder. "Kiss me back, Slade. Let me help."

Wanting to let go of the hurtful memories and move into her healing touch, he made a sound deep in his throat and took her mouth. She was so soft, so warm, so giving. She opened to him, inviting his tongue inside, letting it spar with hers. Her arms encircled his neck as she pressed against him, and Slade felt engulfed in her generosity.

Her body was so very close, her movements as she wiggled making him ache as he grew hard with needs too long suppressed. He swallowed the soft sounds she made as he angled his head, taking her deeper.

This was what he needed, this mindless sensation, the seeking and the finding, the ageless mating dance. He wanted her desperately even though he knew she'd initiated this out of a desire to help him, not out of physical desire. He would take what she offered and make sure she wouldn't regret sharing her special gifts.

Breaking the kiss momentarily, he rolled to his side, taking her with him onto the thick, padded carpeting. Stretching out, he reached out to align her body more perfectly with his, then went back to devour her mouth. She smelled so sweetly feminine, she tasted so wonderful, like something sinfully rich. And tonight he needed her so badly.

The kiss went on and on as Slade's hands began to explore, his fingers fumbling with the buttons of her blouse. As anxious as he, Briana shifted to help him. The top button came free just as the phone in the kitchen rang.

Startled, pulling back, her breath huffed out as she tried to clear her hazy mind. So seldom did anyone call that she dared not let it go. Shifting, she sat up. "I have to get that."

Slade dropped his hands and flopped onto his back, listening to his heart pound. Of all the rotten timing.

Briana picked it up on the third ring. "Hello?"

"Honey, is that you?" Martha Gifford asked hesitantly.

"Yes, Mom. Is something wrong?" It was only ten in the evening, but still late for a phone call from her parents.

"You sound out of breath. Are you okay?" Martha's voice was shaky.

Briana drew in what she hoped was a calming gulp of air. "Yes, of course. Just surprised by your call. Is everything all right?"

"No, honey. It's Gramp. They just called from the nursing home. He passed away an hour ago."

Briana sat in the dining room alcove of her parents' town house on Beacon Hill and accepted the cup of tea from her mother.

"Lemon, dear?" Martha Gifford asked.

"Yes, thank you." Briana took a slice as she slipped off her shoes. It had been a long day.

"It was a lovely service, didn't you think?" her mother asked as she stirred sugar into her own steaming tea.

"Yes." It was the evening of the second day after she'd received her mother's call informing her that Gramp had died. She'd flown out the next morning. The funeral had been this afternoon, followed by a small reception attended mostly by her parents' friends. All of her grandparents' friends were either already gone or lived on Nantucket. No one had flown over for the short service.

Martha reached over and placed her hand over her daughter's. "I know it was upsetting, going to another funeral such a short time after . . . after the last one. I'm sorry you had to go through it."

"I'm all right, Mom." She squeezed her mother's hand briefly. Martha Gifford was a small woman, delicately built with lovely skin and dark hair lightly sprinkled with gray that she refused to color. Briana's older sister, Toni, took after their mother, while Briana had inherited her father's coloring and height.

"At least you showed up." Martha's voice turned disapproving. "I still don't understand why Toni couldn't make the time to say good-bye. Gramp had always been good to her."

Yes, but her sister had been aware as far back as childhood that the Gifford grandparents had favored Briana. "Florida's a long way and there wasn't much time. Don't be so hard on Toni, Mom. She's got a demanding job, one she can't just leave at a moment's notice. Newspaper work is very competitive."

"If you ask me, it's that new man she's moved into her place that she didn't want to leave."

When had her mother become so judgmental? Briana wondered. Toni had always been a handful, a born rebel, one escapade after another as a teenager. She'd totaled a car, run with a wild crowd, and dropped out of school, then moved out at nineteen.

"Mom hounds me constantly," she'd told Brie, "and Dad, when he's home, is too strict. I can't handle either of them, Brie."

Two years younger, Briana hadn't known what to say or

do, so she'd more or less sat back and watched. She loved her sister, but she'd never understood her. Then, somewhere along the line, Toni had straightened out, graduated from college, and gotten a good job, working her way up on a Miami newspaper chain. Apparently, though, she was still going from man to man.

"It's her life, Mom," Briana said, feeling the need to defend her sister. "Maybe this one's a great guy."

"Wouldn't that be a nice change?" Putting aside her troubled thoughts of Toni, Martha fixed her gaze on her youngest. "How are you doing, dear? And how's the house redecorating going?"

"I'm doing all right and the house is really coming along." Something cheery to talk about. She explained what had been done and the rest of the renovation she had planned. "You won't recognize the place in another month."

"Then what? Are you going to sell it?"

"Oh, no. I could never do that."

"Keep it for summer visits, then. I see."

No, she didn't see, but Briana didn't feel like going into more just now. It had been a trying day, saying good-bye to an old, gentle man she'd loved since birth. She took a sip of tea and leaned back as she remembered something. "Did you tell me earlier that I had a message from some attorney?" Things had been so hectic during the reception, then cleaning up after everyone left, that she'd almost forgotten.

"Yes, just a minute, I have his name and number written down." Martha went to the kitchen phone and brought back the note she'd written. "His name is Charles Brewster and he said he was an attorney from Robert's bank. He said he'd been calling your home phone number for some time, trying to reach you."

Briana studied the message, frowning. "Did he say what he wanted to talk with me about?"

"No, just told me to ask you to call."

"All right, I will tomorrow morning." She folded the paper and pocketed it. "Where was it that Dad said he had to go tonight?" Her father had taken off even before the last guests had left. She'd hardly spoken more than a dozen words to him since arriving.

"To his club. They have card games every Thursday evening."

He'd just buried his father and then rushed off to play cards? Briana sighed. She loved her father, *but*. But he wasn't exactly sensitive or sentimental, or even thoughtful or considerate much of the time. But then, he never had been, always more interested in his career, his contacts, his friends than in anything involving his family. Since his behavior didn't seem to bother her mother, Briana wondered why it bothered her.

"You *are* planning to stay for a while, aren't you?" Martha wanted to know. "I mean, it's not as if you have to finish redecorating for a particular deadline. Now that your kitchen's finished, the painting's done, and the carpeting's in, it's mostly just choosing new furniture, isn't that right?"

A picture flashed into Briana's mind's eye unbidden, of rolling around on her new carpeting locked in Slade's arms, passion about to explode between them, just two nights ago. What had begun as comfort had soon escalated into much more. She'd wanted him so badly she'd been trembling, something she hadn't felt in a very long time. Feeling heat move into her face, she stared down into her teacup. He'd overheard her end of the phone conversation and come to her immediately, holding her yet again while she'd wept for Gramp.

No, she didn't have to hurry back to buy furniture, but perhaps for a more personal reason.

"Well, there's still a lot to be done," she told her mother. "I want to get Grandma's garden prepared for winter, make sure the daffodil bulbs are okay for next year. I've ordered new shutters but they haven't arrived yet. The roofing man's coming next week." Briana brushed back her hair, wondering if she could squeeze in a haircut at her favorite shop before returning. She was also wondering if her mother saw through her lame excuses and would ask why she *really* wanted to go back to Nantucket so soon.

"You want to spend some time with Dad yet, though, don't you? And maybe have lunch with some of your friends. Annette and Mary Ann phoned just last week, asking about you. And of course, Craig. He's a persistent one, isn't he?"

"I don't know about lunching with friends right now, Mom, but of course I'll spend time with Dad. Tomorrow." After she talked to the lawyer. Provided her father saw fit to stay home and spend time with her, which he could have done tonight. Would missing his precious card game one evening have been so terrible? "As for Craig, I'm not interested in seeing him. You knew he came to visit me in Nantucket, didn't you?"

"He said he was going to. He dropped in here one day and asked all about how you were doing, what you were up to, were you well, and so on." Martha's eyes narrowed. "Is he just a friend or is he more to you, Brie?"

"Believe me, I consider him only a friend. Anything more is all in Craig's head. I've tried to discourage him, but he just keeps phoning, then popping up uninvited. Tiresome."

"He's a nice young man, Brie. You've been divorced a

long time, dear." Martha's motives weren't exactly altruistic, which bothered her, but only a little. True, Martha wanted what was best for her daughter. But she also wanted Brie to come back to Boston and settle down nearby. This business of staying in Nantucket, which had been her husband's suggestion, not Martha's, was foolish. The poor child needed her family around her.

Briana rubbed her forehead. The headaches she'd so often had before she'd left were back with a vengeance each day since her return. Maybe she was having a reaction to the air around the bay. Or to her mother's incessant questions. "I know how long I've been divorced, Mom, but it isn't relevant. I don't feel anything for Craig and I never will."

"But sweetheart, he's so clean-cut and he seems to genuinely care for you. He could help you get over things, perhaps." Martha's voice was hopeful.

Impatience gnawed at Brie. Why were they having this stupid, useless conversation? "Mom, I'm a little allergic to pressure right now. Craig isn't the answer. I appreciate your concern, but not everything can be solved with a man in your life, or with tea and sympathy. Not in the real world."

"Of course. I just hate to see you alone so much. You're young. You need to find someone, to marry again, to be happy."

Brie's headache was turning into a whopper. "Why, Mom? Because marriage guarantees happiness? I was married and it wasn't even close to wonderful. And I was alone about as much as you are." She paused, took a breath. "Happy? Are you happy, Mom, with a husband who, even now when he's retired, when his daughter is visiting, is home so seldom it's insulting?"

Martha's lips flattened as she searched for words. She hated disturbing discussions. "Your father has . . . has needs separate from mine. Men do, you know."

Staring at her mother, Brie began to see all Martha wasn't saying. "Separate needs? You mean, sex? Other women?"

Toying with her teaspoon, Martha kept her eyes averted as color moved into her face. Her generation, her circle of friends, didn't discuss this subject easily. "Occasionally. But I know he loves only me. Some men are more . . . lusty than others and . . ." Her voice trailed off.

Shock changed to anger. "How do you put up with it? *Why* do you?"

Finally, Martha looked at her daughter, feeling suddenly old. "Because he's my life, Briana." The subject, as far as she was concerned, was closed. She wouldn't think about it, not tonight, or the next. With effort, she put on a smile. "Now, let's talk about something more pleasant. Would you like more tea?"

Tea, for heaven's sake! Martha was back to being an ostrich. Briana felt as if she were the older of the two of them. "No. Actually, I think I'm going to turn in. I'm tired." She'd opted to stay with her parents these couple of days, but tomorrow, she planned to go check on her town house. She wasn't looking forward to the visit.

Gathering up the tea things, Martha's smile faded. "Rest well, dear. I'll see you in the morning."

In the spare room, Briana set down her shoes feeling defeated, deflated. How could her mother live with a man like that all these years, putting up with countless infidelities.

During their teen years, in their late-night sessions in the bedroom they shared, she and Toni had often probed the possibility of Dad's *other women* during his many absences. Now, finally, Mom had admitted it. *He had separate needs.* The hell you say!

Unlike Jeremy, Martha just looked the other way, pretended nothing was wrong. Briana shook her head. Not her problem.

She walked over to gaze out the window. In the distance, she could see patches of moonlight dancing on the Charles River, the leaves on the trees along the bank already turning colors under the old-fashioned lampposts. There was a definite bite to the air.

Autumn seemed to show signs here sooner than on Nantucket, which was surrounded by the sea, but farther south. There the leaves were still green, the trees lush. She wondered how the geraniums she'd coaxed back to health in pots on the front porch were faring with no one to give them a little water, as she had daily. She wondered if the person who'd broken into her house had come back, noticing she was gone. Slade had said he'd keep an eye on things. She hoped he remembered.

Slade. He would never know how much she'd hated to watch him go home that evening so she could pack and get a few hours' sleep before her morning flight. For several breathtaking minutes there, she'd envisioned being held in his arms for long, lovely hours. And much more.

She hadn't consciously made a decision to make love with him that night. But things had evolved in that direction and she'd suddenly felt the time was right. She'd been vacillating, uncertain, for months now about many things, but about that she felt certain. She knew she wanted Slade, and he knew it, too.

The moon drifted behind the clouds, bringing dark shadows. She wondered what he was doing this very minute, if he was outside looking up at the same moon, perhaps thinking of her. A romantic notion, and one she discarded immediately. He was probably asleep and dreaming of no one.

Or perhaps he was having one of his terrible nightmares, the ones he'd told her he had frequently, about the fire that took little Megan's life. She'd been touched and moved by the story he'd told her, and angry that he blamed himself. Naturally, she didn't know Rachel, but if anyone was to blame for a fire so destructive it burned down the entire house, it was the woman who smoked in bed.

Briana was enormously sympathetic with the unknown Rachel over the loss of her child, understanding more than most how the child's terrible death must haunt the mother. But to blame someone else was truly unconscionable. Rachel had lived with Slade, presumably had cared for him. Hadn't she discovered what kind of man he was during all that time? Didn't she realize he would have done anything to save Megan, even endanger his own life?

Perhaps it was better, Briana thought, leaving the window, that she'd never learned the identity of the shooter who'd taken Bobby's life. This way, she had no face, no name to blame except the fates.

Unbuttoning her blouse, she stifled a yawn. Maybe tonight she'd be able to sleep.

Charles Brewster bustled into the conference room of Fidelity Mutual Savings and offered his hand to Briana. "Good to meet you, Mrs. Morgan. Thank you for taking the time to come see me."

Had she had a choice? Brie wondered, studying the tall, sandy-haired man with a full mustache and rimless glasses. When she'd returned the attorney's call this morning, his secretary, in the condescending, cool voice that so many executive secretaries used, had told her that Mr. Brewster would see her at ten. "No problem. I am curious about why you wanted to see me."

Placing his thin leather briefcase onto the table, he gave her a quick smile, then seated himself. "It's about your husband, Robert. About some of the investment accounts he was handling."

She raised a brow. "Robert and I were divorced over three years ago. Even during the time we were married, we rarely, if ever, discussed his clients."

"Mmm hmm." Brewster unbuttoned his suit coat and leaned forward, folding his hands atop the polished mahogany. "There are some suspicious transactions that have recently come to light regarding Robert Morgan's clients. One in particular, a man named Glenn Halstead. Is that name familiar to you?"

"Not that I recall. What kind of suspicious transactions?"

"Let me lay a little background. Mr. Halstead is a powerful, influential businessman, well known up and down the East Coast. It's been rumored for years that he operates on the fringes of the law, although no one's ever been able to prove it. There've been hints of mob connections." He paused for her reaction.

Briana was growing impatient with his cloak-and-dagger routine. "What does this man have to do with Robert? He's been dead for five months. Or with me, for that matter?"

"There's no easy way to put this. We've found clear-cut evidence that Robert Morgan was involved in a rather complicated money laundering scheme, creating false accounts under dummy names, depositing monies in them, then transferring funds elsewhere electronically. To be specific, to a bank in the Cayman Islands where Mr. Halstead has several accounts."

Stunned, Briana could only stare in disbelief for a moment. "That's impossible. Robert was scrupulously honest. Integrity had been drilled into him by his father, who was a state senator. He would never, *ever* get involved in something dishonest or illegal. His career, his reputation, his father's opinion of him meant far too much to him."

Unsnapping his briefcase, Brewster removed a packet of papers and slid them over to her. "I can understand how you feel. But we have proof of the transfers, made over a period of two years, all with your husband's coded number on them."

Her eyes on the top page, Briana frowned. "Coded number?"

"Yes. Each of the account executives puts not only his name on each transaction or transfer of funds, but also a coded number." He pointed to the number in a box on the left side. "That's Robert's code."

The numbers and codes defined on the pages meant nothing to Briana. She looked across the table at the attorney. "I can only imagine someone else typed in Robert's name and code, then. I repeat, he wouldn't have done something illegal."

"I'm afraid you're wrong. We have other proof as well." Again, Brewster sat calmly waiting for her reaction.

Sliding the pages back to him, Briana sat back and crossed her legs. "I don't know what you're expecting of me, Mr. Brewster. I can't, I *won't* believe that Robert was involved in this. But even if he were, what do you want from me?"

The attorney cleared his throat. "It isn't just you we're questioning. The FBI is investigating everyone in Robert's recent past—his family members, his friends, women he's dated since the divorce. There's a great deal of money involved here, Mrs. Morgan. Millions. Not only monies funneled to Glenn Halstead illegally, but large payoffs to Robert."

Skepticism changed to indignation. "Let me get this straight. Are you saying this Halstead paid Robert to do these illegal transactions?"

"Yes, ma'am. His share could be as high as two million. Money laundering is a federal crime. The FBI is working with us on this. Halstead's finances are being thoroughly investigated, but he's a slippery one. I called you in today to tell you that we're freezing Robert Morgan's assets until we can go over everything."

"Two million?" For the first time, Briana felt uneasy. Surely Robert's burning ambition hadn't overridden his good sense, had it? No, she wouldn't believe it. "What assets?"

"Say, for instance, insurance policies, especially taken out recently?"

"The only one I'm familiar with is the insurance company that paid me his death benefit as his beneficiary. Then there's the policy that Robert set up as an educational fund for our son, but he'd only paid several thousand into it at the time of his death because Bobby was only seven." She shook her head, puzzled. "I don't understand. Robert lived in an apartment, owned a nice car, dressed well, but certainly didn't live lavishly. Other than what I've mentioned, I have no idea what assets you're referring to."

Undaunted, he went on. "His bank accounts, his stocks, any bonds, his safe-deposit box. Did you have anything to do with those?"

"No. Only the insurance settlement I mentioned. He had

an attorney. I imagine he might know about those other accounts."

"Yes, a David Rimmer. We've contacted him, as well." Brewster adjusted his tie, looking a shade uncomfortable for the first time as he removed a typed sheet of paper from his briefcase and passed it to her. "We need to check your finances as well, to make certain Robert didn't pass money he obtained illegally to your accounts, perhaps even without your knowledge. If you'd be so good as to sign this authorization letter, we can get this little matter cleared up quickly and painlessly, I trust."

At that moment, the door opened and a man with thick white hair wearing a pinstripe gray suit walked in, a gentle smile on his face. Emmett Brighton, the president of Fidelity Mutual and son of the founder of the bank, walked over and offered his hand. "Briana, my dear. It's good to see you."

Briana tamped down her anger and greeted him. "Mr. Brighton, perhaps you can help clear this up. This gentleman seems to think that Robert was involved in something illegal. He worked for you for ten years. Surely you don't agree?"

Brighton took his time seating himself in a chair next to Briana, angling it so he could cross his long legs. "We hated to have to ask you to come in, Briana. And we hate to cast a cloud over a dead man's reputation, but the facts all point in that direction, my dear."

"I can't, I *won't* believe that." She didn't know whether to laugh or cry. In her wildest dreams, she wouldn't have imagined taking part in this conversation.

"There's a slim chance we're wrong, of course." Brighton's tone was gentle, fatherly, meant to convey trust. "That's why we need to check your assets as well, to see if by chance, unknown to you, of course, Robert was hiding some of his assets by commingling them with your money."

"I'm not certain I want to allow that, Mr. Brighton. I'd like to discuss this situation with my attorney before granting you access." She had nothing to hide, yet to allow them to delve into her finances without checking how this might affect her was something she was unwilling to do. After all, they were talking possible criminal charges here, and the main suspect was her ex-husband. Though she and Robert had been divorced a long time, perhaps they'd try to prove collusion. Even with her limited knowledge, Briana knew the FBI was a formidable opponent.

"Of course, my dear." He rose, laying a hand on her shoulder. "Please do that. Take along a copy of the papers Mr. Brewster's shown you and then get back to us as soon as possible. Good seeing you." With a nod to Brewster, he left.

Annoyed with both of them, Briana accepted the papers from the attorney, slipped them into her purse, and walked out. She was waiting impatiently for the elevator, wondering if Brad Donovan, the attorney she'd used for years, would be able to see her on short notice, when she heard her name spoken. Turning, she saw Craig Walker heading her way. Cursing the timing of the elevator, she put on a smile of sorts.

"Hey, I didn't know you were back." Craig stepped close, his arm sliding round her waist. "But I'm glad you are."

"Just a brief visit, actually, for my grandfather's funeral," she explained as she stepped away from his touch.

Craig's handsome face turned sympathetic. "I'm sorry, Brie. I know he meant a lot to you."

"Yes, he did."

"So, how come you're here at Fidelity? I mean, if you came for a funeral . . ."

She could see the curiosity in his face and wondered why her schedule interested him so much. "Just a little snafu over some of Robert's clients." At least, she hoped that was all it was.

"Why would you be involved with Robert's clients?" he asked, his interest evident.

Briana noticed that the receptionist was pretending not to listen and two young men she didn't recognize walked by, deep in conversation, yet pausing to look her up and down. "Look, Craig, I don't want to go into this here and now."

He glanced at his watch. "Have you got time for lunch? I can clear my schedule. We could catch a cab to the Salty Dog at Quincy. I know you love their oyster bar." He sensed her hesitancy and hurried on. "Come on, Brie. You have to eat."

Maybe she should go and find out if Craig knew anything about this mess. She could call her attorney from the restaurant. "All right."

It was a breezy day but they chose to sit outside on the sidewalk cafe anyway. Brie decided to skip the oyster bar and opted for a shrimp salad, which was huge. She picked at it disinterestedly as Craig cut into his steak.

"Believe it or not, in this city, I get tired of seafood since it's so plentiful on every menu." He offered her a warm roll. "Tell me, are you home for good now?"

"No, I hope to go back tomorrow."

Craig frowned. "So soon? I don't get it, Brie. What's the appeal? I mean, the weather's about the same and you've got the sea here, too. Along with your folks and hordes of friends, to say nothing of your work. Why go back at all?"

She felt her temper climb and wondered why she was so quick to anger lately. "Because I want to." She said it in a way that she hoped he wouldn't challenge, then hurried to change the subject. "Tell me, do you know a man named Glenn Halstead?"

Craig continued buttering his roll. "Nearly everyone's heard of Halstead. He's a mover and a shaker, has his fingers in a lot of pies up and down the coast, mostly investments. Why?"

She gave him an abbreviated version of her disturbing conversation with the attorney and Mr. Brighton. "Can you believe that they honestly think Robert was involved in something crooked?"

"Do they have any proof?"

"They showed me some printouts that supposedly prove that Robert had made some illegal transactions that profited Halstead greatly. They also said that Robert's share was around two million. Isn't that crazy?"

"And they called you in to see if you knew anything about it?"

"More or less, but they also want to examine all my finances to see if Robert was using my accounts to hide money. I'm not the most conscientious bookkeeper, but I'd surely have known if there'd been any large deposits made over a period of a couple of years. It's just not possible."

"So what are you going to do?"

"I'm going to run all this by my attorney. But first, I wanted to know what you thought. I feel disloyal even asking, but did you ever hear Robert mention this Halstead, or did you suspect in any way that he might be skirting the law regarding transfers or dummy accounts set up at some bank in the Caymans?" She took a sip of her coffee, watching him carefully.

Slowly, Craig set down his fork. "It's possible, Brie."

Briana felt the color drain from her face. "What do you mean?"

Trying for casual, Craig shrugged. "You know as well as I how ambitious Robert was. He wanted to be vice president by thirty-five, a millionaire by forty. I'm not altogether certain he couldn't have been tempted. And I hear Halstead's very persuasive."

Her eyes narrowed. "Tempted enough to do something illegal, knowing that if he were caught, he could go to prison? No, Craig, you're wrong. Not Robert. He'd never disgrace himself or bring shame on his father. Or his son."

"You weren't with him much over the last three-plus years, Brie. His ambition could have gotten in the way of his conscience. And remember, no one who does something like this believes he's going to get caught."

Having lost her appetite, she shoved her plate aside, her mind racing. But the more she thought, the more convinced she was that she was right and Craig was wrong. "I'm a little surprised at you. I thought Robert was your best friend."

"He was." Looking earnest, Craig leaned forward. "I knew him better than anyone, Brie. Even you, after the divorce. He wanted to prove to you that you made a mistake in leaving him."

Frowning, she shook her head. "That's not the impression I had, and I saw him every other week."

"For how long? Long enough to hand Bobby over to him?" He also shook his head. "No, you didn't know him."

Upset and confused, Briana glanced at her watch. "Listen, excuse me a minute. I have to make a call."

The phone bank was inside and around the corner from their table. She dialed the number and waited, still mulling over Craig's defection in her mind. Some friend he'd turned out to be.

Brad's secretary came on the line and Briana gave the woman her full attention.

Craig stood, ever the polite gentleman, as Briana returned to the table. He noticed that she wasn't smiling. "Anything wrong?"

"I thought I could turn this matter over to Brad Donovan, but his secretary says he's tied up in court the rest of the week."

Craig wiped his mouth and set down his napkin. "Have you got the papers from Brighton? I could look into it for you and let you know. That way you could get back to your island paradise."

Briana didn't know if it was his sarcasm, his disloyalty to Robert, or his annoying smile that did it, but suddenly she wanted very much to get away from Craig Walker. "Thanks, but I'll handle this myself." Reaching into her purse, she took out a folded bill and placed it on the table as her share of the check, over his protests. She didn't want to be beholden to him for anything, not even a lunch.

Unhappily, Craig stood. "Listen, I'm not sure why you're irritated with me. I'm not the one accusing Robert."

"No, you're the best friend who believes he was a thief. I've got to go." There was nothing to thank him for, so she didn't. Turning on her heel, she started down the street, scanning the street for a cab.

"Wait, Brie!" Hurrying after her, Craig caught up and touched her arm. "Don't go like this. I'm sorry if I offended you. I didn't mean to. You know how I feel about you."

Exasperated, she looked into his boyish face and saw no character lines, no strong chin or eyes shining with intelligence. Instead, she noticed an artificial tan, a petulant slant to his mouth, and a hooded gaze. "Get over it, Craig. We have nothing more to say to one another."

Feeling better having told him how she felt, Briana walked off and spotted a cab turning the corner. Getting in, she gave the driver the address of the bank so she could pick up her car where she'd left it when she'd gone to lunch with Craig. Leaning back, she sighed and closed her eyes.

She'd have thought Craig's reaction would be different, but then, perhaps he and Robert had had words before her ex-husband had died. Nevertheless, it had been a mistake to confide in Craig. She wouldn't do it again.

She'd get her car, take the papers over to Brad's office, and leave them with his secretary, asking him to call her when his current case was over. Then she'd make a quick stop at her town house, pick up a few things she'd been wanting, and return to her parents' place. She didn't relish the thought of spending another night with her mother, but she preferred that to being alone in her condo. Too many memories and too much time to think about this new mess. And tomorrow morning, she'd fly back to Nantucket.

Briana could hardly wait.

Chapter Eleven

It felt like coming home. How could that be? Briana wondered, as her Delta Air Lines Business Express jet broke through heavy afternoon clouds and landed at Nantucket Memorial Airport. All throughout her thirty-minute flight, she'd been eagerly looking forward to returning. In less than two months, the house she now owned on the island had begun to feel more like home than any other place.

The visit to her town house yesterday had been brief and upsetting. She'd checked to make sure there hadn't been any attempts at breaking in despite her new alarm system, listened to a few inconsequential messages on her answering machine, and deliberately avoided going into Bobby's room. She'd packed a bag with some fall clothes and gone to her parents' home.

The evening hadn't been terribly cheery, either. An old navy friend of her father's had just arrived in town so he'd left before Briana had returned, annoying her. Aware now of his *lusty needs*, she wondered if his old friend was female. Her mother irritated her even more by defending his actions, then criticizing Briana for planning to go back to Nantucket the next day. Conversation between them was strained after Martha's confession. Briana hadn't told either of them about the cloud that now hung over Robert's memory. She hadn't felt up to it.

As she'd packed her things earlier today, her mother had brought out yet another camera case, the one Briana had used the day that Bobby had been shot. She'd apparently had it with her at the hospital and Martha Gifford had taken it home for safekeeping. The Pentax inside was an older camera, one she'd bought used from a professional photographer the week she'd decided to get serious about photography. Maybe now, all these months after that dreadful afternoon, she'd have the strength to look at those snapshots, the last she'd ever take of both Robert and Bobby.

Just being on the ground in Nantucket lifted Briana's spirits. Even though she hadn't let anyone, including Slade, know when she'd be returning, she couldn't help but scan the faces of the small crowd waiting for arriving passengers at the gate. Of course, no one was there for her.

Waiting for her luggage, she wondered if Slade would be glad to see her. She'd wager he hadn't thought about her nearly as often as she'd thought about him. The fact that she thought about him at all worried her.

He was a wounded man, one a woman should be cautious in getting involved with, as he himself had warned her. Not for the same reasons though. He thought he "wasn't a nice man" and that he'd "done terrible things." But Briana felt he was much too harsh a judge of himself.

Still, there were reasons to be wary, like the fact that he hadn't come to grips with his parentage since learning that Jeremy Slade wasn't his biological father. Nor even with his inheritance, which seemed to upset more than please him. He was making strides in that department, though, giving away the furniture he disliked and beginning to do over the house to suit himself.

The other thing worried her far more, the fact that he blamed himself for the death of a child and the ruination of her mother. Somehow, he'd have to learn to forgive himself for his imagined sin before he could get on with his life. He no longer trusted his instincts nor trusted too many people, for that matter. An awful way to live. But how to overcome it was the question.

Finally, the bags came and Briana found a cab. The late-afternoon sky was darkening and a distant rumble of thunder could be heard as the cab wended its way northwest along Old South Road. Off to the right, the harbor waters were already choppy. The smell of rain was in the air, drifting in through the open windows, but even that couldn't dampen Briana's mood.

She paid the driver and tipped him generously for hauling her heavy bags onto the porch. As he drove off, she glanced over at Slade's house. No lights on, but then, it was only five. He could be inside napping or out walking or in town shopping.

Or somewhere hurt and in need of help.

Stop that! she told herself. She wasn't his mother or his keeper.

Inside, she found that her plants had been watered, a fact that cheered her, and her mail neatly stacked. She scanned the small pile of bills and ads, deciding it could all wait. The message light was blinking on the new answering machine she'd bought only a week ago. She pushed the button and heard Tom Richmond's voice. Gramp's attorney told her he was sorry to hear that Andy Gifford had died and asked her to call his office when she returned for a reading of the will. The next call was a hang-up. No other messages.

Feeling foolish, Briana glanced around, but saw no note from Slade, no message of any sort. She shouldn't have expected any, she supposed.

It took her very little time to unpack, put things away, and change into jeans, a short-sleeved sweatshirt, and sneakers. Before she could change her mind, she ran next door and knocked.

Two repeats and still no stirring inside. Well, he had no idea when she'd be returning, because she hadn't known herself. She'd tried to get on the earlier flight, but it had been booked solid. She'd briefly considered calling him from Boston last night, then decided that might be misinterpreted. Suppose by now he'd had time to think things over and decided he wanted to back away from her? The last thing she wanted was to be looking forward to seeing a man like some overeager puppy when he preferred she'd go away.

Giving up, Brie went back home and wondered what to do next. She wasn't hungry. She was too restless to read or sit and stare out at the sea. Needing an outlet for her energy, she grabbed the camera bag she'd brought over, rewound the film inside the Pentax even though it had two frames left, and jumped into Gramp's Buick. *Her* Buick now, she supposed.

Setting out for town, she thought about Tom Richmond's message. No surprises in Gramp's will awaited her, since she'd already seen a copy of it. A couple of years ago Gramp had shown it to her, feeling a need to explain why he'd left most everything to her and not Toni or his own son. Briana wondered if this would give Toni still another reason to avoid her family. Probably. Would her father have a reaction? Probably not, since neither of her parents shared her love of Nantucket.

Briana angle-parked in front of the Island Camera Shop and saw that it was just a few minutes before six. The streetlamps were already on and she wondered if Ned Farrell had closed up. Getting out, she spotted him behind the counter and went inside.

Minutes later, she was back in the car, pocketing her receipt. Perhaps this would be the last roll of film she'd take in. Slade had said he'd build her a darkroom in the large walk-in closet between the lavatory off the kitchen and her laundry room. She'd planned on taking him up on his offer, just hadn't gotten around to drawing up a design. She wondered if the offer still held.

While she was in town, she popped into the market and picked up a few perishables before heading back, asking herself all the while why she was such a skeptic, why she thought that four days away and Slade would surely have lost all interest in her.

Because any interest he had in her was reluctant at best, came the answer. Okay, so maybe he wanted her physically. Maybe he even liked her somewhat. But there it probably ended. A man with an unresolved past who didn't trust his own instincts nor most people would naturally want to avoid committing to someone.

Briana wheeled the Buick around the bend and heard a distinct knock-knock from under the hood. A tune-up would likely be in order, she decided.

There was yet another problem with Slade, this thing he had about people moving on. All his life, everyone he'd ever cared about had abandoned him, walked away, left him alone. Jeremy, his mother, even Rachel had shoved him out. He didn't believe anyone would stay for the long haul.

Turning onto Cliffside Road, Briana slowed. Did she want to stay for the long haul with this man? She'd certainly acted like it the last evening they'd spent together. And she'd been acting like it since leaving for Boston, thinking about him every spare moment, even since returning.

Did she love him, then? Slowly, she pulled into the garage, killed the engine, and sat there.

She hadn't thought she'd love again. Love was such an enormous responsibility. Many things about it wound up hurting too much. The thing was, sometimes you didn't have a choice. She hadn't intended to get involved, hadn't set out looking. Yet something inside her had clicked, something had softened, something had reached out.

Was it merely physical? she wondered. As a married woman, she'd enjoyed sex, but once that relationship had ended, she hadn't thought overly much about making love, since she knew no one she wanted to go to bed with. She knew any number of men she thought of as friends. Yet recently her heart had zeroed in on one who was troubled, insecure, and didn't want to get involved. When the heart made the choice, when the body yearned, the head seemed to be outvoted.

Earlier, she'd thought of Slade as wounded. She, too, was wounded. Was that what had drawn them to each other?

Getting out of the car, she walked slowly, lost in her thoughts. She closed the garage door and pocketed the keys. Strolling past his house, she saw that it was still dark. Out by the picket fence, she gazed up and down the deserted beach, then out to a restless sea. She could almost smell some sort of change in the air—rain or a storm, something, although the rumbling had stopped.

Brie didn't want to go inside. The fact was, she didn't know what she did want. She also didn't want to ask herself more questions she didn't have answers to. Leaving the yard, she crossed the road and started down the beach toward the lighthouse.

Perhaps a walk would clear the cobwebs.

Slade was in his favorite spot atop the rocks near Brant Point Lighthouse. In California, he hadn't lived right on the ocean, so he'd never had the opportunity to study the sea up close as he had over the past few weeks. In all its stages, it fascinated him.

He loved the mornings best, with the sun seemingly rising out of the sea on the horizon, pinkening the sky, then spreading the pale blue canvas with streaks of yellow and gold while the water turned from black to dusky gray and finally to brilliant blue. He loved watching the gulls soar and dive, skim the waves, balancing on foam, then sailing off to impossible heights. Down this way, he'd often spotted pelicans strutting along in their comical web-footed gait, then suddenly swooping into the sea and capturing a complacent fish with one gulp of a big bill, sliding it into that odd drooping pouch.

Afternoons, he enjoyed strolling the hard-packed sand, bending to examine shells in all sizes and shapes with the heat of the midday sun warming his back. The days were cooler now but there was much to see still. He hadn't visited the cranberry bogs yet or toured the candle-making factories or strolled the north end of the island. Closer to home, he liked watching the local recreational fishermen seated companionably on the docks, dangling their legs, poles suspended in the shifting waters, buckets by their sides along with coolers. Slade had never fished, but he'd been thinking about getting a pole. He'd found none in Jeremy's garage.

But the sea was most fascinating with night approaching, like now with a storm moving in, heavy clouds jockeying for position in a murky sky, the wind picking up. The moon was there, but mostly shadowed, and the stars were hidden from view. It was a good thing the beam from the lighthouse cast a white glow or he might have trouble climbing down from the slippery rocks.

He couldn't make out the time on his watch, but knew it had to be somewhere between seven and eight. The past few mornings he'd spent reinforcing Irma's front porch. She'd snagged him on one of his walks. It was easy work. What had been difficult was fencing with the sharp old lady, who asked a million questions. But basically, Slade liked her and hadn't minded helping. He'd spent a few hours exploring the island, riding his bicycle and hiking. He'd seen quite a bit, learned a little, and by evening was pleasantly tired if not sleepy. Which had been one of his goals.

He'd even bought a camera, an uncomplicated Minolta that a child of six could operate, or so chatty Ned Farrell had told him. He'd never owned a camera before, either. A lot of things he'd missed out on in his early years that now he finally had the time and money to try. He took pleasure in catching up, in spending Jeremy's money, and wondered if that was what the man had had in mind.

He'd found more papers in a lockbox in Jeremy's desk. Apparently, the company he'd worked for in California had had a retirement plan that matched any money the employee put into it, which was what Jeremy had cashed out when he'd moved to Nantucket. At first, he'd rented the house that was now Slade's, then taken out a mortgage on it with the sale of his first few paintings, finally paying it off only five years later. Had he left all that information there for Slade to find, and if so, why? A puzzle.

The wind was picking up and Slade felt the first few drops of rain. Raising his arms and rolling his shoulders, he stretched, then climbed down. Hands in the pockets of his khakis, he began strolling back, unconcerned about getting wet. It was a fairly warm evening and a little rain never hurt anyone.

Finally, after all his rambling thoughts, he allowed himself to think of the one person he'd been trying not to dwell on: Brie. The truth was, he missed her far more than he'd have imagined.

When had he gone from enjoying her company to looking forward to the next glimpse of her? he asked himself. When had he begun waiting for her smiles like a storm walker searches for the sun? When had he started needing her in his life?

No! Slade felt the air back up in his lungs. Hadn't he seen what caring deeply for someone had done to his mother? His father? Ruined both their lives, that's what. More than half the guys he'd served with in the navy years ago had either been divorced already or had marriages so troubled they'd had no compunction about cheating on their wives. Captain Steve Romero, a man he'd looked up to at the station more than any other, had recently separated from his second wife. Even Irma Tatum had made her way through a few husbands.

Quicksand. He was definitely stepping into quicksand, thinking forever thoughts. Yet, if ever there was a woman he'd even consider such a thing with, Briana Morgan was the one.

A flash of lightning out over the sea caught his attention and he waited for the answering boom of the thunder. It appeared as if Mother Nature were going to put on a show. Slade picked up his pace.

Funny thing about being on this island, about having so much time on his hands to think and ponder and reflect. He'd asked himself countless questions he'd avoided for years, about his puzzling past, this unforeseen present he'd been thrust into, and about his hazy future. He hadn't come up with every answer, but he'd found a few.

What did he want? Briana had asked him on this very beach the night of their picnic. Well, he supposed he wanted what most everyone wanted. Though he'd never admitted it out loud, he wanted acceptance and respect and . . . and love. He wanted to be loved for who and what he was, for his good points and bad, for his strengths and weaknesses.

But he was deathly afraid he'd blown it.

His defenses down their last evening together, he'd told Briana the truth about Megan and Rachel. She'd been wonderfully understanding that night, maybe too understanding. She'd wanted to erase his pain by offering herself to him. And he'd been well on his way to taking her up on it before the ringing phone had put a stop to things.

Maybe it was just as well. She'd left early the next morning and been gone four days now. Four days in which she'd had time to think and rethink and reconsider. Undoubtedly she'd realized in the cold light of day, and the ones that followed, back on her home turf with close family and friends surrounding her, that that phone call had saved her from making a terrible mistake.

Briana was too young, too beautiful, too intelligent to

throw herself away on a misfit like himself. She had talent, for he'd seen the few photos she'd displayed at the exhibition, and money, and a rock-solid family background to draw strength and support from. She didn't need him, never would.

And he wanted no part of a one-sided love affair. He didn't want her pity and that, he'd begun to believe, was why she'd reached out to him that night. She'd felt sorry for him. God, what a terrible basis for a relationship.

The light drizzle had turned into a steady rainfall, not yet a deluge, but coming down pretty hard. The beach was deserted for as far as he could see, with no one else foolish enough to go walking in the rain when a storm was brewing. Slade walked on, already quite wet, unconcerned about getting soaked. What difference did it make? He had no one waiting for him, no one who cared if he caught cold or lived to see another day. Lord, now he was moving into self-pity!

No matter. He'd survive. Others had walked away and he'd survived. Briana would return in her own sweet time and be unable to meet his eyes as she'd explain that she'd thought things over and decided to sell her grandfather's house after all because she was moving back to the mainland permanently. And he'd put on a smile if it killed him, and wish her well. Damned if he wouldn't.

Love was for fools, Slade reminded himself as his Docksiders sprayed wet sand with each step. For a moment, he'd forgotten that, and he desperately wished he hadn't. She'd snuck in during that brief moment, but he'd squeeze her back out. Because loving, needing someone, was the thing that brought a man to his knees.

Slade stopped in his tracks when he heard an unfamiliar sound. Like moaning or sobbing. Glancing around, he realized he was almost upon Mayberry House. He remembered vividly Brie telling him about the tortured ghosts of Josh and Annabel Mayberry, who often cried out for each other on stormy nights.

It couldn't have been real, the sound he heard. But wait! There it was again, an eerie keening. Romantic foolishness, Slade told himself as he turned back. But what he saw then had him halting again.

Someone was walking toward him on the beach, but he couldn't make out who. The globelike streetlamps that dotted the coastal road were dimmed by the falling rain, casting only a small halo of light. Whoever it was had a head bent down, hands in their pockets much as he had, eyes downcast, probably as lost in thought as he. He stood waiting, wondering, unable to stop the sudden acceleration of his heart.

No, it couldn't be, could it?

Perhaps a hundred yards away, the person became aware of him and slowed. Over the sound of the rain, he heard a sharp cry and then she began running toward him. Recognition slammed into Slade and he set off to meet her.

Blood pounding, Brie sprinted to him, abandoning her hopeless thoughts, her fears. Forgetting everything except there he was, the man she'd been hoping to find, the one she wanted above all others.

Heart thumping, Slade reached her, all but colliding with her, grasping her body to his and fastening his mouth on hers. She was here, she was in his arms, she was kissing him like she'd been gone for four years instead of four days. Holding her, he lifted her off her feet and spun around with her, the kiss going on and on while the rain poured down on them. And they didn't care.

Finally, needing air, Brie pulled back, trying to make out his features in the dim lighting. "Is it really you? Are you really here?" Her voice was a little hoarse, a little hesitant. All during her long, long walk, she'd become more convinced with each soggy step that he'd left the island, that he'd gone away so he wouldn't have to deal with the unwanted feelings she'd aroused in him. When she'd looked up and seen him, she wasn't sure if her hopeful heart had conjured him up like an apparition. But no, his arms around her were firm and strong and his hard body against hers was warm and familiar.

"Yes, I'm here. You came back." Slade set her back down on her feet, his hands stroking her hair off her wet face. "I was convinced you weren't going to."

She smiled then, wondering if the dampness on her face was from the rain or her own joyful tears. "I was worried about you. I'd just about convinced myself you'd left Nantucket."

A rumble of thunder overhead sounded almost as loud in Slade's ears as his hammering heart. Could he believe what he was hearing? That was the second time she'd claimed to be worried about him. Could she really want him as much as he wanted her? He didn't have the words, so instead, he bent his head to kiss her again, long and thoroughly, until he scarcely had the breath to pull back.

He smiled then, feeling giddy with the sight and sound and feel of her. His mouth close to her ear, he whispered. "I want you. What do you think we should do about that?"

She nuzzled into his neck. "Find a warm, dry place."

"How fast can you run in this?" he asked, glancing up at a liquid sky.

Her smile was challenging. "Faster than you, I'll bet."

Turning, she began streaking down the beach, clumps of sand flying from her wet sneakers. Grinning foolishly,

Slade started after her. He could run faster now, he knew, because his heart wasn't nearly as heavy.

Feeling mellow, he let her win the race by a hair, as he followed her onto his porch and dug for his key.

Breathing hard, Brie toed off her sodden shoes on the wooden floor. "We can't walk across Jeremy's white carpeting all dripping wet like this."

"The hell we can't. I'm ripping out that carpeting soon, anyway." But when he finally got the door open, he slipped off his shoes, too. "Come here." When she moved closer, he picked her up in his arms, stepped over the threshold, and bumped the door closed with one hip. "Only one set of footprints this way."

Unable to stop smiling, Brie wound her arms around his neck and held on. As he climbed the stairs with her, he pressed his mouth to hers in a breathless kiss, one he didn't break until he'd carried her through Jeremy's huge master bedroom suite and on into his large bath tiled in several shades of blue.

Setting her down, he gazed around. "I haven't used this room yet, but I think it's time. Feel like a shower?"

"Mmm, I think we could both use a rinsing off." Or was it a cooling off? But she didn't want to cool off. She wanted the heat he offered, the sweet warmth she knew he'd bring to her. After the long months, years of being cold, Brie knew she'd found someone who could warm her again.

The shower stall was large, enclosed by smoky glass on two sides in the far corner. Even the oversized tub looked inviting. Through the doorway, she could see the mahogany four-poster king-size bed, the room done in blue and white. "Where do you sleep if you haven't used this room?"

"Down the hall. There are two spare rooms plus the storage room." A shadow flickered over his features, then was gone just as quickly. "I haven't felt comfortable in here, until now."

She wasn't sure just how her presence made a difference, but she was glad he'd overcome another hurdle. With one hand, she gathered her hair to the back, then nodded toward the shower. "Shall I go first?"

His expression unreadable, he nodded as he pointed to a double rack. "Lots of clean towels, so help yourself." He walked out, leaving her alone.

Her nerves skittering, Brie turned on the jets, then slipped out of her wet things, leaving them in a heap in a corner of the tiled floor. Holding up one of the fluffy white towels, she saw that it was generous enough to wrap around herself after her shower. She felt ready to make love with Slade, yet she was just a shade apprehensive, too. It had been an awfully long time, which was just one reason she was glad he'd suggested cleaning up. The first time, at the very least, ought to be special.

Stepping under the spray, she let the soothing water flow over her before picking up the shampoo.

Minutes later, intent on rinsing shampoo from her hair, she wasn't aware that the shower door had opened until she felt a hand on her arm. She jumped back, startled. "Oh!"

"I couldn't wait," Slade said, his voice husky. He saw soapsuds gliding over pale, golden skin, wet blond hair falling past creamy shoulders and suddenly wary brown eyes. In a gesture as old as time, he watched her arm automatically move up to partially conceal her breasts, then drop down as she obviously realized the move was foolish under the circumstances.

"Don't hide. Not from me."

"I . . . uh . . . can step out and give you more room." Perfectly silly to be self-conscious at this stage of the game, she reminded herself, yet that's exactly what she was.

"I don't need more room. I need you." Dipping his head into the spray, he pressed his mouth to her breast and heard her draw in a sharp breath. Her knees seemed to sag so he slipped an arm around to steady her as he continued the intimate kiss. In moments, she seemed to sway closer, her flesh more willing for his attention than her mind was yet.

He shifted his concentration to the other breast and feasted there for long moments. Briana's arms looped over his shoulders and her head tipped back as a soft moan came from between her parted lips. Slade trailed upward, planting kisses along the lovely line of her throat, then captured her mouth. Bodies locked together, they lost track of time.

Finally, tossing back his wet hair, he reached for the soap and held it out to her. "Help me?"

Standing to the side out of the spray, she looked at the soap, then at him. Swallowing around a nervous lump, she took the soap into her palm and began skimming along his shoulders, down over biceps hard as rocks all the way to his fingertips. Back up, she moved to lather his chest, swirling the clean, lightly scented soap in the dark hair there. Never having done this before, never having shared a shower even, Brie couldn't believe how surprisingly sensual it was to feel free to explore and caress the masculine hills and valleys. Her shyness forgotten, her other hand joined its mate to tangle in the incredibly soft hair of his chest, pausing to outline the firm muscles, then slipping down along his rib cage.

There she stopped, looking up at him. "Would you like me to wash your hair?"

His smile was intimate, knowing. "Afraid?"

She stood her ground, though her pulse stuttered. "No."

"Good." But he let her off the hook and pulled her to him. As she raised her face to the spray, he sent his hand on a journey of discovery, inching lower until he cupped her. He felt a response shudder through her, then his fingers found her and moved inside as her knees threatened to buckle.

Whirled into a sea of sensation, Brie could do little more than hang on as desire rocketed through her. His mouth was on hers as his clever touch worked its magic. Needs pounded throughout her system, screaming for a release just out of reach. She groaned into his mouth as she strained against him.

Then suddenly, she was soaring, sailing upward and beyond, falling off the edge of the earth.

Heart thundering in her ears, she clung to him as the aftershocks buffeted her. He held on, letting her slide back, giving her time. At last, her breathing slowed and she opened her eyes to find him watching her, a smile of satisfaction on his face. She'd been on the receiving end, yet he looked enormously pleased.

As she found her footing and eased back from him, thankful that her legs would hold her again, she realized that the water had cooled considerably. Or was it just that her skin was so overheated from his loving attention?

Reaching behind her, Slade turned off the water. He didn't have to ask if she'd enjoyed that. Her lovely face had registered every emotion from stunned surprise to sensual satisfaction. He shoved open the door, stepped out, and grabbed towels for both of them.

But he didn't waste precious time on drying off completely, painfully aware of his erection demanding attention. Quickly, he wrapped his towel around his waist, then reached for another to help dry Brie's hair. She was moving slowly, still in a haze, and he was growing impatient.

Bending, he picked her up, towels and all, and walked toward the big four-poster bed. While she'd started her shower, he'd lighted a chunky candle on the nightstand and shoved back the spread. Pale blue sheets invited them.

"I'm not dry yet," Brie protested. "I'll get the bed wet."

"Sheets dry." He placed her on the bed, then followed her down.

She sat up, rubbing the smaller towel over her hair. "At least I won't soak your pillow."

"*Your* pillow," he answered. "The one next to it is mine." To sleep with her, to sleep holding her. His heart lurched in anticipation.

He took the towel from her. "Here, let me." With strong fingers, he began massaging her scalp, rubbing the soft terrycloth over her head. "I love your hair. Did I ever tell you that?"

"No, I probably would have remembered." Actually, he'd never said much about her looks, but his eyes had spoken volumes. His hands were on her neck now, then on her bare shoulders, his touch light, caressing. She felt a shiver skitter along her spine.

"Are you cold?"

She turned, met his eyes. "With you touching me? I don't think that's possible."

The look held, warmed. "You flatter me."

"I don't need to flatter you." On second thought, perhaps she did, Brie decided. He, too, had to be a little nervous. Perhaps he needed just a touch of reassurance. She would give it to him, gladly, honestly. Removing the towel from her head, she tossed it aside and sank back onto the pillow. "From the first time you touched me, I haven't been able to deny this overwhelming response to you. That sort of thing never happened to me before, not with anyone."

"It's not usual for me, either." How beautiful she looked with her blond cloud of hair fanned out on the blue pillowcase. Leaning down to her, he braced himself on one elbow. "You've been playing hell with my concentration since day one. At first, I wanted to throttle you. Then, even knee deep in paint fumes, all I wanted to do was throw you down on the grass and jump your bones."

Her smile was very female. "Honestly?"

"You don't believe me?" He reached for her hand and placed it on a section of the towel that was still loosely wrapped around his waist, the section that was straining for action.

Her eyes went wide but her fingers tightened on him. "That's only because you've got a naked woman in your shower, in your bed. Most men would . . ."

"I'm not most men and you're not just any naked woman." Ever more impatient, he parted the towel that covered her, revealing breasts so very beautiful and yearning toward his touch. He decided to accommodate them.

Not to be outdone, feeling bolder by the minute, Brie slipped her own hand beneath his towel and went exploring. She heard him groan out loud.

"Listen, I'm having a little trouble here," he confessed, angling back from her, not wanting things to be over way too soon. "I wanted to take this slowly, but . . ."

"Don't go slowly," she told him, arching into his touch. They'd had weeks to built up to this. "I want you too much for slowly."

It was all the encouragement he needed. Yanking aside both towels, he looked down into her eyes. He saw just the smallest hint of uncertainty and a desperate attempt to hang on to her control. He wanted to shatter that control, to bring her to her knees as she'd done to him.

His mouth took hers in a fierce kiss as he gathered her close, her breasts grazing his chest enticingly. Her mouth softened, opened, invited. Her tongue danced with his in remembrance of other kisses they'd shared, in celebration, in surrender. Flesh to flesh with her at last, Slade knew he'd met his match with this fiery woman.

His body was taut and straining, still he held off, raining kisses on her satin shoulders, her throat, and in her ear, feeling her shudder a response. But needs too long held in check pounded at him and he knew he hadn't much time left. Slipping a hand between their bodies, he touched her deeply. He felt her respond with a jolt she couldn't suppress.

But it wasn't his fingers Brie wanted, not this time. Shifting, she reached down and guided him inside her.

Slade swallowed her soft sigh of pleasure as he joined more deeply with her, then began to move, knowing the climb would be short this first time. He'd waited so long, wanted so badly, but he'd make it good for her or die trying.

Brie let the power of his kiss fire her, let the rhythm of their movements take her. This is what she'd been needing, wanting, this mindless giving and taking. Her hands on his back still damp from their shower alternately gripped and caressed. She was peripherally aware of the rain pelting the windows, of the scent of the candle on the bedside table mingling with the aroma of soap and shampoo.

But mostly she was aware only of Slade. Slade on her and in her and with her, taking her higher and higher still. When at last she hit the summit and felt the waves of sweet pleasure ripple through her, she knew he'd been with her all the way.

Chapter Twelve

Briana came awake slowly, very slowly. First, she became aware she was snuggled down under a wonderful old patchwork quilt with her head nestled in a goosedown pillow. She was warm and cozy, her limbs feeling languid, her body still humming. From outside, she heard rain whipping against the windows and pelting the roof, not gently but steadily beating down. Nasty weather just begs a body to sleep late.

Squirming about, she became aware of her physical self more slowly. She wasn't wearing a gown, a surprise, since sleeping in the nude was something she rarely did. With that piece of knowledge came curiosity so she opened one eye. A strange room, semidark, white slatted wooden blinds on the windows, blue carpeting, a heavy dresser against the far wall, the scent of vanilla lingering in the air. A half-burnt candle in a brass holder next to the telephone on the nightstand. Nothing familiar.

The master bedroom in Slade's house, of course. Memories rushed back as heat moved into her face.

Shifting, she opened the other eye at the same time as she inched her right hand toward the other side of the bed. Nothing. No one. She sat up.

Empty, the indentation of his head still on his pillow. The sheets were still warm, so perhaps he hadn't been up long. She glanced toward the bathroom door and saw it was ajar. He wasn't there. She inhaled deeply, but couldn't pick up the scent of coffee. She knew how much Slade loved that first cup of morning coffee. Apparently, though, he wasn't down in the kitchen brewing a pot.

Flopping back, Briana struggled with a sense of loss. Stupid to feel that way, she supposed. One night, great as it was, was hardly a commitment or even a genuine love affair. It was . . . a one-night fling, perhaps. She shuddered at the words, the thought, the implication.

Heaving a mighty sigh, she closed her eyes. Well, what had she expected? A morning after that included awakening to a kiss, then breakfast in bed? She'd had candlelight and been carried up the stairs a la Rhett Butler and several bouts of mind-blowing sex. If that's all there was, she'd have to be a big girl and accept it.

But she wouldn't have to like it.

So cold, so cruel, she thought, leaving her like this. A glance at the clock radio told her it was barely seven. Had he wanted to get away from her so badly he'd gone for an early morning run on the beach in a downpour? Face it, kid, she told herself. Mornings after were the pits.

Her clothes, she imagined, were still in a damp heap in the corner of the bath. Swell. She'd have to borrow something of his to go home in. And since he'd said he never used this bedroom, that meant his clothes were probably down the hall. Terrific.

She'd not been one to jump into a man's bed readily, not even in college away from home for the first time. Perhaps if she had, she'd have known what to expect. She'd been as ill prepared for this as she'd been for a man like Slade to enter her life. Which, translated, meant not at all.

She'd grown up around men like her father, who had two college degrees, spoke several languages, and was a wine connoisseur. And like Robert and Craig, both of whom wore designer suits, bought imported shoes, and had their hair trimmed weekly at a salon. Slade, on the other hand, had graduated from the school of hard knocks, wore his hair a shade too long, probably didn't own a tie, didn't know chablis from champagne, and made beer his beverage of choice.

But her father, though oozing charm, was lousy husband material. She'd divorced Robert and didn't much care for Craig. Slade with his rough edges and blunt talk was a genuine person, a good man. And he could excite her merely by walking into a room.

For all the good that would do her.

She might as well get going. She'd make it easier for him by leaving so he wouldn't have to face her, wouldn't have to make excuses. Flinging back the covers, Brie sat up.

Just as she did, she heard a door downstairs slam, then footsteps on the stairs. Feeling caught in the headlights without clothes, she ducked back under the covers.

The door opened slowly, as if not to disturb anyone still asleep. From under partially lowered lids, she saw Slade creep in and make his way to the bed. His hair was damp and he was carrying a large white paper bag. The unmistakable smell of coffee drifted to her nostrils. Briana opened her eyes.

"Hi, lazybones." A smile on his face, he set down the sack, slipped off his shoes, and sat down. Leaning to her, he trailed a finger along her cheek, then kissed her lingeringly. "Good morning."

Uncertain how to respond to this very different scenario than the one she'd been imagining, Brie smiled back. "You're up awfully early and you're wet."

"It's still raining and I got hungry. We forgot to eat last night." His lips twitched. "Had other things on my mind."

"Me, too. Rather nice things."

"Hold that thought because we're going to come back to it. But first . . ." He reached for the sack, set it between them. "Breakfast."

Scooting upright, propping the pillow at the headboard behind her, Brie pulled the sheet up and anchored it under her arms. "What've we got?" Her mouth began to water.

"Seems I remember a certain someone once saying that chocolate is nature's most perfect food, or something like that." He took out a Styrofoam plate and placed it between them on the quilt before pulling things from the bag, like a small boy revealing his favorite toys. "Soooo, we have chocolate croissants still warm from the bakery oven. Then from Rose's Specialty Shoppe, we have chocolate-dipped strawberries. And from the deli, freshly brewed coffee."

He finished by laying down two paper napkins before tossing aside the bag. "I suppose I should've stopped in the kitchen and fixed these on some fancy plate of Jeremy's and poured the coffee in a couple of those delicate little china cups he has. But frankly, I was in too big a hurry to get back up here to you."

Could anyone resist such a reason? Briana looped an

arm around his neck and pulled him down for a kiss, her eyes suddenly filling. "Thank you," she whispered.

He caught the tears. "What? Is something wrong?" He couldn't imagine what. He'd been gone less than an hour. No one knew she was here so they couldn't have phoned and upset her. "Are you all right?"

Blinking, she smiled. "I'm better than all right. I'm just a little taken aback. No one's ever brought me breakfast in bed before. I feel so . . . so . . ."

"Special? That's how I want you to feel."

"I was going to say spoiled, but your choice is better." She took the cup he handed her, inhaled the wonderful aroma, and sipped. "This is heavenly."

Slade tore off a section of buttery croissant and held it to her mouth, feeling silly, feeling good. He supposed he *was* spoiling her a little. Never in his life had he ever spoiled a woman, or romanced one, for that matter. Rachel hadn't seemed the type and there hadn't been anyone else who'd lasted very long.

No hearts, no flowers, no crystal glasses clinking or walks in the moonlight holding hands. Yet this morning when he'd awakened early, he'd had this irrepressible urge to do something nice, something surprising for Brie. He didn't want to question what motivated his impulse, but the look on her face, the tears in her eyes when he'd returned, were worth having to go out in a downpour.

The warm confection slipped down her throat smooth as melted butter. Brie felt like purring. How could she have been so off base as to imagine he'd turn from her after the night they'd shared? Her self-confidence had to be at a new low. Either that or she'd become paranoid. She'd obviously misjudged him. "Do you do this a lot, cater to women?"

Slade scrunched the pillow against the headboard and leaned back. "I made peanut butter cookies for my mother once. You know, from those refrigerated rolls you slice and bake? I was eleven, I remember, a year after Jeremy left. It was her birthday and she was so sad. She cried when she saw them."

Just like he'd moved her to tears. "She must have loved you very much."

"I guess. But then, I was all she had." But he didn't want to talk about his past. "Do you know it's coming down harder than ever out there. I heard on the car radio that winds with hurricane force were pounding along the coast of the Carolinas."

"That's a long way from us."

"I don't imagine a hurricane's ever hit this far north."

"Actually, it has, back in 1938, or so the old-timers like Irma have said. A couple of others have come close since that big one, but none ever hit right on Nantucket. You don't think it's that bad out there, do you?" She glanced again at the slanted blinds, but could see only gray sky through the rain-streaked window.

"Nah. It's a slow day for news so the guy decided to get people riled up." He took another swallow of coffee, then reached to hand her a strawberry. "I've never tasted one of these, but the woman behind the counter said they were great."

Brie bit into the fruit and had to agree. "Wonderful. Try it."

He did and went on to more. By the time they'd finished the half-dozen strawberries and both croissants, the coffee cups were empty and they were both stuffed. Slade slipped off his jeans and climbed back under the quilt. "I got chilly out there. You'd better come over here and warm me."

He didn't have to ask her twice. Snuggled within his arms, Brie let out a satisfied sigh. "I can't remember when I've had such a wonderful breakfast."

"The best part of any meal is the dessert." He tipped her chin up. "That's you." Lowering his head, he put his mouth to hers, gently brushing her lips with his. Back and forth, back and forth. When she sighed low in her throat, when she opened to him, he gathered her closer and kissed her deeply, like he could never get enough of her. And he was getting worried that perhaps he couldn't.

"Do you know that sometimes when I kiss you, you purr like a kitten?" he asked, smiling down into her eyes. "Soft, smug little sounds from way down deep inside."

Briana pretended offense. "I do *not* purr. Now I'm being tested and graded on my kissing technique, am I? I'll probably flunk out. I'm not very experienced. And I certainly haven't had much practice lately."

His arms tightened around her. "For what it's worth, I can't remember ever having kissed another woman before you. You've erased all those old memories. They probably weren't worth all that much anyway."

Brie felt her heart swell, feelings she'd been fighting swimming to the surface. But she held back, afraid to put words to those feelings. "That's a lovely thing to say."

"It's the truth." The truth. The truth was, he was caught in a trap of his own making, already caring far too much for a woman he knew would one day walk out of his life. Not that he'd blame her. Briana had yet to turn thirty, with a lifetime ahead of her. She needed a whole, complete man, one without a murky past who was lugging around more old baggage than a cross-country passenger train.

He'd known all that last night when he'd seen her on the beach, when she'd spotted him and started running. That was when he should have stopped her, should have told her the deck was stacked against them. But it would have taken a man far stronger than he to turn from her.

"Where did you go?" Brie asked softly, reaching up to brush a lock of dark hair from his forehead. "Where do you go when your eyes get all silvery and secretive like that?"

Slade eased back, huffing out a frustrated breath. He'd told himself to stop obsessing, to enjoy her while he could, and here he was spoiling what little time they had together. "Just thinking. Nothing important."

"Think out loud, then. Don't shut me out, Slade." Were there even more dark secrets hidden inside him? Would he ever share them all? Would he ever trust her completely?

He was thoughtful for several moments before finally turning to her. He wanted to ask her what she'd once asked him. "All right. I've been thinking. Humor me. Do you know what you want, *really* want?"

Briana's answer came more quickly. "I want something to last." When she saw his puzzled expression, she went on to explain. "Nothing seems to last, you know. People move and homes break up, marriages end in divorce or, possibly worse, in shared unhappiness. Relationships dissolve. Everyone moves on, from one person to the next, each searching for something they never seem able to find. I badly want something solid in my life, one thing I can count on, that will always be there, that will last."

There was a message in there somewhere. It appeared on the surface as if they wanted the same thing. Only, Brie wanted something to last and Slade knew there was no such thing. He let out a long breath. "A tough order. Maybe you'd better think of a second choice."

"You don't think what I want is possible?"

"Possible, maybe. Probable, unlikely." He shifted so he

was facing her, his hand trailing down her arm, fingers caressing. "You think I'm a cynic, right?"

"Mmm, but I bet you think you're a realist. And you'd probably call me an optimist. Or a romantic. But labels don't count here. I know what I want and I won't settle for less this time."

This time. Had she before? "You told me earlier that you and Robert didn't really know each other as well as you thought you did when you got married. What did you mean?"

Briana shrugged. "Mostly that we never talked about what each of us wanted out of life, our goals, things like that. I think too often, especially if you marry young, you get caught up in wedding plans, picking out the china pattern, fixing up the apartment. The really important questions never get asked or answered."

"Do you suppose Robert could have known that his ambition would turn him into a workaholic and wreck his marriage?" Any more than Slade himself could have predicted that his past would haunt him forever and ruin any chances he might have with Briana?

"Probably not." Thinking about Robert brought to mind her upsetting encounter with Emmett Brighton and Charles Brewster. Because the whole thing worried her, she decided to tell Slade about it.

He listened quietly without comment until she finished. "Do you think Robert did something illegal to get ahead? I'm not being judgmental here, because I'm sure banking is a field where there's lots of temptation, lots of opportunity, all that money around. But I'd think there'd also be a whole slew of safeguards, with everything computerized these days."

"I can't imagine Robert doing a single dishonest thing.

Not for some altruistic reason necessarily, but because of his father. To bring disgrace on his father, the man he was named after and the man he named his son for, would have been the cardinal sin for Robert." She shook her head. "I can't see him giving in to temptation."

"Yet they claim to have proof. This Brighton, he knew Robert well, too, and he believes something crooked went down?"

"So he indicated." Brie decided she might as well tell it all, so she gave him a play-by-play of her luncheon with Craig. "That was probably more disturbing than Mr. Brighton's loss of faith. Robert's best friend suggesting he might have been dishonest really bothers me."

Craig's lack of loyalty didn't surprise Slade. Craig was the same guy who'd made moves on his best friend's wife right after the divorce. "Maybe they weren't such good friends after all."

She'd been wondering about that ever since her lunch with Craig.

"Tell me, would you say the two of you had a good marriage, except for Robert's penchant for working too hard? I haven't observed too many marriages up close, so I'm curious."

He'd told her a great deal about his relationship with Rachel. She might have guessed he'd be curious about her marriage. "Well, I guess you could say my marriage wasn't exactly made in heaven, though I didn't know that at the time. I was seventeen when we met, twenty when we married, and not very sophisticated or experienced. I was bored with college so I quit, much to the annoyance of my parents, and I took this job in a Manhattan advertising agency with such high hopes. I soon discovered I was nothing more than a gofer. Marriage seemed to offer much more of a challenge. I've always loved challenges."

Slade couldn't help wondering if she looked on him as a challenge, which would explain why she was still here. Fix the poor misfit, like a social worker might, then move on. Where had that come from? he wondered, trying to keep his expression bland.

"Looking back, I believe I really tried to make things work. I went through this period where I wanted to fix up our apartment, be little Suzie Homemaker, make new curtains and gourmet meals, entertain friends and Robert's business associates. Little did I realize that Robert probably wouldn't have noticed if I'd have spray-painted the apartment with glitter, met him at the door wearing only a smile, and served Hamburger Helper seven nights a week. He was hardly ever home and when he was, he was too tired to care."

"You must have seen something in him to marry him. Did you love him?"

Briana forced her memory back to those early days. "Yes, I did. At least I loved the man I thought he was. He'd been so different when we were dating—attentive, romantic, altogether sweet at times. I've never figured out why he wanted me, since as soon as he got the ring on my finger, he changed into this work machine determined to be a millionaire by forty."

Slade took her measure, seeing a woman with lovingly mussed hair, honey-colored skin softer than silk, dark eyes fringed with thick lashes, and a smile that made his heart stutter, and wondered how she could not know. He raised a hand, trailed the backs of his fingers along her cheek. "I know exactly why he wanted you, why any man would want you."

"Do you?"

"Mmm hmm." He wanted to evoke a certain response and wondered if she could read the mischief on his face. "Because, even though you're an ugly little thing, you have a good disposition."

"What?" She'd seen the gleam in his eye and sat up, ready to do battle. "Take that back, J.D. Slade, right now, or I'll . . ."

Before she could get the rest out, he'd taken her arm, maneuvered her neatly onto her back, and was leaning over her. "You were saying?"

"No, *you* were saying that I have a good disposition, but you're about to find out how wrong that is." Hands burrowing between them, she began tickling his ribs.

"Oh, that's how you want to play, is it?" His hands slid under her. "I should probably tell you I'm not ticklish. But I wonder if you are." With that, his fingers attacked.

"Oh, no, don't, please." Laughter bubbled up from deep inside as she squirmed to evade the onslaught, to no avail. "Slade, let me up." She was giggling freely now, wiggling and fidgeting, but he was relentless. And then, just as suddenly, he stopped.

A final laugh erupted before she became suspicious. "What now?"

Bracing himself on his elbows, he gazed into eyes still shining with the residue of laughter. "I just wanted to hear you laugh because I never have."

Slowly, she let out a soft sigh. "I guess I haven't had much to laugh about in a while."

"You have a great laugh. Don't let it get rusty." His mood shifted again as he looked down and noticed that the sheet had slipped from her. "And you have a great body." Unable to resist, he pressed his mouth to her breast and feasted there, the taste more heady than anything he'd found in Jeremy's wine collection.

He was keeping her off balance, taking her from a serious discussion to laughter and suddenly into passion, Brie thought as her skin quivered in response. It was unsettling and nerve-wracking and maddeningly exciting. As his tongue circled a swollen peak, she tried to suppress a low moan.

He lifted his head. "Did I hurt you?"

"No, no. Please, do that again."

Slade was happy to oblige.

She'd wanted to work, Brie had told him, something she hadn't felt the need for in a long while. Since the spring, since Bobby. Slade had watched her pack her camera equipment carefully, like a doctor might check the instruments in his little black bag, and told her he wanted to go along, to watch her work. He'd seen the quick flicker of worry, of refusal leap into her eyes, so he'd hurried on to explain he'd stay in the background, be very still, not disturb her. She wasn't too thrilled with the arrangement, but she'd grudgingly allowed him to accompany her.

It was a sunny afternoon two days after all that rain, with just the slightest nip in the air requiring light jackets. He piled their bikes in his truck and drove to the wildlife refuge at Great Point. Slade parked while Brie ran in to the office for their permits. Her camera case strapped onto the back carrier of her bike, Brie set off on the narrow winding pathway with Slade following closely behind.

"What are we looking for?" he asked.

"Small furry creatures, exotic birds, and if we're lucky, deer. But not till we get in a ways."

It was some time before she found the spot she wanted,

a thick copse of trees, most old, thick, and gnarled. Stately elms and scrub pines grew wild side by side. A blue jay came out of the woods with an annoyed flapping of wings, protesting their arrival. Jumping off, she walked her bike over to a solid maple and leaned it there, grabbing her case. By the time she had her Nikon hanging around her neck, Slade had joined her.

"You've got to walk slowly, watching where you step. If you tromp on twigs or stumble, they'll hear you and get spooked."

"They?"

"Birds, forest creatures, you know." She looked down at his size twelve sneakers and wondered if it was possible to step quietly in those giant shoes. She hadn't wanted to hurt his feelings by not letting him come along, but she couldn't imagine what he'd get out of watching her work. Or perhaps he still viewed a camera as a hobby. She didn't know if she'd ever use any of the shots she'd take today, but she felt the time was right to get back in the swing of things. She'd been out of the loop too long. It felt good to heft the weight of the camera, to anticipate the shots.

"I'm going in. Stay back a little, okay?"

"Right." She didn't seem to understand that he wanted to watch *her*, not woodland creatures. Walking carefully, he followed her into the dim forest. Tiny wrens twittered and flitted among the branches.

They'd been hiking for only a few minutes when he smelled water, then saw the broad expanse of pond just ahead. A swaying limb nearly slapped his face, but he caught it in time. The deeper they went, the more hushed the atmosphere became, like they were trespassing in an outdoor cathedral. The trees, still in full greenery, blocked out much of the sun and cooled the air.

A flutter of wings to his left caught his attention as a russet-breasted robin whipped past him, landing on a higher branch, then cocking her head at him. She wasn't happy with the human intrusion, Slade decided.

Up ahead, he saw Brie climb over the twisted trunk of a semi-uprooted old tree, as surefooted as any deer she might find. Why it was important to her to capture living creatures he couldn't know. On the bicycle path in, they'd passed colorful vines in full bloom and caught glimpses of a magnificent scarlet shrub, vivid against a blue sky. She hadn't even paused. Artists were temperamental and determined, he reminded himself. And a shade peculiar.

He noticed that she kept to the edge of the pond, yet out of sight of anyone or anything trailing along its shores. He felt more than heard the rustle of leaves near his feet and looked down in time to see a chipmunk scurry past. His quick smile took him by surprise. He was surely a city boy.

Turning back, he stopped, noticing that Brie had crouched by a fallen log just ahead. He could tell by her position that she'd raised her camera and was adjusting her lens, setting up her shot. What was she focusing on? he wondered, for he could see nothing but the play of sunlight on the gently drifting pond water, the leafy green of a weeping willow nearby.

Then he saw them on the far side of the pond, a regal swan gliding along the shimmering water under the watchful eye of her larger mate. Her sleek, white neck formed a perfect loop as she drifted, seemingly unaware of the humans invading her private playground. Then the male set out, intercepting her path before falling into formation with her. The two graceful birds swam in unison like perfectly paired professional ice skaters skimming along a silvery rink.

Tired of standing, Slade, too, crouched down and narrowed his gaze, trying to see the scene as she did. Long minutes passed and still she hardly moved as she snapped shot after shot. How, he wondered as his legs began to cramp, could she hold so still without breaking the position? There was more to this photography business than inserting a roll of film and clicking away, it would seem.

Suddenly, he caught a slight tensing of Brie's shoulders, an alertness as she shifted a fraction to the left, then slowly raised her camera, aiming at something in the nearby trees. His eyes burned from straining as he followed her gaze. At last he saw a full-chested owl sitting on a sturdy limb. His feathers were mostly brown with streaks of white and black, and looked to be soft. His eyes were wide open, his sleep interrupted by human interlopers. A light breeze was blowing the other way so he couldn't have picked up their scent. Unblinking, he sat perfectly still, like a statue in a taxidermist's window.

He saw Brie slowly turn her body as she rose, her camera focused directly on the watchful bird of prey. The click of the shutter sounded oddly loud in the dense forest. For the second time, Slade found himself smiling. Now he understood why she'd wanted to come to this quiet place. Nature at its finest was hard to beat.

Light and shadow played hide-and-seek over the rippling water as the untamed swans swam out of sight. Slade watched them disappear around the bend, then glanced back as Brie shifted again. Unbelievably silent wings fluttered wide and the owl took off, scarcely making a sound.

Letting out a breath, Brie finally lowered her camera as Slade came up behind her.

"That was something," he commented, keeping his

voice low, thinking it might still startle some creature in this hushed atmosphere.

"Yes, they're beautiful, all these untamed creatures. I wish we'd run across a doe with her fawn, but the owl alone was worth the trip in."

"I wonder how he knew we were here. We were so quiet."

"Owls have very keen hearing and sight as well. I've read that they can hear a hundred times more distinctly than a human."

"That must make for tough sleeping."

"I wish my darkroom was finished so I could develop these myself." She rose, rolling her tense shoulders.

"Make the drawing. It'll only take me a couple of days to do it. Save the film and develop it later." He took her elbow, helping her over a jagged rock. "I'll bet you got some great shots there."

"I hope so." You could never tell if your hand was steady enough or if the subject moved or if the light shifted at just the wrong moment.

At the clearing by the bike path, Slade stopped. "You probably finished a whole roll in there. When you did your book on Manhattan, how many rolls did you go through?"

"Several hundred, and sometimes I could use only one or two from a specific roll. Night shots are harder, working with artificial lighting. The buildings were easy, but people are more difficult to capture on film than animals. Animals have no guile, no ego to get in the way, and if they don't want you around, they simply run away. Not so people." She repacked her case and anchored it on the bike rack.

"What do people do, get angry and argue with you?"

"Some. Or demand payment. Or want copies or credit in

the book. I always carried release forms with me for them to sign so I wouldn't get sued."

"And did they sign?"

"Some. Not all."

Slade shook his head as he reached for his bike. "Everyone wants their own fifteen minutes of fame, I guess."

"Once a man grabbed my camera and threw it in the East River. Frightening."

"Some vagrant, I suppose."

She looked up. "Not at all. A well-dressed, middle-aged man smoking an expensive cigar. *But* he was strolling along with a blonde young enough to be his daughter, though I doubt she was. The funny thing is, I wasn't even taking their picture. There was an old tug moving down the river that I was trying to shoot."

"Ah yes, a guilty conscience. Makes people do whacky things."

Which brought to mind her cheating father. Why was it that Wayne Gifford didn't suffer from that common malady?

Slade straddled his bike. "You ready to go back?"

Brie glanced up at the lowering sun and noticed more fast-moving clouds drifting in. It had felt good, holding the camera, envisioning the shot, setting up the angle, working again. Maybe she'd call Jocelyn next week and tell her she was ready to consider a second book again.

Pleased with the afternoon's shoot, she smiled at Slade. "I think so. How does pasta cooked in my new kitchen sound to you?"

"Like I can't wait. Let's go."

Brie led the way into her living room, still without furniture but not for long. She'd gone shopping yesterday and found a few good pieces she was considering. "You can make yourself useful and open the wine while I start the sauce. I wouldn't mind a glass while I cook."

"You've got it." While she put away her equipment, Slade paused for a moment in the kitchen doorway. Briana had done wonders with what had been a large, plain room. Recessed lighting, grainy textured wood cabinets with trailing green plants artfully placed on soffits all around. Red tiled floor, copper pots hung over an island sink, an overflowing fruit bowl, a cookie jar shaped like a brown bear with a straw hat. She had a knack for combining warmth and convenience that Jeremy had missed by a mile with his stainless-steel-precision cooking area. But all that was about to change. With Brie's encouragement, Slade was gradually redoing his house.

His house. Another milestone.

Walking in, he bent to the built-in wine rack and read the labels on her small collection. Although he'd been reading a book on wines that Jeremy had, Slade still was a long way from being an expert. But at least he was getting so he liked the taste of some better than others. That was a start.

"Red would be good, right?" he asked as she joined him after changing into a soft yellow sweatshirt and matching loose pants.

"Red would be great." Passing the answering machine, she saw the red light blinking and hit the PLAY button before bending down to search for a big pot.

After a slight pause, a voice came on—low, gravelly, muffled. "You thought you could run away, but you can't. I'm watching you, every day, everywhere. There's nowhere you can hide." A hang-up click followed.

Stunned, Brie straightened slowly, her knees a little wobbly as she stared white-faced at the machine.

Slade's eyes were stormy. "What the hell!" Walking over, he hit the PLAY button again. A second message came on, a woman's voice asking if the resident needed any carpet cleaning done. Annoyed, he hurried past that and pushed the button. Slipping his arm around Brie's waist, he listened again to the playback.

As it finished, Brie shuddered. "Good Lord!" She wished her voice wasn't so shaky. "Who is that?"

Chapter Thirteen

Brie's color was a little better after two sips of the blackberry brandy he'd found in the cupboard, Slade decided. "I don't suppose you recognized the voice?"

"No, but who could? He's obviously trying to disguise it." She realized her grip on the snifter was hard enough to shatter glass, and she carefully set it down. "I wonder if it's the same person who's been calling and hanging up."

Slade's mind snapped to attention. "When did you get hang-ups and how many?"

"Just two. Probably nothing."

"Tell me anyhow."

"The evening I came back from Boston was the first one. The light was blinking and I thought it might be a message from you. But this machine records even the hang-ups and that's all it was. Then again when I left your place the following afternoon, there was another." Worried eyes raised to his. "Do you think we should notify the police and play this for them?"

His look told her what he thought of the local cops. "You mean the same police who've done such a great job of tracking down the guy who broke in here?" The instant the words were out, he regretted opening his big mouth.

A jolt of pure terror straightened her spine, had her envisioning a madman stalking her, watching her every move, phoning to see if she was home, ready to break in again. "You think there's a connection?"

Silently cursing himself, Slade kept his voice level. "I was only trying to point out that the cops don't seem to be on top of things around here." He wrapped his warm fingers around her icy ones. "Listen, this could all be nothing." He didn't believe that for a moment, but he wanted to ease the haunted look in her eyes. "Who doesn't get hangups, wrong numbers? And the break-in was likely kids looking for something to hock." But how did he explain the implied threat of that raspy voice on the tape? "The guy who left that message could have dialed a wrong number."

Ignoring that, Brie brushed back her hair and stared at the answering machine as if it were suddenly an alien thing. "I can't make sense of what he meant. Run away? Hide? What's that supposed to mean?"

Slade had been wondering the same thing. The part that worried him most was when the guy had said he was watching her every day. Who on this island wanted to frighten her and why? Still, if he asked her too many questions, Brie would really get spooked. Maybe he'd do a little investigating on his own, but in front of her, he needed to play it down. "Who knows? Listen, teenage boys—and girls, for that matter—love to fool around with the phones, call strangers, get them jumpy. I used to do it myself."

She sent him a surprised look. "You did?"

"Hell, yes. My mother was never around so this one

friend I had—Gordie was his name—Gordie and I used to make crank calls, especially to old ladies in the apartment building where we lived. No answering machines back then, but we'd say all kinds of nasty things directly to them. There was this one nasty little biddy who was always yelling at all of us kids to keep off the grass, quiet down, don't play ball against the building. She was our favorite target."

Listening, Brie wondered if he was making all that up to take her mind off the real threat. "I wouldn't have guessed you were such a little shit."

He grinned, glad he'd distracted her. "I still am, only I'm bigger now. Did you notice that the caller didn't use your name? Probably just a random dial. Gordie and I used to do that, too. Pick a number, call it, and hope we got a live one."

Relaxing a fraction, she bent down to search for her cooking pot. "Your decadent youth. Did you ever get caught?"

"Nope. We were too smart." He walked over as she straightened and turned her to face him. "Listen, let's chalk this up as a crank call, but keep your eyes and ears open. If you get another call, hang-up, or message, I want to know."

"All right." She would try not to think about this. But she didn't trust the world like she once had. Slade had installed dead bolts on both her doors, plus sturdy locks on all the windows. She was safe here, as safe as it was possible to be anywhere these days. For the sake of her sanity, she had to believe that.

Despite his reassurances to Briana, Slade decided he'd keep her close by his side for a while. He had the uneasy feeling that there was a sicko out there enjoying his game, for whatever reason. Which meant he wouldn't go away easily.

As she lined up onions, tomatoes, and mushrooms for her sauce, three words kept echoing in Brie's mind: *I'm watching you!*

Before they finished eating, another storm hit along the Nantucket Cliffs, battering the shoreline, sending waves arching high overhead, then dashing down to swirl around the distant black rocks, spewing foam. Peering out through her curtainless front window, Brie watched Mother Nature vent her fury, fascinated by the display.

"When are your new drapes supposed to be ready?" Slade asked, standing alongside her. He didn't like this open expanse of window on the seaward side. Anyone walking by on the sidewalk or the sandy shore could look in through the porch screens and see into the living room and on past the arch into the kitchen. If it was dark out and lights were on inside, they could watch Brie undetected for hours.

Of course, who would stand around in a downpour and stare into someone else's home? A sicko, that's who.

"Another week or so," she answered, watching lightning bolts streak from the sky and disappear into the sea. "They brought one set out, but they'd measured wrong and had to take them back."

Bad luck, Slade thought. "Your bedroom faces the front, too, right?"

"The one I've been using does, yes." Maybe she'd move into the back one, perhaps tonight. *I'm watching you.* "But I'm redoing the back one, the one that was my grandparents' room." She didn't want him to know just how much that phone message had rattled her. "Want to see where the sunken tub will go?"

He raised a brow. "Sunken tub, eh? With Jacuzzi jets?"

"As a matter of fact, yes." She led him through the larger bedroom into the expanded bath, still unfinished. "I'm having a wide marble sill put in around the tub, and that's the holdup here. The variegated green marble I picked out is on back order."

"Looks like it'll be big enough for two. Do you like to share?" His hands at her waist, he held her loosely.

"Mmm, depends on who I'm sharing with."

"Let's see. How about someone who thinks you have the most gorgeous hair he's ever seen?" And he thrust his fingers through the blond thickness, his blunt fingers touching her scalp.

"I should have it cut, but I haven't had time."

"No, don't cut it. I like it just this way." He shifted his hands to her face, his thumbs outlining her brows as he studied her eyes. "How about if this same someone thinks your eyes are incredible, a warm brown when you're pleased about something, kind of flinty when you're angry with me. But the best is this rich chocolaty color they get just before I move inside you."

A surge of heat rippled through Briana, weakening her from head to toe. Never had a man talked to her like this, making love to her with his voice. "Wow," she whispered, her voice breathy, "when this ride stops, do I have to get off?"

"No, just hold on to me. And then there's this mouth." With one finger, he traced her lips from side to side, top to bottom, and saw them tremble. "I never knew a mouth could be so responsive, one that could make me want to beg."

Her arms at his back tightened. "Oh, Slade, Slade." Her heart swelled with love. She yearned to tell him, to reveal how she felt, but she held back. What if he wasn't ready, if he didn't want to know? Yet couldn't he see, couldn't he feel how he had her teetering on the edge? "When I'm with you like this, when you hold me, I feel shaky, as if I'm falling."

"You can fall. I'll catch you." He leaned back from her, while from the waist down they were pressed tightly together. How had this woman gotten such a stranglehold on him? "Briana Morgan, what am I going to do about you? I've never known anyone who messed with my head the way you do. You make me *feel* so much and it scares the hell out of me."

Her hands were on his chest, feeling his heart beating wildly beneath her fingers. "Don't be afraid of your feelings. Tell me." Dare she hope they were the same as hers?

"It's easier for you. You were married, you've felt these things before and talked about them freely."

"It wasn't the same." She wondered if she could make him see. "I never felt about Robert the way I feel about you. I never wanted him the way I can't seem to stop wanting you. We met, we married, and we fell into a routine. I knew something was wrong, but I blamed his job, his absences, his indifference. It wasn't until just recently that I've come to realize that what happened wasn't Robert's fault. He was who he was, only I didn't see it until it was too late. It was my problem, my fault for marrying a man who couldn't touch me deeply, who couldn't reach the woman I am. Nothing he could have said or done could have made up for that lack. He simply never could make me feel enough. Because he wasn't you."

She humbled him, and scared him even more with her soft words. "I don't think I can be all you want me to be."

"Why don't you let me decide that?"

"No, that's too easy. I don't trust easy."

"Then trust me. I won't hurt you. I won't leave you." *Unless you send me away. Unless you can't love me back.*

"You'll leave. Everyone does. Didn't you say all you wanted was something that will last? Well, nothing does, no matter how we want it to, no matter how much we care. Everything dies sooner or later." His voice was filled with pain, with the terrible knowledge that what they had, good as it was, was only temporary.

"You're wrong. Love doesn't die, not for everyone. Remember Annabel and Josh Mayberry? Love can be strong enough to overcome anything, even death."

"You're talking legends and fairy tales. That's not real." His hands were rough as he pulled her close, so close even a shadow couldn't have slipped between them. "*This* is real, Brie. You and I together, for now. No promises, no vows, no declarations that we'll have to take back or break. Today is real. No one knows what's going to happen tomorrow."

Her hands hooked around his shoulders, her heart pressed to his, Brie blinked back tears. "That's such a hopeless way to look at things."

"Not hopeless. Realistic. If you don't expect anything, you won't get hurt when you don't get it." His eyes bore into hers. "Here and now, you and me. That's it, that's all there is. Oh, God, Brie, I want you so much. So very much." Bending to her, he took her mouth.

She kissed him back, putting her heart in it, while tears trailed down her cheeks. How had this happened, that she'd fallen in love with a man who didn't believe in love?

Not in its power or its beauty. Why hadn't she seen this coming? Briana asked herself.

And that was her last coherent thought as he backed her through the doorway and pushed her against the bedroom wall, all the while crushing her mouth in a frantic kiss that threatened to blow off the top of her head. A strangled sound lodged in her throat as she struggled to stay upright under his greedy onslaught.

He branded her with bruising kisses as his hands burrowed under her shirt, closing over her straining breasts. If she could have moved, she'd have ripped their clothes aside, so powerful was the need to be flesh to flesh with him. She felt the ache deep inside begin to throb, felt the rush of heat engulf her.

He needed her, Slade finally admitted. God, how he needed to possess her, to make her his, if only for this night. Hungrily, he raced his lips over her delicate throat, the long column of her neck, and back to her waiting mouth. His teeth nibbled and nipped as he felt her legs buckle. His hands slid down and behind to cup her bottom, lifting her to him, to his heat.

But it wasn't enough, not nearly enough.

Through a shuddering breath, Briana gasped out a suggestion. "My bedroom. Across the hall." In this room, there was only newly carpeted floor and a hard wall at her back.

"No. Here and now." His hand slid beneath the elastic of her sweatpants and the panties she wore, shoving down the resisting materials. Testing, his fingers moved inside to find her warm and wet and waiting.

Aroused beyond belief to find her so ready, so willing, he unbuttoned his jeans one-handed and inched the zipper down. Aching to be inside her, he freed himself, then drove in with one hard, swift stroke and watched her eyes glaze over. "Look at me," he demanded, not moving, waiting.

Breathlessly, she did, feeling suspended in time. "I . . . I'm looking at you."

"I want to watch you." To see her climb and then to lose control. He wanted to see her shatter, like she'd shattered him over and over throughout their last incredible night.

His hands returned to support her as her legs wrapped around him. Her skin was damp, her thick hair tumbled around her head like a yellow cloud against the pale green wall, her mouth swollen from his kisses. She was more beautiful than any woman he'd ever known. "Ready?" he asked, knowing she was, wanting to hear it.

"Yes. Oh, yes. Please."

Then he was moving, plundering, stroking, easing back for a heartbeat, then hammering home. Driving her up, driving her crazy, driving her beyond sanity. She cried out at the strength of it, the enormity, the passion.

Eyes locked with hers, he knew the moment her climax began, saw the shocked pleasure on her face, felt the tremulous shudders take her. Finally her head fell forward onto his shoulder. The force of her aftershocks dragged him along for the ride, leaving him breathless with a thundering heart that threatened to explode.

When he was able to move again, he slid them both to the floor, rolling with her on the dark green carpeting. He felt like he'd run the marathon, like he'd tried a free fall from a plane, like he'd climbed the highest mountain where the air was rarefied.

Turning his head toward her, he enjoyed the rosy glow he'd put on her face. "How do you feel?"

Brie drew in a huge breath and let it out slowly. "Surely you aren't going to ask how that was for me, are you?"

His smile came easily. "Probably not."

"Oh, good." She tried to make a fist and found she couldn't. "Lord, what you do to me," she commented, staring at her limp hand.

"I'd say that's mutual. Where'd you learn to be so sexy?"

Lazily, she rolled toward him. "Are you sure you want to have this discussion, because it works both ways, you know?"

"Probably not," he said again.

"Besides, I'm not sexy. I never have been or . . ."

His hand touched her chin, forced her to look at him. "Who told you that? You know what makes a woman sexy to a man? A woman who responds, immediately, totally, freely." His hand snaked under her shirt, found her soft breast and circled. In seconds, her flesh swelled, the peak hardening. "Like that."

No one was more surprised than Brie. She wasn't without experience, yet he was able to get more from her than anyone ever had. "That sort of thing doesn't happen with every man's touch."

"Nor with every woman." Slade was more than a little surprised at how quickly his body had recovered, at how much he wanted her again. "Ready when you are, ma'am."

Stunned, she was sure she couldn't possibly. "Are you trying to kill me?"

"A little death, some call it." He dragged her hard up against his body. "Don't worry. I'll be gentle."

Her mouth was close to his ear. "Who said I wanted gentle?"

The laugh she heard was rich and very masculine.

* * *

The flames were slithering up along the wooden sides of the old house, whipping out the first-floor windows, lighting up the night sky. He was afraid to step onto the creaky porch for fear it would collapse under him, but there was no other way in. Ducking low, he barreled his way into the fires of hell, the poisoned air black as ink, the heat so intense it seemed to sear his throat through his face mask.

He called her name but got no answer. He couldn't see, but knew where the hall was and went that way, staying low. He felt more than saw her on the floor alongside her big double bed, the one they'd once shared. He picked her up and found her dazed, but then she started screaming, somehow recognizing him through all his gear. "My baby. Find my baby, Slade, please!"

He handed her over and went back into the inferno, looking in the child's closet like she'd said. He heard a sound, a frightened cry, but only a mangy cat leaped out and streaked sharp claws down his sleeve before he could stuff her inside his jacket. Down on all fours, he crawled along the hallway, searching, calling out to the child.

Suddenly, all hell broke loose, walls tumbling down, flames devouring everything, the air thick with black smoke. The others dragged him out still protesting, still calling her name. "Megan, Megan, where are you?"

Then he was outside with Rachel as the medics worked on her, seeing the tracks of her tears on her soot-stained face, looking into empty eyes. "Where's my baby? You let my baby die. Your fault. It's all your fault!" Her screams vied for attention with the crackling flames still whirling upward in a macabre dance.

He sank to the ground as they put her in the ambulance. "My fault," he sobbed. "All my fault."

"Oh, God, it's all my fault." Slade's head thrashed on the

pillow, his skin drenched with sweat, his heart pounding. "Megan's dead, Rachel, and it's all my fault. No, no. God, no!"

Briana snapped on the bedside lamp and touched his shoulder. "Slade, you're dreaming." She'd been awakened by his restless flailing about, then heard his mutterings and finally his loud ravings. "Slade, do you hear me? Wake up."

"You're right, my fault. Forgive me, please." He shot upright, his eyes wild, looking about, unfocused.

"You're having a nightmare," Brie told him gently. "It's all right. You're okay."

It finally registered, where he was, who she was. Swallowing around a dry throat, he swiped at his damp face and swung his feet over the side of the bed. He gripped the edge of the mattress, bent his head, and sat there, letting the residue of the nightmare recede. It was always the same one, the one he deserved to suffer with, the one that would never go away.

Briana slid closer, touching his bare shoulder. He'd been hesitant about sleeping over at her house, but it had been raining so hard he'd decided to stay. Had this been the reason why, the nightmares he'd told her he had? She rubbed his arm, wishing she could help, that she knew the right words. "Are you all right now?"

"Should I be? I don't deserve to be all right." Grabbing his briefs, he pulled them on and left the room.

Standing at the bare front window in the darkened living room, Slade stood staring out. The storm had moved out to sea, probably headed for the mainland.

The fist clenched in his gut had begun to ease, the sweat of the nightmare drying on his skin. It was always the same, always like this. He relived his nightmare in brilliant, fiery colors, his failures repeated reel after reel. The helplessness of knowing Megan had been in there somewhere and he hadn't saved her, the hopelessness of facing the mother who knew he was to blame.

Slade braced his arms on the wood frame of the window, seeing not Nantucket Harbor drenched in an autumn storm but a ramshackle house in California disintegrating before his eyes into hot, smoky rubble. When would he ever be able to sleep a night through without those mind pictures startling him awake? What could he do, what could he say to assuage the guilt that dogged his steps from coast to coast? Who would put up with him while he struggled with his demons? No one should have to.

Briana thought she was strong enough. Trust me, she'd said. I won't leave you. She was stubborn enough, determined enough to hang in there with him. But he couldn't let her do that, to waste her life on him. There seemed no end in sight, the shame increasing. When would it end? Maybe never. He deserved to suffer, but she didn't.

She was so very special, he knew, and he'd wanted her from the beginning. At first, he'd thought he wanted only sex, pure and simple. But that hadn't been the half of it. Gorgeous as she was, she was so much more than a beautiful body. It was the way those huge brown eyes looked at him, sometimes so very serious, other times an extension of her generous smile. It was the way she smelled, the way she tasted, the soft sounds she made low in her throat when he moved within her. He wanted no other man to ever hear those sweet sounds, no one but him.

How could he let her go? Yet how could he keep her? She was too kind, too compassionate to walk away from someone in need. And God only knew, he was in need. But how could he chain her to half a man and live with himself? He was tortured, afraid to trust his own instincts, his judgment—and might never get over it. How could he ever forget the dead and broken bodies he'd left in his wake?

How to convince her, for he knew she cared. She'd almost said the words out loud tonight, he knew, but she'd held back. She was afraid he'd fall apart if she told him she loved him. Little did she know, nor would she believe, that he hadn't heard those three important words in more years than he could recall. His mother had sometimes told him when she'd been in her cups and feeling sentimental. Rachel had never mentioned love, only that they were good together and should get married. The other women he'd befriended and sometimes bedded had all been content with good times and good sex. If they began angling for more, he moved on. That was the way his life had been.

Until Briana.

They'd met because of the proximity of his father's house to her grandfather's home. Circumstances had brought them to this island when they'd both been vulnerable. So they'd become closer than either had intended. And never should have.

If only a pleasant attraction and great sex were enough. But they no longer were, for either of them. He saw the way she looked at him, the concern in her eyes, the hope she couldn't hide. And he had concerns of his own. Otherwise, he'd simply enjoy the woman and not overthink things. This time, with this woman, he couldn't stop thinking.

Of what might have been if he were only a whole man free of guilt and ready for an uncomplicated future. She deserved more than him. She deserved a happiness he could never give her.

The raspy voice on the phone machine drifted into his

memory. Was it a wrong number, a coincidence, a prankster? Or was Briana in danger? The very thought had his fists clenching as he straightened. He might not be able to be there for her for all time, but he could and would protect her until they got to the bottom of this mess. He wouldn't let anything happen to her, not if he could help it. He'd failed before, let down people who'd counted on him. He wouldn't fail Briana.

His thoughts as gloomy as the weather, Slade stood looking out.

In the bedroom, Briana lay awake, wondering whether to follow him or stay put. She didn't know which would be right, but she knew she couldn't go back to sleep and pretend nothing had happened. Moving to the closet, she shrugged on her terrycloth robe and padded out to the living room in her bare feet.

She found him at the front window, his very stance suggesting tension. Slipping her arm around his waist, she leaned her head to his shoulder. "Are you feeling better?"

Slade drew in a long breath. "I'm sorry I woke you. I get those nightmares sometimes and there's not much I can do to stop them."

Her eyes finally adjusted to the dark, she looked up at him, but his face was closed down, withdrawn. "Give it time."

That's what everyone said. "I just want to shut my eyes and not see the ghosts from my past, not hear them crying. Doesn't seem like so much to ask, does it?"

"No." She shifted until her head rested lightly on his chest as his arms automatically encircled her. "But I do know what you mean. I have nightmares, too, mostly about Bobby. And always, he's just out of reach, calling to me, and I can't get to him in time. The doctor told me that one day they would stop, but I'm not so sure."

"You're not blaming yourself for Bobby's death, are you? How could you be at fault?"

"Logically, I know I'm not. But when someone we care for dies, we always find some way to blame ourselves. I felt that even when Gramp died. I should have come to see him more often, spent more time talking with him, listening to the stories he loved to tell. Guilt is a hair shirt most of us put on so often we no longer feel the itch. After a while, it becomes comfortable, a way of life."

Looking down at her, he used both hands to brush back her hair, her beautiful hair. "So, Doc, what do you suggest we do about it?"

He'd shoved his demons back for now, which was probably the best he could do, Briana thought. She would do the same. "Let's go back to bed. Come morning, things will look brighter. At least, they usually do."

"All right." Arms entwined, he let her lead him back.

The news broadcaster's nasal voice on the kitchen radio nearly quivered with excitement. "The hurricane of '38 was the largest single disaster to ever hit the New England area, killing over six hundred people. That storm, which was a category four on the Saffir-Simpson Scale, hit on September twenty-first. The weather bureau tells us that there's a very real possibility that Nantucket may be in for another biggie."

Plugging in the coffeepot, Briana glanced up as Slade walked into the kitchen. "Did you hear that?"

"I hope he's wrong." He finished tucking in his shirt and took the glass of orange juice she handed him. "Thanks."

"That hurricane," the announcer went on, "was followed

by Carol, the first great named storm that hit the New England shoreline on August thirty-first, 1954. We enjoyed a six-year respite. The last one to brush along the coast of Nantucket was Donna, the hurricane that hit in early September of 1960. After leaving us, it hurtled north to cut a wide path through Massachusetts and went up as far as Maine. So, ladies and gents, time to batten down the hatches. This one's been named Donald and he's only a two so far, but moving up fast with winds already clocked at over eighty miles an hour. If Donald keeps on this northerly route, the leading edge will be arriving within thirty-six hours."

"Plywood," Briana said, then drained the last of her coffee. "We'll need to get some sheets of plywood and lots of nails."

Slade wrinkled his brow. "Plywood?"

"Yes, to cover the windows. Broken glass is just one problem a hurricane brings."

"Is plywood strong enough?"

"Usually. I was here one fall weekend years ago when a huge storm was scheduled to hit. I don't know if it had been labeled a hurricane, but Lord, it was bad. Everyone was running around nailing plywood over their windows, stocking up on food and bottled water. It hit and pounded on us for seven or eight hours. The electricity went out so my grandparents and I sat in the living room in the dark, waiting it out. I was about fourteen and plenty scared, never having experienced anything like it before. The worst was the sound of the wind. It was eerie, like nothing you've ever heard, and that wasn't even a full-fledged hurricane."

"I'll bet on Jeremy's house all I have to do is close the shutters on the windows that have them, right?"

"I think so. We can check at the hardware store. They'll know." She grabbed her keys and purse. "Can we take your truck?"

Slade glanced at his barely tasted coffee. "You want to go right now?"

"Yes, right now. I'm telling you, that timetable of thirty-six hours is only an estimate. It could hit much sooner. The shutters I ordered haven't arrived." Her frown was deepset and worried. "I . . . I really don't want to lose this house."

"Don't worry. You won't. Come on."

But as Briana headed for the door, the phone rang. In the kitchen arch, she stopped to stare at it, the memory of that raspy voice sending a chill up her spine.

"Don't answer it," Slade suggested. "Let the machine take it."

"No," she said, suddenly straightening. "I'm not going to be frightened out of my own house. Let him confront me in person, the coward." She grabbed the phone. "Hello?"

"Brie, it's Craig."

She nearly sagged with relief, fully aware that her bravado had been just that. Not that she wanted to talk with Craig, but it was far better to hear from him than the threatening stranger. "Craig, why are you calling?" Would the man just never back off?

"I'm calling with hat in hand again, Brie." His voice was contrite, almost humble. "I had no business saying the things I said when you were here that day. Robert was as honest as the day is long, just like you said. I was just sort of playing devil's advocate, examining things from all angles. Old man Brighton's had us all on the carpet since this thing surfaced and I guess I'm a little strung out. Forgive me?"

She didn't particularly want to, since he might take it as

encouragement, but she'd never been one to hold a grudge. "We've all been under a strain, I guess." She noticed that Slade stayed where he was, unabashedly listening. Not that she minded.

Craig had lost his cockiness, sounding almost pleading. "I hope you won't hold that one conversation against me, Brie. I've finally got it in my thick head that there won't be anything more between us than friendship. But I think so very highly of you that I'd hate it if we were no longer friends."

As long as he didn't cross the line, she could agree to his request. "We're still friends, Craig." Brie saw Slade turn his back to her and go look out the window.

Craig exhaled noisily. "Great. I feel a whole lot better. Say, I hear your weather's not the best over there."

"No, it isn't. We've had a lot of rain, and now they're predicting a hurricane may be headed this way." And she was anxious to get moving, to get her plywood so she could secure the house. It was a strain to continue to be polite. "How is it there?"

"Gray skies but no rain so far. Maybe you should consider coming home?"

Same old tune, Brie thought. "Listen, Craig, I'm on my way out. I'm glad you called, that we cleared the air. I'll be in touch soon, but I've got to run for now."

"Yeah, sure. You be careful, you hear?"

"I will, thanks."

"Any message for your folks? I can call them for you."

Impatiently, she frowned. She could damn well phone her own parents. Why was he so solicitous? She fervently wished he'd find someone else to hover over. "No, thanks, I'll be talking with them myself, probably tonight. Good-bye, Craig." Hanging up, she shook her head as she walked to the living room where Slade was waiting for her.

"You're nicer to him than I would have been."

Brie shrugged. "What's the point? Maybe now he'll find someone else to pester."

"Doubtful." He remembered the arrogant way Craig had marched in and pulled Brie into a hard, fast kiss. It rankled every time he thought of that jerk's hands on her. "He's got a real case on you."

Dangling her keys, she looked up at him. "Jealous?"

"Yeah, sometimes I am. But not of some guy who wears *ironed* khakis and loafers with tassels."

"Who'd have believed you'd be a reverse snob?"

"I wouldn't say that. I'll bet he wears paisley suspenders with handkerchiefs to match, am I right?" He shoved open the door and walked through the porch and outside.

Actually, she'd seen Craig in exactly that, Brie thought, following. "You don't like him because he dresses out of *GQ*?"

He stopped, turning back to her. "I don't need a reason to dislike him. I just do. Now, are we going to stand around discussing Craig's wardrobe down to his underwear, or are we going to get moving?"

"I've never seen his underwear."

Slade opened the truck's passenger door for her. "I'm relieved to hear it." Once inside, he turned the key. "Where we going?"

"Wilkins Lumber and Hardware. Just head toward Main Street and I'll tell you where to turn off."

As the sturdy truck bounced through the puddles, Brie forgot about Craig and stared up at churning gray clouds. How much time did they have? she wondered. "I know you think I'm being silly, but this hurricane could be serious. Besides, there's only so much plywood around and . . ."

He touched her arm. "It's okay. I understand." She'd lost her grandparents, her ex-husband, her son, and had two homes invaded by strangers. She couldn't face another loss, even if it was just a house. She was entitled. "Actually, I sort of envy you. I've never been attached to a place, hardly been in one long enough to get that way."

"Even now? What if Jeremy's house got hit and turned into a pile of rubble? Wouldn't that bother you?"

Turning on the windshield wipers against a light sprinkling, he shrugged. "I suppose. But not the way it would bother you if Gramp's house got hit. I haven't any memories wrapped up in that house. Well . . . maybe one." He glanced at her, a smile twitching at the corners of his mouth. "The master shower and bed, now there's a memory that'll warm you on a cold night."

Despite all they'd done together, all they'd been to each other, Brie felt the heat rise along her throat and into her face. The first time they'd made love. Would he hold the memory dear if he didn't care? "Yes, that's a special memory for me, too."

Slade's big hand reached over and scooted her closer to him on the bench seat. "There, that's better." He placed her hand palm down on his thigh and laced his fingers with hers.

Memories, he thought as he followed the curve of the road. He'd best stockpile some special memories for the time when they'd be all he'd have.

Two hours later, they parked in Brie's driveway so Slade could unload the sheets of plywood into Gramp's open garage. The newscast on the car radio had sounded ambivalent, the announcer noting that tracking the probable path of capricious Donald was confounding the best forecasters because of its erratic nature. The uncertainty had nearly everyone on edge, some pounding nails already, others doing nothing, sure the hurricane would hug the coast of the mainland and bypass Nantucket. Squinting into a shifting sky, Slade had a tendency to agree with the latter group, but for Briana's sake, he'd do what she thought necessary.

"Hey, lady," he said after propping the last heavy sheet against the garage wall, "do you suppose, since we skipped breakfast, that we could grab some lunch before we get to this, or is feeding the help going to throw off your schedule?"

"Is that all you think about, your stomach?" she teased, setting the bag of nails on a shelf.

In a flash, he had her turned into his arms and close up against his warm body, his smile lascivious. "I wouldn't say that."

Laughing, she kissed him lightly. She'd feed him, she'd even clown with him a bit, but she badly wanted those windows covered. The thought of anything damaging Gramp's house was more than she could bear just now. "Come on, then. How about a sandwich and some fresh coffee?"

"Sounds good." Stepping on the front porch as Brie unlocked the door, Slade noticed a package in a plain padded manila envelope on one of the rocking chairs. "Looks like the mailman's been here." Picking it up, he followed her inside and handed it over.

In the kitchen, Brie checked out the typed label. "No return address."

Looking over her shoulder, Slade frowned. "There's no postmark, either. This didn't go through the mails. Someone had to have hand delivered it." Carefully, he took it from her. "I'm not sure you should open this, Brie."

Fear prickled along her spine. "You're scaring me. What do you think we have here, a bomb dropped off by our friendly neighborhood nutcase?"

He examined the package, his fingers pressing gingerly. He could feel no wires, nothing suspicious. He was far from an alarmist, but something didn't seem right here. "Let's at least go out back and open it, all right?"

His concern was contagious. "All right." She followed him into the backyard. "We're going to feel stupid when we find some curtain samples or something in there."

Cautiously, holding the envelope at arm's length, ready to toss it should he hear or feel something wrong, Slade ripped off one end. Nothing happened. Relieved that there was no danger, he shook the contents out onto the grass.

Briana gasped as she recognized what she was seeing. Scattered on the ground were remnants of Bobby's size-one seafoam-green beach shoe cut into chunks and jagged pieces, as if done by a very angry, very vicious hand. Wild-eyed, she looked at Slade. "I left that shoe in the house, in my bedroom. Oh, God, Slade, he's been in my home!"

Chapter Fourteen

Sheriff Stone stooped down to examine the thick pieces of slashed plastic. Thoughtfully, he examined first one, then another, and still more. There had to be a dozen. Straightening, he held the chunks in his big hand. "Not many scissors would cut through this stuff. Had to be a very sharp knife, like a fish-boning knife, or one a butcher might use."

Standing white-faced and silent, Briana just stared at the remains of the small mutilated shoe that had once belonged to her son.

Her outward calm didn't fool Slade; he knew inside she was breaking into more pieces than the shoe. Perhaps he could hurry the slow-moving sheriff along. "Brie remembers leaving that shoe in her bedroom closet. After the break-in, I put deadbolts on both doors and reinforced the window locks. How in hell he got in is a mystery."

Stone pursed his lips. "How many keys and who has them?" he asked Briana.

"Two keys and I have both."

"Where are they?"

"One's on my key ring and the other's in my dresser drawer."

"You want to check for me that it's still there?" Stone watched her walk away without another word. He turned to Slade. "You didn't keep a key, did you?"

He'd been expecting the question. A good lawman would ask and not care who he annoyed. "No, I didn't."

Stone turned the padded manila envelope over, checking both sides. "The label's common enough. You can get them at any drugstore. The printing's block letters, black pen. No clue there." He sighed heavily, then glanced toward the house. "Briana's not been herself since her son died. Do you think she might have left the shoe outside and forgotten about it?"

Slade remembered in great detail the day she'd stumbled across the shoe and run inside where he'd found her weeping in the kitchen. He'd noticed the shoe on the counter, then seen her take it into her bedroom after his attempt at comfort had turned into more. "No, it was definitely inside the house. She's also had several hang-ups on her answering machine and one message that you should listen to."

The sheriff looked as if he'd rather be anywhere else. "All right, let's hear it." He followed Slade into the kitchen just as Brie came in.

"Here's the other key, Sheriff." She held it up. "And here's the second one on my key ring." She showed him that as well.

"Were your keys ever out of your sight when you were away from home, Briana, like maybe you forgot them somewhere and had to go pick 'em up, or maybe at a restaurant while you went to the rest room?"

Annoyed that he'd think her so careless, she shook her

head. "I always keep them in my purse, or in my pocket if I'm out on the beach."

"I thought the sheriff ought to hear the message on your machine," Slade told Briana. He saw her nod, then brace herself to listen to that disturbing voice again.

Stone listened to the tape, a frown on his face. "Have you had any calls since this one?" he asked Briana.

She thought of Craig's annoying call and the company wanting to clean her carpets. "Yes, two."

"No use dialing Star 69 then, to trace back the last caller." The sheriff's eyes narrowed behind his rimless glasses as he looked from the tape to the envelope containing the slashed shoe. "I can't imagine who'd be pulling this stuff on you, or why." Drawing in a breath, he leaned against the counter. "I'd like to tell you we'll find this guy, Briana, but whoever he is, he's sly. There'd be no tracing a call like that, over and done in less than a minute, even if we had your phone under surveillance. I'll contact the phone company, see if they can get me a list of your incoming calls. But even then, some phones have their numbers blocked for privacy."

Frustrated, he paced the kitchen. "Is it connected to the hang-ups? Who knows? The man can't walk through walls, yet he got in here somehow and took that shoe, went home and did his dirty deed, then snuck over and left the envelope on your porch. It was handled by both of you so even if there were prints, we couldn't pick 'em up. Chances are, careful as he seems, he wore gloves. We didn't pick up a single print, not even a partial, from the window that was broken earlier."

So the sheriff thought the incidents were connected, too. Brie shivered, despite being warmly dressed in sweater and slacks. "You think it's the same person, then?"

Stone shrugged. "It's possible. I don't trust coincidences." He glanced out the window at the gray sky. "You've heard, I suppose, that there's a big nor'eastern headed our way. Maybe, while the planes are still flying, you ought to go back to the mainland. Give us time to work on this a bit."

"I thought you said there wasn't much to work on," Slade interjected.

"There isn't, but I could set up a surveillance, have a deputy swing by the house regularly, check things out."

Brie crossed her arms over her chest, feeling vulnerable yet again. "I don't see what good that would do. Apparently, he's trying to frighten me, for some reason. If I leave, I doubt he'll come back. No one broke in while I was in Boston recently."

The sheriff was feeling impotent and he didn't much like it, especially with J.D. Slade's eyes on him. "I need you to think real hard here, Briana. Is there anyone who might have reason to harm you?"

"I *have* thought hard, Sheriff." Hadn't she been through this with the Boston police about the shooting? "I don't know of any enemies I might have, but surely, it's possible. The thing that puzzles me most is that he's here on Nantucket. I've had nothing but pleasant times here. I can't recall ever having even a minor altercation with anyone on the island." Shoving both hands through her hair, she walked away. "I don't know why this is happening."

Slade thought of something. "Is Caller ID available in Nantucket?" Noticing Brie's blank look, he went on to explain. "It's a box you can hook up to your phone and each time someone calls, their name and number appear as a readout. If this guy called back, even if he hung up, we possibly could trace him that way."

"Yeah," Stone said, "I know about Caller ID. But phone customers can choose to have their name and number blocked, just like they can choose to have unlisted phone numbers. Do you suppose a guy who's making threatening calls would be dumb enough to phone from his home?"

"Maybe," Slade commented. "Maybe he's not aware of Caller ID or maybe he's not very smart."

"He's smart enough to keep me on tenterhooks." Briana was tired of the discussion, tired of the situation, and very tired of being afraid. "Sorry to have bothered you, Sheriff. I guess there's not much you can do."

Stone set the bag on the counter. "Wish there was, Briana."

"I know. Thanks for coming out."

The sheriff glanced up at Slade, remembering that he'd been here after the last incident. Seemed like these two were pretty friendly. Maybe that would help Briana. "Since she's not leaving, maybe you can keep an eye on her, eh?"

"I'll do that." Slade walked outside with him.

"She's a special lady. Hate to see anything happen to her." Stone opened the door to his cruiser.

"That makes two of us." He watched the sheriff drive off, then stood back as Irma's BMW replaced the sheriff's vehicle in the driveway.

"Just the man I'm looking for," the widow said as she stepped out of the car, favoring her left foot. "I feel silly driving less than a block, but I was afraid I'd slip and fall on this wet pavement." She stuck out her bandaged leg. "I've got a bad sprain as it is. I don't need another."

Walking around, Slade took her arm. "What happened?"

"Getting clumsy in my old age, I guess. Stumbled over an uneven step on my porch. Nothing broken, thank God, but it hurts like the devil. At least it's my left so I can still drive." She peered up at him through rose-tinted glasses. "How have you been? I've called you any number of times, hoping to catch you, but you're never home."

"Oh, I'm around, here and there." Irma was wearing a Western shirt complete with fringe and jeans with a wide belt fastened around her middle. The red wig was back. Despite the outfit, she looked more frail than usual.

"Uh huh." Irma glanced at Briana's house. "Around here, most likely. That's why I came over. Thought I'd find you at Brie's."

"You caught me." Holding on to her, he led her up the steps. "You mean to say there's something wrong with your porch after I reinforced it?"

"No, not that porch. The one in back." She let him open the door for her, stepped into the living room, and spotted Briana in the kitchen. "Company, my dear. Uninvited, but I'm here."

"Irma, it's good to see you." Brie came forward to hug the older woman, then stepped back to check out her bandaged leg.

Irma went over the story again, then dismissed the injury. "Let me tell you, kids, it's hell to grow old, but considering the alternative, I'll take it."

"I'm just making some lunch, Irma. Come join us." Glancing out the window, Brie saw that it wasn't raining yet, but the sky looked ominous. She wouldn't think about threatening phone calls or mysterious packages, but rather concentrate on this simple meal and then on getting the plywood sheets in place. She had a bad feeling about this pending storm. "How does a roast beef sandwich and coffee sound?"

"Actually, it sounds pretty good," Irma admitted. "I haven't had much of an appetite lately." She'd been to see

Doc Winslow in town and he'd done his usual exam, finding nothing new. Yet she seemed to have no energy these days.

"Your mouth will start to water as soon as you smell Brie's cooking." Slade settled Irma at the kitchen table. "It's one of her specialties, made like a Reuben with Thousand Island dressing and melted Swiss cheese."

Irma watched him walk to the counter where Briana was working and place a hand on her shoulder, gently caressing. Quite unconsciously, Brie leaned into his touch for the briefest of moments, then resumed fixing lunch. So that's how it was, Irma thought, hiding her smile. There was no mistaking the familiarity of touches between two people who've been intimate. She'd seen enough to recognize the signs immediately.

She hadn't been in favor of J.D. Slade when he'd first arrived. Rumors of his drinking had bothered her and she'd mistaken his inborn reserve, his shyness with strangers, for aloofness and arrogance. He'd stood up well to her hardline questioning the evening they'd spent at the art exhibit. But it wasn't until she'd asked him to work on her porch while Briana had been in Boston that she'd come to know and understand him better. And finally, to like him a great deal.

He had problems, she knew, but then, who didn't? If you were alive and in the mainstream, you had problems. The only problem-free people were tiny babies and dead folks. The question was, was he strong enough to overcome his problems? And equally as important to Irma, who loved Briana like the granddaughter she'd never had, would he not add to that lovely woman's problems, but rather, help her over the heartache of losing her only child?

The jury was still out on that one.

Briana placed a huge hot sandwich on each of three plates while Slade poured fresh coffee. Sitting down with her guests, Brie found a smile for Irma. "I'm so glad you came by."

Irma tried her coffee before responding and found it hot and robust. "It's good to see you as always, Briana, but I must admit I came looking for Slade." She cocked her head at the man who was already halfway through the first half of his sandwich. "I figured when he didn't answer his phone that he'd be here."

Idly, Brie wondered who else had noticed their togetherness, not that she cared. "We drove into town to get some plywood to cover the windows. The newscaster warned that the storm could hit by tomorrow."

Slade wiped his mouth. "We have enough for your windows, too." Brie had had him buy out half the supply, it seemed.

"Oh, that would be so kind of you." Relaxing, Irma finally tasted her sandwich. "I heard the news, too. I can't get around too well with this ankle and the boy I use for odd jobs went back to the mainland to college."

"No problem. I'll fix that step, too, and check out the rest. Meantime, you'd better stay off that back porch."

"I intend to. My house is old, you know. Creaky like me."

"Irma, stop fishing," Briana said, mock seriously. "You know you don't get older, just better."

Irma reached over to touch her arm. "You're so good for my ego."

"Well, it's true." She glanced at Slade. "Shall we tell Irma about our latest crisis over here?" It was a slim hope, but maybe the woman who knew everyone on the island would recognize the owner of the raspy voice.

"Not another break-in?" Irma had heard about that all around town. Such incidents were rare on the island.

"Worse." Briefly, Briana told her, then went to the answering machine and hit the PLAY button. She found herself gritting her teeth as the message replayed and was glad when it ended. "You wouldn't know him, would you?"

Irma shook her head. "I only wish I did. It's obvious he's good at disguising his voice, the bastard. What on earth does he want, calling you like that? And that business with Bobby's shoe! That's a sick mind. Did you call the sheriff?"

"Oh, yeah." Finished, Slade sat back. "He'll never find the guy with the little he has to go on right now."

"You need to come stay with me, honey," Irma said, making up her mind just that quickly. "I've got a shotgun that belonged to my second husband. It hasn't been fired in a while, but I believe it'll still work. And I still remember how to shoot."

Briana struggled with a smile. "That's sweet of you, but I'm not letting some coward hiding behind a disguised voice and no return address on a package scare me out of my home. I'm not denying that he scares me. But I'm staying put."

Slade drained his coffee and set down the cup. "There's something here that bothers me, Brie. Never mind how he got in, the man got a hold of Bobby's shoe. What I wonder is how he knew that cutting up that particular shoe would bother you the most. In order to know that, he has to know you, know about your son dying, and therefore know how to strike a chord in you."

She sat back, a little stunned. "I never thought of that, but you're right."

"I would imagine," Irma said, joining in, "that nearly

every permanent resident of this island knows about your loss, Briana. That doesn't exactly narrow down the field."

"No, but I think it eliminates the possibility of this being random, as I'd originally hoped," Slade said, thinking out loud. "The calls, maybe, but not the shoe incident."

"Perhaps they're not even connected," Brie said, rising to clear the table and top off their coffee.

Slade noticed that although he and Irma had clean plates, Brie had scarcely finished half a sandwich. All this was getting to her far more than she let on. "I know you don't want to leave this house, so you should stay. But until this is over, I'm staying with you. He's not going to creep in here again without running into a great big surprise or two."

Irma looked at her young friend with troubled eyes. "I think that's wise, Briana. If, God forbid, this man is watching you, stalking you, he'll not make a move with Slade by your side. Not if he has a few working brain cells left."

"Hey, guys, you're preaching to the converted. I have no intention of being stupid about this, nor in minimizing the danger. But I just don't want him to win. He's *not* driving me away."

A gusty wind rattled the back kitchen window, drawing their attention. Briana saw that it looked as if rain might fall any minute. "Look, let's leave these dishes and get moving. We need to board up the windows before things get really bad out there."

"You're right." Irma rose, cautiously stepping down on her foot. "I'll drive home and be ready to help when you get around to my place."

Slade shook his head. "Irma, this is a two-person operation. I hold the sheets in place and Brie hammers home the nails. You've got a bum leg. Tromping around on the uneven ground out there is no place for you right now."

Noticing that Irma was feeling a bit left out, Brie slipped her arm around the older woman's waist. "You get to stay in and make us one of your wonderful soup recipes for afterward, okay? We'll probably be chilled all the way through, especially if it rains. And you've seen how Slade loves to eat."

"Sounds good to me," Slade added.

Hobbling to the door, Irma finally agreed. "All right, if you're sure."

"Absolutely." Brie saw her into the car, then hurried to the garage where Slade was already hauling out the first sheet.

"We'll start with your house because mine will be easy. Mostly just locking down shutters."

Briana grabbed the hammer and nails. "I'm right behind you."

It was seven before they finished Irma's house and after eight when they swallowed their last spoonful of mushroom and barley soup in Irma's cozy kitchen. The radio kept them updated as the weather bureau tracked Donald, and the news so far was good. The hurricane had detoured slightly, veering into Cape Hatteras, delaying its northerly ascent along the Atlantic coast. Speculation ran high that Donald seemed whimsical enough to jump off course and stray far east into the Bermuda Islands.

Sporadic rain buffeted buildings and drenched the shoreline while screaming winds bent younger trees nearly in half. Then the downpour would turn misty and the air almost breezy, giving people a false sense of security before it all began again.

But the actual hurricane hadn't arrived yet and predictions had it showing up in a wide time range anywhere from midnight to the following midafternoon. Nerves were stretched taut with anticipation as Nantucket waited.

Standing in the doorway of her grandfather's porch, which was the only place she and Slade could look out with all the windows boarded up, Briana watched the sea behaving as she'd never seen before. She had taken a shower and put on a sweatshirt and jeans and an all-weather jacket. Wrapped in Slade's arms, she felt safe yet awestruck at the powerful electrical light show.

"It's unbelievable. Something you have to see for yourself."

Slade watched the wind-driven water lift the ocean waves to what looked to be easily ten to twelve feet high, then saw them surge onto the sloping shoreline before sucking sand in huge gulps on their return journey. Their houses were off the beach, up a grassy incline and on the other side of the coastal road. Still, he wondered if the sea might reach their yards and even farther.

"I've never watched anything like this," he confessed. "It's frightening, but it's also fascinating."

Above the roar of the wind, Briana could hear a distant loudspeaker, but couldn't make out the words. "That's probably the sheriff's deputies telling everyone to keep off the streets. I only hope that any tourists still here listen to the warnings and stay inside. People have a tendency to want to watch the show, not realizing the danger they're in. I've heard that those waves can get as high as twenty-five feet and actually hurl inland as far as Main Street, dragging all kinds of sludge and mud with it."

"You saw that happen?"

"No, I didn't, but Gramp told me he was here during the

big one. The next morning, when they finally were able to go out, they saw bridges dangling, cut in half, roads all blocked from uprooted trees, buildings picked up and dropped back down, lying in a heap like so many broken matchsticks. It sounded awful."

"Lots of people died, I imagine." He'd seen heavy rains and mud slides in California, but never watched anything like this.

"Yes, and many more were injured. Oh!" She watched a tree just down the street snap in half from the force of the wind, the broken section whirled along down the beach. "See that? Can you imagine what chance a person has out there if a tree can't withstand that wind?" She shook back her hair but the wild gusts continued to whip the strands about her face.

The sky was an eerie yellow, making the lightning bolts appear vividly orange. The rising wind was slapping moisture against the house now, whether rain or from the sea, Slade couldn't be certain. "We'd better go inside. I don't know how solid this porch is." Taking her hand, he led the way to the door, surprised at how difficult it was to cover the ten feet of space against a wind so strong it felt as if a large restraining hand was holding them back.

Safely inside, he put his back into it and shoved the door closed. "You know, if I hadn't seen this with my own eyes, I couldn't have imagined it." The keening sound of the wind whirling torrents of water up and around outside made his skin crawl. "The noise. I wonder how long that keeps up."

Brie shook the dampness from her hair, then shrugged off her jacket. "Until it's over and the hurricane blows out to sea and goes on to plague some other city. Although there's a lull that happens when you're right in the eye of the storm, or so I've read. It gets real still and very quiet, but it doesn't last long. Then it picks up and blows even harder."

The rain continued to pound and the wind to scream. The electricity had cut off hours ago. One of two oil lanterns Slade had lighted cast a red glow around the kitchen. The other was in the bathroom, otherwise the rooms were eerily dark. Briana had set out several candles and two big flashlights in case they needed them.

She paced to the front even though she couldn't see out the window. A sudden sound to her right had her jumping. "What was that?"

Slade joined her, cocking his ear, trying to hear above the storm. "Sounded like glass breaking. Maybe one of the shutters on my place blew loose." He knew it would be disastrous to go out now and try to secure it. Instead, he reached for Briana, thinking that if he didn't look worried, she'd follow suit. "No big deal. I'll clean it up later."

Thank goodness he didn't want to rush outside as she'd feared he might, Briana thought, placing her head against his chest, soothed by the steady beating of his heart. "I wish we'd insisted on bringing Irma back here, especially with that sprained ankle. What if she stumbles in the dark over there?"

"We lit two lanterns for her, remember? And she has that big flashlight if she needs to walk to other rooms. She'll be all right. That woman's survived worse than this." He stroked her hair gently. "And we'll be all right, too."

Briana let him hold her for a while, then became as restless as the storm outside. Returning to the kitchen, she flipped on Gramp's battery-operated shortwave radio.

" . . . winds tracked at 123 miles per hour . . . traffic lights dancing on their overhead wires, two falling to . . .

huge tree limb zinging through the air like a child's toy . . .
garbage can hurtling past our second-story window as I
stand looking out our small peephole . . . four of our windows have popped despite being boarded up . . . glass
spraying everywhere like shrapnel . . . advise everyone
who can hear me to open your inside doors slightly to re-
lieve the pressure . . . oh, no! The roof across the street
lifted right off and . . . brick wall two doors down caved in
. . . giant live oak over a hundred years old now blocking
Main Street . . . Hurricane Donald's a big one, folks." The
interruptive static took over completely.

Swallowing hard, Briana turned down the volume. Her
hand to her mouth, she closed her eyes, praying they'd
make it through this. All of them. Property could be repaired, replaced. But lives couldn't. She knew firsthand
how quickly a life could be snuffed out, a loved one forever silenced.

Slade did as the reporter had directed, propping their inside doors slightly ajar. He could hear the wind spiraling
upward and sideways, the sound like a banshee wail.
Thunder seemed to rattle the very foundation of Gramp's
house, one that had been standing firm for decades. He
hoped it would hold for decades more.

Returning to Briana, he stroked her back, trying to ab-
sorb her fears, to ease her mind, though he knew that was
a tall order this time. He knew she wasn't materialistic
enough to be concerned about losing the house because of
its value, but rather because of its sentimental connection.
He also knew she was worried about the people on Nantucket, the ones she'd known since childhood. "It's going
to be all right, Brie. We have to think positive here."

She didn't answer, just held on to him more tightly.

In his own way, he was worried, too. Whatever time the

storm moved on, he knew that would be when the real work would begin. Fires were the biggest danger when gas lines were broken and electrical connections severed. If the radio announcer was to be believed, whole buildings were falling. People would be frantic once the wind and rain died down, looking for loved ones.

It would likely still be dark, and rescue trucks from the fire department and police wouldn't be able to get through on the flooded streets. Would the water be safe to drink, the food spoiled after hours without electricity for refrigeration? Would the hospitals be able to accommodate the injured, the dying? Were there enough medical people available on this small island to take care of a disaster of this magnitude?

He didn't have answers, just questions.

The sudden silence was ominous and suspicious. Slade got up from the floor where they'd been huddled together in the corner of the living room, and walked to the door. Listening, he could hear very little. Was this the respite, the calm during the eye of the storm? Cautiously, he cracked open the door leading to the porch.

Briana leaped up and rushed to his side. "Do you think you should?" she asked, a nervous hitch to her voice.

Not answering, he grabbed his jacket and opened the door wider, then all the way, walking onto the porch. It was still raining, but the wind was almost a gentle, shifting breeze. Lightning streaked down the wall of the night sky, illuminating briefly a tumultuous sea, but not a threatening one right now.

"I'm going to go fix that shutter," he said, pulling open the porch door.

She grabbed his hand, suddenly afraid again. "Let it go,

Slade. The damage is already done. This could all start up again any minute."

"I read once that this calm lasts about ten minutes, sometimes a little longer. I'll be back long before then." He squeezed her hand. "If I'm not, go back inside and shut the door." He hurried down the stairs before she could stop him.

It was the side shutter over the small, high window into the hall bath, Slade discovered. He didn't have time to get hammer, nails, and a ladder from the garage right now. He decided that of all windows, that one broken would do the least damage. Quickly, he ran around the perimeter of Jeremy's house, checking for other problems, but found none.

Ignoring the light rain, he did the same for Gramp's house, but found that the plywood had held far better than he'd expected. The storage shed in the backyard lay on its side, some of the contents spilling out and jamming the doorway, but he passed on by, unwilling to waste time on a minor problem right now.

As he rounded the front again, he felt the wind pick up slightly. His head down against the rushing air, he hurried down the street. Irma lived a block away, which should only take him minutes to cover. He wanted to be able to tell Briana that her elderly friend was all right.

Two doors from her corner house, he saw that Irma's picket fence was gone, nowhere in sight. Odd, because the one in front of Briana's place was intact. Donald was fickle, it would seem. Blinking against the rain beginning to pound at him with its needlelike spray, he saw that her roof was undamaged, the porch he'd reinforced still standing.

As he turned to inspect her backyard, a fierce gust of

wind shoved him against the neighbor's privet hedge with the force of a battering ram. Slightly dizzy, Slade got to his feet and knew he had only a few minutes to get back to Briana.

Briana. She was what he was rushing back to, her warm hands, her loving arms, her giving heart. Out here, fighting the elements as he'd never seen them, Slade came face-to-face with a truth he'd been unwilling to admit. He needed her.

It was as simple as that, and as complex.

That need wouldn't be enough to keep her, but he knew without a shadow of a doubt that he needed her and always would. It wasn't Jeremy's house, now his, that pile of mortar and stone and wood, that he was worried about. It wasn't even his own safety that concerned him. It was Briana. He had to get back and get there safely, for Briana.

He'd avoided even thinking the "L word" for so long that even now, it gave him pause. Loving someone made you so damn vulnerable and open to the pain of losing them. Hadn't he learned that the hard way—Jeremy, his mother, Megan, even Rachel? Yet Briana had made him realize that *not* loving might have a higher price tag.

Starting along the path homeward, he glanced down the beach and thought he saw a man struggling to stay upright, much as he was. Stopping, he peered into the sporadic darkness and saw someone who wasn't dressed for the weather any more than he was. Slade didn't recognize the guy, whose head was bent low, so he hurried to retrace his footsteps. Whoever he was, Slade hoped he'd find his way.

Briana was at the door, reaching to yank him inside, her heart slamming against her ribs. "Damn you, why'd you have to go out there and scare me half to death?" She was pulling him to her, yet pummeling his back with tightly curled fists. "I saw you walk around the house, then a few minutes later, you started down the street. I leaned out and called to you, but you kept on going."

"I went to check on Irma and . . ."

But Briana wasn't listening. Another good whack, followed by a third and fourth. "How could you go, knowing I was here worried and frightened and . . ."

On the porch, with the wind howling and the rain whipping in through the open door, he kissed her. It was the only way he could think to stop her frightened babbling. He knew that nerves were fueling her feverish punishment, that worry had pushed her to the edge.

Breathing in, choking back a sob, Brie kissed him back, her mouth bruising his, taking over. She'd thought she'd lost him, thought he'd simply walked out of sight, been swallowed up by the storm. He'd been gone so long and she'd been scared out of her mind. Her hands moved up into his hair, gripping, kneading. She couldn't lose him to a stupid storm, not when she'd just found him.

Needing a breath, feeling the wind whipping into them at his back, Slade broke the kiss and guided them quickly into the house before closing the door and shoving the dead bolt in place. "Now then, where were we?" he asked, removing his wet jacket and looking at her in the flickering light of the oil lantern.

But Briana's nerves were far from settled. She thumped him with an openhanded slap that landed on his chest, then turned and moved down the hallway, swiping at her tear-streaked face as she walked. Damn, but he'd had her crying, nearly sobbing, then he'd sashayed back in like he'd been to the corner store for a pack of cigarettes on a sunny day. "You did that on purpose, staying away so long just so I'd miss you."

Brushing back his wet hair, Slade found himself smiling despite the absurd situation. Or maybe because of it. "That doesn't make sense. Why would I want you to worry or to miss me?" He caught the towel she threw at him, but just barely.

Taking a moment, he rubbed his hair with the towel, studying her in the glow of the second lantern sitting on the bathroom counter by the sink. She was working up a full head of steam. "Tell me why I'd want to do that."

"Because you're perverse, because you like getting me worked up, because you don't give a damn about my feelings." She sniffled, reached for a tissue from the box on the counter, and patted her face dry.

"That's crazy." Slade draped the damp towel around his shoulders, watching her. "You know I'm not like that." God, but she was even beautiful when she was angry, when she was crying.

"Maybe I don't know you. Maybe I don't know anything, not anymore." She crossed her arms over her chest defensively, then glanced up at the bathroom window as something heavy crashed against it, the next moment drifting away. "I thought I was getting a handle on things, that maybe with a little more time I could put that terrible day behind me and start over. But then you came along and screwed around with my head and my feelings, and now I'm a mess all over again."

If she didn't look so serious, he might have smiled. "And just how did I do all that?"

She was too exhausted from worrying, from trying to cope, to lie or to turn away. Damn him again for being so calm, like the eye of the storm, always in control. Which she decidedly was not. Her eyes downcast, studying the floor, she spoke quietly. "By making me fall in love with you."

Slade let out a whoosh of air and looked at her a long moment. "No, I've made you *think* you're in love with me. Big difference." Nerves skittering, he tried to keep his mind thinking clearly when inside, his heart urged him to pull her close and never let her go, to believe exactly what she said. "Brie, we don't have a chance."

"That's about what I expected you to say. Ever the optimist." Her anger surfacing again, she looked up at him, her eyes growing bright. "You don't know the first damn thing about loving someone. Did you think I *chose* this situation? Did you think I *wanted* to fall in love with a man who's pessimistic enough not to even believe in love? Do you see me as totally masochistic?"

"No, I . . ."

"Well, there you are. I didn't want to care about you. I stayed clear of you, let you be. *You* came after *me*."

"Yes, and I shouldn't have." He moved closer, took hold of her arms, blotting out the sound of gale winds rattling through the rafters and rain clawing against the boards covering the windows like the talons of some prehistoric bird trying to break through. Like he was trying to break through to Briana. "You and I are from different worlds. You're from a well-to-do family where everyone loves each other and . . ."

"That's not so. My father's been cheating on my mother for years. She finally admitted it this last time I was home. So much for Ozzie and Harriet."

He wasn't about to be put off by a minor correction. "That aside, they loved you, they stayed together, they raised you in luxury, and they still care. That's totally opposite from my early life."

"What does that have to do with the price of eggs?"

"Opposites may attract, Brie, but they soon revert to their roots and get tired of living with someone who can't keep up."

"Keep up how? I'm the one who quit college and you finished, even though it took you a while. Travel? You've been places I've only read about. Money? I'd wager you have more than I do by far. Socially? Okay, maybe you've got me there, but I was never a part of the country club set that my parents are so fond of. Nor do I wish to be."

She was doing one hell of a convincing job. He fervently wished he could believe her. "You'll leave, Briana. We both know you'll walk away one day, go back to Boston where you're comfortable."

Brie struggled to hang on to her patience, which was rapidly slipping way along with her foolish courage. "I don't know what more I can say after I've said it repeatedly. I'm not like the others. I won't leave you."

"You'll leave Nantucket. There isn't enough to hold you here. It's not as sophisticated and polished and intellectually challenging as Boston or Manhattan or . . ."

"Bullshit!" She whirled about, thrusting trembling hands in her hair, angry with herself now. "Why am I trying so damn hard to convince you? Let's face it, pal. You're afraid. Afraid to just let go of the past and take a chance on loving me back. Loving is damn risky. I know. I took the plunge once and freely admit it didn't work out. But I'm knee-deep again and *I'm* not a coward. I won't bolt. *You're* the one who's ready to run for cover."

One word had his back straightening. "I'm not a coward," he said emphatically.

"Aren't you?" she challenged. "All right, let's find out. I want you to answer one question for me, just one. All other things aside, my past, your past, my problems, your problems. Just one question: Do you care about me?" She'd gone so far, risked so much, yet hadn't been able to make herself ask if he *loved* her. She knew it'd be easier for him to admit he cared than to say those three fearful words.

Glaring down at her, Slade pressed his lips tightly together. She just couldn't leave it alone, could she? "Yes."

The small ray of hope that had been fluttering around inside her spread just a little. "Say it."

His hands moved to curl around her arms, his fingers tightening. "I care about you, Briana, but it doesn't make any difference."

Brie let out a rush of air. Albeit reluctantly, he'd admitted he cared for her. It wasn't exactly what she'd wanted to hear, but it was definitely a step in the right direction. She rose on tiptoes, her mouth a scant inch from his, her eyes filling. "It makes all the difference in the world."

"I don't know . . ."

She grabbed his hand just as a thunderclap reverberated throughout the house. Pulling him to the bedroom floor, she settled her arms around him. "Make love to me, Slade. Let's make the world go away, for just a little while. Don't think about anything else. Just love me."

He was pretty sure he already did, Slade thought, just before his mouth found hers.

Chapter Fifteen

Distant sirens woke Slade. His eyes popped open and it took him a moment to orient himself. He wondered how long he'd been asleep. A glance at his watch in the wavering light of the oil lamp told him that he and Briana had been lying in each other's arms on the bedroom carpeting for about six hours.

He sat up slowly, feeling a little stiff from the awkward position, and noticed that Briana must have gotten up at some point and found a quilt to cover them. He pushed it aside and got to his feet, the movement awakening Brie with a start.

"What time is it?" she asked, shoving back her tangled hair.

"Five-thirty," Slade answered, bending to pick up the clothes he'd removed so hastily last night. He reached over and flicked the light switch but nothing happened. "Still no power."

"It's so quiet," Briana said, uncertain whether to trust

her ears. "I can't even hear rain. Do you suppose it's over?"

Slade had been wondering the same thing. Pulling up his briefs, he said, "I guess there's no predicting how long these things last." As he climbed into his jeans, he watched her yawn and stretch, then reach to yank up the quilt that had slipped down to reveal her bare breasts. Desire engulfed him just that quickly. He fell to his knees beside her. "Pretty funny, your modesty after last night."

Briana felt a smile form. Her hand moved to where the snap of his jeans lay open, and she trailed a finger along the edge. "I've always thought a man in unbuttoned jeans was one of the sexiest sights ever."

"Is that a fact? I guess we can wait another little while before going to check on the storm." He settled down alongside her, his hand snaking under the quilt to find the breast she'd hidden from his sight.

But a pounding noise that seemed to be coming from the area of the back door had him changing his mind. Hopping up, he grabbed his shirt. "I'll see who that is."

Brie rose, feeling achy in more than one place, thinking it was probably a good thing the interruption had come along. She was stiff as an old woman from a night spent on the floor. Nevertheless, it had been a memorable night.

By the time she'd gone into the bathroom and put on some clean clothes, Slade was back, slipping on his shoes. "That was Chris Reed from in back."

"Pam's all right, isn't she?" Brie asked, tying back her hair. "I've heard that storms can cause a woman who's near her due date to deliver early."

"Chris says she's fine and so's Annie. Their house escaped damage, but one garage wall caved in. He came over to check on you and found me. He seemed a little shocked to see me." He glanced over his shoulder at her. "Does that bother you?"

"Why should it? You mean because you were obviously just getting dressed? I don't think our being together is anyone else's business. Besides, Chris is a nice guy. Why, did he say something?"

"No, he just looked kind of surprised. He said he's going to walk around, see if anyone needs help. I told him to wait for us." He picked up his jacket on the way through the living room and saw that it had pretty well dried out, so he put it on.

"Hi, Chris," Briana called through the back door as she grabbed her jacket. "Looks like we can't make coffee without electricity, just when we could really use some caffeine."

"I had a Coke before I left. Want me to go get you two some?" His red hair stuck up in tufts as if he'd slept on it funny or had spent a rough night finger combing it.

Slade came out holding two flashlights and held the screen door while Brie locked up. "Nah, we'll catch something later."

He led the way around front, gazing at a gray sky streaked with pale yellow clouds. The ocean waves were thundering in to shore as always, only slightly more foamy than usual. Seaweed was clumped along the edges of the sand like ragged fringe on the hem of a dress. Bobbing around out aways were pieces of debris, what looked like a wood garage door, some kind of child's toy that gleamed bright red, and a sailboat that had capsized. Seagulls dipped and rose, searching for breakfast as if it were a normal day. "Almost like it never happened," he commented.

Stunned at the comparison of last night to this morning, Brie gazed around. "It's barely chilly and there's hardly a breeze, much less a wind. Amazing. Oh, I should've tried the radio."

"I had the shortwave on," Chris said as they began walking. "Lots of damage downtown, mostly to storefront windows. A few rooftops and one or two old buildings collapsed. Over by the airport, a small private plane got picked up by the wind and flipped right on top of a hangar."

Slade glanced over the rooftops toward the direction of new sirens. "Listen to that. I wonder how many fires are still burning."

"Quite a few," Chris answered, "according to the news report. The problem is that many of the streets are water damaged and impassable so emergency vehicles can't get through."

"Hey, look over there!" Briana saw a group of people gathered around the side yard of Irma's house. "Oh, no. I hope Irma's all right." She broke into a run.

Right behind her, Slade and Chris followed. Slade reached the back area first, circling the small crowd and pushing through. His face grim, he peered at the broken boards and siding that had once been Irma's back porch, now neatly severed from the rest of the house as if sliced by a very large, very sharp knife. But that wasn't the worst of it.

"Oh, my God," Briana said, her hand going to her mouth. The side wall of Irma's house had collapsed in on itself, causing a gaping hole in the floor of the kitchen. The opposite wall was still standing, but it was engulfed by flames and curling black smoke. Broken bricks from her corner fireplace were scattered everywhere, interspersed with the jagged edges of the ruined plank flooring. The tiny basement beneath could be seen through a cavernous opening, as well as severed pipes leaking water. "Tell me Irma's not in there."

" 'Fraid she is, Briana," a thready voice said at her elbow. Jake McGrath, his bony face a maze of worry lines, leaned on a bent stick as he stared into the fiery rubble that was Irma's place.

"What happened?" Chris asked.

"There was a funnel cloud that came along with the hurricane," a tall stranger with a bushy mustache explained. "Happens sometimes. The thing swept along here, looks like, hitting things randomly. Chopped off this porch and when that happened, it broke the foundation of the house at the rear. See up there," he added, pointing to the next block. "It must've whirled through the yard between those two houses, knocking bricks and roofing every which way. Then it went on down toward the sea, apparently, 'cause the ground looks kinda scorched across the way."

"Where is Irma?" Briana wanted to know.

"Inside, trapped on the floor of the kitchen over that way," Jake answered, pointing. "We had a firefighter here couple of minutes ago. He tried going in after her, didn't get far before another section of the floor fell down to the cellar. He crawled back out and said he was going for more help, but with things the way they are, he didn't know when he'd be back."

"Irma," Slade called out, "can you hear me?" Listening hard, he stepped closer to the wreckage of the porch, peering over as he shone his flashlight in an arc around the kitchen area.

"I just don't know . . ." a woman in a raincoat began.

"Shush, will you?" Jake told her. "Let the man hear."

"Irma?" Slade called again. "It's Slade. If you can hear me, call out so I know where you are."

They waited for what seemed a long while before at last a weak voice could be heard. "Over here."

Slade swung the light in what he thought was the right direction, but didn't see her. "Again. Yell out again."

"Over here, Slade."

Finally, the light found her, but Slade didn't feel much better. She was trapped, all right, lying in an awkward position on her side in the far corner near where the kitchen sink had once stood. Several thick boards had her pinned in and it looked as if one had her legs caged. "I see you. Are you hurt?"

"My one foot, a little," came the shaky reply.

"Irma," Briana called from alongside Slade. "Hang on. Help's on the way."

Yeah, but when would it arrive? Slade wondered. Something caught his eye and he flashed the beam over to it. "Damn," he muttered.

"What is it?" Briana wanted to know.

"See where those flames are trailing slowly along? They're heading in the direction of that gas line. There has to be a break somewhere."

"Yup, that's what it is," Jake chimed in. "Firefighter fella said his guys have been trying to get to the main gas line to shut it off, but hadn't managed to yet. That's another reason he came back outta Irma's place. Said if those floorboards gave way, that gas line could blow the place sky high."

"So how does he plan to get Irma out of there?" Chris asked.

Jake rubbed a trembling hand over his unshaven chin. "He didn't say."

Because he couldn't say, Slade thought. Getting Irma out would take a miracle, what with the precarious way the back section of her house was now situated and the additional threat of a fire explosion.

He'd no sooner completed the thought than they heard the unmistakable sound of a blast coming from the street over. Flames shot into the sky, followed by billowing smoke. Grinding his teeth, Slade knew they were looking at the forerunner of what Irma's place could be in short order. Those patient flames were inching along steadily.

"Someone's got to do something," Briana murmured. "We can't just let her die in there." She grabbed hold of the dangling end of the broken porch, testing its strength. "Why don't I crawl in there? I'm lighter than that fireman who was here, I'll bet, and . . ."

"No!" Slade's voice was low but firm. Hadn't he known the moment he stepped over here that it would come to this? To wait for the firefighter to come back was to waste valuable time. He would have to go, yet could he do it?

He felt sweat drip down his back despite the chill morning air. What if he failed, what if he set off the explosion and sealed Irma's fate by taking things in his own hands, by not waiting for the proper authorities? What if Briana and this whole town blamed him for yet another death? He wasn't afraid for himself, but rather afraid of mishandling the rescue. Was his judgment any better now than a few months ago?

Maybe not. But looking into Briana's tortured eyes, he had to try. He couldn't live with himself if he didn't. "I'll go," he told her.

If anyone could do it, that man would be Slade, Briana knew. She wanted him to try, but what if she lost the both of them? Yet there was something in his eyes, something that told her there was more involved here than the rescue of one woman. It was a test he needed to take, for himself.

Reaching up, she touched his cheek and felt her heart lurch when he turned his face into her palm and placed a kiss there. No words were said. None were needed.

Chris Reed wanted in on the action. "I'll go with you."

"Can't risk the weight of two men, and I've done this sort of thing before. You can help by getting as close as you can and shining the light exactly where I tell you." Slade would need his hands free to climb over the rubble, and the flashlight was big and awkward. What he wouldn't give for his gloves, an ax, his mask.

"Right, just tell me where." Chris took the flashlight Slade handed him.

The fire crackled and climbed the far wall, the smoke thick with bits of charred debris flying about. With careful, measured steps, Slade climbed over the wreckage of the porch and stepped gingerly onto the rim of the kitchen flooring. The gaping hole was just to his left. He'd have to circle it and cross over the exposed gas line. Fire sputtered from the area of the uprooted stove. He gave it a quick glance only. "Over here, Chris."

The wide beam of light showed the hole into the basement more clearly. Slade began inching around it. "Hold tight, Irma. I'm coming."

"No, Slade. I'm an old woman. If I die here in my home, it won't be so terrible. Don't risk your life for me." It was a long speech for someone hurt and frightened.

"Save your strength." Testing each board as he stepped ever so carefully, he moved slowly, coughing as the smoke swirled around his head. He crouched, ducking lower as heat shimmered in great waves. One step, then another. Then .... his foot skidded on a slippery section where water had seeped. Sliding to the edge of the hole, he managed to hold on, to catch himself before going over, but just barely. The creak and moan of the old house told him he didn't have much time, as the weight shifting was loosening things even more.

Despite his best efforts, his memory took him back to another fire, inching along that smoldering floor, trying to find a little girl. There'd been smoke then, too, and a sizzling, scorching heat. And fear. Just like now.

What if he failed again?

"Slade, are you all right?" Irma asked, barely able to see through the smoke and without the glasses she'd lost in the fall. Not only that, but her wig was turned around and hanging crookedly, her best black one. She knew crying wouldn't help, but she felt like it anyhow.

Regaining his footing, Slade continued on his path, climbing over a broken maple chair. "I need some light over here, Chris." The beam raced along the floor and finally he could make out Irma's form. "There you are."

"A sight for sore eyes, right?"

"You fishing, Irma?" he asked, grabbing hold of the section of fallen beam that had one of her legs trapped. Damn if it wasn't wedged in there good. Kneeling so he could put his upper body weight into hefting the beam, he got a good grip. "When I give you the word, you see if you can move your leg out, okay?"

"Okay."

It took three tries, but Slade raised the beam perhaps half an inch. "Now!" Irma's leg moved, but not enough. Grimacing, Slade held on, knowing if he dropped it back, he could sever her foot or break her ankle. "Okay, once more," he said, grunting with the effort, and lifted it higher. Nervous sweat trickled into his eyes, but he saw her leg pull completely free. Muscles straining, he lowered the beam slowly, trying not to cause the floor to shift.

It shifted anyhow, sending chunks of debris hurtling into the cellar while bits of the ceiling rained down on them. Placing his hand on Irma's ankle reassuringly, Slade held perfectly still till everything was once more quiet, then he cautiously inched closer. "Okay, what hurts, anything?"

"My ankle like the fires of hell and maybe my pride," she confessed. "Can't believe I let myself get in this mess."

"Hurricanes aren't anyone's fault, Irma," Slade commented drily. This was no time to debate. Still on his knees, he glanced over his shoulder. The wall fire was gaining ground. When the structure was weak enough, the remaining wall would fall right on them. He prayed they had enough time to make it out before that happened.

Slade brushed at the sweat pouring into his eyes with the back of a sooty hand. There was no way he would be able to pick her up and carry her out the way he'd come in, knowing the precarious floor wouldn't hold their combined weight. A long rectangular window was just to the left. It would be tricky, getting her to it over the fire line that was lazily hissing and sputtering. But there was no other way.

"Chris, can you find something to knock out that window with? I'm going to have to hand her through to you. Can't risk backing up with the two of us. Floor's gonna give any minute."

"Right." Glad to be able to do something more constructive than holding a flashlight, the young man carefully made his way over and, using the solid end of the heavy flashlight, began smashing the glass out. He did a thorough job, scraping off the jagged edges. Then he turned the flashlight beam back to where Slade knelt alongside Irma, who was now sitting upright. "All set."

"Do you think you can stand, Irma?" Slade asked.

"I will, or die trying." Holding on to him, she slowly pulled herself up.

But as she did, the boards under their feet shifted, a large section breaking off. Irma cried out, fear causing her heart to pound.

"Hold on to me!" Slade yelled. Oh, God, he couldn't lose her now, not when they were so close. Had he misjudged yet again?

A shower of ceiling rubble fell onto both of them, battering them with chunks of tile, covering them with gray dust. Irma almost stumbled to her knees, but the iron grip of Slade's hands held her, kept her with him. "Don't move," he told her.

The waiting was wearing, but he didn't budge, not until he felt sure the shifting had stopped. He could hear the hissing of the fire raging behind him, inching closer. Carefully looking down, he saw that they had no more than a foot and a half of board left to stand on. He couldn't waste another second. Over his shoulder, he saw that the other fire trail had snaked itself across the room and was now perilously close to the main gas line.

"Chris," Slade said, "I'm going to pick her up and hand her out. You ready?"

"Ready," Chris answered, propping the flashlight beam so it would provide some light. Overhead, the sky was beginning to clear, but inside Irma's house, it was dim and dank. He held out his arms, waiting.

Trying to be careful of her injured foot, Slade picked Irma up, realizing that although she was tall, she probably weighed no more than a hundred pounds, all skin and bone. Still, that weight added to his could send them plummeting to the basement, where chances were they'd never get out again.

Pulling his mind back to the job at hand, he silently thanked Irma for wearing slacks instead of one of her long, flowing skirts. Each step took forever as he tested the board for stability. At last at the window, he handed Irma into Chris's waiting arms. He caught a glimpse of Briana on the lawn, her face tight with tension.

The searing heat licked at his back. "Everyone get back!" he ordered.

As soon as Chris stepped from the window, Slade took a rolling dive through the jagged opening, landing on the grass. Hurriedly, he jumped to his feet, annoyed that too many people were still just standing around. "Everyone, let's move away from this house. It's going to blow sky-high any minute."

That got things moving. The bystanders began scattering, running, dashing away. With Irma in his arms, Chris hurried down the block just as an ambulance came careening around the corner. An eerie popping sound could be heard. Finally, only a few stragglers were left. Slade grabbed Briana's hand and ran with her.

"I knew you could do it," she told him, tears trailing down her cheeks. "Thank you."

They stopped some distance away, but Slade didn't respond. He felt numb, like a man sleepwalking.

Time, Briana thought, noting his sudden pallor beneath his dirt-streaked face that even the heat hadn't reddened. He needed time to assimilate and assess all that had happened this morning.

Halfway up the street, Chris was settling Irma into the ambulance. Briana rushed over, Slade at her side. Just then, they heard a low, rumbling sound followed by a fierce explosion that had fire spurting upward from the back of

Irma's house, followed by a huge billowing cloud of black smoke. Those nearby fell to the ground.

It was several long minutes before Slade dared to raise his head, his body still covering Briana's where he'd guided her beneath him, instinctively protecting her.

After several minutes, Slade rose, helping her up. He stood watching the greedy flames devour Irma's home, feeling dazed and infinitely sad.

Inside the ambulance on the gurney, Irma saw the remains of her roof crash into the interior. "Well," she said, "I'd been wanting to remodel anyway."

Briana climbed up to her and hugged the older woman. "I'm so sorry you lost so many of your lovely things."

"Pshaw! If there's one thing I've learned in my eighty-two years, it's that people are more important than possessions." She brushed away a tear. "I do wish I could have saved my photo albums."

"The insurance will help you rebuild your home. The important thing is that you're okay."

Irma gazed over at Slade and Chris standing near the ambulance doors. "Yes, thanks to these two young men." She felt her eyes fill. "How do I thank you for risking your lives to save an old woman?"

"By getting well." As the attendant settled a blanket over Irma, Slade glanced at her ankle, badly swollen and lacerated where the heavy board had trapped it. "You'll be up and dancing in no time."

"He's right, Irma," Chris chimed in. "First dance is mine."

"You've got a date," Irma told him, adjusting her wig somewhat clumsily. "Briana," she said, taking hold of her young friend's hand and pulling her closer, "I was wrong about Slade at first. But no more. He's quality goods, honey. Don't let him get away."

Brie looked over at Slade, who'd turned back to silently watch the flames reduce Irma's house to ashes. Was he remembering that other fire where Megan had died? Was he in shock? "Don't worry. I don't plan to." She kissed the wrinkled cheek. "I'll be by to see you at the hospital as soon as things settle down." She hopped out of the ambulance.

The attendant closed the double doors. "They're running out of beds at the hospital, but I hear medevac helicopters are on their way over from the mainland to give us a hand. The National Guard's coming too, to prevent looting. I don't know where your friend will wind up, but you can call once the phone lines are working again. They're setting up some kind of hot line."

"Thanks." Slade watched the ambulance drive off, feeling filthy, exhausted, drained. A hand on his shoulder had him turning to see Chris looking at him.

"You did one hell of a job in there," the redhead said quietly. He already admired the man for finding his daughter that evening. But what Slade had done just now had taken nerves of steel and courage not many men had. Chris had grown up on Nantucket, had known and cared about Irma Tatum all his life, yet he'd been afraid to go in. They'd gotten her out with mere seconds to spare before the house had blown.

"Couldn't have done it without you." Slade took the hand Chris offered and shook it.

"I'm going back home," Chris said. "I don't want to leave Pam and Annie alone too long. Looks like the emergency people are getting things under control. See you guys later." He started to leave, turned back to Slade. "Listen, you ever need anything, *anything*, you know where to find me." And he walked off.

Pulling in a deep breath, Slade looked out to sea. The sky was lightening, turning blue, and a weak sun was breaking through.

"Will you look at that?" Briana asked. "It's going to be a nice day after all." She looked up at Slade. "You're a hero, Slade. Irma wouldn't be alive if not for you."

Frowning, he shook his head. "I'm no hero." He'd saved one life, but cost a child hers. That hadn't changed, not really. He'd managed to carry Irma out this time, but did that mean he could trust his instincts the next time? How many times before he could feel secure and confident once again?

Brie took his hand into hers, saw he was cut and bleeding. "Let's go back to the house and I'll fix this for you."

Shaking his head, he pulled free. "I can do it." Looking down, he noticed that his shirt was torn and dirty. "I need to clean up." He started walking back toward their houses, his steps slow, lumbering.

Brie followed, frowning. "Slade, what's wrong?" He'd done a heroic deed, yet he seemed to be blaming himself for something. He was shutting her out. What was going on in his mind?

He held out a hand, as if to keep her at arm's length. "I need some time. I need to be alone for a while." He glanced at her, saw the pain and confusion in her eyes. He'd put it there and wasn't sure how to make it go away. "Come on, I'll walk you back."

Brie slowed, then stopped. "No, you go ahead." Shoving her hands into her pants pockets, she turned to gaze out to sea. "I'll be along."

Irritation flooded him, at her, at himself. "Look, I don't mean to hurt you. I just . . . I'm not an easy man, Briana."

That was an understatement, she thought, feeling her eyes fill, keeping her head averted.

"I warned you that you shouldn't get involved with me."

So the onus was on her. All right, she'd play along. "Yes, you did."

He gazed down at his sodden, ruined shoes, but saw only her sad brown eyes. "I don't know what I'm feeling right now. So many things. I need to sort things out."

"All right." After all the hours and days and weeks, he still wasn't certain about his feelings. After coming to grips with the truth about his father and his mother, after redeeming himself by rescuing Irma, she'd thought he'd be celebrating. Instead, he was pulling back inside that protective shell he'd arrived with.

There was nothing to do but let him go.

He didn't know what else to say, didn't know if he ever would. Despite everything that had happened, he was still the same man he'd been before, one filled with doubts. Things would never work between them because he wasn't like other men. If he couldn't trust himself, couldn't respect himself, how could he ask her to?

He would be doing her a favor to walk away now before things went any further.

"I . . . I'll call you later." Eyes downcast, he walked away.

Briana watched a brave new sun breaking through the wispy clouds. Gramp used to say that things always looked better in the morning. Not always, Gramp, Briana thought, blinking back the tears that wanted badly to fall.

I care about you, but it doesn't make any difference.

Maybe Slade was right and she'd only been indulging in a pipe dream.

Slade climbed onto his porch and went inside, wishing he could simply turn off his mind. He flipped the switch and saw that the electricity was back on. He walked through the downstairs, turning on lights as he went since the windows were still shuttered up, looking over everything. A stroke of luck that nothing here had been damaged except the upstairs bathroom window, while just a block away, Irma's house was in ruins. The gods, it seemed, had been with him. He hadn't lost his house, just the woman he cared for more than his next breath.

Oh, he could still have Briana, for he'd seen it in her eyes. But how long would her warm feelings last if the demons that lived inside him never went away? She deserved better. He cared too much for her to put her through that. He'd always been a loner and he would continue to be, foisting his dark moods on no one.

He badly needed a shower and some rest. His head hurt and the cuts on his hands were stinging. The external aches would heal long before his internal pain.

On his way upstairs, he paused in the dining room, noticing the mail he'd tossed there two days ago, before the storm had hit. He'd been on his way to Briana's and hadn't even glanced at it. He never got much of importance, anyway.

Casually, he fanned through the small pile until one envelope caught his attention. It was addressed to him in a tight, feminine handwriting. He flipped it over and saw that the sender was Edith Crane, Rachel's mother. Tapping the envelope against his palm, Slade debated whether or not to open it. There was no way it was good news.

For all he knew, Rachel could be suing him, perhaps on some wrongful death suit. Lawyers were always willing to take on such cases, especially if the accused involved had money to go after. He'd given Edith his address when he'd left, explaining that his father had died and he was going to Nantucket to check things out. He hadn't had contact with either of them since.

Why put it off? he decided, and ripped open the envelope as he walked into the kitchen. He sat down at the table. He was bone weary and thought he shouldn't learn bad news standing. Slumped in the chair, he began to read. By the third paragraph, he was sitting up, narrowing his eyes at the page. He finished the letter, then read it again, just to make sure he hadn't misinterpreted what Edith had written.

Could it really be true?

On the one hand, he was saddened by the news she'd sent him. On the other, he was most grateful she'd written, and suddenly elated by what Rachel's mother had revealed. Pulling in a calming breath, Slade put the letter back in the envelope.

This changed things considerably. His first thought was that he wanted to share the news with Briana right away. And he would, as soon as he cleaned up.

Was it possible that there might be a small measure of hope for them yet? His heart racing, Slade took the stairs two at a time as he hurried up to shower, unbuttoning his shirt as he went.

Maybe the gods would smile just one more time.

Chapter Sixteen

In her laundry room, Briana stripped down to skin and tossed everything she'd had on, including her canvas shoes, into the washer. The acrid smell of smoke lingered. Adding soap, she pushed the button and started the cycle.

How strange life was, she thought, wrapping a large towel around herself and walking to the kitchen. Something as devastating as a hurricane undoubtedly destroyed much property and even, she supposed, cost a few lives, though so far the shortwave hadn't detailed any actual casualties. Yet there were also isolated instances of heroism. And heroes who didn't wish to be recognized.

At the refrigerator, she took out the orange juice and poured herself a glass. Sipping, she wandered to the back door, peering out through its small, high window, the only one that hadn't been boarded up. The storage shed lay on its side, but other than that, the old house and grounds had sustained no damage. A good testament to how well built these homes were, and to the capricious fates that had spared this end of the block.

With her heart in her throat, she and several others had stood watching Slade slowly make his way to Irma. She'd been afraid for the old woman, but afraid for Slade, too. Yet she'd felt strongly that he could do it, even though first, he'd had to set aside his own fears.

And miraculously, he had. He'd also overcome the hesitancy of the area residents to accept him. After seeing Irma brought to safety, she was certain that the people who'd witnessed his selfless act had told half the town. Irma's savior was none other than the reticent newcomer, J.D. Slade.

Many were probably saying they'd known all along what a fine man he was. People enjoyed taking credit for spotting the good in others. Yet no one, including Slade himself, had truly believed like she had.

But what did all the faith matter if he didn't believe in himself?

He'd offered to help her with the house when she'd been less than pleasant to him. He'd rescued a small girl's kitten when the memory of another kitten rescue was part of his nightmares. He'd found Annie when she'd wandered away and handed her over to her grateful parents. He'd rebuilt a widow's porch, then saved her from a fiery death. And he'd healed her own tattered and torn heart. As Irma had said, Slade was quality goods. Why was he so reluctant to acknowledge that?

Time healed all things, another cliché she was beginning to doubt. After Slade thought things through, would he come around? There was a time she'd have quickly said yes, but after the way he'd looked, the way he'd walked off today, she was no longer certain of anything.

With a final glance out into the backyard, now bathed in sunshine, Briana drained her glass. And if he didn't come around, well, she would cope. Somehow, some way. She'd lived through worse. She had learned that a strong person could survive almost anything.

But, dear God, she didn't want to lose yet another person she loved. A lump clogging her throat, she went to shower.

The water wasn't exactly hot, since the power had been off for hours and along with it, the hot water heater. But it was warm and wet and cleansing. Stepping out, she wrapped a small towel around her wet hair and dried off with a big one, rubbing her skin until it was rosy. Slipping on a yellow T-shirt and clean jeans, she slid her feet into scruffy slippers. Fluffing out her hair so it would dry, she walked back to the kitchen. She'd put on some coffee because maybe Slade would change his mind and . . .

"Oh!" Startled, Brie paused in the kitchen doorway, hardly believing what she saw. Craig Walker, looking uncharacteristically dirty and disheveled, was standing just inside the door. "What are you doing here?"

"Brie, I've been wandering all over, looking for you." Looking exhausted, he pulled out a kitchen chair and dropped into it.

Confused and annoyed, she stayed in the archway. This was something she really didn't need right now. Craig's timing was rotten. "How'd you get in?"

"Your back door was unlocked." He rubbed a shaky hand across his face. He was unshaven and his eyes were bloodshot. "I don't suppose you have any coffee?"

The door had been left unlocked? How could she have been so careless? Her mind filling with questions, she answered, "I was just about to make some." She filled the pot with bottled water she kept in the fridge, just in case there was a problem with the island water, all the while keeping a wary eye on him. "I just talked with you, wasn't it yesterday?" She remembered the odd, conciliatory conversation they'd had where he'd apologized, sounding more humble than she'd thought him capable of.

"I told you then that we were having hurricane warnings." When had they closed the airport? she wondered. "Why would you come over, knowing that?"

"I just have to get this over with, to finish. I had to see you because . . . because time is running out. I only have until the first and . . ." Seeming to realize he was rambling on, he licked his lips nervously, glancing toward the back door. "I got caught in it, you know. I wanted to come see you, but I couldn't find a cab on account of the weather. So I started walking." He shook his head, his face bleak. "Damn rain. I got drenched, then you weren't home. The winds were so strong. I wound up going into this movie theater just to get out of the rain."

Eyebrows raised, she glanced at him. "A movie theater was open during the hurricane?"

"No, I broke in. I had to get out of the rain, don't you see? And it was too far to go walk back to the Nesbitt Inn where I'd checked in. No cabs running."

Briana remembered he'd stayed at the Nesbitt the last time he'd visited. If he'd gotten a room, it must mean he intended to stay awhile. She really didn't want to deal with him right now. But she plugged in the pot, then turned to face him, leaning against the counter. Keeping her distance. Something wasn't right here. Craig was acting very much out of character and she needed to find out why. "I don't understand what was so important that you couldn't wait until the weather improved. You didn't mention anything pressing on the phone."

But Craig seemed focused on something else. "I stopped to help this woman on the way over here. She was pregnant and she'd fallen. I tried to get her over to this clinic. She kept telling me she was going into labor. Jesus! I don't know anything about delivering babies."

He wasn't making sense. Usually he was so centered, so in control. Was he just overtired? Had the hurricane freaked him out? Perhaps if she played along, he'd finally get his story out. "What happened to her?"

"This cop came along and I handed her over. I didn't know what else to do. Then there was this old man. He was caught in this building and the roof had blown off. A wall had caved in and he was trapped under some furniture. You could hear him yelling out on the sidewalk." He shook his head, as if it were all too much for him.

"Did you help him?"

"Yeah, but it took hours. These two guys showed up— big, strong truck driver types—and the three of us shoved and pushed and pulled." He glanced down at his hands, dirty and scratched. "I didn't think we'd do it, but we finally got him out." His hazel eyes seemed to plead for understanding as they met hers. "I'm not a bad guy, Briana."

Puzzled now, she frowned. "I never said you were, Craig. You've already apologized and I told you we're still friends. There certainly was no need for you to come in person. I mean, what more can I say?"

He waved a hand, dismissing that. "No, this isn't about that. It's about . . . oh, shit! I never wanted things to get out of hand like this."

Thoroughly confused, Brie poured them each a mug of coffee, took his over to him. As she placed it on the table, she noticed that he smelled like whisky. "Craig, have you been drinking?" It was about nine in the morning. Had he needed some liquid courage after the incidents he'd described to her?

"This cafe on Main Street was passing out free drinks to rescuers, guys who were helping out, so I had a couple. To warm up, you know." He glanced down at his ruined Armani suit. "Damn, but it was cold in that rain. And the wind!" Shivering, he picked up the mug and sipped the coffee.

Brie went back to stand at the counter, keeping the island sink and counter between them. This whole conversation was making her uneasy. She supposed he couldn't be faulted for having a drink or two. Perhaps he'd even been in shock. By the look of him, he might still be. "Listen, I still seem to be missing something here. Just why is it you felt it necessary to come back over here?"

His hands folded around the mug, as if trying to get warm. "I stopped at the Island Camera Shop before coming here," he said, totally ignoring her question. "The owner was there, cleaning up the plate glass window that had blown in. He said you'd picked up the film a couple of days ago." He looked up frustrated, angry. "Just give it to me, all right, Brie? Forget what you saw and I'll go away and never bother you again."

Unease turned to apprehension as Briana noticed his sudden shift of mood from beseeching to demanding. "What film?"

"Don't play games with me!" Craig shouted, rising. He didn't go to her, but instead began pacing his side of the kitchen, his muddy shoes leaving a trail of footsteps on her new tile. "You have to know I never wanted it to come to this. If only you'd cooperated in the first place, everything would have worked out."

"Worked out how? I'm not playing games. I really don't know what you're after." Heart thudding, she watched his agitated pacing, wishing Slade hadn't picked today of all days to pull back from her. She'd give anything if he'd suddenly appear at the door, walk right in. She'd known Craig for years, yet his behavior was scaring her. And his raving about some film she was supposed to have was really off the wall.

Pausing at the table, he gulped down the rest of the coffee, hoping to steady his nerves. He had to make her see. This was his last hope. "There's not much time left," he said, rattling the loose change in his pants pockets. "There's so much at stake. There are others involved here, people who won't hesitate to kill me if I can't continue to produce. If I blow my cover. I can't risk being identified and exposed, not when I've come so far."

Blow his cover? Calm. She needed to stay calm, even though she was having trouble following his ramblings, trouble thinking clearly. He was acting so irrational, so crazy. She'd read where in the face of someone threatening, someone obviously disturbed, the thing to do was to appear calm. "I still don't know what you're talking about."

"The goddamn film! I know you have it, so just hand the pictures over."

She clutched her coffee cup in both hands. If he came at her, she would throw it at him, mug and all. The coffee was no longer hot enough to do any real damage, but it was her only defense. He was watching her closely now. Her knives, unfortunately, were on his side of the room. Why hadn't she left Grandma's big iron skillet out where she could easily grab it? Dear God, she prayed, don't let it come to that.

"I don't have any pictures you'd be interested in. The roll I picked up from Island Camera was taken months ago, snapshots of Bobby on . . . on his last day. And I . . ." The scene popped into her mind, snapping pictures of Bobby walking away, his hand in Robert's, the green balloon bobbing along. She'd continued taking pictures after they'd reached the other side of the street. Then the sounds, the car that had sped by.

Her eyes widened as a terrible thought slipped into her consciousness, but it was too awful to consider. No! It couldn't be, could it? "Is that the roll of film you want?"

"I can tell you haven't looked at them yet, right? Maybe there's nothing there, but I need to see for myself. I need to make sure." He took a step around the table, towards her.

"Make sure of what?" Brie asked, her voice steady as an icy calm settled on her. Surely what she was thinking wasn't so.

"That no one can ID me, damn it!" He'd been through so much, couldn't she see? He hated for her to hear the truth, hated for her to look at him with loathing the way she would. Maybe if he told her all of it, she'd understand. "The others who're involved, they're not patient men. I have to come through. It's the domino effect, don't you see? If they catch me, my arrest will lead the investigators to others. These are violent, dangerous men. I couldn't convince Robert of the danger. He just wouldn't listen. As soon as he found out, he confronted me, told me I had to confess, to make restitution or he'd expose me. I couldn't let that happen so . . ." He paused, as if searching for the right words.

As if in the middle of a bad dream, she stood perfectly still. "Go on."

Sweat poured down his face, but Craig ignored it. "I never intended to kill Robert. I . . . just wanted to scare him, you know. He stood there that day, arguing with me, telling me I had until Monday to make it right or he was going to Mr. Brighton. He was so damn *sanctimonious*, so judgmental. I told him, everyone skims a little here and there. You just have to be careful."

His voice cracked in his anxiety to explain himself. "But not Saint Robert. He wouldn't bend the rules a little, not even for his best friend. So I knew I'd have to do something, scare him so he wouldn't turn me in. The shot was meant as a warning, supposed to just graze him, but I was nervous. Driving fast, my fingers sweaty. My aim was off and the first shot hit the kid. Damn!"

The kid! The first shot hit the kid! Briana felt a choked sob burst from her.

Craig struggled with tears. "I wouldn't knowingly have hurt Bobby for the world, Brie. You know that. You have to believe me. It was an accident."

The horror of his words struck Briana like a fast, furious fist to the gut. "You killed my son. But why?"

"For the money, of course."

"You shot Bobby for a little money?" She wanted to understand, needed to.

"Not just a little money, Brie. Two million dollars. But that's not all. If I'm exposed, if my face or the license plate of my rental car is in any of your pictures and Glenn Halstead's men find out, I'm a dead man."

She felt as if she were climbing up through a thick, gray fog. "Glenn Halstead. The man Mr. Brighton told me about. So it was you, not Robert, who'd been laundering il-

legal money through dummy accounts. And you tried to
convince me that Robert was guilty, that his ambition led
him to do something dishonest, when all along, it was
you." Brie's hands flew to her face as a wave of nausea
swept over her. "Oh, God, how could you compound your
dishonesty by killing your best friend and an innocent
child?"

Distraught at the condemnation in her eyes, Craig
scrubbed a hand over his face. "You have to believe me,
Brie. I had no idea Bobby was going to be with Robert that
day. He told me to meet him at Beacon and Charles, that he
had an appointment and didn't have much time. How was
I supposed to know it was his day with the kid?"

"How dare you! His name was Bobby and he'd be here
right now, this very minute, if it weren't for you." She
swung around, away from that sniveling face, closing her
eyes as bile backed up in her throat. "Get away from me,
from here. I never want to see you again."

"Oh, no, we're not finished." He came all the way
around the table and grabbed her arm, jerked her around,
his hot breath hissing in her face. "I haven't come this far
to give up now. I tried everything to find out where those
pictures were without involving you. I broke into your
condo in Boston, and they weren't there, not in any of your
cameras. I broke in here, twice, and nothing! I tried to
scare you off the island, so you'd come back where I could
get the information out of you one way or another, without
hurting you. But not even the phone calls scared you. It
wasn't until I talked with your mother after you left this
last time that she mentioned she'd given you the camera
bag you'd had that day. I had to come, don't you see? I saw
you taking pictures that day on the Common. I have to get
that film, the one that might expose me. They warned me

that if I didn't take the film to them soon, they'd kill me. I tried, God knows, and then this blasted hurricane came along. Damn it, Brie, if you'd have just cooperated."

Trembling inside, Brie was determined not to let him see. Lord only knew what he'd do if he realized how truly frightened she was. A crazed man was totally unpredictable. Stalling for time was her best bet. Maybe Slade would have an epiphany and come over.

Pushing back the horror of what she'd learned over the past few minutes, Brie tried to shake off his hand, but he held her in a steely grip. "I'm really sorry I didn't roll over and play dead for you by handing over pictures I had no idea you wanted."

Craig was running out of patience. "Just tell me where they are, give them to me and I'll leave."

She knew exactly where she'd put the packet of pictures she'd picked up the day she and Slade had stopped at the hardware store. She'd held the envelope in her hand, but hadn't found the courage to look at the last photos she'd taken of Bobby. So she'd put the packet in her nightstand in her bedroom. Last night, she'd slept on the floor of the master bedroom with Slade and hadn't given the pictures a thought.

Would he ever hold her like that again?

She'd have to get away somehow, to mislead Craig and do a good job of it or, by the look of him, he'd hurt her. He'd killed two people already. And if he got ahold of those pictures and negatives and destroyed them, she'd have no proof that he'd been the shooter that fateful morning.

"I don't remember where I put them, Craig. I was in a hurry the day I picked them up. There was a hurricane coming. Pictures were the last thing on my mind." Then, as if struck by a thought, she looked up. "Oh, I'll bet I left them in the glove compartment of the Buick. I made several stops that day and . . ."

Craig swiped his free hand across his face, brushing back his sandy hair, his fingers tightening on her arm. "You wouldn't try to snow me, now, would you, Brie? 'Cause if they're not there, I might just have to hurt you. I don't want to, but you see what a position I'm in here? If I don't get those pictures this trip, if Halstead finds out I failed and the paper trail fingers him, I'm going to be joining Robert in hell."

She didn't think she could swallow her fear and let anger take over, but she surprised herself. "I don't believe Robert's in hell. He didn't take two lives."

She'd said it so softly, so finally. Craig wished he didn't have to send her to join her son and ex, but he saw no way out. Not after that. She hated him. He'd hoped she'd understand, especially since she'd divorced Robert years ago. She might have understood if it hadn't been for the kid. Tough luck about the kid.

Nervously, Craig glanced behind him, thinking he'd heard a noise, but he couldn't see anything. It was spooky in here, the windows all boarded up, even with the light on. He'd get the pictures, take care of Brie, and get the hell off this damn island. Then Halstead would get off his back and he'd be home free. The careful way he'd set up Robert to take the fall at the firm, old Brighton would never suspect him. Then, with the payoff of his two million, he'd kiss the company good-bye and be off for the South Seas.

On the far counter, he noticed the rack of knives stuck into a wooden block. Convenient. He hadn't been able to bring his gun, with the tough laws imposed by the airlines these days. Now he'd find out if she was telling the truth.

Pulling her along with him, he selected a long one that looked especially sharp. "Nice," he commented, testing the blade with his thumb. Craig twisted Briana's arm behind her back, applying just enough pressure to make her want to cry out. Only, she wouldn't give him the satisfaction as she gritted her teeth.

"One more time. Where are those pictures, and don't you *dare* lie to me. I've got nothing to lose by killing you. Afterward, I could set a match to this place and blame it on the hurricane. Tell me, Briana. *Now!*"

"I am telling you. They're out in the glove box." She prayed he'd believe her. Once outside, she'd think of something to do, distract him, call out, fall down and trip him, anything.

He tightened his hold on her. "I don't believe you. Time's running out. Talk!"

He was close enough behind her that she could smell his whisky breath. She'd have to take a chance, because this was getting them nowhere. "Let me think . . ." Then she brought her free arm back hard, her elbow slamming into his midsection.

"You little bitch!" Craig was slight, but wiry and strong. Never letting go, he maneuvered her down to the kitchen floor and captured both her wrists in one hand while he held the knife to her chest with the other. Grinning, he straddled her. "Thought you were too good to go out with me, didn't you? Never gave me a tumble. That was a mistake, Brie."

Eyes dancing fire, she glared up at him, his weight sitting heavy on her. Her one arm was numb with pain from his twisting. She bided her time, waiting for him to glance away, to lose his train of thought, and she'd try again. But she had to watch that sharp knife in case he . . .

Craig slashed down the front of her shirt, easily cutting the thin cotton and exposing her breasts, his eyes growing huge. "Well, well. Maybe we're not in such a big hurry after all. Since we've waited so long, maybe we deserve a little reward." Almost playfully, he trailed the knife tip slowly down between her breasts. A thin line of blood oozed out.

That did it. She'd find some other way to expose him without the pictures, but she wasn't going to let him mark her up or . . . or worse. "All right, you win. I'll tell you where the pictures are."

"Hold your horses, Miss Eager Beaver." Craig's eyes were riveted to her flesh. He let go of her hands and lowered his to reach down and . . .

"No!" Briana bucked her hips beneath him, upsetting him while batting at him with her hands, trying desperately to avoid that knife. "Get off me you . . . you murderer, you sadist."

Furious now, Craig lashed out with the knife just as Briana's arms flew up to protect her face. The blade sliced along the inside of her right arm several inches above the elbow. Blood spurted out immediately, spraying Craig as she cried out.

"Now look what you made me do. Damn it, Brie. Why couldn't you have cooperated? Why couldn't you just give me the damn pictures?" He was almost sobbing now, watching the blood pump out of her as her arm fell limply onto her chest.

"Oh," Brie moaned. The deep cut burned, but that wasn't as bad as watching her blood seemingly pouring out of her. He must have severed an artery. "Craig, please, I need a doctor. Don't do this. Don't add another killing to your list."

He couldn't listen to her. He had to ignore the blood and ignore her words. Gripping the knife in fingers slippery with nervous sweat, he leaned down to her face, holding the silvery edge to her throat. "Just tell me where the goddamn film is and I'll get you to a doctor."

Gray dots danced in front of her eyes, then receded. Briana licked her dry lips as her heavy arm slid off her chest, slippery with blood. "I need a tourniquet, Craig. Are you going to let me bleed to death?"

"The pictures! Where are they?" he screamed.

"Hey!" came a voice from behind him, then someone grabbed his hair hard and hurled him backward. Though he went flying, Craig lashed out with the knife, trying to stab his assailant. Missing, he cursed as he scrambled up and saw the guy from next door looming over him. Before he could react, a thick fist rammed into his chin, sending him sprawling again.

Flat on his back, he made to get up, but a large shoe stepped on his wrist, the pain causing him to drop the knife with a clatter to the kitchen tile. "Wait a minute," he sobbed out.

But Slade wasn't waiting. Grabbing Craig by his shirt front, he hauled him to his feet only to punch him down again. And again. Then he leaned over him and pummeled both fists into his pretty-boy face, not stopping until he heard the satisfying crack of Craig's nose breaking. One more time, he picked him up, but Craig was deadweight by then, passed out, slumping to the floor.

Turning, Slade looked at Briana, who was trying to get up. His mouth went dry. So much blood, everywhere. On her chest and arm, her torn shirt soaked through. Down on one knee, he bent to her. "Where did he cut you?"

"My arm," Brie said, the gray spots in front of her eyes

turning black, growing in number. Trying to rise with his
help, she swayed as a wave of nausea hit her. "Going to be
sick." But she swallowed it back. No, she couldn't pass
out. Not yet.

"Let me help you." He'd come around back and had
been about to knock on the door when he'd heard shouts.
He'd eased the door open and seen a man on top of Briana,
a man with a knife, and blood all over. It wasn't until he'd
pulled the guy off that he realized the man's identity.
"Craig. What's he doing here?"

Brie drew in a shaky breath. "He's the shooter. He killed
Bobby and Robert." She swallowed again. "Long story.
Slade, I need a tourniquet."

Hell, yes, he should have thought to stop the bleeding.
Rummaging through one of the drawers, he found a shoestring and bent to her. "Let me see where to put this."

She lifted her arm and he saw the open, gaping wound.
Not a pretty sight. Hurriedly, he tied the shoestring in
place. "I'm taking you to the hospital."

"Tie him up first. We'll call sheriff." A wave of dizziness
had her swaying again. "Thirsty. Water, please."

"Right away." From the refrigerator, he took a bottle of
cold water and held it to her so she could drink. "Hold on
a minute." He'd spotted a piece of clothesline in the
drawer. Grabbing it, he hurriedly bound Craig's hands and
feet tightly behind him.

A quick dash to the bathroom to grab two thick towels,
then he returned and knelt down to her. Carefully, he removed her bloody shirt and bound her wound with one of
the towels. Yanking off his own shirt, he helped her into it,
knowing she'd want to be covered. Then he picked her up
in his arms, his mind racing. He had to get her to the hospital. She was losing so much blood.

"Double lock the door," she told him as he stepped outside. "So Craig can't get away."

"Don't worry, honey. He's not going anywhere." He looked down at her as her head rested on his shoulder. So small and fragile, yet with a core of steel. She would need it.

He settled her in the truck, her head on his lap, and drove as fast as the flooded roads would allow. His eyes kept returning to her, noticing how pale she was, how shallow her breathing. She drifted in and out. And the towels he'd wrapped around her wound were already soaked through as her blood pumped steadily out of her.

Slade had never been a praying man, but he prayed now. *Don't let me lose her, please.*

The hospital room was dim and quiet. It was early evening and the night shift of nurses had just come on. The middle-aged one assigned to Briana's private room had just left after checking her vital signs and telling him that she was holding her own.

Holding her own. What the hell did that mean?

He'd rushed into the ER with her in his arms, her clothes and the two thick towels red and slippery with blood, and still it had taken some time before she'd been taken into a cubicle. Didn't he realize there'd been a hurricane, that dozens of injured people were filling the rooms, lining the hallways? one weary young doctor had asked him. It had taken all of Slade's control not to throttle the man, though he knew his anger was misdirected.

It should be him lying in that bed, not her, he thought as he took her slim, cool left hand into his. His pride, his self-indulgence, his unwillingness to bend had almost cost Briana her life. If he hadn't walked off to lick his wounds, if he'd gone with her, Craig never would have been able to carve her up. Once he made up his mind, he was as stubborn as the man he was named after, the one he wasn't even related to.

"No more, honey," he whispered, though he knew Briana couldn't hear him. They'd stitched her up, sedated her, and transfused her. Even now, two tubes were flowing into her, one in her good arm, the other at her ankle. She was dehydrated, the young, harassed doctor had finally told him. They'd replaced most of the blood she'd lost from her severed artery. She was young and strong and otherwise healthy. She would probably come out just fine.

Probably?

"Here you are," Sheriff Stone said, entering quietly and speaking softly as people in hospitals do. "How's she doing?"

"Holding her own," Slade told him, never taking his eyes off Briana's pale face.

"Just thought I'd come by and let you know we got the man who did this to her out of her house and in our jail. I called the Boston P.D. and talked to the lieutenant in charge of the Morgan case, told him about this Craig Walker guy. Said he'll be sending a couple of their men over in the morning to pick him up. I guess I'll get Briana's side of the story once she's better."

Slade didn't answer.

"Thought you'd like to know, those calls on her phone been coming from the Nesbitt Inn. We found a key in Walker's pocket from there. Found another key that looks like it might be to Briana's house. Guess we've got our mysterious caller and B&E man."

It didn't matter to Slade. Nothing mattered except getting Briana well.

"Guess I'll be going then." Stone walked to the door, turned back. "Don't you worry none. Briana Morgan's a fighter. She'll come through this."

Slade didn't look up, just sat running his thumb along the smooth skin of her hand. The doctor had said she probably couldn't hear him, but he began to talk anyhow. Slowly, softly. "I was wrong, but I guess you know that. You were right. I was coming over to tell you so when I found you like . . . like this.

"I guess I'm more like Jeremy than I ever knew. Stubborn, refusing to see all sides of the picture, unforgiving. In this case, I couldn't seem to forgive myself. But I'm changing, Brie. Because of you."

He swallowed hard, blinking. "Now the rest is up to you. You have to get well. You promised you wouldn't leave me, remember? I'm going to hold you to that."

Rising, he leaned over and kissed her cheek gently. *Love can be strong enough to overcome anything.* "I love you, Brie."

It felt as if she were coming out of a thick fog, trying to find her way. The vapory air swirled around her as she struggled to open her eyes. So heavy. So much easier to just stay this way, no hassle, no pain. Floating.

But something made her try, and try harder. Finally, Brie's eyes opened and she blinked. A hospital bed, a hospital room. She still felt pretty floaty. Sensing someone, she turned her head.

He was asleep in the chair he'd pulled up to her bed. The man who'd saved her life, the one she'd feared she'd never see again. What had made him change his mind and come back?

Slade's eyes popped open and he nearly scooted from

his chair when he saw she was awake. Not only awake, but smiling at him. "Hey, lady," he said, leaning to her, "you sure gave me a scare."

"Did I? I didn't mean to."

"Are you in pain?"

"No. Floating." Her brow wrinkled. "Is it bad? Scar?"

"Just like a woman. A little scar, maybe." He took her hand then, afraid to squeeze too hard, yet needing to touch her.

She studied him for a few moments. "Why did you come over?"

He drew in a deep breath. "Because I love you. Because I . . ."

"No. Never mind the rest. That's the only reason that counts." Smiling, she closed her eyes and went back to sleep.

Two days later, they agreed to release Brie from the hospital, provided she had someone to care for her. That someone was Slade, who'd scarcely left her side. She was still weak, having lost a good deal of blood, but feeling much better.

That night, curled up in the big four-poster in the master bedroom, she finally found the courage to look at the packet of pictures. She'd given a similar set to the sheriff, who'd in turn handed them to the Boston police. With Slade at her side, a comforting presence, she showed him Bobby in all his smiling, seven-year-old wonder. She'd captured him hamming for the camera, laughing at the antics of the ducks on the pond, swinging from a tree limb, and climbing up for his green balloon.

"He's beautiful, Brie," Slade said, and meant it. The boy radiated childhood at its carefree happiest. He felt a lump form at the thought that her son had been taken from her, the pictures bringing home the message more clearly than her earlier words had. He reached to fold her hand in his. It seemed these days that he couldn't get enough of just touching her, holding her.

"He was, wasn't he?" She would at least have that as a memory she'd store away forever. Her son had been happy and loved.

The next picture showed Robert and Bobby walking away, Bobby waving to her across the street, the balloon tied to his wrist. In the following snapshot, a dark car could be seen in the right-hand corner, more of it visible in the next photo.

"You can easily make out the license plate number," she told Slade. "Craig said it was a rental car."

"It can be traced to him, I'm sure. Why would he have rented a car if he hadn't intended to do something? That proves premeditation. That means old Craig is facing more than just prison bars."

Brie stared at the shadowy form of a man behind the wheel of the gray car. "If I blow this up, and I will, I'll bet it'll identify him as the driver. This is the picture he was afraid of." A shudder shook her body as she set aside the photo. "Oh, God. The horror of someone planning such a thing, carrying it out so cold-bloodedly, his first shot killing an innocent little boy who just happened to be in the wrong place at the wrong time. Then he shot again."

She felt Slade squeeze her fingers, letting her get it out. "To think he met me at the hospital that terrible day and I was so glad to see him. He pretended to be grieving right along with me. He's a monster!"

"Yeah, he is. But he's going to get what's coming to him.

Finally, it's all over. No more phone calls, no more threats."

Briana blinked back her tears. "You're right. We can get on with our lives, finally."

It was Slade's turn. He reached across to the nightstand for the envelope he'd had in his pocket on his way over to see Briana that fateful morning. "And speaking of getting on with our lives, this is a letter from Rachel's mother. I'd like you to read it."

He didn't look upset, she thought, taking the single sheet of paper. Had Rachel finally forgiven him?

Briana read quickly, emotions shifting on her face. Finishing, she raised suddenly damp eyes to his face. "Oh, Slade." She reached to hold him close. After a moment, she leaned back. "How do you feel about this?"

He stared at the letter, trying to put his feelings into words, something he was getting better at. "I feel terrible that Rachel thought the only way out was to overdose on pills, but I know what guilt can do to a person. She couldn't handle living with the knowledge that *she*, not I, had caused Megan's death."

"I can't believe she locked that small child in her closet to punish her for getting into the cookie jar. That's such a kid thing to do, one probably every child tries at one time or another. Was she that harsh with Megan when you lived with them?"

"A little, but apparently she got worse after I left. Maybe that guy she'd had living with her for a while hadn't liked kids and complained a lot about Megan. So, being a weak person, Rachel followed his lead."

"After you told me that Megan was afraid of the dark, of enclosed spaces, I couldn't imagine that she'd gone into a closet willingly." Brie's maternal heart went out to the child. "The poor little thing."

"I'm sure Rachel had intended to punish her for just a short time by locking her in her own bedroom closet while she lay down on her bed. But she fell asleep. All these months, how she must have suffered, knowing what she'd done."

"Doubly so because she'd let you believe it was your fault. She hadn't been able to own up to her own guilt." Brie sighed, feeling sorry for the woman whose judgment had cost her dearly, yet unwilling to overlook the fact that Rachel had allowed Slade to blame himself all this time.

"I hope she's found some form of peace now." As he hoped that Jeremy had.

She laced her fingers with his. "So you see, it wasn't such a bad judgment call you made back in California. And besides, what you did for Irma would have wiped the slate clean in anyone's book." She'd had Slade check on Irma's condition while she was still in the hospital and learned that their friend had a fractured hip and a badly bruised ankle, but she was doing well.

Brie studied Slade's face, saw that he was still thoughtful. "What are you thinking?"

"I'm wondering why it takes a near death to wake up some people. Damn, I almost lost you. Longest night of my life."

"You didn't and you won't." She raised a hand to stroke along his cheek, then back up to trace the small scar above his left brow. Lord, how she loved this man.

He smiled down at her. "All right, then, if you're sure, maybe we should do the thing."

"Am I to understand that's a proposal, then?"

Slade held her close, his fingers tracing her full lips. "It is."

"Can I perhaps hear you say those three little words?"

"I love you. I want to be with you always, Brie. I want to go to sleep with you beside me and wake up holding you. I want to have a child with you." He watched her eyes fill, soften. "I know Bobby can never be replaced. But we can have another child, one you and I make together."

Blinking, Briana nodded. "I want that, too."

"Is that a yes, then?"

"Definitely."

The kiss was long, tender, breathtaking. Opening his eyes, Slade glanced across the room at the window open to the sea. The sun was just setting, streaking the sky gold and red. "Look at that, a red sky tonight."

" 'Red sky at night, sailors delight,' " Brie quoted from the old mariners saying.

Slade snuggled down with her. "A delight. I like that. Maybe it's an omen. Only good things ahead. All the bad times are behind us."

"I know they are." With that, she turned into his kiss, filled with the promise of bright tomorrows.